COLORADO

Clara F. Hall

COLORADO

BY

LOUIS BROMFIELD

Harper & Brothers Publishers

NEW YORK AND LONDON

For

my old friend

JOE PASTERNAK

begetter of

Destry Rides Again

and

MARLENE DIETRICH

who sang

"See What the Boys in the Back Room Will Have"

this story without social consciousness

or self-consciousness

COLORADO

PART I

XXXXXXXXXXXXXXXXXXXXXXXXXXXXXXXXXXXXXXXXXXXXXXXXXXXXXXXXXXXXXX

THE TRAIN MOVED ACROSS THE VAST SEA OF BURGEONING GRASS LIKE A stub-tailed and languorous snake. The single track, put down a little over ten years earlier, was still unsettled especially in those parts where the foundations had been washed out and repaired each year or heaved up by a climate in which the temperature ranged from thirty degrees below zero in winter to over a hundred and ten degrees above in summer and violent floods alternated with burning drouths.

For nearly two days the train had been moving through dead flat country, treeless and covered by the green of early summer grass which rippled as the wind played over it like the waters of the ocean itself. For nearly two days the passengers of the train, save at watering stations and maintenance camps where a few Irish or Chinese gathered around it when it stopped, had seen but three human creatures animating the vast and monotonous landscape—a man and a woman standing outside a sod hut shading their eyes to watch the train pass, and a lone rider on a spotted cayuse picking his way up the dry bed of a stream toward the sunset. Once there appeared on the crest of a low rise in an endless sea of grass a dozen buffalo, last remnants of a dying race. The air, if it moved at all, was like the breath of heat from the opened door of an oven.

This was the vast world of the Great Plains which somehow had been passed over by settlers hurrying farther west to the bonanza country of the Rockies and the Pacific Coast where gold and silver were to be had for the effort of picking it up and orange trees grew wherever a passer-by dropped a seed.

The valiant, puffing little engine, with its great oversized funnel, drew a train of eleven cars. One was given over to the United States

Post Office, two to freight of a wide assortment, ranging from mining equipment to new gadgets for Mrs. P. J. Meaney, wife of the King of Silver City, and eight coaches for passengers. Of the eight, seven were crowded to overflowing by a wild assortment of people—miners, peddlers, whores, laborers, loafers, cheap gamblers and immigrants only recently arrived on the far distant Atlantic shores. None of them carried much money; they were all bound for the Promised Land to get rich. They were going west toward the setting sun with a little small change in their pockets and a few bank notes hidden in a shoe or sewed into the lining of a jacket or the lining of a bustle. Among them was an eternally optimistic old man of eighty making his twentieth fresh start in life and there was a baby which passed its third-month birthday in a wooden-seated railway coach filled with dust and the smell of sweat, overflowing spittoons and fragments of sandwiches which with coffee was the only food the passengers had seen since leaving Kansas City. By the second day neither the train nor the passengers smelled very good and as the train crawled across the hot, endless plain it left behind it a clouded aroma which sent gophers scurrying into their holes.

They were fleeing the crowded East and the particular Great Depression of their times. They had had enough of the East and the filthy, overcrowded cities and the farms where you worked your life out fourteen hours a day for gains that were not worth the effort. They were all going west into that country where the mountains were filled with gold and silver and copper, where there was sunlight and oranges and you didn't have to buy coal to keep warm, westward into that land of opportunity, of wealth, of freedom, into the New Country of which the handouts scattered by the railroads sang as angels sing of Paradise.

The eleventh railroad car was different from the others, so different that the car itself and the people in it seemed to belong to another world. It was higher than the others and wider so that it made the train from certain angles resemble a combination of a caterpillar and a fat-tailed North African sheep as much as a stub-tailed copperhead viper. On the outside were painted the words PARLOR-SALOON, and from the outside the Chinese and Irish laborers, who peered through the windows at each watertank stop, saw the passengers through wide sheets of plate glass bordered by looped-up curtains of red plush hung with ball fringe. The Parlor-Saloon car was the effort of a new and rich nation feeling its way toward the luxury which was appropriate to a country bursting at the seams with coal and gold and silver and oil and timber and rich black prairie land, a country divided between the wealth of an industrialist East and the incredible, scarcely touched wealth of a fabulous West.

There wasn't any royalty in the car. There wasn't even any nobility; but the Parlor-Saloon car was an expression of hunger for such institutions and of a groping for civilization in terms of mechanical and material expression. Today people, living in a world of streamlined luxurious continental trains and planes which cross the whole continent in a few hours, laugh at the old engravings of such things as the Parlor-Saloon car but at that time it was looked upon as fabulous and breath-taking in its elaborate vulgarity.

Inside, the car was certainly as luxurious as the red and gilt outside and the ball-fringed curtains implied. Also it was stuffy and dusty, especially for travel across vast plains shimmering with the fierce heat of late June and clouded by the dust that rose in clouds from the roadbed, rushing upward through every crevice and crack of the car. The Parlor-Saloon car was an experiment in design, one of the latest, and put on the Kansas City-Denver run because P. J. Meaney, the great magnate of Silver City, Colorado, owned a large share in the railroad. At one end there were sleeping compartments for six people who, among them, paid twice the fare of a whole carload of the shabby and hopeful adventurers in the cars ahead. Not only did they pay well, the passengers in the Parlor-Saloon car, unlike the anonymous mob in the cars ahead, were important enough to have their names recorded on a card, carefully hand lettered, in the possession of the conductor.

They read:

> PROFESSOR ALONZO DA PONTE
> MADEMOISELLE LA BELLE DA PONTE
> MR. RICHARD MEANEY
> MR. CECIL M. CHATSWORTHY
> MR. JONATHAN WRIGHT
> MR. CYRUS L. LAIDLAW

Five men and one woman, or rather five men and one girl.

In addition to the six sleeping compartments, the Parlor-Saloon car had seats for twelve people with tables between them upholstered in green baize for the benefit of those who wished to pass the time at cards. These were covered when not in use for gambling by red plush "throws" bordered by ball fringe which matched the elegant red plush curtains. At the far end of the car there was a compartment six by ten feet in size in which lived, ate, slept and cooked a fat, rather squat negro with a bald head and a fringe of curly white wool, who looked rather like an elderly monk in black-face. It was his duty to cook and serve food to the six distinguished passengers and at frequent intervals to go through the car with a broom, a feather duster and a cloth to stir up the dust that settled over everything in thick clouds—clothes, red plush, brasswork, spittoons and mahogany.

The people huddled like cattle in the cars between the freight wagons and the Parlor-Saloon have little part in the story, save as background—that background of milling, hopeful, gambling, breeding, pathetic, tragic, unruly humanity—which was crowding into the West at a time when the East seemed to be already overcrowded. They will be there all along, working deep under the earth in mines, running saloons and gambling establishments, herding cattle, building railroads and digging ditches and dams to hold and release the sweet waters that would turn millions of acres of desert country into fertile land, the people who changed the whole of the West from a wilderness to a cornucopia of fertility and wealth. They will be with us all along, working in P. J. Meaney's mines and on P. J. Meaney's ranches, in P. J. Meaney's general stores, on P. J. Meaney's railroads, watering and plowing P. J. Meaney's land and setting out his orchards.

In the Parlor-Saloon the six passengers did not get on too well. Perhaps this was so because among them there was very little conversation, even less indeed that was of common interest. But there were other elements as well, of personality, of ambition, of secrecy, of suspicion and of fear which set people apart even on a miserable, hot, and dusty journey in a parlor car deluxe across the vast unsubdued plains of the western Mississippi Basin during the latter half of the nineteenth century.

Mr. Cyrus L. Laidlaw was a small man with a potbelly and a chin beard. He carried with him a metal-bound wooden box filled with papers which were mostly contracts or covered with column upon column of figures. He had no lips to speak of and his eyes were an indeterminate shade of cold grey-blue. He appeared to have no interest in the other passengers but spent most of his time at one of the green baize-covered tables poring over the papers or writing letters of which he made many copies in a small machine which required the dampening of the paper each time a copy was made. He was a combination of banker and lawyer and had important connections with Jay Gould and Jim Fisk in the East as well as P. J. Meaney in the West.

Mr. Jonathan Wright was a lawyer for the railroad company and kept mostly to his room. When he came out of it to eat he sometimes talked with Mr. Richard Meaney and Mr. Cecil M. Chatsworthy. He was traveling on a pass with all his expenses paid and was a tired, grey man of about sixty-five, with a full black beard which in relation to his greying hair was like an exclamation point.

Both of these gentlemen will disappear from the story for a time at Denver, a bustling city, half-metropolis, half-frontier, full of silver dollars, gilt and plush, fast women and fabulous yet commonplace stories of the rise from pick and shovel to palace. Their only importance is that they too are very much a part of the background, along with the sweating, dirty people in the coaches ahead, for they too played a big part in the manipulations which brought about the opening of the fabulous West. They helped to provide the capital and to make and break the laws which made possible the wild, swift development of the riches which lay within the earth and in the forests and the streams of the new El Dorado.

Mr. Cecil Chatsworthy was a thin young man of perhaps twenty-seven or eight, rather owlish in appearance, who wore heavy gold-rimmed spectacles. His clothes made of obviously good tweed, a material rare in America, set him apart and made him seem a foreigner, which indeed he was. His bearing during the crossing of the whole continent had been marked by behavior notable for an excitement which seemed strange in a man so delicately built and so apparently bloodless, for his skin had a waxlike pallor and usually he preserved a rather bored and studious calm. Early each morning he rose and left

[5]

his room to sit at the window of the Parlor-Saloon, looking out, sometimes talking in a low voice and with a very odd accent to his friend and traveling companion, Mr. Richard Meaney. He and Mr. Meaney, alone among the gentlemen on the Parlor-Saloon, did not make use of the spittoons. He retired late, only when the sun had gone down and the landscape fell into darkness. The baggage he carried with him consisted of two Gladstone bags made of heavy plaid material. In his own room, after he had retired, he read by the light of the brass-plated kerosene lamp at the head of his bed, long and thick volumes with strange names and written in an obsolete tongue. But for the glasses and the pallor, he would have been a good-looking fellow, with his slim figure and curly dark hair. He had nice, full-curving lips and a straight nose and the general look of what was considered in the Eighties distinguished and well bred.

Mr. Richard Meaney was the son of P. J. Meaney and was recognized as such and treated with great, if somewhat reserved, civility by Mr. Laidlaw, the banker, and Mr. Wright, the lawyer. He was a big fellow with curly, sandy hair and a freckled face. He too was dressed in tweeds which would have made him, like Mr. Chatsworthy, seem foreign but for something unmistakably rugged and American in his walk and bearing, in the big shoulders and in the grin that from time to time illumined the friendly face. You felt that the big strong hands could straighten a horseshoe or that the big fists could in short order clear a barroom filled with brawling men. An expression and manner of obvious good humor made it evident that he had no quarrel with life nor any part of it. On his young face, life had as yet left no record. It was a face filled with the light of health, of friendliness, of eagerness —a face whose brilliance and charm was likely to warm any heart, and certain to arouse tenderness in the hearts of all women, especially older women.

Professor da Ponte was what might be called a flashy dresser. Mr. Laidlaw and Mr. Wright, the banker and the lawyer, regarded him with distaste. Mr. Laidlaw saw in him a certain resemblance to Jim Fisk, a friend of Mr. Gould's who liked champagne and the French opera and had come to an untimely end at the foot of the grand stairway of the Astor Hotel when he was shot in a brawl over a fancy trollop called Josie Mansfield.

The Professor wore striped trousers and a long frock coat with a fancy checked vest crossed by a heavy gold watch chain from which hung a heavy seal of agate engraved with the figure of a naked woman. When he got down at the water stops for a bit of air he put on a grey top hat over a curled and fancy reddish-brown toupee which no longer matched the greying fringe of hair which surrounded it. His face was pitted with much drinking and his nose was bulbous and cherry-colored between two twinkling very bright blue eyes. He was, he said, a professor both of music and of phrenology, which meant the analysis of character by feeling the bumps of the head. He had offered his services free to Mr. Laidlaw and Mr. Wright and had been coldly rejected by both.

Miss La Belle da Ponte remained during the whole of the trip from Omaha to Denver somewhat of a mystery. She was only seen twice, both times when she emerged from her compartment to take the air on the arm of the Professor—once at Cotchecatche, Nebraska and once at Hangman's Leap, Kansas. Each time she was regarded with silent and celestial awe and admiration by the Chinese track workers who had never seen a woman so upholstered in bustles, passementerie, tassels and feathers, and with frank, loud, and vulgar admiration by the Irish; and small wonder it was, for it had been months since many a man at the water stops had seen any woman at all and it is probable that never in all their lives had any of them seen a woman so lush and so stimulating at so tender an age.

For it was clear despite the sophistication of her modish clothes and the elaborate and intricate structure of puffs, braids, and curls which adorned her small head, that she *was* young—very young indeed. Also it was clear to the most cynical and experienced eye that she had, even beneath all the upholstery, a superlative figure—a waist that could be encircled by two fairly good-sized masculine hands, with voluptuous swellings both above and below, the latter exaggerated by an elaborate bustle adorned with long fringe which swung and swayed tantalizingly as she walked up and down the rough path that separated the train from the watertank. Atop the elaborate coiffure, she wore a tiny hat adorned with cherries and tilted slightly forward at a pert angle. The hair was a tawny gold color and the large eyes were blue

[7]

with long dark lashes. The mouth was curved and generous and even voluptuous and the snub nose tilted a little.

To a young man, she was an awesome spectacle which made him feel hot and awkward. To an experienced man she was all that was desirable save that her obvious youth and unlined face augured an uninteresting lack of experience. To the old lecher, she was the type which induced drooling. In any case, one could not fail to notice her. The sauciness, the costume, the false demureness of the modestly downcast gaze, the flamboyance of the costume were all designed to attract, startle and excite. It was then small wonder that the Chinamen were struck dumb and the Irish were rendered vocal and demonstrative.

This then was the group which occupied the Parlor-Saloon car that was the latest contribution of designers of luxurious travel in the largest and richest country in the world. It was an ill-assorted group. Mr. Laidlaw, the banker, had long ago become more susceptible to columns of figures and crooked manipulations than to the charms of women and Mr. Wright, the lawyer, got more pleasure at his age out of torturing phrases of the legal code than in studying the female form. Both regarded Miss da Ponte once, put her into the dusty mental pigeon-hole where trollops had once been filed away, and went back to the work in which had been sublimated long since whatever interest in females they had ever possessed.

The two brief glimpses of Miss da Ponte merely terrified the Englishman, Mr. Chatsworthy, and his young American friend, Mr. Richard Meaney. In all their experience, even on rare visits to London in the past, they had never encountered anyone quite so stimulating and so frightening. It was clear that Professor da Ponte was guarding her with all the strictness of a Spanish duenna, from what the whistling of the Irish track workers made clear but for what they did not know. Both young men, being shy and inexperienced, did not discuss her even with each other. The most they learned about her came from the Professor who, unasked, explained that he was her uncle, that she was a singer of remarkable talents and that she was going west on a tour and would appear presently at several grand concerts in the Denver Opera House.

"She has sung," the Professor said, "in all the great opera houses of Europe. Kings and Princes have thrown pearls and diamonds at her feet." He added, "She is very sensitive—a real artiste—very full of temperament." Then he sighed and rubbing his hands and looking away into the distance out of the plush and ball-fringed bordered windows, he observed, "I sometimes wish that she was less sensitive and more sociable. I am certain that you young gentlemen would find her stimulating company. But I cannot induce her to live in the world, *among* people." Again he sighed and added philosophically, "I suppose that is the way artistes are."

Then he pulled out a silver flask from his hip pocket, summoned the old negro who brought glasses and offered both young men drinks of Bourbon. "Good Bourbon," he said, "from my brother's ancestral home in Kentucky."

Meaney and Chatsworthy accepted the drink but did not like it very much. Chatsworthy had never tasted Bourbon and young Meaney, who had only recently begun to drink anything at all, had tasted only Scotch which he did not like very much. The Bourbon he liked even less. Then the Professor took out a pack of cards, shuffled them in a professional way and asked, "Would you gentlemen be interested in a little game of cards to pass the time?"

But neither Mr. Meaney nor Mr. Chatsworthy had ever played cards. Mr. Chatsworthy returned to reading Suetonius and Mr. Meaney and the Professor continued a rather stilted conversation which led nowhere. Mr. Chatsworthy only looked up from his reading now and then to regard the vast, inhuman, terrifying expanses of flat country lying beyond the windows and to murmur to Meaney, "What a country! What a huge country! What can anybody do with it?"

Once, early in the evening of the third day sounds of discord came from the compartment of Mademoiselle da Ponte. The voices were those of the Professor and of the oversensitive Mademoiselle. Clearly they were quarreling but very little of what they said could be overheard. It was only when the train stopped for a moment at a watertank, that a phrase or two became audible as the Professor opened the door to descend from the train for air. As the door opened, the two young men heard the voice of the fragile Mademoiselle da Ponte saying, "Well, I'm goddam sick of being shut up in here!"

As the Professor turned and saw them and knew that they had

heard, he said, "The diva is having a little temperament. It means nothing—nothing at all."

He swept airily off as if he would be through forever with the two young men once they arrived at the end of the journey. He had found them difficult and uncommunicative and at last was ready to dismiss them as two young men of moderate means going west like himself to make their fortunes and so of no use or interest to him. He did not at the moment know that he was passing up a great opportunity for he did not know that young Dick was the son of the great P. J. Meaney, King of all the Calamares Country. Indeed, he was not quite sure who P. J. Meaney was, although he had heard the name or read it somewhere many times.

Nothing much of interest happened during the remainder of the trip. Presently at ten in the evening the train drew into the depot of Denver, a great sprawling, new city built where the vast expanse of the Great Plains rises, at first imperceptibly, into the terrifying vastness of the Rockies. Mr. Laidlaw, the banker, and Mr. Wright, the lawyer, disappeared into the noisy, vulgar depths of the city. The two young men went to the biggest and newest hotel and the Professor and his niece disappeared in a horse-drawn hack with four trunks loaded on the roof. They made no mention of their destination.

Beyond Denver lay the western world—that new world toward which men, women and children were trekking like ants across the Great Plains. Already there were thousands of them settled here and there, in ramshackle cities, in rich valleys, on the edges of the vast forests, in watered places in the desert. Deep in the mountain there were mines and indeed whole cities which had grown up around the mines, yet close at hand just beyond the limits of the towns there were vast wildernesses where one could journey for days without ever seeing a house or indeed a human creature. There were deserts where prospectors and immigrants sometimes lost themselves to be discovered later, if at all, merely as a heap of bones picked clean and white in the dry air by birds and wild animals. The white man was filtering into the huge wilderness, wandering along trails in streambeds, always a little startled by the grandeur and color and beauty of this new country where the sky seemed bigger than anywhere else in the world, and the stars more brilliant and the air more clear and tangy. Even the most coarse and sodden experienced a new feeling of dignity and breathed a little more freely in the presence of the great mountains, reaching snow-capped into the blueness of the sky, of the brilliant walled canyons, the clear rushing streams, the deep, dark forests and the still, high lakes mirroring the deep cobalt skies.

In all that mountain-desert wilderness there was not much man-made order, not too much law and sometimes little more than a rude and primitive justice.

Young Mr. Meaney, home from three years spent in England, was returning to his native country, his heart overflowing with nostalgia for the mountains, the streams, the high mountain meadows. In his heart, although he never mentioned it even to his tutor, Mr. Chatsworthy, he felt a little as if he had spent the last three years in a cramped hall bedroom, for he belonged to this wild, free country. He was among the first white men born there. All his brothers and sisters had been born farther east—in Pittsburgh, in Chicago, in Omaha, in St. Louis, during the wanderings of a father who was always trying something new, always hoping to strike it rich.

Young Meaney was the youngest of the family, younger than his nearest sister by ten years, born after his father P. J. Meaney had struck it rich, and so he was different from the others, as his father had wanted him to be. P. J. Meaney had long had an ambition to be a gentleman and when it became evident, even to himself, that he never would be, he had concentrated all his desires for gentility upon his youngest son. That was why he had sent young Dick east to school and later to England to continue his studies at Oxford. Young Dick, the old man had determined, was to be educated so that he would know how to get the most out of his money, instead of just spending it to buy *things*.

But young Dick hadn't liked the plan too well. He had submitted to it but all the time he felt cramped and uneasy at the school in the East and later on at Oxford. More perhaps than any of his brothers and sisters, he *belonged* in the West.

[11]

And now in a hotel bedroom in Denver which he shared with Mr. Chatsworthy he was on his way home, so happy and so excited that he could not sleep all the night before the final leg of the long, slow journey from England. He would have gone out to explore the garish splendors of the new city but for the fact that his companion was exhausted and wanted only to sleep. Unused to the rocky swaying and bumping of the long train journey across the plains, Mr. Chatsworthy had scarcely slept at all. But he was suffering too from an exhaustion of the spirit brought on by the fact that since his arrival in the barbarous New World he had been constantly overwhelmed and stunned by the vast size of the United States, by the great cities, the endless expanse of rich farms, but most of all by the terrifying emptiness and size of the vast grass-covered plains. Very plainly Mr. Chatsworthy, who had spent most of his life in a sleepy, ancient university town in little England, was so flabbergasted by the grandeur, the size, the noisiness of this new and growing world, that he was completely exhausted.

In background he was about as far away from young Dick as it was possible to be, for he had been born in the vicarage of St. Dunstan's Church at Cowperdown, a village in the neat, tight, ordered parklike country of Gloucestershire where he was never out of sight of a house and on each hill there was a neat compact little village of ancient houses. The vicarage itself had been built in 1691 and the church had been there since the thirteenth century. And during all the time that intervened there had been a tight human continuity of installations, of habits, of customs, even of incomes. Mr. Chatsworthy was the son of the Vicar, who in turn was the youngest cousin of the Earl of Cantwell. There had always been a living from church and state and a small income from the Earl's estate. Nobody in that world had ever thought of adventure or making a fortune or even of money, for money was always there in sufficient quantities to provide for sturdy and good solid English food and an occasional modest trip to London or the Continent. Whatever spirit of adventure there was in Mr. Chatsworthy had been confined up to now to the exploration of Greek and Latin literature or the finding of sympathetic "diggings" in the town of Oxford. He had been a little startled when one day he had found himself tutoring a big, rather awkward American boy called Richard Meaney from a place with the outlandish name of Silver City, Colorado, and even more astonished to find that he liked the boy and his quick, eager mind and that there was a remarkable sympathy between the two of them, perhaps because each wanted to be, at least a little, what the other already was. But the astonishment of Mr. Chatsworthy knew no bounds when at the end of three years young Dick said, "I am going home next month, back to Colorado. How about going along with me?" And Mr. Chatsworthy was even more astonished to hear himself saying, "Yes, I'd like to. That new country must be very interesting."

From that moment on Mr. Chatsworthy blew hot and cold regarding the tremendous project of a voyage into the barbaric wilderness. One moment the quiet, ancient peace and security of Oxford and the vicarage drew him back and the next some obscure strain of that adventurous spirit which lies buried, however deep, in every Englishman, drove him on. Now in the hotel bedroom with the sounds of a wild, new city which never slept rising from the streets below his window—the screams, the laughter, the drunken shouting, once even the sound of gunfire—the struggle still went on. Trembling a little he thought, "Maybe I don't belong here. Perhaps I have made a serious error. Perhaps I should turn back."

The terror and astonishment of the long journey still clung to him and the memory of the strange rough people packed like cattle in the part of the train ahead of the Parlor-Saloon car, the sight of the Chinese and the Irish at the tank stops. At home laborers like the Irish knew their places. They did not make mocking remarks about people's clothes nor bawdy sounds at the sight of someone like Mademoiselle da Ponte. In this new country there didn't seem to be any distinctions of class except, of course, those of money which created the colossal gap between the people in the railway carriages ahead and those in the Parlor-Saloon car.

Both Professor da Ponte and Mademoiselle da Ponte had disturbed him, for in the narrow circle of life at the vicarage, in the sleepy scholastic life at Oxford, or even in the rare trips to London, he had never seen anything like them. He had actually found himself unable to speak in response to the overcordial, loquacious sallies of the glib-tongued Professor himself. He had tried to rationalize them and protect himself psychologically by telling himself that the pair—the Professor and the young diva—were something out of Dickens like the Crummles family in *Nicholas Nickleby*.

The pair had made an impression on both young men. This was especially so of Mademoiselle da Ponte, although neither young man was quite certain of the implications of the impression. Like most virginal Anglo-Saxon young men they did not understand the full implications of love until they had actually experienced it. Although they never mentioned the subject of Mademoiselle da Ponte, they both felt strongly the effect of that strange combination of freshness and provocation, of innocence and voluptuousness, of which she was an extraordinary example. Young Meaney fell asleep thinking of her and Mr. Chatsworthy found in the end, when he at last fell asleep, that her image far outweighed his terror and astonishment at the size, noisiness and crudeness of the New World.

At eight the next morning, the train for Silver City, Leadville, Meeker's Gulch, McGovern's Peak and "points west" stood in the Denver depot taking aboard passengers. A good many of them, like young Meaney and Mr. Chatsworthy, had been passengers on the train west across the plains and were simply using Denver as a junction and transfer point.

The Silver City train resembled very much the train that had crossed the plains, save that for one car it was infinitely more dilapidated. That one car outdid in elegance even the Parlor-Saloon car in which the young men had traveled across the dusty prairies. It was painted a bright blue and inside all the fittings were of mahogany and gold plate, even to the spittoons. The curtains were also blue, not the blue of plush but of expensive velvet and were ornamented with gold fringe. On the outside in gold letters was the legend, "The Colorado Blue Bell, P. J. Meaney, Silver City, Colorado." It had been sent all the way down the valleys, mountains and canyons, past Indian encampments and prospectors' diggings to meet the youngest son of the Meaney family on his return from England to the domain of the regal Meaneys.

It was toward this car that the two young men, having overslept, made their way at the last minute. Indeed they were actually late, but the train dispatcher was holding the train for them on the pretense that there was something wrong with the engine, although the real reason was that P. J. Meaney owned the whole of the railroad and the train dispatcher would catch hell and probably be fired if he allowed the train to depart without Meaney's youngest son.

On the platform bedlam reigned. Families pushed mattresses and bags through the windows. Babies squalled. Men fought for seats. The platforms were jammed with people and the train dispatcher was kept busy shoving people and baggage off the roofs with the warning that at the first tunnel (known as Ma Meeker's Diggins) all would be swept off.

In the midst of the bedlam stood the Professor and Mademoiselle da Ponte surrounded by six large trunks and several bags and paper parcels obviously containing hats. The Professor, already a little under the weather, kept shouting in a regal manner for aid with the trunks but in all the confusion no one paid him any heed. Beside him Mademoiselle da Ponte, elegantly dressed, enveloped in the now familiar air of innocence and voluptuousness, stood quietly with downcast eyes.

It was young Meaney who spied them first. He said to Chatsworthy, "Look! There's the Professor and Mademoiselle!" And Mr. Chatsworthy in his turn spied them with a sensation of alarm.

"They must be taking this train. I thought they were staying in Denver."

Then young Meaney went up boldly and addressed them saying, "Good morning. May I help you?"

The agitated demeanor of the Professor changed with the speed of lightning to one of suavity and cordiality.

"Good morning, sir," he said. "You could help me to get someone to load us on the train."

The train dispatcher, a tough red-faced Irishman, who had worked his way up from the lowly station of pick-and-shovel man by knowing on which side his bread was buttered, interrupted them. He took off his hat and addressed young Meaney, "Good morning, sir. I'm glad to see you back. We've been holding the train for you."

Young Meaney held out his hand and the train dispatcher took it with a glow of pleasure. Young Meaney said, "You can get someone to help us get our luggage aboard and help out this gentleman and lady. The train looks full."

"Full, sir," said the train dispatcher, "there'd be more room in a can of sardines."

"Better put them and their trunks in our car." He turned to the Professor. "How far are you going?"

"To Silver City," said the Professor.

"That works out fine," said young Meaney. "We're going to the same place." To the train dispatcher he said, "Better get started. We're late already and Pop'll be mad if it's my fault."

"All right, sir. Don't worry! I'll tell the engineer to make it up. You'll be there on the dot or ahead of time. Don't you worry, sir."

He turned away and out of nowhere appeared a half-dozen men who shouldered the trunks and bags and swept them aboard the Colorado Blue Bell.

Then for the first time, Mademoiselle da Ponte raised her downcast eyes (at least *openly* she raised them, for from under the dark lashes she had been observing the two young men all the while with stealthy sidelong glances). She said prettily, "Thank you, sir. I don't know what we would have done without you."

Young Meaney took off his hat and bowed slightly. "It's nothing at all," he said. "From now on you needn't worry. This is my father's territory."

Despite the liquor the Professor had already consumed—the early morning drinks which he described as "phlegm-cutters"—his senses became astonishingly alert. He regarded the young man in a new light.

"Come along," said young Meaney. "We'd better get aboard." And he bowed again to permit the young lady to lead the way toward the Colorado Blue Bell.

He followed and then came the Professor and finally the pale Mr. Chatsworthy with misgivings in his heart. For two thousand miles across the vast continent he had watched the demeanor of his young charge gradually changing from one of dignity and reticence to one of gusto and greater freedom and cordiality. It was as if, like an artichoke in the process of being consumed, layer after layer of reserve had been peeled off. The whole slow progress from the spires of Oxford to the bawdy noisiness of Denver had worked so remarkable a change that for a moment Mr. Chatsworthy stared through his thick spectacles at young Meaney as at a stranger.

Suddenly the engine gave out a series of shrill blasts and the small army which had been carrying the luggage aboard the glittering Colorado Blue Bell took up positions in formation along the side of the train and went to work on that element of the prospective passengers which had not yet found places in the crowded train. They pulled some off the roofs of the cars, some off the platforms. Others they beat back to a safe distance so that the train could start without running over any disappointed passengers. One woman separated from her children who were already aboard the train, screamed and beat two of the guards over the head indiscriminately with her umbrella and then made a dash for it. Two tough customers received bloody noses and one man was knocked out. Finally with another series of shrill blasts, the wheezy engine got under way, carrying those who were lucky enough to find places aboard and make the second stage of their journey into that fabulous new country where all of them planned to make a fresh start in life and become millionaires.

The train moved slowly, gradually picking up speed, until the sound of the wails and imprecations of the travelers stranded on the platform were no longer audible.

Inside the Colorado Blue Bell the four passengers settled down among the blue velvet and gold-plated spittoons to the routine of drinking and fighting the heat. The Professor had Bourbon, the young men Scotch and soda and Mademoiselle da Ponte contented herself with a glass of barley water tinctured with lemon. The drinks were prepared by a colored boy called Esau, dressed in a strange costume of blue velvet with gold buttons and yellow lapels. It was part of his duties to meet and welcome young Meaney and Mr. Chatsworthy but his first descent in costume from the private car had aroused such a sensation among the bawdy, noisy immigrants on the platform that he had retreated quickly and remained under cover while the station master and his strong-arm squad had welcomed the young gentlemen and taken care of their baggage.

Now that the train had pulled out and he was no longer greeted by the shouts and hoots of the white trash in the coaches ahead, he was enjoying once more the color and cut of his celestial blue uniform.

At first the conversation was somewhat strained. Even the Professor, knocked out by all the splendor of the blue velvet and gold-plated spittoons, found his usual loquacity dried for a time at the source. It was not until he had taken out a pair of canary yellow gloves, a little worn at the seams and donned them, did he completely recover his composure. Then he explained the misunderstanding which had caused him and his niece to pause only for a night in Denver and then go on to Silver City.

The misunderstanding, he said, concerned dates. There had been some confusion about months. In one contract, he said, the month mentioned for Mademoiselle da Ponte's appearance at the Denver Opera House had been noted as July, in the other, August. So they now had a month to spare and having heard that there was a splendid Opera House in Silver City, he had decided to go there and seek an engagement for his niece during the extra month.

"Why, yes," said Dick Meaney. "My father owns and operates the Opera House there."

Again the Professor brightened perceptibly. "Perhaps he would give my niece an audition?"

"I'm sure it can be arranged," said young Meaney.

Now that he had left Denver, he had begun, to Mr. Chatsworthy's alarm, to expand even more and to shed more and more of the artichoke leaves of reticence and dignity.

In his corner, like an alarmed and watchful mouse, Mr. Chatsworthy was in his heart growing more and more terrified. Outside the window as the train began to climb, this way and that along the swift flowing rivers, on the edge of deep canyons, through low and suffocating tunnels, the country grew steadily more magnificent and awful and frightening. There were mountains alone bigger than a whole English county. The scenery became more and more savage and overwhelming. Even the colors struck him as crude, violent and even terrifying. There were whole mountains of blue and purple and red, splotched with the

[18]

bright green of the summer foliage of the hardwood trees and the black green of pines which seemed to grow out of nothing as if they were glued precariously to the sides of the brilliant precipices which rose straight up and up into infinity by the side of the train.

But these things alarmed him perhaps even less than the behavior of the Professor which became steadily more and more intimate under the pressure of P. J. Meaney's excellent Bourbon. Mr. Chatsworthy was also alarmed by those warm glances which shone out every time the dark lashes of Mademoiselle da Ponte fluttered over her barley water, and by the extraordinary costume of the negro boy, Esau. He was accustomed to the white stockings and powdered wigs worn on state occasions by the innumerable footmen of his cousin, the Earl at the big house in London, but they seemed mediocre and insignificant in comparison with Esau's *habillements*. The only time he had ever seen such costumes, they were worn by the end men of an American minstrel show giving performances on the quay at Brighton.

But what troubled him even more was the spectacle of the Professor's skill as a spitter. Not only did the Professor keep himself well elevated with Bourbon, he began, as he warmed up and the atmosphere grew more cordial, to chew tobacco as well. The action, new to Mr. Chatsworthy, appeared to produce incredible quantities of saliva of which the Professor relieved himself at frequent intervals by spitting a considerable distance into one of the gold-plated spittoons. When Esau proposed to move the spittoon a little nearer to him, the Professor waved the colored boy away with a grandiose gesture of his yellow-gloved hands, saying, "No! It's just the right distance for me. That's my best distance."

It seemed to Mr. Chatsworthy that as rapidly as the Professor absorbed Bourbon and water, he rid himself of the excessive moisture by spitting. Mr. Chatsworthy, like all Englishmen, had an admiration for skill in sports and could not but admire grudgingly the accuracy with which the Professor landed a stream of tobacco juice across Mademoiselle da Ponte, straight into the opening of the gold-plated spittoon, an action which the young lady accepted with the calm and confidence of a female target in a knife-throwing act.

As the train wound through the mountains, higher and higher up canyons and through tunnels, Mr. Chatsworthy noticed something

[19]

else from the windows of the Colorado Blue Bell. At each stop and at every small cluster of houses set precariously on the edge of the canyons or in a clearing of mountain pines, Mr. Chatsworthy discovered the name P. J. Meaney. It adorned the fronts of the ramshackle general stores, grocery stores, and meat markets. It even appeared painted on at least two shacks that served as depots—Meaneytown and Meaney-ville. It seemed to him that the name Meaney in this wild, vast country was like the crown and the coat-of-arms which marked buildings, institutions and palaces and post boxes belonging to the King.

"King P. J. Meaney," Mr. Chatsworthy reflected, trying the sound over in his head. "King P. J. Meaney, the First," and looking at his friend he thought, "Richard, Duke of Silver City."

But his friend, by now, was deep in animated conversation with the Professor and Mademoiselle da Ponte. They were planning Mademoiselle da Ponte's first appearance in Silver City at the Opera House as Violetta in *La Traviata*. It was one of the two roles which she knew. The engagement would fill in nicely during the wait for the opening of what the Professor referred to as "The Denver season." Young Dick, enthusiastic by now, was sure he could arrange the engagement.

PART II

%%

THE WHOLE OF SILVER CITY LAY IN A VAST HOLLOW WHERE THE DEEP, narrow canyon which contained Rattlesnake Creek widened out for a space of seven or eight miles. Above and around it rose the high, multicolored mountains, pierced by the mines which kept pouring out more and more silver ore, more indeed than the world wanted or needed. The town itself had begun as a single street and gradually spread out in a ramshackle manner over the whole of the open expanse closed in by the mountains.

Most of the houses were little more than shacks built from lumber hauled painfully up the mountains by P. J. Meaney's railroad or from rough green timber sawed out of the trees, owned by P. J. Meaney, that clustered on the lower slopes of the mountains. The principal street, named Eudora Street after P. J. Meaney's eldest daughter, was lined with buildings notable principally for their false fronts. There were general stores, government offices, saloons, gambling houses and brothels. If you looked merely at the fronts you had the impression of viewing a rich town notable for the ornate and elegant architectural fantasy of its façades. These were in various styles ranging from the classical Greek of Moe Hirshbein's Clothing Emporium through Gothic, Renaissance and late U. S. Grant. Seen from the backside these same buildings were the source of great disillusionment. They were shabby, ramshackle, boxlike and innocent of paint, the brothels and saloons cluttered by a remarkable number of crudely built outside stairways which permitted their clients to make quick exits under the stress of adverse circumstances.

On the whole, however, the effect was one of exuberance and gaiety like the gilt and glitter of a carnival or a circus. Adding to the air of

[21]

gaiety was a population which appeared to live in the principal thoroughfare, day and night, twenty-four hours a day. If anything, Eudora Street was gayer and certainly noisier at three in the morning than at three in the afternoon. It was a population largely made up of miners, trollops, prospectors, gamblers and sheep and cattle men from the high, vast plateau north of the town which ran way up into Utah. All evening and all night there was the sound of music, the clatter of chips, the neighing of amorous mares and stallions along the hitching rails, punctuated by the distant periodical sounds of blasts being set off in the high mines on the mountainside or by the rattle of pistol shots in the near vicinity where there was a ruckus in one of the brothels or gambling houses or among the eternally feuding cattle and sheep men, who, carrying their feuds within the borders of the town, began taking pot shots at each other,

Among the fragile and garish façades and the ramshackle houses, three buildings raised an air of substance and durability. These were Mrs. Sowers' Grand Hotel and Boarding House, the Silver City Grand Opera House and the Castle. Mrs. Sowers' Grand Hotel and Boarding House appeared vast in comparison to the surrounding buildings. It was constructed of wood and, although architecturally pretentious and ornamented with a good deal of jigsaw work, had by some oversight, never been painted. This fact gave it an air of impermanence as if Mrs. Sowers felt that Silver City was not here to stay and that the whole thing might collapse at any time. The Grand Hotel had a vast wooden veranda running around three sides of the building where her boarders sat out in rocking chairs of rustic design, made by the neighboring tribe of Palomel Indians, of native pine at the price of thirty-five cents a rocker. Within its depths, in boxlike rooms, each equipped with a durable pitcher, washbowl and slopjar, dwelt most of the transient visitors to Silver City—the gamblers, the medicine men, the government agents and the members of the Silver City Opera Company during the season.

The Opera House itself was a building of impressive size built of granite from the quarries which P. J. Meaney had opened in the mountain that dominated the city on the north. It was constructed in pseudo-Moorish style, with archways, a grand stairway and an auditorium with gilded boxes which seated two thousand music lovers. Its season ran through the month of August when even the high, clear air of Silver City grew too hot for the comfort of two thousand people crowded into one room with no provision made for ventilation.

The third majestic building, known as the Castle, stood on a low hill just above the city and was the residence of P. J. Meaney himself. It was a vast pile, constructed, like the Opera House, of native granite. The walls, as Meaney himself always pointed out to visitors, were two feet thick, a provision possibly necessary to support the crenellated towers which rose from all parts of the structure in imitation of the battle towers of ancient Florence. The whole was surrounded by an enormous, closely clipped lawn, naked of all vegetation save for large groups of cannas, kohlia, salvia, begonia, geraniums and other ornate or variegated flowers set out in beds made in the shapes of stars, crescents, pentagons and hexagons. A long, sweeping driveway bordered by kerosene lamps on cast-iron posts led up to the elegant porte-cochere and grand hall.

The grand hall was famous throughout the West. Nothing quite like it existed even in rich, polygot, wide-open San Francisco, while in Los Angeles, the nearest approach was little more than a hut or adobe.

As you entered the house by the doorway opening from the porte-cochere you were faced by an immense stairway with balustrades of pink marble with the newel posts ornamented by female figures (discreetly draped) holding aloft gilded lanterns. From the balcony overhead hung "verdure" tapestries of no particular merit save that they existed by the square yard and were expensive. On the tessellated marble floors stood a small jungle of potted palms from among which at intervals appeared suits of armor and four immense stuffed grizzly bears. In the very center of the hall there was a figure wearing armor mounted upon a life-sized horse. Both horse and man were realistically painted.

On the left of the hall there was a huge "parlor" furnished with heavily overstuffed and buttoned crimson brocade furniture, ornamented with ball fringe. On the walls hung row upon row of oil paintings which P. J. Meaney had bought upon the basis of size. The most expensive was an immense canvas, very dark and "antique" by some unknown painter, depicting "The Feast of Belshazzar"—a picture in which very strange dubious orgies were taking place beneath the thick fog of varnish.

On either side of the great folding doors leading into the hall stood life-sized easel portraits of P. J. Meaney and his wife, Ellie-May, draped at the top with swags of crimson, ball-fringed brocade velvet which matched the furniture and the lush, elegant curtains.

Room after room the house extended upward and outward, a monument to P. J. Meaney's success and to his power over a whole kingdom larger than many a state ruled by an Indian potentate. There were rooms, indeed whole suites of rooms, for his four sons, his invalid daughter Eudora, himself and his wife, as well as suites for the senators, congressmen, governors and politicians so necessary to the maintenance, preservation and growth of the Meaney Kingdom.

At the moment the shabby, puffing engine with the Colorado Blue Bell attached came puffing through canyons and tunnels higher and higher toward Silver City, P. J. Meaney himself was seated in his office. This was a large room on the second floor, occupying a whole floor of one of the battlemented towers. It contained a half dozen stiff, uncomfortable, heavily carved chairs, placed at intervals about the walls, a vast teakwood table inlaid with mother-of-pearl, a roll-top desk, a huge and comfortably upholstered swivel armchair and above it on the wall an over-life-size portrait of P. J. Meaney in a long frock coat standing in a statesmanlike attitude beside the teakwood table and holding in one hand a scroll of papers of mysterious origin and content. The swivel chair P. J. Meaney employed to turn from table to roll-top desk and back. The desk he kept locked except when he was in the room.

As the Colorado Blue Bell puffed toward Silver City, P. J. Meaney faced across the great desk a lean, tall man called Henry Caldwell, quiet in appearance for all the gaudiness of his cattleman's clothes, with a long, straight back supporting a well-shaped head covered with sandy hair. The eyes were steel grey and the hands large, beautiful and heavily veined, the nose large and straight and the lips full but well-shaped. He sat opposite P.J. on one of the stiff, uncomfortable carved chairs.

[24]

Across from him in the swivel throne chair between the teakwood table and roll-top desk sat the great P.J. dressed in his usual long frocked statesman's coat. He was a big man and a hairy one, black and scowling in appearance. His black hair, beginning to show signs of grey, was naturally wavy and a source of vanity. He kept it heavily oiled and shining. Beneath beetling black eyebrows which he never trimmed and which his barber combed and oiled carefully into place each morning, the features were coarse and even brutal and their coarseness was not alleviated by the heavy black mustache which partly covered the big, heavy-lipped mouth. He had wrists like the pistons of the locomotive that drew the Colorado Blue Bell and hands like hams. Black hair growing in a pattern like the hair on the paws of a chimpanzee covered the backs, running well up on to the knuckles. On the table before him lay a six-shooter, the size of a small cannon which he kept there during all interviews. Always it pointed directly at the visitor who sat on the straight chair opposite him. At the moment, Henry Caldwell, unawed, was looking straight into the muzzle.

"And let me tell you further, Henry Caldwell, that there's no place in this territory for any radicals. This here is *my* territory—P. J. Meaney's territory—and the Calamares range is P. J. Meaney's range and any cattle caught on it is *his* cattle. And his son Buck will see to it that there ain't any arguing about that fact."

The visitor interrupted him, saying, "But there's enough grazing on the Calamares range for ten times the cattle that's up there."

P. J. Meaney had an answer for that one. He said, "Is it my fault that the Lord only provided for a range cow to have one calf at a time and half of 'em bulls? We're fillin' up that range as fast as we can. Give us three more years and there'll be cattle enough to clean up every blade of grass on Calamares range. I wish to God them longhorns had litters instead of solos." He picked up the six-shooter and began to examine it. "It looks to me, Henry Caldwell, as if you was one of them natural born trouble-makers. I'm talking to you as an old friend. I think it's a good idea to keep off'n that Calamares range and what's more, it's a good idea to keep right out of Silver City, even during the "Opry" season. There's been some trouble lately among the miners and I ain't so sure you ain't had a part in it. I aim to fire the trouble-makers. I got some new help comin' on the train that's puffin' up the canyon right now. When they get here the trouble-makers is takin' the first train out of town."

Henry Caldwell studied the inside of the big weather-beaten hat he held in his gnarled hands and then said, "Is that your last word, P.J.?"

"That's my last word and my last word is my final word!"

Henry Caldwell didn't say anything. He just stood up and walked across the wide expanse of floor separating P.J.'s teakwood table from the door. He did indulge in one gesture of defiance. He put on the big weather-beaten hat before he reached the door, in the very presence of P. J. Meaney.

When the door had closed on Henry Caldwell, P.J. sat for a time staring at it, thinking. He had always liked Henry Caldwell but he couldn't understand him. Once, long ago, Henry could have been his partner in the building up of the Silver City kingdom, but there had come a point when he refused to go along. And lately he'd been getting all sorts of radical ideas, even to running for Congress, as if he had a chance against P.J. and the machine. He didn't like having to talk to Henry as he had just done, but there didn't seem to be any other way out. Henry was as stubborn as a bone-headed off-ox, never seein' what side his bread was buttered on.

P.J. concluded his thoughts with a monumental sigh and turned quickly, as was his habit as a man of action, to other things. He picked up the six-shooter, put it in the table drawer and took out a gold-plated mirror. Then he unbuttoned the frock coat and looked at his watch which he wore attached to a heavy gold chain, draped across the front of his spotless white waistcoat. When he had checked on the time he replaced the watch and took from another waistcoat pocket a small gold comb and a small phial of verbena-scented Macassar oil. One drop of this he placed on the gold comb, rubbing it with a giant forefinger to spread it over the surface. Then replacing the phial in his pocket he picked up the mirror and, regarding himself carefully, he applied the comb first to his wavy hair, then the bushy, flowing eyebrows and finally to the flowing mustaches. When he had finished he put away the comb and put the mirror back in the drawer in its accustomed place beside the six-shooter. Then he picked up the black broad-brimmed statesman's hat and walked out into the vast hallway.

For some distance he walked between the second-floor potted palms until he came to the door of the room leading into the big sitting room of his wife, Ellie-May's suite.

In more than twenty years, he had not crossed the threshold with amorous intent, but he liked going there to talk now and then with the tired little woman he had married nearly forty years earlier. It was the one place in all the kingdom or indeed in the whole State of Colorado where he could rest and be himself, where he did not have to carry himself like a pouter-pigeon and receive the plaudits and flattery of the crowd. It wasn't any good sticking out his chest in front of Ellie-May because she didn't even notice it. She had been through the whole of the long struggle that began long ago in migrations from town to town with a growing family and a thin pocketbook, while P.J. was trying to find his "opportunity." When at last it came, and he found a country, a society and a condition suited to his peculiar talents, she wasn't impressed at all by the money he made and the power he wielded. Sometimes he thought she didn't appreciate him. It was as if she had liked that other life better when they were knocking about, living in cheap boarding houses, leaving town when the bills got too big.

He couldn't complain that she didn't do as he asked her. When the governors or senators or bankers and lawyers from the East came to the Castle, she dressed herself up and sat at the head of the table and did what the wife of a man like P. J. Meaney was expected to do. The rest of the time she kept pretty much to the two rooms she had fitted out for herself on the second floor after Richard was born and that woman Tessie Burkhart made the shooting scrape right in the middle of Eudora Street and Ellie-May said she wouldn't live with him any more.

As he opened the door, he found Ellie-May seated at the new-fangled sewing machine which she had coveted more than tiaras and diamond necklaces. She was a small, slight woman with sandy hair, turning grey and a prematurely aged face which must once have been very pretty. Now it was like a rather puckered, withered pansy. As he entered, she looked over her shoulder and said, "These new inventions are wonderful, P.J. I'm running up a new nightgown for Eudora. She wears them out so fast always being in bed."

She never called him anything but "P.J." or "Mr. Meaney"—the one to his face and the other in front of distinguished guests. For nearly twenty years he had never heard her use any term of endearment.

The room was a comfortable and cosy room with well-worn furniture and white Nottingham lace curtains at the big windows. Outside each of the windows there was a big flowerbox where Ellie-May grew mignonette and night-scented stock and all the flowers she loved, for which there never seemed to be any place in the big ornate flowerbeds which decorated dubiously the vast, well-clipped irrigated lawns. Their scent, warmed by the heat of midafternoon now drifted in through the open windows and as P.J. became aware of them, he felt suddenly soft and nostalgic.

He said, "If you want any more new-fangled things, Ellie-May, just you say so and I'll have Bascomb send 'em on from New York."

He noticed that she was wearing a well-washed gingham dress and said, "It's time you got dressed for the reception. The train'll be here in half an hour."

She said, "You go on to the depot without me. You know I don't like riding through the streets in those showy carriages."

"Don't you want to meet Dick and Mr. Chatsworthy?"

"I can wait," said Ellie-May, still pedaling at the sewing machine. "I've waited over three years to see Richard. Another half hour or so won't matter. Anyway, I don't like greeting Richard in front of all that crowd."

P.J. was silent for a moment. Then he said, "Richard is kind of your favorite, ain't he?"

"Yes," said Ellie-May, without looking up from the sewing machine, "he sure is." Then as an afterthought she said, "I'll be waiting and ready in the front hall."

He went out, closing the door behind him and went down the vast marble stairway to the porte-cochere where three Victorias decorated with plumes and paper streamers were waiting.

After being married to Ellie-May for nearly a half century, he still couldn't make her out. In all the world, she had always been able to stand up against him and he still didn't know how she managed it. She never raised her voice and sometimes she didn't even bother to answer back. When she addressed him as "P.J." or "Mr. Meaney" there was no coldness or resentment in her voice. She spoke quietly and with dignity; but in nearly twenty years she had never used the term "honey" which she had employed in her southern way during the first, hard years of their life together. It was as if Ellie-May had some inward spirit with which he had never been permitted to become acquainted, even in those distant first years. He could never make out what she was really thinking and sometimes he had an uncomfortable feeling that she looked down on him from the very beginning and that her contempt had grown, the more rich and successful and powerful he became.

Of course, he knew that she had begun to call him "P.J." only after Tessie Burkhart had winged him through the left shoulder, shooting from the upper window of the El Dorado Casino that day on Eudora Street. From then on she seemed to take no interest in him or his philandering.

And there was the business of Richard. He knew well enough that the boy, born long after the others, was her favorite, yet she never raised a protest when he proposed sending him east to school and later to Oxford. He had wanted at least one solid gold gentleman in the family. Buck and Shorty and Black Pete—the three eldest boys—were good enough he-men and they knew how to manage their respective provinces of the kingdom, but it would occur to no one to call them gentlemen. Buck handled the cattle, Shorty, the mines, and Black Pete, the sheep. It worked out fine that way but all hell and lightning couldn't have made gentlemen out of them, like Senator Wilkinson who had been to Harvard. Very shrewdly, long ago P.J. had discovered that if you couldn't be a gentleman, the next best thing was to be a character. That's what he and the older boys were—characters—known from Boise to Albuquerque and Denver to San Francisco as men you couldn't meddle with. They were black and hairy like himself. They were chips off the old block. Richard was different, with red-gold hair like his mother's people and a fair, clear skin.

No, he couldn't make Ellie-May out. Now after Richard's being away for over three years she wouldn't even go down to the depot to meet him. He crossed the hall between the palms and the suits of armor, and stepped into the first bedecked open Victoria.

[29]

Two of his older sons, Buck and Shorty, were already in the two carriages which followed his. They sat sprawled out in store clothes, looking for all the world like twins, dark, hairy, heavy-boned men with a certain animal good looks. At sight of him they sat up and said, "Howdy, Pop!"

Shorty, who ran the mines, lived in Silver City. Buck had come in for the occasion from the range where he kept a Calamares Indian woman with two half-breed kids.

Blackie who was unmarried and looked like his brothers, but was stocky and built like a bull, hadn't been invited because he and Buck always fought over the rights of the cattle and the sheep to the grazing land. P.J. had long since given orders that they were never to be in Silver City at the same time.

P.J. said, "Good morning, boys!" as he stepped into the first Victoria, which settled down on one side under the great weight of his frame and said, "To the depot. The band is meetin' us there!"

When P.J. closed the door, Ellie-May pedaled away a little longer at the new sewing machine until she had Eudora's new nightgown assembled. Once it was stitched together she would cross-stitch the cuffs of the long sleeves and the high neck with red and then sew "valenseens" lace outside the collar and the cuffs. Eudora didn't have many visitors—only Mrs. Mintz from the Primitive Methodist Mission and Reverend Pearlsides of the Church, Miss Rachel Hirshbein, daughter of Moses who owned the Clothing Emporium and Myrtle Higgenbottom, who, like herself, had never married. But Ellie-May liked her to look nice when she received visitors.

Ellie-May kept humming a hymn as she pedaled. She was quite happy, occupied as she was all day long with a million small things like cross-stitching Eudora's nightgowns and watering the window boxes and going on endless shopping expeditions given over to the purchase of countless small and inexpensive articles such as patent eggbeaters, dress snaps, pneumatic bustles, antimacassars, etc. She was in reality, gadget-minded, although the flow of "gadgets" which marked the advance of future generations was only beginning to appear on the shelves and counters of Silver City. Apparently the only satisfaction she found in P.J.'s rise to great wealth was the fact that she could afford to spend as much money as she liked on all the little things she had never been able to afford in the nomadic period of the Meaney family life when P.J. was looking for his opportunity.

P.J. was generous with her. She could have spent thousands or hundreds of thousands on travel, perfumes, jewels, clothes and her extravagance would have raised no protest, because P.J. never really knew how rich he was and because he would have looked upon such extravagances in his curiously realistic flat-footed way, as "conscience money" which he owed her in return for his philandering, in recompense to her for Tessie Burkhart, Madge Beakymer and all the others. But all the luxuries meant nothing to Ellie-May. She was, in her simple way, a singularly wise and happy woman.

She had none of the appetite for great wealth and power which constantly devoured her dynamic husband. Within the orbit of the Castle, the Kingdom, the whole Empire which P.J. had built up, she had created a world of her own, a small neat world encompassed by patent sewing machines and gadgets and window boxes filled with mignonette and night-scented stocks. It was a world preserved out of her own southern background—genteel, placid, sentimental, romantic, unreal and limited—in which she was safe and cosy. Her own rooms in the vast Castle she had managed to make, despite their high ceilings and walnut doors, resemble the rooms of the well-managed and spotlessly clean cottage in Independence, Arkansas, from which she had come as a girl long ago.

Sometimes, in the rare moments left her from her fussing and fidgeting and housekeeping, she reflected upon her own past and the past of P.J. and always came to the conclusion that the wellsprings of P.J.'s vast ambitions for wealth and power lay in the remote past when P.J. as a peddler had been looked down upon by her family and forbidden the premises of the parsonage house of the Methodist Church back in Independence. She fancied—inded she was quite sure—that P.J. had built a whole empire simply to show that he was as good as her own family.

In these odd moments of reflection the stream of reminiscence carried her back into a past when P.J. had been a young man, tall, slim, dark and strong, who had swept her away on a stream of passion which still startled her even years after it had waned and died. Many things had killed it, the overwhelming and insatiable concupiscence of P.J., his fabulous egotism, the gradual hardening of his character in the process of worldly success and the fact that P.J. himself had changed from a tall, strong, dark passionate lover into a kind of grizzly bear—coarse, hairy and growling, altogether too much for her mild, mid-Victorian tastes in love. Sometimes, looking at the big hairy man, she wondered that he could ever have been the young fellow who so upset all her southern upbringing and good behavior that she had defied her family and run off to marry him in the frontier town of Kansas City.

Now he did not bother her. He had not bothered her for nearly twenty years. She was aware in her simple, quiet way that he had strong tastes in women, and the strong tastes, even when carried out and satisfied, did not trouble her much since she was not a jealous woman and, in her extraordinary position, she was not subject to humiliation. Living in the Castle, apart from the town of Silver City, absorbed and secure in the small details of the cosy life she had made for herself, like the nest of a bird or a rabbit, within the gawdy orbit of P.J.'s world, she was not subject to humiliation, even though the whole town knew about Madge Beakymer.

Ellie-May even had an objective, detailed, and almost scientific interest in Madge Beakymer on the rare occasions when she passed the big, florid, dyed-blonde proprietress of the El Dorado in the streets of Silver City. Objectively she speculated upon what Madge and P.J. talked about when they were together in Madge's flat above the gambling rooms and even allowed her simple mind to speculate upon the amorous goings on of the pair. It must be, she thought—knowing P.J. and speculating about the big buxom, blonde Madge—a bull-in-a-china-shop performance with the furniture flying in all directions and the floors, walls and ceilings bulging in and out. At times, as the picture grew in her imagination, she even found herself laughing quietly.

Whenever Ellie-May got enough of housekeeping and the pompous life of the Castle, she fled to her retreat in the high valley above Silver City. This was a log cabin of three rooms, simply and comfortably furnished, with a little garden watered from one of the valley lakes that reflected the brilliant blue skies of the Colorado country. Sometimes she would get Eudora out of bed, wrap her up well and take her along, to resume her bed-ridden life in the cottage, but these visits of Eudora's grew less and less frequent as her daughter complained that the altitude and the journey brought on "poor spells."

P.J. was never allowed to come there. That was the only thing she ever demanded of him—that he absent himself altogether from the place. When she found herself growing fretful and intolerably bored with life at the Castle, she would return to the cottage in the high valley, sometimes even in the midst of winter when she had to put on snow shoes and plow through the snow that was many feet deep, accompanied by Esau, the colored retainer, who cut wood and made fires for her and sometimes shot the timber wolves that came and howled outside the windows.

Some people, failing to understand Ellie-May and the life she had arranged for herself, felt sorry for her but they wasted their pity. Untormented by envy or ambition or jealousy, she led what was undoubtedly the happiest and most placid life in Silver City, or perhaps in Colorado or the whole of the nation.

When she had finished the major construction of Eudora's new nightgown, she laid aside her work, rose, opened the door and crossed the hall to the room where Eudora lay, as she described it, "chained to her bed."

Eudora was thirty-one years old and she was monstrously fat as a result of a total lack of exercise and an appetite which seemed unaffected by her "malady." She had lain in her bed for seven years, ever since she was thwarted in love. Since the trips to the cottage had come to an end, she never left her room or her bed save when she was moved from bed to armchair by the window overlooking the shacks, the houses and the turbulent life of Silver City—a proceeding which prevented bedsores.

As Ellie-May entered the room, Eudora was sitting propped up on pillows cutting out texts and bits of moral poetry which she found in books and magazines and in the Bible itself. These she pasted on bits of cardboard and sent to the inmates of the local jail and the newly established state penitentiary. All around the texts she pasted clusters of forget-me-nots, buttercups, and eglantine which came with the backs already covered with glue. P.J.'s New York agent had found them for her and kept forwarding them constantly in great quantities—one of the many strange tasks he was called on to perform in order to hold his job and satisfy the whims of P.J.'s family (another was providing pictures of nude women for Blackie who managed the sheep business on the high and lonely range).

The cutting out and pasting of texts kept Eudora busy and comparatively happy, especially since the opening of the new state penitentiary which had increased the field enormously. Within the past three years she had clipped into ribbons two hundred and sixty-three copies of the New and the Old Testaments. In her selection of texts she was shrewd and moral, avoiding the more lewd, voluptuous and stimulating passages like the Song of Songs, the story of Lot and his daughter, the unfortunate experiences of the young angels on their visit to Sodom and Gomorrah and many others. In this she exercised tact as well since many of the recipients of her texts were in jail or in the state penitentiary as a result of statutory charges as age-old as the stories of the Old Testament and not entirely unrelated to them.

Eudora's misfortune and the cause of her tragedy in love was the direct result of the fact that she resembled her father P.J. instead of her small, feminine mother. She was very dark, with the heavy, rather oily skin that was shared by P.J. and her three eldest brothers and she had the same heavy, black eyebrows which grew a little bushier each year. She also had the big limbs and in addition a huge bust for which Ellie-May had to make structural allowances in the creation of her nightgowns.

Eudora's one romance and the one which had blighted her life occurred with a young eastern lawyer who saw, for a time at least, the prospects of a brilliant and opulent future in marriage with the daughter of P. J. Meaney. He had became engaged to her, but as the date set for the wedding approached and Eudora's wedding dress, made by Ellie-May, "was on the bed," he had weakened and sent a long letter explaining that his New England family would not permit the marriage. On receipt of the letter, Eudora fainted, they put her to bed and from then on she never arose from it save on the occasion of the now abandoned excursions to the cottage or to sit in the armchair by the window overlooking Silver City.

Ellie-May with that curious, quick, realistic wisdom, which informed the whole of her existence, had come to the conclusion that "under the circumstances" Eudora had found a very satisfactory solution to her existence. She was able to lie in bed most of the day and to eat all she wanted of the rich and varied dishes prepared in the distant kitchen of the Castle by the French chef. Her creative instinct seemed wholly satisfied by the cutting out and pasting up of texts and bouquets. She was, Ellie-May observed, much happier than most people in this world and not half so driven and harassed.

And in a way, Eudora carried on an active life through her friend, Rachel Hirshbein who called nearly every day with detailed accounts of all the local happenings. Rachel, like Eudora, was a virgin, "through choice" as she put it, and would have made a fortune two or three generations later as a gossip columnist. She knew not only the major facts of any scandal or shooting but she discovered or divined the inner essence and the more morbid details of every murder or crime of passion. The two women spent many happy hours together going over the more scandalous manifestations of life in Silver City, dissecting, speculating, re-creating the more intimate and morbid details. One of their most harried subjects was the romance between P.J. and Madge Beakymer. Sometimes Rachel brought her mandolin and played for Eudora the new songs they were singing at the El Dorado or Jake's Place or the Parisian and Gates Ajar bars.

There were, of course, occasional periods when even Eudora grew a little bored. At these times she had what she referred to as "poor spells." Ellie-May had long ago discovered that the best cure for these poor spells was brandy. It seemed to be the only thing that could bring Eudora round.

That afternoon the conversation between Eudora and her mother concerned mostly the subject of Richard's return.

Eudora, cutting out her texts, seemed brighter than usual and even a little excited at the prospect of seeing her youngest brother. The other three, so like herself in appearance, paid her little heed and seldom if ever came to her room, but Richard, ten years younger, so blond and clean looking, had always been her favorite, and the imminence of his arrival allayed any possibility of a "poor spell" overtaking her. For weeks she and Rachel had spent many happy hours speculating about him, whether three years in the Old Country had changed him, whether he had had any experience with women, whether or not he would have acquired an English accent, and what the tutor, Mr. Chatsworthy, would be like.

At sight of her mother, Eudora merely looked up and went on cutting out texts. She had struck a rich vein in the Proverbs where almost any line seemed to suit the cases of her unfortunate friends in the jailhouse and the penitentiary. The trimmings of paper lay spread across her vast bosom like drifted snow.

"Is the train on time?" she asked.

"I guess so," said Ellie-May, "or Merle Hardenfelt down at the depot would have sent word. Your Pa has just gone off with Buck and Shorty."

"I wisht I was well enough to see the welcome," observed Eudora. "Where's your telescope?"

"Over there. I'm going to sit up for a spell and watch." She sighed a martyr's sigh. "But it ain't the same as bein' there."

It was one of Ellie-May's crosses in life that all her children but Dick not only looked like P.J. but talked like him, as if his dynamic personality and physique had left an impress even upon their speech. They said "ain't" and used similar colloquial words and phrases which Ellie-May had learned to avoid in her refined southern parsonage upbringing. Even Dick, as a small boy, though he in no way resembled P.J. either in physique, or coloring or character, showed signs of similar lapses. That was one of the reasons why she had not only given in to P.J.'s suggestion that they make a gentleman of Dick by sending him east and to the Old Country; she had actually urged it.

"Well, I expect he'll be in before an hour's up," said Ellie-May.

"Ain't you excited?" asked Eudora, looking at her mother, who showed no outward signs.

"Of course I'm excited," said Ellie-May and thought, "It'd scare you, if you knew how much." Then she added, "The chef is making up one of those gatto St. Ornerys especially for you. You know the kind —whipped cream, honey, sugar, chocolate and almonds."

A watery look came into Eudora's eyes and for a moment the scissors paused in mid-air.

"You look good," said Ellie-May.

Again Eudora sighed, "I ain't so bad this morning. Dick's coming home makes me feel better. I'm kinda curious about this here Mr. Chatsworthy."

"Any good letters from the jail today?" asked her mother.

"Nothing out of the ordinary."

Her mother referred to the vast correspondence which had arisen between Eudora and the recipients of her texts. The correspondence had grown to considerable proportions, occupying a great part of Eudora's time and brightening her spirits greatly. Sometimes they reached as many as ten or fifteen a day. Some were pious, some groveling, some obscene since both the local jail and the state penitentiary were somewhat new and primitive affairs where there was no censorship, but all of them displayed an awareness that Eudora was the daughter of P. J. Meaney who possessed great power in the state. Eudora never showed the obscene ones to her mother but kept them locked away. Occasionally she took them out and let her friend Rachel Hirshbein read them. They kept both women abreast of the latest expressions in the underworld and instructed them in many strange goings on in the world of amorous experience.

Eudora said, "I seen Henry Caldwell leavin' here this mornin'."

"Yes," said Ellie-May quietly. "He was trying to settle that fight over the range lands with your father."

"It's a shame he and Pop had to take to fightin'. I like Henry Caldwell and I miss him."

Ellie-May sighed, "I always said your father was wrong and that wrong never won out over right." A little glint of fire came into Ellie-May's pale blue eyes. "He'll find it out one of these days."

"Rachel says that she hears Henry Caldwell is fixin' to run for Governor. That would make Pop mad."

"If Henry got elected your father would have to curb some of his high-handed ways." She sighed deeply, "But I guess Henry wouldn't have a chance."

"I don't know," said Eudora. "Rachel says people are gettin' sick of Pop runnin' everything. She says there's more and more talk agin him even right here in Silver City."

"Well, a revolution is bound to happen some day, but your father won't believe it. He's a pig-headed man."

Eudora sighed again, "I guess the Meaneys is all pig-headed."

Then suddenly from far down in the town below the Castle there came the sound of music, the playing of a brass band. It drifted into the room and Eudora put down her Bible and scissors.

"I guess Dick must be arrivin'," said Eudora.

Three shrill blasts of a locomotive whistle came through the air. "Yes, there's the train now."

Ellie-May went over to the bed and Eudora swung her great unwieldy body to the edge, placing her bare feet on the floor. Then she stood up and took the arm of her mother and together they went to the window where Eudora sat in her armchair and took up the telescope.

"Well," said Ellie-May, "I guess I'd better go and get dressed up."

As she walked across the hall, a faint smile crinkled her lips and a light came into the pale eyes. She was thinking about Henry Caldwell. She knew something none of the rest of them knew and that secret had supported her for more than twenty years and made her invulnerable to anything that P. J. Meaney might do or say and to the dullness of all her life in the Castle and in Silver City. It was something she clung to and hugged close to her breast. The only pity was that Henry Caldwell and P.J. had taken to fighting and Henry couldn't be there at supper tonight when Dick came home. But anyway he was in Silver City. That was something. And probably he'd see the parade of welcome.

By two o'clock even the inside of the Colorado Blue Bell had turned really hot. It was the dry heat of the high mountains, a heat such as Mr. Chatsworthy had never experienced in his whole life in England. It was accompanied in the high clear air by small tornadoes and whirlwinds of dust which were broken up almost as soon as they were born by the intervening rocks and precipices. From the sides of the canyon through which the train passed, heat was reflected with redoubled intensity. It seemed to penetrate the car even with the blue plush curtains drawn.

Presently conversation died and the soporific effect of the Bourbon made itself felt upon Professor da Ponte who fell asleep, high collar, yellow gloves and all, and dozed peacefully with his mouth open.

Mademoiselle da Ponte nodded in a discreet and refined way and young Dick slept on the black walnut sofa. Only Mr. Chatsworthy really remained awake. He did so for fear of missing something— anything—in this wild, ferociously beautiful new country.

As the train climbed, the canyon grew narrower and higher until even by thrusting his head out of the open window at the peril of losing it altogether, he could not see the top of its lofty walls. He was exactly in this position when the engine gave a series of shrill blasts, almost deafening him as they reverberated from side to side of the rocky walls. Clearly it was some kind of signal and the shrill toots were arranged in a series of dots and dashes. Filled with alarm, as if the shrill whistles had been directed at himself for thrusting his head out of the window, Mr. Chatsworthy drew in his head and a moment later the canyon walls which had been pressing in upon the train were no longer there and the train was crossing a wide open space bordered by mountains and filled with a few trees and a great number of shabby huts and houses, arranged in no particular semblance of order.

As the train advanced, it signaled its shrill code again. Dick wakened and sat up. Mademoiselle da Ponte discreetly withdrew to the ladies salon, and the Professor, disturbed in his sleep, began talking to himself.

Outside, the houses and shacks became more numerous and closer together and their quality improved a little and then on an eminence above them appeared a vast, castellated granite structure surrounded by bright flower beds. The contrast with the shabby houses was so great that Mr. Chatsworthy turned to Dick and asked, pointing, "Is that a jail?" And Dick replied sleepily, "No, that's home. This is Silver City!"

Then the noise of a brass band playing, "There'll Be a Hot Time in the Old Town Tonight," drowned out the sounds of the train wheezing to a stop.

"Damn and hell!" said Dick. "They're welcoming me home!"

It was the one thing he had dreaded. He had wanted to return home quietly and he had even written twice asking his father to permit him a quiet entry, but in his heart, knowing his father, he knew that the noisy welcome would be inevitable. P. J. Meaney was not a man to overlook an opportunity for advertisement and glory for himself or for any member of his family. Dick's brothers would not have minded. They would have taken it in their stride sullenly or philosophically, planning all the time the celebration was going on how quickly they could get away to the flashy delights of Eudora Street. But the "welcomes" for them were few and far between as they came and went to and from Silver City almost continually.

Mr. Chatsworthy was at the window as the train pulled in, witnessing a spectacle such as he had never seen before even in London on the Queen's birthday. The whole depot platform was filled with people, even more wild in appearance than those who took part in a costermonger's crowning of the Pearly King and Queen, and they were dressed even more fantastically than the costermongers in bright shirts and pants made of cowskin fringed from thigh to ankle, in checked suits and red ties. A great many wore silver ornaments on belts and on shields strapped to their wrists. Here and there appeared a stolid Calamares Indian squaw in a bright-colored blanket carrying other blankets and articles made of bright-colored beads and glass.

The train stopped and then suddenly a dozen tough-looking men wearing railroad caps began beating through the crowds to make a passageway. When a way had been cleared another group of station hands moved from the depot to the steps of the Colorado Blue Bell rolling a red carpet before them. Behind them as they rolled moved the majestic figure of P. J. Meaney, hair and mustaches glistening, dressed in a top hat and Prince Albert coat. Behind him came his two sons, Buck and Shorty. While the manner of P.J. was full of triumph and dignity, that of the brothers, Buck and Shorty, who while waiting had helped themselves too generously from his flask, had a hang-dog and embarrassed quality.

On the platform beside the Colorado Blue Bell, the meeting between father and son took place. The full dignity and impressiveness of the occasion was somewhat disturbed by the presence of the Professor and Mademoiselle da Ponte whom no one had expected. The Professor's costume, with the yellow gloves, the checked vest, the heavy gold watch chain and the gold-headed stick created a sensation even among the bright, eccentrically dressed members of the crowd, but he was overlooked almost immediately as the crowd caught a glimpse of Mademoiselle da Ponte. All the crowd knew P.J.'s son and at least had heard, long since, that he would be accompanied by his English tutor who was unmistakable by his quiet, mouselike demeanor, his tweeds and his deerstalker's cap, but who were the tall stranger in the yellow gloves and the voluptuous young lady?

Within the crowd whispers of speculation went around and at last most of the onlookers settled for the theory that the Professor was at least an English Duke and Mademoiselle da Ponte, his daughter, and at least, the prospective fiancée of young Dick.

All through the handshaking welcome the eye of P.J. had kept wandering toward Mademoiselle da Ponte and when at last Dick was able to introduce them and explain a little of her story, P.J. said with enthusiasm, "Bring them right up to the Castle! We'll double up and they can have a carriage to themselves."

Outside the depot the Silver City Gold Cornet Band kept up its blaring noisy music and after P.J. had arranged the seating in the Victorias, the band, leading the way, behind two stalwarts carrying between them a banner bearing the legend, "Welcome Home—Young Dick!" set off up Eudora Street.

In the first carriage rode P.J., his youngest son Dick and a bewildered Mr. Chatsworthy. In the second rode the Professor and Mademoiselle da Ponte and in the third the two dark, hairy brothers, sullen, bored, a little drunk and looking as much alike as two black-eyed peas. In the rear came about thirty of P. J. Meaney's cowhands on prancing and bucking calico ponies, occasionally punctuating the noise and excitement with loud whoops and pistol shots.

As the procession moved up Eudora Street, everyone turned out. From Moe Hirshbein's Emporium, customers left the counters and crowded to the wooden sidewalks. Those patrons of bars and saloons still able to navigate came through the swinging doors into the street. All activities ceased even in the establishment of Madge Beakymer. As the procession passed the El Dorado all gambling ceased and Madge herself leaned out of the upper window in an aura of bleached gold hair, resting her ample bosom on the window sill to give P.J. a special smile and cheer.

"Yes, indeed!" thought P.J. It was a great success, a real tribute to his popularity and power. The occasion served as a symbol signifying the strength of the dynasty that would carry on after he was dead. But that was a long way off. Riding up Eudora Street, lifting his black hat and bowing right and left like royalty in acknowledgment of the tributes of the crowd, P.J. felt indestructible and immortal. He had never felt stronger than at the moment he raised his eyes and encountered the smile and wave from Madge Beakymer.

Outwardly the "welcome" was all that it should have been, all that P. J. Meaney had planned down to the smallest detail—all perhaps save for one thing. He could not change the sullen faces of a great number of men and a few women who stood among the crowd displaying no sign of pleasure or excitement. They were among the number of citizens whom P.J. had bullied or wronged or cheated or robbed through his bank, on his cattle and sheep ranges, in the gambling houses and brothels which he owned. There were more of them than P.J. liked to consider and their numbers were growing every day. Among them too were a lot of people whom he had never harmed directly who were simply sick of corruption, injustice, power and vulgarity. In short they were sick of P. J. Meaney. Among them, in front of the El Dorado, stood one man who swore and spat with disgust as the noisy procession passed. It was Henry Caldwell. What he muttered to himself was, "I'll get the sonofabitch if it's the last thing I do!"

From her invalid's chair at her window, P.J.'s daughter, Eudora, watched the progress of the procession through her telescope with a gasping excitement which became very nearly unendurable as the band and carriages turned from Eudora Street up the avenue leading to the Castle, for at that moment the figures of the Professor and Mademoiselle da Ponte came clearly into focus—the Professor still in a warm haze of Bourbon, bowing left and right as if the plaudits of the crowd were meant for him alone, Mademoiselle da Ponte holding a fan delicately in front of her face to shield herself from the "whoopees" and whistles and pistol shots which she accepted at once as a special tribute to herself rather than to P. J. Meaney. What she did not know was that many an exuberant male looked upon her as a new addition to the establishment of Madge Beakymer whom P.J., as a special favor to Madge, was parading through the town (a procedure usually conducted by Madge herself in her own Victoria).

As the Professor and Mademoiselle da Ponte came into focus, Eudora, for the first time in seven years felt a terrible inclination to put down her telescope, take up her bed and walk. Instead, however, she compromised and, clinging to her telescope with one hand, she picked up with the other the large cowbell by her side which she used when she wanted attention and rang it with all the vigor of her 250-pound frame. The size of the cowbell was determined by the degree of audibility and presently Ellie-May in her apartment putting the last touches on the toilette designed to welcome her son, heard its call and crossed the hall to Eudora's bed-chamber.

As she entered, dressed in a black taffeta frock, sprigged with flowers and wearing a bit of heliotrope in her graying, sandy hair, Eudora turned, held up the telescope and asked, "Look! Who's that?"

Ellie-May, raising the telescope to her eyes and changing the focus to suit her own vision, knew at once whom Eudora meant, for the others in the party were her own husband and sons. With one eye closed, she stared for a moment and then said, "I'm sure I don't know. Richard didn't say he was bringing anyone but Mr. Chatsworthy."

Eudora took back the telescope and re-examined the two figures in the second barouche. They were nearer now. Without lowering the telescope, she said, "You don't think it's a Duke or something?"

"I'm sure I don't know," said Ellie-May.

"Oh, dear!" said Eudora, "I wish Rachel would hurry up and come."

"She'll be here as soon as she can get through the crowd," said Ellie-May. "I must go down now and receive them."

Ellie-May had gone into her second personality. She had abandoned the personality which lived in her own little world, pumping the sewing machine and tending the flower boxes, and taken on the personality which she employed in the role of "consort" to the great P. J. Meaney and hostess of the Castle. This second personality was not so artificial as might be supposed. At heart, Ellie-May was a romantic, and to some extent a thwarted actress of the romantic school. The consort personality was a crystallization of Ellie's-May's dreamlife and all the reading she had done as a girl. It was compounded out of *Ivanhoe* and *Kenilworth*, out of the writing of Mrs. E. D. N. Southworth and of a new writer called "Ouida" whose books were shipped west to her by P.J.'s agent in New York along with the gadgets, the paper flower garlands pasted by Eudora on her cut-out texts, and the pictures of nude women for Blackie, the sheep-herding son.

And now as Ellie-May started down the great marble stairs into the vast hall filled with potted palms, armor and stuffed bears, she became Rowena and Amy Robsart and all the "fast" worldly heroines of Mrs. Southworth and "Ouida" rolled into one. The transformation was perhaps less a shift of personality than an impersonation but it was good and often deceived distinguished senators and bankers from the East who visited P.J. for reasons of politics and investment in the fabulous riches of the West. They were likely to say, when they reached home in the East once more, "Oh, yes! P.J. is quite a character. Ha! Ha! A diamond in the rough. But his wife is quite different. Charming and obviously a lady! She really has the grand manner. I can't imagine where he picked her up. Arkansas, he says . . . but that seems unlikely."

Now in her consort personality, Ellie-May descended the stairway slowly, her feet close together so that she seemed to float rather than walk. The slight stoop acquired during the hard, early years of struggle when she and P.J. had traveled from cheap boarding house to cheap boarding house raising a family, was gone as she walked, proudly as Rowena the Saxon Princess or Amy Robsart moving toward the hidden trap door that was her doom.

She timed the passage so that she arrived at the grand door of the porte-cochere, held open by the negro servants in the same blue and gold livery worn by Esau, at the very moment the procession arrived.

Upstairs, Eudora became frantic as the cavalcade turned into the porte-cochere and out of range of her telescope. In her extremity it is probable that she would have dressed herself, left her room and gone downstairs, shattering forever the illusion of her invalidism, but for the fact that one thing, a physical fact beyond her control, prevented her from yielding to temptation. She had no clothes! For the first time she realized the inconvenience of being *accepted* as an invalid. For when Eudora had announced at the moment of the jilting, seven years earlier, that she would not arise again from her bed, Ellie-May had not argued with her. She had simply given away all her clothes to the Methodist Mission. Thus whether by design or accident, Eudora, who had inherited her father's cantankerous, strong appetites and temper along with his physique, had been delivered into Ellie-May's hands.

Now her impatience and curiosity grew to such proportions that she felt the symptoms of a "poor spell" coming on, a development which always caused much trouble to the household. The symptoms were checked only by the timely arrival of her faithful hand-maiden and reporter, Miss Rachel Hirshbein, by way of the back stairs.

Rachel was tall, thin and dark with a mustache of fine dark hair now glistening with perspiration from the climb on foot through the heat up the hill to the Castle. As she came in the door, Eudora said pettishly, "Where have you been all this time?"

Rachel explained and Eudora said, "Who are these people?"

But Rachel knew no more than Ellie-May had known. Their arrival, she said, was a sensation in the town. All kinds of speculations were afloat from the theory that the girl riding in the second barouche was Dick's fiancée to the speculation (and here Rachel blushed a little) that she was a new girl Madge Beakymer had brought to town.

The attachment of P.J. for Madge was no secret to Eudora or Rachel. Although virgins, they both knew the facts of life and a great deal more gathered from Eudora's heavy correspondence with jailbirds. The two talked freely of Madge and P.J.'s romance. Both decided however that even P.J. would not have the boldness to parade one of Madge's new girls through the streets or bring her to the Castle.

They were still gossiping and speculating as Eudora's impatience grew when clearly and unmistakably the sound of music came from belowstairs. Into that stuffy invalid's room, smelling of medicines and red flannel, the music drifted up the great stairway through the door and in at the open windows. It was the music of a piano being played by someone who played professionally and brilliantly. It began in a series of roulades, glissandos and arpeggios that went off like fireworks at the celebrations marking the announcing of Silver City's tenth anniversary.

Such a thing had never before been heard in the Castle. Indeed, the sound of music was never heard even in the vicinity of the Castle save when late in the evening Ellie-May's quavering voice was heard sometimes singing hymns or old songs like "Let Me Fly to the West to the Eagle's Nest" to the accompaniment of the square piano in the withdrawing room.

Presently the fireworks stopped and real music began, music that was unfamiliar both to Eudora and Rachel listening in the invalid's room abovestairs, but music which touched the thin, vicarious thread of life which moved in both women, music created by a thin, consumptive, tragic little man, dead long ago who had poured out the whole of his own frustration and longings into its fragile beauty. As the music of the grand Polonaise and two nocturnes drifted up through the darkness into the open window of Eudora's room, the two women, Eudora and Rachel, allowed their chatter to die away while they sat listening, embarrassed and uneasy as if the music somehow touched and illuminated their own baffled, narrow little lives. When it ceased abruptly, they sat for a moment in silence and then Eudora, unable any longer to control the pangs of her curiosity, took up the cowbell and again rang it lustily in a loud commanding way.

The sound of the cowbell traveled into the hallway and down the stairs through the great hall into the withdrawing room where as the beery applause died away it became clearly audible. As the sound reached Ellie-May sitting on a sofa beside her youngest son with her hand clasped in his, she turned to him and said, "That's Eudora's bell. She probably wants to know what's going on. You'd better run up and see her. She might go into a poor spell."

So Dick rose and made his way through the crowd into the hall and up the stairs to the room where Eudora and Rachel were waiting.

In one corner of the withdrawing room, shrunken into as small a space as possible like a cornered wren which hopes against hope it cannot be seen, Mr. Chatsworthy had found refuge. He was tired and wanted only to be a quiet spectator; and so pale was his personality and so great the curiosity and interest in the Professor and Mademoiselle da Ponte, that no one bothered to speak to him save one or two members of the band, dressed in their scarlet and gold uniforms, who approached him from time to time to ask, "How about some more beer, Bub?"

Wanting in his heart to be cordial and fit into the startling spectacle of which he was but an onlooker, Mr. Chatsworthy accepted beer after beer until presently he felt as inflated as a balloon.

[46]

He had expected the strain, the excitement, and most of the great procession of welcome itself to die away and vanish at the door of the Castle, but to his astonishment he and the other members of the party were followed into the great hall, not only by the band itself, which deposited its instruments in one corner behind the potted palms, but by a nondescript gathering of cowhands, local businessmen and politicians, who had marched behind the procession up the hill to the Castle. Unknown to the ways of P. J. Meaney he did not understand that these processions were always followed by "receptions" at the Castle itself to which were invited the important members of the community. It was part of P.J.'s power that while he ruled as a tyrant, he acted the part of a democrat. He talked a great deal about the virtues and the hard lot of the common man.

The thirst of the party was replenished constantly by steins of beer drawn from two large barrels hidden among the palms of the hall, each spot marked on the tessellated marble flooring by a growing pool of liquid. The marble which covered the whole of the lower floor of the Castle had great advantages since after one of P.J.'s receptions a mop and a pail could quickly destroy all evidence of cigar butts and beer.

The guests crowded about Dick and Ellie-May and the Professor and Mademoiselle da Ponte, and the members of the band, learning that the latter pair were musicians, at once took them to their hearts and pressed more and more beer upon them. The Professor upon whom the effects of the Bourbon imbibed during the trip aboard the Colorado Blue Bell had begun to wear off graciously accepted, and consuming all the beer offered him began presently to regain his old nonchalance. When at length the beer content of the Professor had reached a certain point and the members of the Gold Cornet Band learned of his talents, the performance of Chopin at the square piano became inevitable.

At the sound of the opening fireworks, the members of the band, recognizing technique if not great music, fell silent, their beer mugs paused, listening. Only now and then did one of them, peering over the shoulders of the others at the flying, agile fingers of the Professor, mutter, "Jees! Look at him go!" or "That's what I call lettin' fly, brother!" And the Professor, encouraged by his success, played on and on before an enchanted, beery and fascinated audience.

[47]

Meanwhile, abovestairs young Dick sat with Eudora and Rachel, satisfying the aching void of their curiosity. He explained that the Mademoiselle was a concert and opera singer and that the Professor was a pianist, a fact which by now needed no explanation, and the impressario of the young diva. He did not know their nationality although they spoke perfect English.

"Pop," he said, "has fixed it all up. Mademoiselle is going to sing at the Opera House. They're going to live at the Grand Hotel for the season."

Beyond the Castle the sun had long since gone down in a blaze and triumph of color, of mauve and crimson and green, as the high mountains, falling into the blue shadow which crept slowly across the valley, turned cobalt and indigo at the base below the pink-lighted peaks. Mr. Chatsworthy, filled with fatigue and the beer which had been pressed upon him in vast quantities as a visiting stranger from the Old Country, was still alert enough to be aware of the incredible beauty and glory of the spectacle of twilight and sunset at Silver City. Two things astonished him—that all the others took that beauty for granted as a routine part of their daily lives and gave no heed to it and that in all his experience, he had never witnessed a people so filled with unquenchable vitality or with so vast a capacity for drinking.

As he watched the magnificence of the fading day and the blue glory of the night enveloping the shabby town, he became dimly aware that the music of the piano had been augmented by the music of other instruments—flutes, fifes, cornets, trombones and even a tuba as the members of the Gold Cornet Band, one by one, retrieved their instruments from the pile hidden by the potted palms in the hall and, one by one, joined the group gathered about the square piano and fell into the cacophony of instruments played tipsily with a high and original talent for improvisation. Beyond the cluster of musicians, all blowing, tooting and whistling, there gradually formed a circle ten deep, composed of those who possessed no talent for instruments but were the possessors of loud, strong, masculine voices which it clearly gave them the vast pleasure to utilize and exercise.

And then Mr. Chatsworthy became aware, as he leaned back with his head drooping on his chest, of the presence of a very still and demure figure seated beside Ellie-May. It was Mademoiselle da Ponte whose admirers had gradually drifted away toward the group about the piano as the influence of the beer gradually gave music the advantage over sex. She looked a little tired but sat bolt upright, fanning herself gently. Hazily Mr. Chatsworthy speculated again upon her origin and background and the mystery which surrounded her. She seemed to accept the whole of the noisy spectacle as casually as she had accepted the noisy tributes which greeted her progress through the streets of Silver City.

About eleven o'clock the first casualty occurred when the tuba player fell sound asleep in his chair, still entwined like Laocoön, in the brass convolutions of his instrument. After that one by one the band and guests either began to fall asleep or to return singly or in noisy groups in an uncertain progress down the hill from the Castle to the town.

At this point Mr. Chatsworthy felt that if he acted quickly he would still be able to make his bedroom under his own power. He rose and approached his hostess, Ellie-May, who still sat in her sprigged taffeta like a Duchess receiving at a garden party.

He managed to say, "I think I'd better go and lie down." And Ellie-May rose and with the strange dignity of her consort personality led him, aiding him at times, to a vast room with a huge carved bed of black walnut.

When she had left him and closed the door, he lay down on the bed and almost immediately fell asleep, to spend all the rest of the night fully dressed in his tweeds, undisturbed save for fitful dreams in which he was being chased by a tribe of naked redskins.

Down the hallway, Rachel, as she observed from the window all the signs of a party breaking up, helped Eudora to her bed, bade her good night and left for the town to relate the details of the party to her parents who always sat up in the rooms above the Emporium until their maiden daughter returned safely through the bawdy perils of Eudora Street.

As the guests drifted off, a carriage appeared at the porte-cochere and P.J. himself led Mademoiselle da Ponte and the Professor, by now considerably the worse for wear, down the steps and helped them into it.

To the driver, he said, "The Grand Hotel, Mrs. Sowers is expecting them."

As it drove off, the Professor said to his companion, "Well! Well! That was quite a party!"

When he got no answer he looked up and said, "Well, wasn't it?" And Mademoiselle answered, "Yes, of course." And then, "It's a pity you can't always play like that." And it was the Professor's turn to fall silent. He sighed heavily and there was no more conversation until they reached the Grand Hotel where Mrs. Sowers was sleepily awaiting their arrival.

She was a tall, thin, angular woman of about fifty-five with the rough-hewn features and the bitter expression of disillusionment which afflicts women when the scales of love have fallen from their eyes and they discover that the heroes they have married long ago are nothing but drunken liabilities. Mrs. Sowers had such a husband who already lay in the marital bed soundly snoring. For twelve years Mrs. Sowers had had to earn the living, supporting herself and a once flamboyantly handsome consort who had long since lost his good looks and his virility. She did a good job of it but her ability and character did not make of her a soft and sympathetic woman.

Managing the Grand Hotel and Boarding House was no simple or easy job. It required force, intelligence, vigor and at times muscular strength, all of which she either possessed as a natural endowment or had developed under the stress of necessity.

She was waiting up, sleepy and physically worn by the battles and skirmishes of the day, only because P.J. had ordered it, and what P.J. ordered she had to carry out, for P.J. owned, along with most of the rest of the town, the structure which Mrs. Sowers managed with considerable profit. She held a contract which he had the power to break at any time and the hotel was too good a thing to lose. Not only had she waited up to welcome his guests but she had evicted, partly by vituperation and partly by physical force, two cowhands who the night before had gone to bed with their spurs on and ripped to ribbons two good sheets before they sobered up in the morning. And she had also thrown out a flashy red-haired woman of forty who had tried to bring a battered, grizzled old prospector up to her room. Mrs. Sowers was having none of that. There was, she said, a proper place for that kind

of goings on, on the opposite side of Eudora Street, in Madge Beakymer's establishment.

Mrs. Sowers received the newcomers with a semblance of cordiality
and led them to their respective rooms where the trunks had already
been installed. The line of progress led them through a reception room
equipped with rocking chairs, dusty artificial palms and spittoons, for
half a block through a long cheerless hallway and finally up a creak-
ing flight of stairs to the second floor. After asking them whether there
was anything they wanted, she bade them good night and left,
troubled and a little softened in her heart, for out of her rich experience with what might be called the flotsam and jetsam of the human
race, she recognized signs of trouble. The girl was too young and too
pretty and the man was clearly a tipsy, broken-down, defeated member
of the human race. She only hoped that they would not stay long
enough for the trouble to materialize. She knew that P.J. had a way
of "discovering people" whom he would enjoy and exploit for a little
while only to abandon and even persecute them, once he had had
enough of them.

When Mrs. Sowers left, Mademoiselle da Ponte locked the door (a
precaution she had learned long ago in her strange, disordered life)
and sat for a moment on the bed, looking about the room. The bed
was pitch-pine, still bearing on its footboard the imprints of the cowhands' spurs. The walls were pitch-pine, painted a bilious tan color.
In the corner there was a pitch-pine washstand with pitcher, basin
and slop-jar. A rocking chair stood in the opposite corner and above
it, fastened into the wall, was a row of wire hooks. There was no
cupboard and the cotton netting, tacked to the windows against the
assaults of mosquitoes, shut out whatever air was stirring on that hot
night in Silver City. It did not, however, shut out the sound of music
and revelry coming from Eudora Street on the opposite side of the
hotel.

After a long time Mademoiselle rose and, lifting the mattress and
sheets in turn, examined them for signs of bed bugs of which she found
none. Then, sighing a little, she began taking off her clothes, layer
upon layer of them down at last to pants bordered with cheap lace and
the whaleboned corsets which gave to her figure the engaging curves
and bulges. These she removed last of all and finally in the heat she

stood up as nature made her, poured water into the washbowl and began taking a sponge bath.

As slowly she took off layer after layer of the chrysalis of modish upholstery which enclosed her figure, it became more and more evident that the figure beneath was not possessed of that fragile voluptuousness which it appeared to have. Divested of appurtenances and accessories in the form of whalebone, lace, tassels, passementerie, bustle, stuffing, plush, taffeta and silk, the figure appeared boyish and strong and healthy. But for the handsome breasts and certain other features one would have said that it was the figure of a tough young cowhand. When in the midst of the sponge bath, she lifted one tin trunk off another on to the table, it was with the ease and strength which marked the baggage handling of the men who threw the trunks on and off the baggage cars of P.J.'s railroad.

When she had finished the sponge bath, she began taking down the elaborate structure of hair that crowned the genuine beauty of her young face. Knots were untied, hairpins and combs taken out, braids unbraided and finally false curls unpinned and attached, like the trophy of a Calamares brave in the days of the early settlers, to the frame of the mirror hanging above the bureau.

Then opening the trunk, she took out a nightgown with long sleeves and high neck, donned it, blew out the kerosene lamp and lay down on the bed.

Despite all the confusion, uproar and weariness of a long day, she could not fall asleep at once. The day had begun as one thing and ended as another. Early that morning the Professor had wakened her and said, "My dear, I think we had better get out of Denver."

She did not ask him why, for she was long since familiar with these sudden departures and knew that they were always occasioned by one of the scrapes into which the Professor was forever embroiling himself.

She did not protest. She only asked, "Where to?" and he had answered, "We'll go to the station and see."

She knew too what that meant. He would inquire concerning trains leaving in all directions and then glean information concerning their ultimate objectives and the characters of the towns along the way. At last he would make a choice and, with the trunk containing their costumes, his juggling equipment (balls, hoops and unbreakable chinaware, painted white), they would set out upon an adventure the end of which neither of them was ever able to foresee.

Very often the end of a day or journey turned out fantastically different from anything they imagined or planned, but never had any day turned out more fantastically than this one.

At the station in Denver the Professor had found there was not a great choice either in trains or in their objectives, since, save for one trans-continental railroad there were only two or three lines. The reports he received from strangers and railroad men offered several possibilities—Leadville, Tombstone, Virginia City, Silver City and a few smaller, less animated and spectacular communities, little suited to the scope and variety of their talents. Silver City was the nearest and a train already awaited prospective passengers but it was the sight of the blue and gold Colorado Blue Bell attached at the end of the train which led the Professor into a decision. He read the legend "P. J. Meaney, Silver City, Colorado" on the side and said, "Meaney? Meaney? Wasn't that the name of the boy on the train coming out? It's an omen! Silver City it will be!"

When young Meaney and his companion appeared and took them into the Colorado Blue Bell itself, the Professor was more than ever convinced that fate had taken a hand in their affairs and that from now on all would go well.

It had gone well—too well—reflected Mademoiselle in the pitch-pine bed at the Grand Hotel. Here they were, under the wing of P. J. Meaney who was clearly a great man and clearly a millionaire, with their hotel bills paid and the chance of singing Violetta. The Professor had sold her as a great singer and if things continued as they were already going she would have to sing whether she wanted to or not.

And presently she thought, "I'm nearly twenty years old and nothing has ever really happened to me, except knocking about in boarding houses and music halls, running from one town to another." She thought, "I want to be somebody. I want to have a home of my own and a carriage and a family. I'd like people to say when I drove down the street 'There goes the Judge's wife!' "

And she knew she would never have any of these things or even the opportunity for them so long as she was tied up with the Professor, for sooner or later he always got found out for the fraud he was. Yet in her heart she knew there was no being rid of him until he died. She could neither turn him out nor run away from him, because without her he would simply fall to pieces and end in the gutter.

At last, like the healthy young person she was, she fell asleep despite her troubles, despite the noise of the revelry and the sound of occasional pistol shots from Eudora Street.

In his own room the Professor was undergoing a second "poor spell" in one day, for the beer too had begun to wear off and he was suddenly tired and old. But worst of all he was alone, which was for him a terrifying thing. When there were people about—even one person—he would be gay and entertaining, pompous, comic, fabulous, noisy all in turn or at the same time. He needed an audience and, even though his performance and his personality were often quite unreal (less real than the result of histrionics or impersonations), he was able to command the situation and usually to dominate it. It was only when people began to grow a little tired or bored that the fraud became discernible and the whole illusion blew up in his face. Because his own life had been a failure and because his own talents had been wasted, because he was perpetually being defeated and exposed, he came to live a large part of his life in fancy and in make-believe which in the end came to absorb him completely. In all of this alcohol played a large part; it gave him confidence in his performance and helped him to believe the world of fantasy in which he lived and the preposterous lies which he told.

But now as he sat on the bed, the color had gone out of his face, even out of the roseate nose of the alcoholic. The face, so animated, almost gay, when there were people about and plenty to drink, seemed as shriveled and sagging as the stooped, collapsed figure.

The shrinking and collapse had come about far less because the effects of the beer and Bourbon were wearing off, than because he was alone now with himself behind the locked door. It was the spectacle of a man guilty of the worst sin, a man who had denied and wasted his own talents. The brief moment of triumph, when, keyed to the proper point by alcohol, he had quieted all those tipsy, noisy people in the withdrawing room of the Castle by the virtuosity of his playing, only made it worse now that he was alone for, in his heart, the old man

[54]

knew that once he could have thus swayed and enchanted whole audiences in London, Paris and New York. The failure was the failure of character—that all his life he had refused, in favor of the cheap, the easy, the transient, the sacrifices that would have brought success and even triumph. It was this weakness which in the end had driven him to seek refuge in the alcohol that enveloped all the failure and disillusionment in a rosy, spectral glow and made the false triumphs achieved by clowning, by talk, by fabulous stories partake of the fabric of real triumph, acclaim and respect.

It had been a long time now since he had transferred what remained of his ambitions and aspiration to his "niece." He meant, in those transient moments when his self-respect returned, that she should have the success which was denied his own talents. He meant in his sober moments to make of her a great singer, a great artist—the artist he might once have been, before it was too late. She had, he knew well enough, all the endowments but two and those were the desire and the temperament. She had all the beauty, and health and vitality, and a good voice but she did not want the rewards, the triumphs these things could bring her. She wanted, indeed her absorbing hunger and ambition was, to be a respectable married housewife.

After a long time, the old man found strength at last to rise from the bed and take off his clothes and put on his nightshirt. As he blew out the light, he heard, during a brief and rare moment of quiet in Eudora Street, a phrase or two spoken in a booming, oratorical voice coming from outside the hotel and, tracing the sound, he found that it came from a second-floor room in the ramshackle building on the opposite side of the thoroughfare. The room seemed to be a kind of meeting hall with a platform and table at one end. Through the window he could see the speaker, a big burly man who stood before the table orating at a score of other men and three or four women.

Professor da Ponte, during the brief lull in the mingled uproar of yelling, brawling and music which arose from Eudora Street, heard the orator say, "This glorious new State of Colorado, endowed by a benevolent Almighty with all the blessings that can be bestowed upon humankind, has been for too long blighted by the skulduggery and the black tyranny of P. J. Meaney. It is time, I say, for rebellion and revolt!"

[55]

Then as a burst of cheering and applause drowned out the speaker, the customary sounds of Eudora Street rose again in a wave and the Professor heard no more. Quietly he crawled into bed and fell into the fitful slumber of a tired, disappointed old man.

The fragment of oratory thrown to the surface of the flotsam and jetsam of Eudora Street which the Professor overheard and promptly forgot came from a meeting of The Association of Independent Voters being held in the meeting hall over Holbein's Meat Market. There, in the very heart of P. J. Meaney's kingdom, sweltering in the heat, were gathered a handful of rebels. They included some cattlemen, a handful of adventurers, a few battered prospectors, a number of the miners who worked in P.J.'s silver mines and a sprinkling of cantankerous citizens of the type described by P.J. as radicals and "agin everything." The bull-throated orator was a foreman from the Ellie-May Mine who was among those miners who had been fired two days earlier by P. J. Meaney for protesting over the conditions in the Ellie-May boring where sulphurous water dripped from the roof and sides of the mine and where the workers waded in the stinking water up to their knees. He was an Irishman and a natural born orator and he had already been speaking for an hour and was now reaching his climax. Finally, after many unrealized hints that the end was approaching, he paused for nearly a full thirty seconds. Then in a low voice, as near a whisper as could be produced by the bull-throat, he said, "What we need is a campaign—an organized campaign. And what such a campaign needs is a leader. We have this night launched a great movement that will change the history of this glorious God-endowed State of Colorado, and bring down in a thundering crash the tyranny and despotism of P. J. Meaney. What we need is a leader and we have that leader in our midst tonight." Here he turned toward the sandy-haired weather-beaten man seated at the table in the chairman's place, "His name is Henry Caldwell. I now nominate Henry J. Caldwell, as the Democratic candidate for the office of Governor of this glorious, God-endowed State of Colorado."

The end of the declaration was lost in the uproar and shouting and applause punctuated by pistol shots fired by two or three of the cattlemen in an excess of exuberance. The sound for a moment drowned out even the noises of Eudora Street and reached the second-floor room of Madge Beakymer's establishment where in the seclusion of her "boodwar" she was entertaining P. J. Meaney himself.

The "boodwar" was a room on the second floor of No. 69 Eudora Street, overlooking the cheap houses and shacks which stretched away toward the magnificent multicolored cliff where the valley broke away into the high mountains. Being at the back of the house, the noise of Eudora Street and of the big mirrored reception room downstairs came through the walls muffled and distant. The "boodwar" was as near a quiet place as could be found in the whole of the Street. It was just quiet enough for P. J. Meaney who liked the feeling that there was always life, people and whoop-de-do somewhere near at hand.

It was a box-shaped room with a Turkish cosy corner, ornamented with shields, spears, Cashmere shawls and pampas grass plumes. Before the cosy corner stood a teakwood table encrusted with designs of inlaid mother-of-pearl on which rested a hookah that remained forever dry and unused. The walls were hung with life-size paintings of four nudes depicting the four seasons. The rest of the furniture was gilt Louis Philippe, a suite including six chairs, a round table and sofa. It was here that P.J. returned when he wanted relaxation in the company of Madge.

He had come here after the party broke up at the Castle. Still unexhausted by the celebration which had occupied most of the day, he wanted company in which he could find both enjoyment and repose. Certainly he would not find these things in the company of his "invalid" daughter Eudora nor with his two dark, sullen, beetle-browed sons, Buck and Shorty, whom he regarded as not quite bright, and certainly he could not find them with Ellie-May, with her indefinable and maddening air of superiority and her habit of going to bed early so that she could rise, as always, at 6:00 A.M. And his son, Dick, always a stranger to him, was now, since his return from the Old Country, even more a stranger.

Obviously Madge Beakymer offered the relaxation he needed from a long, hard day. Now, seated opposite each other, P.J. and Madge

[57]

talked quietly like an old married couple or a pair of congenial business partners. They were drinking champagne, chilled by the ice from the Grand Kalmath Glacier of which P.J. imported two carloads every other day in order to keep Eudora Street and the Castle in ice. P.J. believed none of those superstitions about mixing drinks and had no objection to shifting from Bourbon to beer to champagne all in one day.

Having taken off his Prince Albert coat and winged collar, P.J. was at ease. He sat now with his shirt sleeves rolled up and his shirt open at the throat, so that he resembled in his dark hairiness a gorilla with Macassar-oiled hair and mustaches, dressed in man's clothing. Madge wore a pale pink evening dress with bustle, cut low to expose her extravagant overblown charms. Her only jewels, in the form of an elaborate butterfly of diamonds, rubies and emeralds, she wore fastened into the intricately arranged mass of brassy yellow hair.

P.J. told her about the party, slapping his big thighs now and then in delight over its success, a feature which he always measured in terms of noise. And presently Madge got around to what was on her mind. She asked, looking directly at P.J., "What about this Mademoiselle what's-her name?"

P.J. looked back at her for a moment and then understood her. He said, "Nothing doing! She's too smart and high class!" He drank another glass of champagne and added, "You know what I mean!"

Madge sighed, "Too bad! I could do a lot for that girl. I'd put Clarissa out of the Rose Petal Room and give it to her."

"She ain't interested," said P.J. "She's singing in the Opera. There's more in it for her. She's high class!"

Madge sighed again, "Too bad! The place is full tonight with a line waiting. Somebody spread a story that she was a new girl I'd brought to town." She emptied her glass and observed philosophically, "Funny how news travels. There's cowhands here tonight that's come all the way from Hinkley's Gap and Meeker's Gulch. Somebody must have rode all the way at topspeed."

This was one of their quiet, homey evenings, disturbed only when Madge was called belowstairs to settle a fight between the cowhands and the sheepherders in the gambling rooms or throw out a drunk who had become obnoxious—a feat she had done single-handed many times without disturbing either the convolutions of her coiffure or the diamond butterfly fastened to it. P.J. was feeling cosy rather than amorous.

On amorous occasions, the behavior and the results were quite different. He was a big man and Madge was a big woman and what went on was never discussed by the others in the house, but the Turkish cosy corner always seemed to be the chief casualty. On the mornings after, the colored porter was always summoned to put the room in order. He found the chairs and sometimes the sofa of the Louis Philippe suite overturned and sometimes broken, but the cosy corner was always in the same condition, reduced to a heap of spears, shields, pampas grass and Cashmere shawls which had always to be reconstructed according to the original plan. On such a morning the porter would reappear downstairs reporting that "P.J. had knocked hell out of the cosy corner again!"

But tonight the cosy corner was safe. P.J. said presently, "I'm kind of worn out tonight. Have you got a bed for me?"

"The house is full up," said Madge, "but I guess I could turn somebody out."

"Thanks," said P.J. "I need a good quiet night's rest."

At that moment from the Assembly Room two doors away came the outburst of cheers, screams and shooting which for a period drowned out the other noises of Eudora Street. P.J. listened for a moment and said, "What the hell's that?"

"It's a reform meeting," said Madge. "They're trying to get Henry Caldwell to head it up. They want to clean up Colorado and Silver City."

P.J. leaned back and laughed. "A hot chance they've got."

But Madge didn't join in the laughter. She said, "I wouldn't be too sure, P.J. I've been through a lot of these reform movements. Sometimes they get out of hand. Henry Caldwell's nobody's fool!"

"Henry Caldwell is anybody's fool. He could be a millionaire like me but he wouldn't play along. He couldn't lead nothin', not even a herd of sheep."

But Madge didn't share his confidence. "Just the same," she said, "it's just as well to nip things like that in the bud."

In the Castle the last light burning was in Ellie-May's room where, divested now of the sprigged taffeta and her consort personality she sat alone at last talking with her son Dick. Throughout all the long afternoon and evening she had watched him hungrily and with misgivings, troubled by the fear that somehow he had changed, that in all his experience in the East and in the Old Country, he might have forgotten her or lost, on his side at least, that bond of understanding which had always existed between them. It was a bond which had never existed between her and the three black, sullen sons and the ponderous swarthy Eudora. Even as babies, when she had seen them immediately after birth, it had seemed to her that there had been some mistake—that these dark red babies with thick thatches of black hair must belong to some other woman. It was a sense of strangeness which had increased rather than diminished as time went on.

And now, seated opposite him in the clear, harsh light of the carbide gas lights with which the Castle was furnished, she knew that everything was all right. There was the same humorous twinkle in Dick's eye that had been there since the day he was born, and that same flash of understanding which came suddenly between them and made words unnecessary. He, like herself, regarded his brothers and sister as definite characters who were unwittingly humorous.

He said, "Eudora seems better." And Ellie-May answered, "One of these days Eudora is going to get up and walk right down into the middle of town and forget she was ever ailing. It's getting so her curiosity can't stand being cooped up any longer. It isn't as if she was a real invalid. She's as strong as an ox and her strength keeps gnawin' at her."

"What would she do if she got well?" asked Dick.

"That," said his mother, "is something I'd rather not ponder over."

They talked a little about Buck and Shorty and Black Pete but none of them offered much material for conversation and as subjects quickly became exhausted. It was P.J. they talked about most. Ellie-May told her son, casually and without rancor or emotion that he had taken up with a woman called Madge Beakymer and it seemed to be a good thing because Madge kept him in order and prevented him from running around and getting into scandals like the one he got into the time Tessie Burkhart potted him in the shoulder. She guessed that Madge was a sensible sort. She managed at least to run her establishment with a minimum of disorder.

[60]

"But in other ways your Pa is gettin' out of hand," said Ellie-May, "and it troubles me. He's just about got to thinking that he's God Almighty himself out in this territory. Now he's aspirin' to spread out and take over the whole State of Colorado. It's like the whole story of the frog who was jealous of the ox and tried to inflate himself up to the same size. That's what's goin' to happen to your Pa if he doesn't look out. Some day he's goin' to pop from the pressure."

Then young Dick asked about Henry Caldwell and a delicate flush came over Ellie-May's face. She said, "I don't see much of him any more, less and less since he and your Pa broke up. He looks about the same and every now and then I get a government postcard from him and when your Pa finds it out he gets ravin' mad. Henry Caldwell is about the only man P.J. has ever been real jealous about."

"Well," said Dick, "I'm going to look him up."

"That's right," said Ellie-May. "He was always a friend of yours from the time you were a little boy and because your Pa can't get on with him is no reason why you shouldn't see him—especially now you're back to stay." She looked at him anxiously. "You are going to stay, aren't you?"

Dick grinned, "Sure I'm going to stay. This is my country and all the time I've been away I've been homesick for it. I used to lie awake nights and think about the cottage and the canyons and the range and the fishing. In places like Boston and Oxford it was just as if I couldn't breathe properly."

"You certainly speak English awful nice," said Ellie-May. "It's nice to have a gentleman in the family. Your Pa never was a gentleman and nothing could ever make a silk purse out of a sow's ear and your brothers and sister took after him. But he's the kind that will be proud of you because you're a gentleman. Why, only the other night when Senator Higginbottom, from Boston, was here, he was already boasting before he saw you. He was saying, 'Wait till you see my son, Dick. There's a real gentleman for you and a smart fellow. I wouldn't be surprised he'd be President some day.'" She looked at him sharply and said, "I guess he's got plans for you to take over the railroad and the shipping business. Did he speak to you about it?"

"No," said Dick, "he hasn't. But I'm not going to do it. I'm going

[61]

out on my own. I've got a lot of ideas about ranching and cattle and I'm not going to be just P. J. Meaney's youngest son."

She had heard what she wanted to hear. All the rest did not matter now. She settled back and said, "Well, I wouldn't be too forward about telling him that. Just you play around until the end of the summer and show your friend Mr. Chatsworthy the sights. There's plenty of time to set out on your own. Just pretend to your Pa that you're going to do as he wants till the time comes. And by that time he's likely to forget about it and want something else. That's the way I've handled him for nearly forty years." After a moment she said, "Maybe when the time comes you might make a tie-up with Henry Caldwell. He's gone into the ranching business in a pretty big way already. It might make your Pa mad but he'd get over it. He has before!"

At about three o'clock in the morning young Dick rose and kissed his mother good night. On his way to his room he looked in on Mr. Chatsworthy and found him asleep, fully dressed even down to the deerstalker's cap, on the bed. After a moment's hesitation he resolved to let Mr. Chatsworthy go on sleeping, and went to his own room across the hall from Eudora's room from which emanated the faint smell of red flannel and medicines.

The old room, next to the bedroom of his mother, was unchanged, exactly as he had seen it three years earlier, with the heavy walnut bed, the pictures of "Pocahontas Saving the Life of John Smith" and "The Wreck of the Hesperus," the heavy plush curtains with the curtains of Nottingham lace underneath, the big washbowl and slop-jar, the collection of Indian spears and scalping knives, the stuffed birds in a glass case.

Looking at the room and its furnishings young Dick understood for the first time how much he himself had changed. The room, it seemed to him, was a kind of measuring stick. It had belonged to the Dick who went away, an awkward half-civilized cub, to see the world, to acquire a growing and different sense of values, to undergo an alteration of tastes and standards of judgment. A crude, half-developed boy had gone away and a civilized man had come back.

Out of all that had happened to him, out of all he had learned in lecture halls and from the contacts with people whose very lives were steeped in tradition and form and manner, two things, he was aware, had remained unchanged in his character and his feeling. One was his passionate love for this western country with its great mountains and forests, its high ranges, its wild magnificent sunrises and sunsets, its streams and high mountain lakes. He knew now, how fully the town of Silver City was a gaudy, shabby place, but he knew too that Silver City would one day change. Either it would die or become civilized. And in a way he loved even this excrescence of man's encroachment upon the wilderness, for its vitality, for the promise of the future which lay in the brawling, coarse vigor of its people.

The other thing which remained was his respect and feeling for his mother. If these things had changed at all they had increased, for he *knew* now what he had always suspected, that his mother, whether in her homely manifestation pumping her new-fangled sewing machine or in the grandeur of her role as consort to P.J., was a great lady, and that this quality in her would be recognized anywhere in the world, in any society, as it was recognized in Silver City where she was one of a handful of women ever spoken of with respect. She had established her position with a rocklike security. She had survived and even dominated the philandering and grossness of her husband's career, so that in the estimation even of the ladies of Madge Beakymer's establishment, she was the one who achieved respect and honor without pity. She had maintained the solidity and dignity of the family itself even in the face of the essentially disreputable behavior of P.J. and his three sons. She had coped, calmly, with the problem of Eudora. All of these things she had achieved through the greatest of all virtues, integrity. She had neither deceived herself nor allowed herself to be defeated. If, someday, the whole kingdom of P.J. collapsed, she would still be there amid the wreckage unhurt and untouched—Ellie-May Meaney— exactly as she was before, because the things upon which P.J. placed such great value meant nothing to her. She lived by different gods and standards, less transient and less precarious.

[63]

PART III

THE SILVER CITY OPERA COMPANY BEGAN ASSEMBLING AT MRS. SOWERS' Grand Hotel and Boarding House about the middle of June. They came from all parts of the country, from San Francisco, from Boston, from New Orleans, from Chicago and New York. If they had arrived all at once on a single train the effect would have been that of a circus coming into town, but they kept coming in one or two at a time to be assembled at last in the big hall of the Grand Hotel and on its wide wooden verandas. People along Eudora Street first became aware of the imminence of P.J.'s opera season through the bedlam of strange noises which began about the middle of July to emerge from the Grand Hotel, increasing in volume until at last the whole of the troupe was assembled. The effect was that of aural rather than visual fireworks. From various windows on all sides of the block-sized boarding house came roulades and scales and whole arias, against a background of cacophonic and somewhat tinny pianos supplied by P.J. for the practicing period.

None of the singers was very good for P.J., while he enjoyed the idea of providing half of Colorado with a season of what the cowhands referred to as the "French Opry," was unwilling to spend the money asked by the big singers who were starred in the billings of the French Opera House in New Orleans or Jim Fisk's New York Opera House. So what he got was the coloraturas who could trill like birds but were unable to stay on pitch, the tenors with frayed, strained voices, the lyric sopranos who had seen better days, asthmatic baritones and now and then a young beginner, for it was one of P.J.'s delusions that he had a genius for "discovering" people in the realm of the arts as well as in the realm of business and politics.

[65]

By the time the Professor and Mademoiselle da Ponte arrived in Silver City, most of the Silver City Opera troupe had arrived and were already installed in the Grand Hotel and Boarding House. Most of them were veterans of earlier seasons and knew their way about, and among them were two who were the ringleaders and shared jointly the dictatorship of the troupe and the Opera House. Both had had long experience in the politics of opera houses, the most complicated and intricate form of politics yet evolved by the human race in its long climb upward from the primeval ooze. These were Signor Malatesta and Signorina Baldacie.

The Signor occupied the joint position of general manager and conductor of the orchestra. He was a small, fiery man, Sicilian in origin, with a bald head and fiery black eyes. He was thin, nervous and temperamental. He wore pince-nez attached to a long black ribbon which hung about his turkey-thin, wattled neck and a fringed, oiled and dusty black toupé which deceived no one but himself. His companion and joint dictator, Signorina Baldacie, was a large woman of about sixty, with an immense bust and a jutting posterior. Born in Turin, her family who operated a spaghetti and pasta shop discovered that she possessed, even at an early age, a natural birdlike voice. She could trill and execute glissandos and roulades with the facility of a nightingale and appeared, as a child, to enjoy these complicated exercises. Her parents, quickly seeing in her possibilities of fame and fortune, and the elimination of all future work for themselves, fastened their attention upon her to the exclusion of their remaining fourteen children and dug into their earnings almost daily in order to take little Gisella to La Scala to hear all the great coloraturas of her time.

Almost at once it developed that little Gisella had not only the vocal organs of a nightingale but that she was gifted with a remarkable memory and talent as a mimic. She could return from an evening at La Scala and entertain her parents and a large circle of admiring neighbors and friends by repeating whole arias. More than this she was able to improvise and garnish the most florid arias with improvisations of her own. Gambling upon a great future and fortune, the Baldacie family saved money by eating the spaghetti and pasta which had grown moldy during the damp winter season in Turin, and used the money saved for the education of the prodigy, Gisella.

In all their speculation they had overlooked one element, a vastly important one in the career of any singer. Among the good fairies who stood about the cradle of little Gisella saying, "You shall have the voice of a nightingale," "You shall have the looks of a passionate and beautiful woman," "You will astonish thousands by your gifts," there was one malicious old witch who ruined everything. Perhaps unseen among the others, she stood over the cradle, and said, "But you will have no sense of pitch."

And so it was. Through at least fifty-two of her sixty years, Signorina Gisella Baldacie, managed to astonish those who were ignorant or insensitive to music or those whose standards of music were determined by pyrotechnics and agility, but in the end she never sang in any but third-rate opera houses, sometimes for little more than board and room, because always she sang flat and the longer and more florid the aria, the flatter she got. She could *feel* herself singing, and even at the age of sixty still became self-hypnotized and intoxicated by her own performance exactly as she had done at the age of eight standing on a table outside a *trattoria* in her native Turin. But she could not *hear* herself singing, and so, fortunately perhaps, was quite unconscious of where she ended up at the end of a long aria. This unhappy faculty, or lack of faculty, had on occasions in the Old Country in provincial opera houses like those of Vicenza and Padua (which represented the highest level of her attainment) given rise to jeers, boos and whistles and what sometimes developed into actual brawls and routs between the partisans of pyrotechnic and agility and the partisans of pitch in music. In the end, Gisella, billed as the "Turin Nightingale," came to lose even her engagements at provincial opera houses and migrated at last at the age of forty to the New World in search of new, cruder, less impassioned and perhaps less discriminating audiences.

Her first appearance at the French Opera in New Orleans was very nearly as full of disorder as her earlier appearances in Vicenza and Padua and presently she drifted westward, a little further each year, until she found the audiences which fully appreciated her curiously lop-sided talents. This was among the cowhands and miners of wide-open towns like Silver City where they cheered the remarkable roulades and glissandos and trills which seemed to emerge effortlessly from her aging and steadily augmenting figure without any necessity

[67]

for breathing. At the end of one of the long stretches of fireworks she would be greeted by cheers, stamping of feet, and loud applause, sometimes by the throwing into the air of chairs and beer bottles and even by occasional pistol shots from an exuberant audience which remained blissfully undisturbed by the pitch on which the aria ended. On the brawling frontier of the great West, Gisella Baldacie, born in the back room of a spaghetti shop in Turin, came at last into her own as the "Eyetalian Nightingale" in Silver City, Tombstone, Leaping Rock, Nevada City and Leadville.

Throughout twenty-odd years of the career Signor Malatesta was her consort. The arrangement began in passion and, after a long period of cooling off in which finally all passion became spent, degenerated into an arrangement of business and of necessity. They were held together by the bond of indispensability. The "Eyetalian Nightingale" refused to accept any engagement, whether in the bars and gambling houses where her occasional appearances in bugles and aigrettes gave tone and class to the place, or at the various "Opry" Houses, unless the contract included the services of Signor Malatesta as accompanist or conductor of the orchestra. On his side, Signor Malatesta was indispensable to Signorina Baldacie because, being in truth a rather remarkable musician, he had evolved a system of transposing the accompaniment on the piano and even with a pliable orchestra so that he could partly persuade the audience that it had been wrong and that the "Eyetalian Nightingale" had ended up approximately on pitch. Signorina Baldacie knew that if the aria was a comparatively short one with a reasonable pause in the accompaniment while she executed trills and roulades, she could drop in pitch one full note of the scale. If it were a long aria with an exceptional embroidery of fireworks, she could drop two full tones and survive the results. With considerable agility, Signor Malatesta was able to resume the accompaniment at approximately the point where Signorina Baldacie ended up. This was comparatively easy if he were accompanying her on the piano. It was more difficult with an orchestra and in an opera, especially since it was intolerably disconcerting to the other singers and required unquestioned loyalty from every member of the orchestra and the cast. On occasion the trick had been known to drive the more sensitive individuals of the audience from

[68]

the auditorium into the street, and on one occasion during the season in Leaping Rock, had caused the suicide by shooting on the steps of the Opera House of a man who had seen visions and heard things out of the air and was already partly convinced that he was going insane.

Thus the pair became yoked together by bonds far more rigid, inflexible, and indestructible than those of mere passion or of matrimony which as artistes they had ignored throughout their long association. Both shared a talent for intrigue and blackmail, fostered in the case of Signor Malatesta by early association with the Mafia, and in the case of Signorina Baldacie, by long experience in the slums of Turin and with the intrigue of the provincial opera companies of her native land.

Before the party at the Castle had finished, the news that there was a new opera singer in town (traveling by the Silver City grapevine, a lightning method of communication), had reached Mrs. Sowers' Grand Hotel and Boarding House and been passed from one member of the assembling opera company to another. The effect of the news was exactly like that of a strange dog appearing suddenly in the midst of a well-established pack. Figuratively speaking, and in the case of the dilapidated Latvian basso, Monsieur Blavatsky, literally speaking, it caused the hair to rise and bristle on the backs of every member of the company. The news that the new singer was young and very pretty only made the situation worse. Within opera circles sex plays a small if not invisible-role; hatred or quarreling between two women is as nothing compared to the hatred between the tenor and the soprano when one of them receives more applause than the other or the hatred aroused by one singer who plays his or her scene a little nearer to the footlights than another. And in the case of the Silver City Opera Company each member felt himself established and regarded any newcomer, regardless of age, sex or physique, as an interloper and a threat. Since none of the members of the Silver City Grand Opera Company could have found employment outside the Leadville, Silver City, Tombstone circuit, which they regarded as a good thing and their own property, the threat of any newcomer immediately caused the whole of the company to gather in a circle, facing outward, snarling with bared fangs.

Thus the reception of Professor da Ponte and Mademoiselle at the

Grand Hotel was not what could be described as cordial. In the morning when they descended for breakfast in the large, fly-specked dining room, the other members of the company were already assembled at their tables to inspect the interlopers. At their entrance, the buzz of conversation in countless tongues and accents died away abruptly leaving a great and bottomless pit of silence through which the Professor and his companion, escorted by Mrs. Sowers who was still giving them special attention, reached their table.

Once the pair were seated the buzz began again with equal abruptness. The comments, many and voluble, but all of the same general tone, could have been summed up in the remark of the "Eyetalian Nightingale" herself, who to Signor Malatesta, Monsieur Blavatsky and the others consuming corn pone, fried ham, calves' liver, eggs and bacon at the same table, said "Basta! She has no chest! She has no place for her breath. How can she seeng?"

It was true that in comparison with Gisella Baldacie, the girl seemed flat-chested and tubercular, but it was clear from the attention given by Signor Malatesta and Monsieur Blavatsky that they did not altogether share the opinion of the big coloratura. From time to time they kept shifting their positions for better views until the Signorina became aware that their interest was less musical than amorous and made a scene during which the neighboring cowhands, traveling salesmen and gamblers were treated to a lively discussion conducted in several languages on the subject of chests and accompanied by gestures indicating objects of various sizes and shapes ranging from tomatoes, through cantaloupes to watermelons.

Not one member of the company left the dining room until the Professor and Mademoiselle had finished and gone out. Then in a body, all gesticulating and talking at once, they followed.

At eleven o'clock on the same morning in P.J.'s office in the Castle, the great man was in serious conversation with his youngest son, Dick. The boy sat, like any caller, on a stiff chair separated from the great upholstered chair occupied by his father on the opposite side of the big teakwood table. They had been talking about the future of young Dick, now that his education was finished.

P.J. taking a big cigar from his mouth, said, "I've no objection, son, to your taking a vacation for the summer. There's plenty of money. Move around. Get acquainted with Silver City and the boys up on the range. Buck and Shorty and Black Pete will help you out. They know all the ropes and they learned the hard way like their old man. They began at the bottom of the ladder."

He said all this with a straight face, looking squarely at the son who knew that very little of it was true. He knew the story of how P.J. with his aggressive pride had pushed his sons ahead. He knew all about how Henry Caldwell had been jockeyed out as viceroy of the cattle and sheep kingdom to make way for Buck and Blackie. And he knew how incompetent his brothers were and how unpopular. But he did not choose to argue these points since he knew, equally well, that arguments rarely got anywhere with P.J.

And then P.J. said, "There's one thing, son, you can do for me, better than anyone else. It ain't hard to do."

"Yes," said young Dick obediently.

"It's to look after Professor da Ponte and Mademoiselle. I want you to see they get everything they want and that they don't get pushed around by them other Russians and Eyetalians. The Professor and his niece are a credit to Silver City. They're high-toned. You can see that right away. I ain't heard her sing but the old man can certainly tickle the ivories. If you can handle the rest of them Wops and Polacks so they don't make life too tough for the Professor and his niece you'll be doin' a good job."

He crushed out his cigar and lighted another, looking up shrewdly at his son and saying, "And you might get some valuable experience. If I wasn't so old and so heavy I might be interested myself, only she ain't quite my type. I like the full-blown rose type." He made a gesture similar to those employed earlier by Signor Malatesta, Signorina Baldacie and Monsieur Blavatsky during their animated argument in the Grand Hotel dining room. "You get what I mean?"

"Yes," said Dick.

The old man leaned forward, narrowing his eyes, "I suppose by now you must be pretty experienced after living over there in the Old Country. You are, ain't you?"

"No," said Dick, "I'm not!"

[71]

"You mean to say you're twenty-one years old and you're still a virgin?"

"Yes," said Dick.

P.J. leaned back in his chair almost overcome by his astonishment. He blew out a great cloud of cigar smoke and said, "Well, I'll be damned!" And after a moment, "You're wastin' a lot of time. Now you've got an opportunity—a big opportunity all ready made. See what you can do about it!" Then he chuckled, thinking back over his now remote youth and added, "I guess there's some things you can learn as a drummer that you can never learn in one of them high-falutin' foreign colleges."

At that moment P.J.'s "typewriter," a middle-aged, rather gaunt woman called Miss Beals, who wore a black skirt, a starched high-collared shirtwaist and nose glasses attached by a small gold chain to the gold fleur-de-lis on her flat chest, came in briskly and said, "Excuse me, P.J., but two of those opry singers are askin' to see you."

"Which ones?" asked P.J.

"I can't ever rightly remember their names," said Miss Beals. "But it's the man who leads the band and that big fat soprano who does all the trills."

"Oh *them!*" said P.J. "Tell 'em to wait a minute and I'll see 'em." Then he turned to his son, "I guess they've come up here to raise hell about bringing a new singer into the company. You're gonna have trouble, son, but it'll be good experience. If you can handle that bunch of Dagoes and Polacks and bring your friends through without a bein' massacreed, you can do anything." He stood up, regally, with the air of dismissing his son as he dismissed all his callers, save the politicians he needed in his business.

"Good luck to you. And if you get yourself or your friends into a jam, don't come to me about it. It's up to you!"

"All right!" said Dick and went out. In the hallway he passed Signor Malatesta and the "Eyetalian Nightingale" but he saw neither of them very clearly for his eyes were blinded by anger.

A second later Miss Beals appeared and said brusquely to the pair, "Mr. P. J. Meaney will now see you."

She bristled from the tops of her high-topped, pointed, patent leather shoes through the starched shirtwaist to the elaborate coiffure in which was stuck an assortment of multicolored pencils. She disliked foreigners principally because they were, in her opinion, both emotional and inefficient, and she did not like opera because, as she said, "Opry was so false to life." But more than all that she was aware that the pair lived in open sin and knew delights far beyond her own somewhat arid experience. So, after leading the pair into the office, she slammed the door as she left them facing P.J.

He did not rise but invited them "to take seats." Signorina Baldacie, somewhat taller than her companion, was an imposing figure in a purple dress with a yoke and high collar of Battenberg lace, carrying a sunshade and wearing several strands of false pearls. The whole creation was topped by a large picture-hat covered with aigrettes made of processed crow's feathers. Signor Malatesta wore a Prince Albert coat and carried a cane and top hat. His heavy mustaches, dyed like those of P.J. himself, were waxed into pin-point perfection.

"Glad to see you back in town again," said P.J. "What can I do for you?"

The pair did not go at once to the point but talked of the weather, the repertory, the new curtain at the Opera House which consisted of a colorful Italian landscape surrounded by garlands of flowers within which appeared advertisements of the El Dorado Dance Hall, Moses Hirshbein's Emporium, The Paris Grille and other Eudora Street establishments, including a discreet notice which simply bore the legend "Madge Beakymer—Entertainment." The curtain more than paid for itself from the revenue of the advertisements. Only Madge's notice had been painted without charge through the courtesy of the management.

As the small talk grew a little drawn out, P.J. began to grow impatient, for with his many projects and responsibilities he was a busy man. He finally said, "Well, what is it you wanted?" And Signorina Baldacie said, "It's about this new singer. Meester Malatesta don't know anything about her. . . . How does he know if she can seeng or not?"

"She can sing all right," said P.J.

"But in my contract," protested Malatesta, "it says I must give approval."

P.J. leaned forward amicably and even Signorina Baldacie knew that was a bad sign. When he grew genial it was the prelude to bullying. Now, in his softest, most engaging voice, P.J. said, "*Mister* Mala-testa, I am P. J. Meaney. Every year I pay a loss of thousands of dollars in the Opry House. I do it because I like a good show and like music and for the culture of Silver City. *I* am the only contract. If I want a new singer the new singer is going to sing."

Signorina Baldacie and her companion already knew all this, and they knew that they could not do much about it. It was not only that they could not afford to lose the salary of the Silver City season, they knew that, contract or no contract, P.J. could throw them out without paying them and that they could do nothing about it. But it was not the money alone; they could not afford to lose the prestige of being members of the Silver City Opera Company, a far more pretentious outfit than anything existing in Tombstone, Leaping Rock, Leadville or even Denver.

"Eet is an outrage," said Signor Malatesta, the "Eyetalian Nightingale" merely making a snorting sound.

"Well, that's the way it's goin' to be," said P.J. "The Opry Company needs new blood. Why, there ain't a singer in the company under fifty."

The Signorina's aigretted hat quivered. Her mouth opened and closed as if she meant to deny that she was a day over thirty. But P.J. did not give her time. He said, "When they're playin' Camille to music I'd kinda like to see a woman playin' Camille that a feller could want to sleep with."

This, of course was a direct insult to the "Eyetalian Nightingale" who had always considered the role which P.J. referred to as "Camille" as her private property. Indirectly it was an insult to Signor Malatesta as well since it was well known that he was the Nightingale's lover.

P.J. rose in a grandiose gesture of dismissal. "And I don't want any monkey business!" he said. "If there is anything you want, consult my son Dick. I am a very busy man. Good afternoon!"

At the same moment, Miss Beals appeared and held the door open, leaving the pair no choice but to leave. Indignantly they bowed and went out the door which Miss Beals closed behind them, snorting again with indignation.

On the way down the hill the Nightingale and Signor Malatesta talked and gesticulated wildly, but most of their indignation they took out in talk for there was little else they could do. On arrival at Mrs. Sowers' Grand Hotel the Nightingale retired to her room and had hysterics.

In the days that followed at Mrs. Sowers' Grand Hotel, the Professor and Mademoiselle became aware slowly of the fact that they had become the pariahs of the establishment. Only the cowhands and the gamblers spoke to them with civility and, in the case of Mademoiselle, sometimes with an undisguised warmth. From the assembled members of the Silver City Opera Company, they received at best only the most casual nods of recognition and more often than not, cold stares illuminated by actual hatred. When it came to the question of securing the use of one of the tinny pianos for practicing, it was discovered that all the pianos were constantly in use at very nearly all hours of the day and night. Even Mrs. Sowers herself, resentful of P. J. Meaney's absolute control over her and her establishment, was both uncordial and uncooperative.

The experience was not altogether new either to the Professor or to Mademoiselle for the Professor had lived most of his life "in the profession" from concert hall to cheap vaudeville and circuses, and Mademoiselle had discovered at a very early age that while her youth and good looks could prove an asset under certain circumstances, they could under other circumstances, and particularly where women were concerned, arouse only alarm, jealousy and hatred. Since she was eight years old when her mother died in a boarding house in Philadelphia, she had led the same precarious existence under the protection of the Professor—a life of cheap boarding houses, of escaping bills and unpaid accounts for room and board, of traveling on poor and cheap trains and fighting for the right merely for shelter and at least two meals a day.

In the beginning it was the Professor who had done all the bitter plotting and trickery which kept the two of them clothed and alive, but for a long time now she had become aware that, more and more, the task of making ends meet, of finding shelter and food, was falling upon her own shoulders. She knew why this was so—that drink was quietly and steadily destroying the talent, the wits and the courage of her companion as he grew older and more tired. She also knew that

[75]

but for him she would long ago have been sent to an orphanage to be shut up as if she were a delinquent and be dressed in dingy grey like all the other girls in the institution. She knew that on the day after her mother died the proprietor of the Philadelphia boarding house had made all the preparations to have her sent away, and would have succeeded save that the Professor had intervened and had even adopted her legally. From then on the threads of their two lives had been bound together.

She had no memories whatever of her father and the memories of her mother had grown steadily dimmer with the passing of years. Her mother existed now only as a sort of wraith—a pretty, frail woman, struggling always against consumption to provide security for herself and her daughter by taking small parts in a company of actors who played perpetually "Colleen Bawn" and other Irish plays before audiences of homesick Irish immigrants in Boston, New York and Philadelphia. Then one night when Mademoiselle was eight years old, her mother, coughing until the blood gushed from her mouth, sent her to fetch the landlady and when she returned, her mother was dead. Of her father, all she knew was that he had been handsome, and an actor good enough to have been understudy and substitute for Dion Boucicault himself. The Professor who bore the name of Alonzo da Ponte played the piano in the orchestra of the same traveling Irish Company. Since the day of the adoption they had never been separated.

She owed him, she knew, more than protection. She owed him for all the education she had ever known. It was the Professor who, on trains and in boarding houses, had taught her to read and write. It was the Professor who had directed her reading. It was the Professor who taught her to sing and to play the piano and to stand on the stage without fear, acting as his assistant in the juggling act which supported them in the remote little towns in the Middle West where the only other entertainment was revival meetings. It was the Professor who taught her to sing *two* operatic roles, always believing that one day opportunity would come their way and that she would, overnight, become a famous star of the opera.

She was aware, with a kind of clairvoyance, that things were coming to a dead end for herself and the Professor. She was herself no longer a child—indeed, being many times wiser and more experienced than girls of her age—she had never been a child, and for a long time now she had watched the Professor disintegrating slowly, like an old, worn-out clock, running down and going to pieces. She had watched the old confidence go out of him along with the old zest for impersonation and humbuggery. She had watched him growing more and more weary. The old gaiety was wearing out and each time he drank to give himself courage and defiance, the effect grew a little less and lasted a little shorter time. All too often he became not gay but merely drunk. Something, she was aware, had to happen soon. That something was inevitable.

The treatment from the other members of the Opera Company did not disturb her, partly because she had expected it and partly because, in her precocious knowledge and wisdom, she felt resentment for the poor battered troupe less than a mixture of pity and ridicule. In any case since she was old enough to reason at all her life had constantly been a choice—either to yield or fight. Because of her youth and appearance, the opportunities to yield were endless and varied. To have yielded even once was, she knew, ruin. So she had always chosen to fight, and slowly her virtue and honor had become far more important and cherished than that of the daughter of a Methodist Deacon. Gradually and vaguely it had become the most precious of her possessions—far more precious to her than the fine bosom, the entrancing blue eyes, the blonde hair and the figure with which Nature had endowed her. She was, in quite simple language, able to take care of herself and she had always done so. She was used to attack and all the weapons of seduction and knew how to cope with them all. She was aware too that the most valuable of all weapons in her armory for the defense of her chastity was the dovelike air of innocence. For all its falsity, it was in most circumstances an invincible weapon. Because, save for the Professor, she had never known in their wandering life any companionship or had any friends, loneliness, which occurs only to those who encounter it suddenly, did not exist for her.

As for the opportunity to sing at the Silver City Opera House, she accepted it as an opportunity—perhaps a way out. She meant to sing too because the others were against her and willing apparently to resort to all sorts of trickery to prevent her singing. She meant to show them!

So on the third day when Mrs. Sowers knocked on her door and said that one of P.J.'s sons—the youngest—had called at the hotel and wished to see her and the Professor and was waiting in Mrs. Sowers' private parlor, she kept him waiting for a time while she put a faint touch of rouge on her cheeks and gave her complicated coiffure a little special attention. Then she went to the Professor's room and when there was no answer to her knock, she opened the door to find him asleep on the bed, his mouth open a little, snoring. She knew all the signs. Somehow he had gotten out into Eudora Street without her and met up with "friends." There was, she knew, no use in trying to rouse him since even if she succeeded in waking him, he would be useless in any interview with young Mr. Meaney.

Mrs. Sowers' private parlor was a room which, under ordinary circumstances was sacred to the uses and privacy of that estimable lady. It was a room just off the hotel office, furnished with a suite of gilt furniture, with enlarged and tinted photographs of herself and the derelict Mr. Sowers hanging over the organ which, on its many shelves and projections, carried a whole garden in the form of aspidistras, begonias and miniature potted palms. Here, seated precariously upon the edge of one of the rickety gilt chairs, Mademoiselle found young Dick.

At sight of her, he rose and bowed—a courtesy which out of long experience she distrusted as the first step in an attempt at seduction. (The Old Southern Gentlemen were the worst with their fancy manners and their talk of the sacredness of womanhood.) He did not begin the conversation by any pretty speech. He said, "My father told me to call on you and ask if there was anything you needed."

She invited him to sit down and seated herself on another of the gilt chairs. "Thank you," she said, and waited.

The boy grew a little red in the face—a reaction which was new to her—and said, "He has asked me to look after you during your stay. He is very enthusiastic about your becoming a member of his Opera Company."

"Please thank him for me and my Uncle," she said, with an air of querulousness, and the conversation immediately lagged. After a painful silence which Mademoiselle seemed quite able to endure, he said, "I'm afraid the hot weather has set in very early this year."

"Yes," said Mademoiselle.

[78]

Another silence and the flush appeared again on young Meaney's face. After a pause, he said, "I suppose Mrs. Sowers has provided you with a piano."

"No," the girl said, "they are all in use."

"Then I'll see that you have one. The rehearsals begin in a week. I suppose you have met Signor Malatesta, the conductor."

"No."

"I shall see to that."

Again a silence and then, "What do you think of Silver City?"

"It's all right."

The boy tried desperately to think of something else to say and came out with, "Perhaps you would like to see more of the town?"

"Thank you. I shall be very busy rehearsing."

Again she waited without saying anything more. It was an old trick of protection. The technique made any advances difficult for the potential seducer and gave her time to watch him and divine something of his character and his motives.

Then young Dick stood up suddenly, "Thank you for seeing me," he said. "I will see that you have a piano and that you meet Signor Malatesta. If there is anything further you need, please let me know."

Mademoiselle rose and held out her hand with the air of a great prima donna expecting her hand to be kissed. Young Dick shook it awkwardly.

She bowed her head a little, "Thank you again," and he went out leaving her to look after him with an expression of bewilderment on her face. Never before had she met a man, young or old, quite like this one.

In the big parlor of the Grand Hotel Cecil Chatsworthy was waiting in a big rocking chair beneath one of the dustier potted palms which forested sparsely the big hotel parlor. The sense of wonder and excitement still enveloped him. Each figure that came through the swinging double-door was new and strange—the cowhands, the Indian squaws, half-buried beneath their stocks of blankets, beaded moccasins and baskets strung like necklaces about their fat throats, the slick urbane gamblers, the miners, the wildly foreign members of the Opera Company. He was aware, as he had been from the beginning, that among them all he was the strangest figure, the most exotic, the one which attracted the greatest attention, for, although he sought psychologically and spiritually to shrink into invisibility, he still remained the one figure in which all the passers-by showed the greatest interest. In his tweeds and deerstalker's cap, so uniform, so conventional, so unnoticeable at home, he stuck out, in this new world, like a sore thumb. Even the squaws seemed aware that here was something new and exotic. One squaw circled three times the rocking chair in which he sat, studying with her staring, pupilless, opaque black eyes every detail of his costume, finally giving complete reign to her tactile curiosity by approaching closely and feeling the material of his checked tweed jacket. After she had felt the beautiful softness of the tweeds, she felt in turn the texture of one of the blankets she carried over her broad shoulders and looked at him with a broad toothless grin as if to say, "See! Indian squaw make good stuff too!"

These attentions Mr. Chatsworthy received with an inward shrinking and suffering. By nature he was a mouse, seeking only to conceal himself and lose his identity in the protective coloring of his surroundings. At Oxford, in London or at the vicarage this was easy enough for he had looked exactly like every other typical Englishman, even to the slightly protruding row of somewhat damaged upper teeth, but here in the vast foyer of the Grand Hotel he was a curiosity. No one had ever seen anything like him, not even among the bearded eastern bankers who always wore either Prince Alberts or dark tight-fitting suits which caused them at times to be mistaken for undertakers. In England he had achieved that anonymity, that colorlessness which was the very goal of his exemplary and conventional existence. Here in Silver City in the midst of the glowing, wild, eccentric West, he became a curiosity and the center of all attention as if he were something out of a menagerie.

So he welcomed with relief the reappearance of young Dick who, in a checked shirt, cowhand chaps and high-heeled boots, attracted no attention whatever but faded into the colorful background like the mouse which Mr. Chatsworthy wished he could become.

Together they walked out of the hotel parlor through the swinging doors into Eudora Street bent upon the errand which was the reason for Mr. Chatsworthy's descent from the realm of the Castle into that of the town. The errand had obsessed him ever since the moment he had been the center of attraction and hospitable offers of more and more beer on the occasion of the party to mark the return of young Dick.

He was going to purchase suitable clothes.

As they walked along Eudora Street, Mr. Chatsworthy remarked that his companion gave rise among the populace to two kinds of re-action—one a welcome so hearty that it approached the realm of falsity and groveling, the other a sour nod or an averted face. For the first time it occurred to him that in the kingdom of P. J. Meaney all was not well and that loyalty to P.J. and his dynasty was not al-together undivided.

As they walked, young Dick pointed out various characters and establishments. He explained about the Hermit, an old man with long matted hair and beard, clad only in a breechcloth and a necklace of bear's teeth who led a life of mystical contemplation in one of P.J.'s worked-out mines. And he explained about Dangerfield Ravenel, the king of the gamblers, who had given up the Mississippi River boats for the richer pickings among the cowhands and prospectors of the Silver City, Leadville, Tombstone, Leaping Rock circuit. Danger-field was a tall, thin man of about fifty, dressed all in black with curling mustaches and an imperial air. His hair was long, black and well-oiled and he wore a wide-brimmed black hat and a large false diamond in his black ascot tie. He would, young Dick explained, bet on anything at all. And as they passed the El Dorado Dance Hall and gambling establishment, a loud, cheerful voice called out, "Hello Dick," from a balcony overhanging the street and looking up they discovered Madge Beakymer herself, dressed in peignoir and holding a palm-leaf fan, leaning over the railing.

Young Dick called back, "Hello, Madge."

Madge said, "Welcome home! Come up and have a glass of champagne!"

For a moment young Dick hesitated, planning to make excuses, and then thought better of it and said, "Sure, thanks!"

And Madge called back, "You know the way?"

Young Dick led the way through the swinging doors into a huge room echoing with noise and music which caused the eyes of Mr. Chatsworthy to pop out of his head. The room was filled with tables crowded with gamblers, tables given over to all kinds of games which Mr. Chatsworthy had never before seen. There were tables for faro, for poker, for roulette, for blackjack, for dice, for red-dog. At one end there stretched into smoke-filled space the longest bar Mr. Chatsworthy had ever seen, lined with cowhands, prospectors and gamblers. At the opposite end of the room was a stage where at the moment a kind of female minstrel show was in progress. A fat female with a voice so loud it dominated even the uproar of drinking and gambling was singing, supported by a row of Madge's girls all in purple tights with bodices embroidered in bugles. Around their posteriors hung gold fringe which swayed enticingly with each movement of their voluptuous bodies. No one, either drinkers or gamblers seemed interested in the entertainment, no matter how loud the brazen-voiced singer sang or how much the girls swung the gold fringe. Around the whole of the room ran a wide balcony furnished with tables and chairs where other drinkers were crowded. The whole place smelled of cows, sheep, sweat and stale beer.

Mr. Chatsworthy would have enjoyed staying there for a time but for the fact that his tweeds and deerstalker's hat again became embarrassingly the focus of attention. As he passed tables in the wake of young Dick the gamblers even turned from their game to regard him, making such comments as, "Well, I'll be goddamed!" and "Where in hell did that come from?" or "What the hell is it?" and "Where did young Dick find that?" With crimson face, he followed Dick across the room to the stairway leading up to the apartment of Madge Beakymer. As they crossed the room, the big singer interrupted her song to call out in a stentorian voice, "Hey Limey!" The sally was greeted by a wild shout of laughter and Mr. Chatsworthy, accustomed only to the grey protective coloring of Oxford, wished suddenly and passionately that he could shrink through the floor.

Over his shoulder Dick said, "Don't mind, Cecil! It's all meant in a friendly way."

Then they climbed the stairs and went through Madge's parlor, with the gilt chairs and the Turkish cosy corner to the second floor veranda overhanging Eudora Street where Madge usually passed the hot afternoons, when everything was going smoothly in her establishment, rocking and exchanging sallies with old friends passing on the sidewalk below.

In accepting Madge's invitation to drink champagne, young Dick wasn't doing what he wanted to do, he was doing what he thought he should do. He knew all about Madge and P.J. He knew that between them they ran all Silver City. He had no doubt as to their relationship and he knew that the only course was to accept the relationship. As to the morality of the situation he was not greatly concerned because he had been born and brought up in Silver City and knew since childhood the facts of life. The question of taste—a matter of small concern in the life of Silver City—troubled him. It didn't seem right that the pair should be so brazen about everything. But he thought too that Cecil should get to know the life of Silver City and who was a better guide than Madge and what establishment a better school than the El Dorado?

As they passed the Turkish cosy corner and walked on to the veranda, Madge's booming voice called out, "Hello, boys!"

Dressed in a flowered peignoir she sat rocking and fanning herself beside a silver champagne bucket filled with the ice P.J.'s train brought down every other day from the Grand Kalmath Glacier. She looked hot, handsome and florid, like an overblown Maréchal Niel rose. All during the summer months she conducted her business from the veranda above hot Eudora Street, summoning passers-by from the street, dispensing favors and interrupted only occasionally by the necessity for going belowstairs to quell the disorder whenever a crisis arose. She settled many a problem or bestowed many a favor which she felt was too insignificant to bring to the attention of the great P.J. Those who had the favor of Madge had the favor of P.J. Those who were summoned from the sidewalks of Eudora Street to have a glass of champagne were among the anointed.

Dick said, "This is my friend Cecil Chatsworthy."

Cecil bowed and Madge said, "Sure, I know. P.J. told me all about him." Then she turned and said, "Bring a couple of glasses off the table."

Dick obeyed her and she leaned down to the silver bucket beside her, raised the bottle of champagne and filled the two glasses. Raising hers she said, "Over the burning sands!" and they all drank.

Then Madge wiped her lips with a handkerchief of mauve lace

and said, "It's a hell of a hot day for this time of year," and in the same breath, turning ladylike, she leaned forward a little toward Cecil and asked, "How do you like our town? Quite a place, ain't it?"

Cecil, who had never seen anything quite like Madge said, "Yes . . . yes . . . yes . . . Indeed it is!"

"I always say there's no place like it—not Leadville or Tombstone or Leaping Rock. They're all country towns compared to Silver City. If you want to enjoy yourself this is the place to come." Again she turned to Cecil and said, "Silver City, brother, is what they call a wide-open town!"

"Yes! Yes!" said Cecil. "It is indeed wide open!"

She raised her glass again as the big diamond on her carefully crooked little finger glittered in the harsh reflected sunlight. Then she said, "Richard, you ought to get him some clothes. He looks kind of funny in that outfit. He sticks out kind of like a sore thumb."

"That's where we're headed," said Dick, "for Moe's store."

"That's a good place. Moe's got the best stuff at easy prices too!" She sighed heavily, "I wisht I made as much money as Moe." Then she said, "Hold up your glasses, boys," and lifted the bottle again.

When the glasses were filled, she said, "How's your mother, Dick?"

The boy felt the color rising in his face but he managed to say, "She's fine, thank you!"

"I always say that's the finest woman in Silver City, a real old-fashioned woman. She reminds me of my own mother. She was a little woman too. Ran a rooming house back in Cincinnati . . . took in only teetotalers." Again she sighed, "Poor Ma. She went to an early grave from overwork. She could never relax. . . . And Eudora? Is she still poorly?"

"Yes," said Dick, "just the same."

"Poor Eudora. It's a terrible thing to be disappointed in love!" She looked away, as if for a moment she were lost in memories of her own long and colorful past. Then quickly pulling herself back into reality, she said, "Now you're home again, I suppose you're going to stay a while."

"Yes," said Dick.

"Well, I hope we see a lot of you . . . and you, too, Mr. Chatsworthy . . . that's the name, ain't it?"

Cecil nodded.

"You must come down often. We have a lot of fine entertainment . . . anything you want . . . all first class."

At that moment there arose from somewhere inside the establishment the sound of screams and curses and breaking glass at which Madge suddenly put down her glass and sat upright listening. While she still sat poised, the inside door of the parlor opened violently and old Hiram the colored porter appeared. As he crossed the room he said, "It's on the balcony. They're fightin' over Irma. They ain't begun to shoot yet."

At the news, Madge rose quickly, fastened the front of her peignoir and went into action. As she passed Dick and Cecil, Dick rose and said, "I'll help you," but she brushed him aside saying, "No, you boys had better keep out of this."

Then the sound of two pistol shots gave wings to her feet and she disappeared through the parlor, followed by the porter.

For a moment Dick and Cecil sat looking after her. Then very meekly Cecil said, "Do you think we might go and look?"

"Sure," said Dick, "come on."

When they reached the balcony, they found Madge standing, with a gun in her hand beside an overturned table surrounded by broken glass. On the floor lay two men, one short, squat and swarthy and the other a red-headed, skinny, freckled fellow in cowhand's clothes. Against the wall stood one of the girls whom a little earlier they had seen on the stage. She kept screaming in a monotonous rhythmic way. Belowstairs one of the big mirrors was shattered by a bullet. From under the tables gamblers and drinkers were beginning to emerge with caution.

Madge was holding forth, her fine bosom rising and falling beneath the flowered peignoir. She was saying, "Now, get the hell out of here, both of you and don't come back! I don't give a damn who the hell you are!" She prodded the swarthy man with her foot. "And that means you too, Blackie!"

Then she turned to Dick and said, "I guess it's his living up there on the range with all them sheep that makes him so ornery. The Meaneys is an ornery family when they get started but Blackie's the worst."

[85]

By this time the swarthy man had managed to stand up. It wasn't only that he was ornery; he was also very drunk. Reeling a little, he leaned against the table for support. Then dully, recognition came into his eyes and looking at Dick, he said, "Hello, sister!"

Young Dick's face grew red. Quietly he said, "Hello, Blackie!"

"Is Mamma's darling going to stick around a while and do some work?"

"Shut up, Blackie!"

Then Blackie looked at Cecil and said, "Where did you get that?"

Here Madge intervened. Taking Blackie by the scruff of the neck she shook him and said, "Mind your manners, you black-hearted skunk! I'd call you something worse if I didn't respect your little mother. Mr. Chatsworthy is a stranger from the Old Country and you ain't fit to wipe his boots."

Blackie shook himself free and began, "You and my old man . . ." but he got no further. The speech was suddenly shut off by the impact of Madge's hand slapping him across the mouth.

"I told you to shut up! If you ain't got no respect for your kinfolk, I have!"

The blow sobered him and he stood sullenly looking at the floor and wiping the blood from his cut lip with the hairy back of his hand.

The red-headed cowhand had disappeared and Irma, her screaming quieted, stood watching with concentration the tactics of Madge.

Dick turned away and said to Cecil, "Come on! Let's go!"

As Cecil started to follow him, Madge turned and said, "I'm sorry you had to be mixed up in this Mr. Chatsworthy. You mustn't get the wrong impression. This is a refined place. I hope you'll come back to see us often and drop in any afternoon when you feel like a glass of champagne." Then, in a kind of parenthesis, she repeated, "All the Meaneys but Dick and his mother is ornery, but Black Pete is the orneriest of the lot." She turned to Blackie and said, "Ain't I right, Blackie?" And Blackie still holding his cut lip said, "You sure are, Madge. I sure *aim* to be the orneriest."

Then she shook Cecil's hand warmly and he followed Dick who was already halfway down the stairs. Madge turned to the girl, Irma, and said, "Get back to your room and wash your face!" and went back to the rocking chair, the palm-leaf fan and the champagne.

She reached there about the time Dick and Cecil emerged from the room below into Eudora Street. Leaning over the rail she called out, "Come back real soon, Mr. Chatsworthy, and we can have a real good talk!"

"Certainly," Cecil called up, "I enjoyed myself outrageously."

In the street the two walked for a time in silence past the tethered horses, The Paris Grille, the saloons and eating places and presently Cecil said, "Don't take it so hard, old chap! We all have skeletons in our family closets. I had a cousin who was deported to Australia for swindling and an aunt who has been kept for years by a rich pawnbroker."

Dick didn't answer him. He wasn't even thinking about Blackie, because Blackie had long been a part of his life from the time when as a small boy Blackie, as a much older brother, had tormented and abused him. Blackie and Buck and Shorty, like his father were in the pattern of things in Silver City. They had always been there since the day when Dick first became aware of the world about him. Doubtless they would be there for the rest of their lives. They were, oddly enough, a part of the whole of this world which he loved so much and for which he had been homesick all the years he had spent away from it. The brothers, his father, Eudora, Madge, indeed all the bawdy life of Eudora Street were a part of that world, along with the great mountains, the high ranges, the canyons, the waterfalls. He had passed over Blackie, suffering only a mild embarrassment that Cecil should have encountered his brother for the first time in the midst of a brawl in Madge's establishment. He was touched by Cecil's remark about his own relations. He understood that Cecil was trying to make the scene easier for him, not understanding that the scene was a part of the whole thing.

At the moment he was thinking, as he had been thinking even while they sat drinking champagne with Madge on her veranda overhanging the street, about the girl with whom he had held so baffling and incomplete a conversation in Mrs. Sowers' parlor. In all the years away from home, he hadn't learned much about girls—he had never seen one like Mademoiselle—but his instinct told him that there was something peculiar and unnatural about her suspicious constraint. He was aware that she had a certain sullen beauty, but it wasn't that which occupied and stimulated his thoughts at the moment. Largely it was annoyance with himself—that he had seemed so stupid there in Mrs. Sowers' parlor and in the background of his mind there was still a sore place, a tiny clot of resentment over P.J.'s mocking remarks about his lack of experience with women.

Then he heard Cecil saying, "Is this the place?" and looking up he saw they were at the door of Moe Hirshbein's Emporium.

The establishment had an ornate front of red and yellow. The shop windows were almost covered with signs advertising special bargains in socks, in chaps, in shirts, in boots and shoes. The store, like the other buildings in Eudora Street, was all front, receding from the pavement into an ugly and unpainted two-story wooden structure. The store occupied the ground floor and overhead lived Moe, his wife and Eudora's girl friend, their daughter Rachel.

Young Dick had known Moe and his wife and daughter from the time he was a small boy when Moe had made him gifts from time to time out of the vast assembly of cheap toys and junk which made up what was known as the "bargain bazaar" at the rear of the store. He knew Moe was a good citizen and Mrs. Hirshbein as a large-bosomed, dark woman who spent her days as a saleswoman in the Emporium and her nights in keeping the books and in thinking up ways by which she could help other people. Together with his mother, she had formed the first Civic Improvement Committee which put an end to dumping garbage and even chamber pots into the street and organized a street-cleaning service to take care of the droppings of the cowhands' ponies that lined the hitching rails of Eudora Street all day and most of the night. It was the two of them who set up the first organization to help out the poor families which dwelt in shacks along the cotton-wood bordered river during the cold winter months. Indeed, the two of them, with occasional help from Henry Caldwell, had been the principal civilizing influence in Silver City.

So, on entering the store, with its long counters piled high with ticketed merchandise, young Dick had a great welcome from both Moe and his wife. Mrs. Hirshbein even pressed him against her great bosom and kissed him with an emotion so great that tears came into her great dark eyes. Their welcome of Cecil as a friend of Dick's was scarcely less warm and emotional.

And then Dick said, "We want to buy some clothes for Cecil."

Moe regarded Cecil for a moment from head to foot and then as if they were beyond control his fingers stole toward Cecil's tweeds. As he felt of the material he said, "Fine stuff! Fine stuff! That is the real thing," and then, "And what do you want?"

Dick explained to him the purpose of the visit—that Cecil was tired of being stared at because he was dressed differently from everyone else in Silver City. He wanted to outfit himself in protective coloration, the brighter and gaudier the better.

There began at once a great hub-bub over outfitting Cecil from head to foot, in which Mrs. Hirshbein took a leading part. The process began with socks and belts and then he turned to shirts, chaps, boots and hats. In all the selections—even the belts and socks—Cecil displayed a predilection for color. He chose the brightest socks and the gaudiest of shirts and when it came to chaps, selected a pair made from the skin of a piebald Pinto of remarkably gaudy coloration. The whole was topped off by the purchase of two wide-brimmed hats. As the outfitting progressed the eyes of Cecil became brighter and brighter and the cheeks pinker and pinker and at last he said, timidly, but with enthusiasm, "Perhaps I could change into these things now?"

So they went to a small room at the back of the Emporium and while Mrs. Hirshbein withdrew discreetly, Cecil took off the tweeds and the deerstalker's cap. Divested of his outer clothing, he stood before the mirror as nature had made him—scrawny, thin and pallid, unadorned save for a kind of sagging unionsuit with sleeves reaching below the elbow and pants that reached below the knees. Upon this unpromising basis Moe draped one by one the articles of clothing selected earlier—first a shirt of the most violent red and black checks, then a pair of tight blue denim pants and next a pair of brilliant emerald socks and a pair of high-heeled boots in a filigreed design of black upon white. Finally the chaps made of the piebald Pinto's skin were buckled on and above them a wide, leather belt heavily ornamented with silver. One of the two broad-brimmed hats was placed on his head and the transformation was complete.

Moe stood back with the air of a great Paris dressmaker regarding his creation and, rubbing his hands together, said, "Well! Well! You'd never know it was the same feller."

But Moe's pleasure was as nothing compared to that of Cecil himself. In front of the mirror he turned from side to side looking at himself and his new finery from every angle and, slowly, there broke over his pale face a grin of satisfaction that was beyond his best efforts at repression.

Neither young Dick nor Moe distracted his show of satisfaction and presently when he had satisfied himself, at least temporarily, he turned to Dick and asked timidly, "Could I have a gun?"

"A gun!" said Moe. "I have the finest assortment of guns in Colorado! Come!" he said, and led the two of them back into the Emporium where he kept an assortment of firearms in a glass case.

Cecil's taste ran to the largest and gaudiest of the six-shooters and he was dissuaded from purchasing the largest of all only by young Dick's suggestion that not only would he find such a gun unmanageable but that he might even have difficulty in holding it in one hand. In the end he was persuaded to choose a more modest and serviceable weapon.

"You may need to use it," said Dick. "You'd better get something your size that you can handle."

A holster to match the broad silver ornamental belt was purchased to carry the new gun and Cecil's costume was complete. He had once more to regard himself in the mirror and be admired by Moe and at last he and Dick left the Emporium followed by the fond and admiring regard of Moe and Mrs. Hirshbein.

It was a new Cecil who stepped out of the door of the Emporium into Eudora Street. He felt himself no longer to be a curiosity but a part of this enormous, exaggerated, grandiose world where there seemed to be no people but only characters. He would have walked with a swagger—indeed he attempted it—save that the uncertainty of the high heels, which pitched him forward on his toes prevented it. By the time they passed the Grand Hotel on their way to the Castle, he began to feel the faint qualms of a new disappointment. Now no one seemed to notice him. On the wooden sidewalks among the other residents and visitors of Silver City, even the brilliance of the red and black checked shirt and the Pinto-skin chaps attracted no notice.

As they turned up the hill toward the Castle into the range of Eudora's telescope, he became lost in speculation. "What," he thought, as he still tottered on uncertainly on the high-heeled boots, "would Cousin Herbert think if he could see me now!" Cousin Herbert, of course was the Earl.

Eudora had finished cutting out and pasting her texts for the day and sat now by the window watching the town through her telescope. Her friend Rachel was with her, crocheting a chamber muffler in a matching design of pansies, while she gossiped. Eudora, from time to time, reported over her shoulder to Rachel what she observed through the telescope.

"They've opened the Opry House," she said, "and are cleaning it. I guess rehearsals will begin soon."

To which Rachel replied, "It's all over town that Signorina Baldacie is mad because that new girl is goin' to take her place. The Signorina goes around everywhere making threats."

"I guess it's all Pa's doing," said Eudora. "Every year he does something to rile up them Dagoes and Polacks. He kind of enjoys it, I guess."

"I don't think that new girl is so pretty," said Rachel. "I don't know what they're all talking about. She's got a hard chin and jaw. I'd hate to set her against me. And I don't believe she's as young as she pretends to be. I'd guess she was thirty if she was a day."

"I ain't seen her except through the telescope," said Eudora. Then her attention became focused suddenly on Madge Beakymer's veranda overhanging the street. "Well, I declare!" she said, "it's Dick and Mr. Chatsworthy! They're drinking champagne with Madge!"

Rachel sighed heavily, "I think it's a disgrace the way Madge sets out there every afternoon drinkin' champagne and calling up men from the street . . . leading citizens, too. You'd think she was queen of Silver City. Your Pa ought to do something about it."

But Eudora didn't hear the latter remark. She leaned forward concentrating all her interest into the barrel of the telescope. "There's some kind of row going on inside the El Dorado. The Old Darky just come and got Madge. They're all goin' inside. I wisht this telescope could see inside. Is that shots I heard?"

Rachel nodded, "Sounded like it to me." She crocheted the last stitch into the design of pansies and turned the half-finished chamber muffler to begin the creation of an intricate border.

For some time there was nothing for Eudora to report from the telescope and the conversation lagged. Presently Rachel asked, "Did you get any good letters from prisoners today?"

"Nothing special," said Eudora. "Just one sayin' that the texts I sent him made him see the light. He's gettin' out soon and wants Pa to give him a job. Nothing very interesting."

"Heard any more from that fellow who killed his wife and the peddler?"

"Nothin' for three weeks now. Could be he climbed out and ran away."

"It's a pity they hung that Simpson feller," said Rachel. "He wrote such gentlemanly letters. I always calculated he was educated in the East."

Then Eudora reported, "Dick and Mr. Chatsworthy have just come out of the El Dorado." And then a moment later. "Why there's Blackie comin' out. He musta got into town this afternoon."

"You'd think," said Rachel, "that he'd come to the Castle first."

"He always goes to the El Dorado first," said Eudora. "As soon as he comes down from the range—straight as an arrow to the mark."

"I guess all them sheepherders are alike," observed Rachel.

Then a long silence intervened broken only by minor and unimportant reports from Eudora. Nothing of great interest turned up until Eudora reported with some excitement. "Dick must have left Mr. Chatsworthy in town. I hope he won't get into no trouble."

"Why?" asked Rachel.

"Dick's comin' up the hill with a cowhand, all dressed up fit to kill. Wonder who it could be? Maybe you'd better look. Your eyes is better than mine."

Rachel put down her crocheting, rose and took up the telescope. After a moment's silence, she said, "Why, I do believe it's Mr. Chatsworthy himself. They musta been to the Emporium and fitted him out. Why, sure enough, it *is* Mr. Chatsworthy. And he don't look like the same man. They sure fitted him out. He's got a gun and everything."

"Let me see!" said Eudora impatiently and took back the telescope. After a moment she said, "Why, it sure is and he looks kinda good got up in them cowhand's clothes."

There was a little silence and Rachel, looking up slyly from her crocheting beneath her heavy oriental eyelids, asked, "How do you like Mr. Chatsworthy?"

"Oh, I like him all right," said Eudora, still watching through her telescope. "He's an elegant talker. I like men that talks like him."

The look of slyness in Rachel's dark eyes sharpened a bit.

"He seems very refined," she observed, and while she spoke, it occurred to her for the first time that Mr. Chatsworthy resembled to a remarkable degree, both in physique and in manners, the fiancé who had walked out on Eudora at the last moment when her "wedding dress was on the bed." Rachel was aware that both the telescope and Eudora's attention were still focused upon the approaching men. As they progressed up the hill leading to the Castle, the telescope was gradually lowered to keep them in view until they reached the portecochere and were no longer visible.

Then Eudora put down the telescope and said, "He was better lookin' than I thought. Them cowhand's clothes certainly make a difference to a man."

Once inside the Castle, Dick left his companion and went directly to his mother's sitting room. As always he walked in without knocking and found that she was not alone. Seated in the rocking chair by the window was Henry Caldwell. At sight of Dick an expression of pleasure came into Henry's grey eyes. He held out his hand and said, "Well, Dick, it's good to see you back. You're looking fine."

"It's good to be back," said Dick and then he noticed his mother Ellie-May was smiling. Indeed, it was more than that. The look was one of complete happiness such as he rarely saw on her withered face.

She said, "Henry and I have been talking about him runnin' for Governor. It seems a lot of people want him to run and he's considerin' it."

"I wanted your mother's advice," said Henry. "She has remarkable good sense and she knows a lot more about what's goin' on than most people give her credit for."

"What does she think?" asked Dick.

"She's for it," said Henry.

"Pa won't like it much," said Dick.

Then suddenly and unexpectedly Ellie-May grew tart. "It doesn't matter what your Pa thinks. He's had things his own way in Colorado long enough. People are gettin' sick of him and if it goes on someday somebody is goin' to shoot him as full of holes as a sieve. And anyway it would do him good to be taken down a bit. Lately he's been actin' like God Almighty Himself!"

They fell to talking of the prospects. It seemed that the revolt had spread beyond the limits of Silver City through the whole of the new state. People, Henry said, were getting sick of having state officers that were no more than the puppets of P. J. Meaney. And they were getting sick of corruption and mismanagement.

"I hate to break your father considering what friends we were in the old days," said Henry. "But it ain't like it used to be. As your Ma says, it would be for P.J.'s own good to get defeated a couple of times. He's had his own way so long he's forgotten that this is a free country and a democracy and someday he's goin' to run into trouble. Even if he does run Colorado, there's still the government of the United States and outside Colorado people haven't even heard of P. J. Meaney." He looked at Dick sharply and said, "What are you goin' to do now?"

"Pa wants me to take over the railroad for him, but I'm not interested. It's not the kind of work that interests me."

"What about politics?" asked Henry. "The state could use a young fellow like you."

Dick frowned, "I couldn't go right into politics against Pa as soon as I got home."

Surprisingly, Ellie-May put in a word, "Not now, maybe, but later on . . . after Henry has won and cleaned things up a bit."

"I don't know," said Dick.

The truth was that he was finding the whole business of readjustment a great deal more difficult than he had expected. In the years he had been away, and particularly during the last few months before his return when the homesickness had become overpowering, he had wanted only to return to that wild, beautiful country, believing that there would be no difficulties, that he could begin again where he had left off at the age of sixteen, hunting, fishing, riding the range. But more and more each day he was discovering that the return was not so simple. All the things he had learned out in the world, indeed everything he had been and done during his absence contributed now to the difficulties and the complexity of readjustment. It wasn't at all as he had remembered it, not because the life at home had changed in any way, but because he himself had changed and he saw the whole life of Silver City and even the members of his own family, P.J. and Eudora, Blackie, Shorty and Buck all differently, all except his mother who remained as stable and unchanged as the great mountain which dominated Silver City itself. He knew now that he would never agree with his father or work for him. He knew that any desire he had once felt to find a place in P.J.'s vast kingdom was dead. And there was the disturbing business of this Mademoiselle which troubled him far more than he had thought any girl could possibly trouble him.

And as he sat there he was aware of another thing—that the meeting here in his mother's sitting-room with his mother and Henry Caldwell seemed comfortable and pleasant and right. It was as if he himself belonged here rather than in the other rooms of the Castle, as if Henry and Ellie-May and himself constituted one family and all the others made up another. He began to think, looking back over the past, that he had not properly understood and appreciated Henry Caldwell, perhaps because in the past he had always taken Henry for granted, because Henry in the old days was always overshadowed by the robustness of P.J. himself. Henry was quiet but tough. He had helped more than most people knew to build up the great empire which P.J. now dominated from his fortress-Castle. He had only parted company with P.J. when P.J. began, as Ellie-May said, to act like Almighty God and become guilty of a lot of things which Almighty God would never have undertaken. There was a lot of fight and a lot of principle in the wiry figure in rancher's clothes seated in the rocking chair opposite him, a lot of toughness despite all the gentleness of his appearance and manner. And he remembered suddenly the legends of Henry Caldwell's youth—how he was the best shot on the frontier and how he had cleaned out the evil Jenkins gang single-handed. If Henry had been the kind of man to put notches in his gunstock he would have had several to his credit. Everybody in the state knew Henry's name and the legends that had grown up about him and that wouldn't be any disadvantage in politics.

Henry was saying again, "We could use you in the State of Colorado, Dick—not only now but in the future. Colorado is goin' to be a great state and Denver a great city. Someday there'll be Meaneys in the United States Senate and Meaneys who are leaders and society people. The state ain't ready for that yet and the Meaneys ain't, but it would be a good thing to bear in mind, even if it does set you up against your Pa."

The sun had begun to slip down behind the great mountains and the blue of the shadow began slowly to creep up the sides of the granite Castle, higher and higher toward the window boxes outside Ellie-May's room. As the vast shadow crept upward the cool of evening moved with it, releasing slowly the scent of the flowers which Ellie-May watered and tended so carefully. Seventy miles away, the snow-capped peaks of the high ranges began to turn slowly and almost imperceptibly rose-colored, and young Dick felt suddenly and sharply once more the sense of peace and of cosiness here in the room with Ellie-May and Henry Caldwell and the sense of almost measureless color and splendor in the world outside. And he knew suddenly that Ellie-May and Henry Caldwell were experiencing the same emotions and that they loved this country as passionately as himself. But none of them would or perhaps could express what they felt.

Abruptly Ellie-May said, "Where every prospect pleases and only man is vile."

The remark seemed to embarrass Henry Caldwell who rose suddenly and said, "Well, I must be goin'. I got a long ride after the train gets to Meeker's Gulch. Thank you for the visit, Ellie-May. It seemed like old times." To Dick he said, "Think over what I've been tellin' you. And remember someday the Meaneys are goin' to be prominent in society in Washington and New York. It's about time they were thinkin' of turnin' respectable."

When he had gone, Dick turned to his mother and asked, "What would Pa say if he knew Henry Caldwell was visitin' you here." And

Ellie-May answered tartly, "Don't worry about your Pa. I always managed him up to now and I can still manage him. The truth is that your Pa is showin' signs of crackin' up. He still thinks he's in his teens but he ain't." She looked at him with narrowed eyes. "I'd keep in mind what Henry said. It makes sense. The Meaneys are ready for the second step upwards, I mean. They've either got to go ahead or go back and it looks to me that your Pa and the boys are goin' back. It's kind of up to you, son."

Dick said, "Blackie's in town."

She displayed little interest but asked, "Where did you see him?"

"At the El Dorado."

"Yes, he always goes there just like he couldn't wait." She sighed and strangely enough repeated what Madge had said, "All the boys are kinda ornery but Blackie's the orneriest of all." She spoke with detachment and objectivity as if she had never given birth to them and claimed no connection now.

At this point, further conversation was interrupted by the sound of Eudora's cowbell, ringing violently and Dick said, "I'll go and see what she wants. You lie down and rest." Then he added, "You must get awfully sick of Eudora at times."

"It isn't that," said Ellie-May. "I just wish she'd show more gumption and get up. There's nothin' the matter with her at all. It's not right for a girl to carry on like that because she was disappointed in love."

When he had gone, Ellie-May did not lie down. She went back to the sewing machine and resumed the work which had been interrupted by the visit of Henry Caldwell. She was making flannel underdrawers for the children who lived in the ramshackle huts along the river. Winter would be coming on before anybody noticed it and it was up to her and Moe Hirshbein's wife to see that the children didn't starve and freeze to death. It made her feel good to have a stock put away so they wouldn't run short when the wind began to whistle down the canyon and the snow to pile up in drifts along the wretched shacks where the miners and their families lived.

Across the hall in the room smelling of patent medicines and flannel, Dick, answering the imperious call of Eudora's cowbell, found his sister sitting up in the chair by the window. The room for once seemed to be in order, with the bits of cut paper and the paste pots and scissors put away. Eudora herself was changed too. She wore a purple silk wrapper with a wide bertha of white lace, and had her hair done into an elaborate coiffure with false curls. Rachel Hirshbein, who had spent a good half hour getting the room straightened up and concocting the elaborate coiffure out of Eudora's heavy Indian black hair, sat near-by in attendance.

Dick said, "Ma was busy so I came to see what you wanted."

Rachel giggled suddenly but Eudora came to the point, "I thought Mr. Chatsworthy and you might like to have a cup of tea up here with us."

For a moment Dick found words difficult. Nothing like this had happened in his memory. "I'm sure he would," he said. "I'll ask him."

Across the hall he pushed open the door of Cecil's room and came upon a remarkable scene. Cecil, still clad in the finery purchased at the Emporium, hat, gun and all, stood before the long gilt pier-glass. He held the gun in one hand pointed at his own reflection. Suddenly, with an expression of intense ferocity on his face, he would take one step abruptly toward his reflection, bring the gun to his hip, and say, "Put 'em up!"

So absorbed was he in this exercise that he performed it three times without being aware that he was no longer alone. Then Dick retired, still unobserved into the hall and made a new entrance, this time knocking on the door to give warning.

When he made his second entrance in response to Cecil's "Come in," Mr. Chatsworthy had restored the gun to its holster, taken off his hat and appeared to be in a sane condition.

Dick said, "My sister and Rachel Hirshbein would like us to have a cup of tea with them. How about it?"

"Of course," said Cecil, "but do you think I'm dressed properly?"

For a moment Dick felt laughter coming up inside him. With an immense effort he managed to control it and said, "Yes, it's perfectly all right. I think she'd like to see you dressed like that."

The tea party turned out to be a great success. It had been a long time since Eudora and Rachel had entertained any young men and they entered into the spirit of the occasion with enthusiasm. Cecil told them about life at Oxford and the vicarage and in turn they told him legends and bits of scandal and gossip about Silver City which even Dick had never heard before.

When he reported later to his mother, he said, "You know, Eudora behaved almost like a human being. I think she's feeling better."

It was not only the purchase of his first cowhand's clothes that had an effect upon Mr. Chatsworthy. The purchase of the clothes was indeed not the cause but rather an effect of many other things. First of all there was the air. The change from the damp, sluggish air and the atmosphere of antiquity which hung over Oxford to the brilliant clear, dry air of the high mountains had slowly but certainly brought about a remarkable change in Mr. Chatsworthy's metabolism. In the beginning he had experienced merely alternative periods of elation and depression, accompanied by a remarkable dizziness which overtook him, as on the afternoon of the reception, after the first swallow of beer. It was not that he was unaccustomed to beer; he had, along with quantities of heavy victuals, drunk beer at Oxford, but the effect there had merely been to throw him into a kind of torpor which led to long periods of heavy sleep in which he dozed like a digesting anaconda. Here the beer was different, or at least seemed to be.

The high, clear, dry air also had a remarkable effect upon his appetite. It became ravenous, and where before he had regarded food like many of his countrymen, merely as so much fuel to stoke up and keep operating the human organism in a damp, cold climate, he now regarded with excitement the menus placed on the table at each meal by the chef. These were written in elaborate script in French and until Mr. Chatsworthy and young Dick returned, they had remained a mystery to the household of Meaney's Castle who were content merely to see what turned up. Ellie-May, in her calm philosophy of accepting what existed, had never made any protest about these mysteries, but like Eudora, waiting aloft in her room with the anticipation of a hungry python, had accepted the French names (which had no English alternates) and produced names of their own in imitation of the French ones which after a time the French chef came to understand and identify. For example *bombe glacé* became "that glassy bomb you make" and *gâteau St. Honoré* became "gatto St. Ornery."

But Mr. Chatsworthy knew French and during his somewhat brief experiences at the house in London of his cousin, the Earl, had learned the French names of many dishes. So as he ran over the written menu each day the salivary and gastric juices began to work overtime. It was not only that he had discovered that food could be a sensual business, almost as sensual as the passions and desires which he had read about but never experienced, but that the change of air gave him a ferocious appetite. The change from an Oxford diet of boiled mutton, potatoes, greens, puddings and beer to one of filet mignon, paté de fois gras, omelette Norvegienne, gâteaux St. Honoré and champagne was, to put it mildly, a revolutionary one.

And there was also that sense of grandeur, splendor and space in this new country which continued to affect him. The first terror of the size and of the vast uninhabited spaces had worn off a little, but the sense of exaltation remained. It overtook and swamped him at unexpected moments, at sunrise or sunset or when a vast thunderstorm, of proportions inconceivable in his own neat, tight, placid England, formed over the mountains and broke over Silver City releasing tons of water as if someone had pulled a chain. The food and the appetite affected his glands which began to function to a degree hitherto unknown on the diet and in the climate of England. His tendency to constipation began to disappear and the rather pasty complexion, like one of the suet puddings which had largely induced it, began to clear up and color began to appear in his cheeks. Alas, it was too late for these revolutionary elements to affect the jut of the horse-teeth which spread from beneath his upper lip like the struts of a Japanese ivory fan.

Spiritually the same growth began to take place. He felt himself, not without alarm, expanding, growing reckless and carefree. He found himself neglecting to keep the drawers of his huge black walnut bureau in meticulous order. He just tossed things into them or pulled things out at random, because in this stimulating new world there seemed to be no time for such things. He found himself neglecting his reading of the trunk of books which he had brought all the way from England to be read and digested for the definitive volume he had planned to write upon "Prostitution, Secular and Sacred, Through the Ages." He had begun, after his visit to Madge's El Dorado to suspect that he might gain more extensive and authoritative information and material out of the daily life around him.

At times in his more sober moments when he lay in the darkness, falling asleep, he became alarmed at the change in himself.

The encounter with Blackie at Madge's place had startled him. He was aware that there were characters more or less like Blackie in abundance in Silver City, but it had never occurred to him despite the knowledge of black sheep and family skeletons in the Earl's family, that anyone was related by blood to such people. That Blackie was the brother of young Dick seemed impossible, and yet, somehow, exciting. The physical dissimilarity—the difference between young Dick's fresh blond, almost adolescent cleanness and Blackie's sinister, dark brutishness, seemed shocking.

What he did not know was what went on inside Blackie's curious, twisted mind—that Blackie suffered like many another before him, from being the son of an overwhelming personality like P. J. Meaney. Without P.J. in the background, Blackie might have been a dull and fairly respectable average citizen, but P.J. had distorted the character of Blackie as indeed he had distorted the characters of all his children, even Eudora, except young Dick, who had, largely through Ellie-May's calm and calculated maneuverings been saved from the blight. The truth was that P.J. was as much a tyrant inside the Castle as he was in the world outside—a tyrant with all but Ellie-May. He had wanted each of his children to be the image of himself, not only in physique, but in vitality and ruthlessness, yet each time one of them displayed any of his own qualities, that child was promptly beaten down and suppressed. And so each of his own sons had grown up, it might be said, with one arm raised psychologically above his head to protect himself from blows. On the other hand each of them had inherited the unholy vitality and physical strength of old P.J. They had also inherited something of his zest and lust. Of all of them Blackie was the most acute example of suppressed tyranny, zest, lust, and general violence. All of these things smouldered inside him like the fire of a magnesium bomb and the long months on the sheep ranges only served to aggravate rather than suppress these forces.

The result was that when Blackie paid a visit to Silver City, all hell generally broke loose. Throughout the visit he lived at Madge's place, gambling, drinking, whoring, fighting. If he had been anyone but P.J.'s son, Madge would long ago have thrown him out for good, but P.J. always said indulgently, after one of Blackie's carousing escapades, "Leave him stay, Madge! He ain't bad at heart! It just ain't human to live up there on the sheep range most of the year."

So Madge had never yet barred him from the place—a penalty she reserved for only the worst characters of Silver City.

Once or twice during a visit, Blackie would put on store clothes and go up the hill to the Castle on a visit of ceremony. On these occasions he sat at meal-time largely glum and largely silent, swarthy and sullen, and smelling of sheep and sheep dip, looking always as if he were in need of a shave and a haircut. In the beginning Ellie-May had tried, as she had tried with all her children, to give him manners and refinement, but as with all the others save young Dick, she had long ago abandoned the struggle and now merely sat back observing them with detachment and objectivity as if all of them were specimens which had nothing to do with her.

There is no need in repeating the conversations between Blackie and the other members of the family because there was no conversation to repeat beyond the "yes" or the "no" which Blackie gave out in reply to questions aimed at him. The only real conversation took place in P.J.'s elegant office when Blackie was called to report upon the condition of the six hundred thousand sheep which were in Blackie's charge on the vast, disputed and isolated Calamares range.

Three days after the brawl in which Mr. Chatsworthy had made his first acquaintance with Blackie, one of the ceremonial visits to the Castle took place. It proceeded along the usual lines and when noon-day dinner was finished Blackie shook hands with Ellie-May (she had long since given up kissing him since it would have been like kissing a Longhorn bull or a Merino ram) and set out down the hill to get out of his starched collar as quickly as possible and back into his sheepman's clothes Very likely that was the only thought which occupied his mind until he reached the big veranda of Mrs. Sowers' Grand Hotel and Boarding House. Then just as he passed the veranda there appeared at the top of the steps a vision of the kind which haunted his dreams night after night during the long months on the sheep range.

It was a pretty young woman, fashionably dressed, with a remarkable figure and a face in which innocence and voluptuousness were remarkably blended. For a moment Blackie's steps faltered and at the same time the young lady, noticing his hesitation and perhaps the look in his eye, appeared suddenly to have forgotten something urgent and, instead of descending the steps, turned, crossed the veranda and went inside the hotel.

Now Blackie was not the sensitive type nor one to be easily rebuffed, much less when he had glimpsed for the first time in the flesh the image created out of the suppressed desires of months and years. All unconsciously, he gave out a low whistle, hiked up the store pants that were always slipping down because he had no hips to support them, climbed the steps, past the rocking chairs occupied by Signor Malatesta and the "Eyetalian Nightingale" and entered the hotel. He went through the door just in time to discover the vision disappearing through the door on the opposite side of the big parlor.

Hot on the trail he crossed the room and followed the vision down the steps onto the wooden sidewalk where it progressed to the corner and turned into Eudora Street. As he followed it along the street he observed that he was not the only one who found the vision desirable, for as she progressed the glances of cowhands, sheepmen, prospectors and gamblers turned slowly in her direction. Occasionally one of the admirers gave out a low whistle. But Blackie pursued his quest alone. The others merely grinned at his enthusiasm. As he passed along the hitching rail lined with horses and rigs, one cowhand called out, ironically, "Good luck, Blackie!" And another observed, "Wastin' your time, buddy." For by now it was well established that Mademoiselle was *not* one of Madge's importations, but that on the contrary, she was on her own but impregnable.

Undisturbed by the advice of his more experienced friends, he continued the chase with the persistence of an old Merino ram, and as they neared Moe's Emporium he quickened his pace and came up opposite her. As he did so, he lifted his hard hat and said, "Good afternoon, Ma'am!"

But Mademoiselle, through the medium of reflections in the store windows and the remarks passed by the loafers along the curb, had been aware throughout her short excursion that she was being followed.

At Moe's Emporium she turned in, still well in possession of her dignity. Being followed was not a new experience and she did not allow it to disturb her. Once inside she went down one of the long aisles between piled-up counters of merchandise until she reached the counters where ladies unmentionable garments were sold. As it happened, here Rachel Hirshbein was presiding at the moment. She stood tall, thin and forbidding, her protruding eyes staring from behind thick glasses, all her attention concentrated upon the approaching figure of Mademoiselle. Her own interest was scarcely less intense than that of Blackie, for Mademoiselle was an actress and opera singer and she was young and very pretty.

As Mademoiselle arrived at the counter she said primly, "Good afternoon."

"Good afternoon, Mademoiselle," gushed Rachel. "Can I do anything for you?"

"I would like to see some drawers."

"Yes, indeed," said Rachel. "What kind—long, full or skimpy? With or without lace and about what price?"

"Just plain," said Mademoiselle, "and about a dollar."

Then as Rachel turned to the shelves behind her, she saw Blackie who until that moment had not come within the narrow range of her thick glasses. He too was standing at the counter piled high with ladies' drawers. At sight of him her heart skipped a couple of beats, partly because she was afraid of him and partly because he had always fascinated her as a symbol of all the vice, passion and disorderly living of which she possessed so little first-hand information. She could not believe that even he would have the effrontery to come into her father's establishment to buy ladies' drawers. Moreover his behavior was peculiar in the extreme. He was standing very near to Mademoiselle, fingering the eyelet embroidery of a pair of long, full drawers marked at three dollars and fifty cents. But his attention seemed less directed to the embroidery than to the lady by his side.

Rachel thought quickly and desperately. Clearly it was impossible to display drawers to a lady customer with him present. It did occur to her that, even in his store clothes, Blackie appeared more like a bear than a man but she had been carefully brought up by Mrs. Hirshbein and she realized that, man or bear, the drawers department was not the place for Blackie. With another part of her mind she was aware that the situation would make an excellent tid-bit to report to Eudora.

She acted quickly. Turning with the dignity of a queen, she asked, "Is there something I can do for you, Mr. Meaney?" And at the name Meaney, even through her thick eyeglasses, she was aware that Mademoiselle made a slight movement of interest and surprise.

"No," said Blackie, "I was just lookin' around."

Rachel, trembling inside with the memories of stories concerning Blackie's wild behavior at the El Dorado, acted courageously.

"If there's nothing that interests you in this department, I would appreciate it if you would move along quietly so that I might serve the lady who is waiting."

Blackie looked at her with a sullen eye and rubbed the back of one hairy hand over the other. "All right! All right!" he said and moved away as far as the hardware counter.

By this time Rachel was fully aware of the true object of Blackie's interest and she was also aware that the way had been opened for conversation and even perhaps friendship with the glamorous newcomer to Silver City.

She said, "Has the gentleman been annoying you?"

"Yes," said Mademoiselle. "He's been following me all the way from the Grand Hotel and he doesn't follow like a gentleman. He was practically walking on my heels. Did I hear you say his name was Meaney?"

"Yes," said Rachel, "he's P.J.'s son."

A look of astonishment came into Mademoiselle's face, "You mean he's related to that nice young Mr. Dick Meaney?"

"He's his brother," said Rachel, "but they're not much alike." Rachel was eager now and a little breathless. "Maybe you'd like me to walk back to the hotel with you."

"No, thank you. I think I can manage him."

Rachel felt disappointment stealing over her. She said weakly, "He's a bad man . . . a real bad man!"

"I think I can manage him. If he gets too fresh I'll sock him."

Mademoiselle picked up a pair of drawers as if to indicate that the conversation was ended. "And now about the drawers," she said.

The rest of the discussion was entirely technical and impersonal, regarding sizes, styles and amount of embroidery. Mademoiselle selected two pairs and Rachel wrapped them for her in businesslike fashion, exchanging the package for the two heavy silver dollars which Mademoiselle took out of her reticule. A side glance from Rachel revealed the fact that Blackie in his store clothes was still standing by the hardware counter.

Then as she left Mademoiselle suddenly turned gracious, "Thank you, very much," she said. "I don't want you to think that I don't appreciate your kind offer but I'm used to mashers like that. I think I can manage him."

She placed the package under her arm, grasped her parasol firmly and set off down the aisle. Rachel observed as she moved away that Blackie lost all interest in hardware and followed down the aisle. He followed out of the door of the Emporium into the street.

As Mademoiselle turned toward the Grand Hotel, Blackie turned with her, walking very near. Twice he repeated his greeting, "Good afternoon, Ma'am," and twice she turned her head in the opposite direction. Then after a moment she said between her teeth, "If you don't stop following me you'll be sorry."

"I only wanted to get acquainted," said Blackie. "I don't mean no harm. You're mighty pretty."

Then in silence they walked together for a time side by side less like the strangers they were than like a long-married couple in the midst of a quarrel. And presently Blackie said, "Aw, Come on! Give in! I'll carry your package for you."

"I won't warn you again," said Mademoiselle between her teeth.

By this time they were approaching the Grand Hotel where most of the Silver City Opera Company, resting like pythons after a heavy noon-day dinner, were seated in the rocking-chairs. Mademoiselle had almost reached the steps when Blackie's hand reached out and touched her arm. It was as if he had touched a hair-trigger attached to a charge of dynamite. The package containing the drawers fell to the sidewalk and Mademoiselle taking a firm, quick grasp upon the handle of the umbrella, raised it and brought it down on the top of Blackie's hard hat.

The quickness and violence of the action so astonished him that for a moment he was dazed and completely blinded by the brim of the hat which had been forced down over his eyes, pressing his ears outward. Before he was able to recover, Mademoiselle had picked up her package, hurried up the steps and was inside the hotel, and the whole of the Opera Company had burst into a chatter of mixed languages like a troupe of macaws in an aviary.

Once inside the door, Mademoiselle moved quickly toward the stairway but as she neared it she found her progress blocked by the figure of young Dick. He stood, hat in hand, smiling, and as she came nearer the smile faded out, for it was clear that Mademoiselle was in no congenial mood. He was aware, however, that it was impossible to beat a retreat now, so he said, "Excuse me. I was waiting to see you."

She answered him quickly and with a rudeness he had not expected. She said, "Thank you, but I don't care to see you. I don't want to speak to anyone called Meaney."

And with that she hurried past him and up the stairs, leaving him standing there, bewildered, hat in hand, aware that he was being observed with amusement by all the others in the room. After a moment, he put on his hat and walked out feeling completely a fool. He had come to tell Mademoiselle that she and the professor should use the piano in the big drawing-room of the Castle since all the other pianos, he had been told by various members of the Opera Company, were in use twenty-four hours a day.

He thought, "To hell with her if she's going to act like that!"

As he went out the door Mademoiselle reached the second floor and went straight toward the room of the Professor. She knew what she had in mind. She was sick of Silver City and the whole thing. She didn't want to be an opera singer. All she wanted was to get out as quickly as possible, while the full fury of her humiliation by Blackie in Eudora Street was still upon her. She meant to pack up and take the Professor with her on the train that left that evening for Denver.

At room No. 27 she knocked on the door once and then twice without getting any response and then turned the knob and opened the door. Inside in the heat the Professor was lying on the bed asleep, still fully clothed. She might have gone away and returned later but the full fury of her indignation burned high with the impetus to escape from Silver City, from Signorina Baldacie and Signor Malatesta and Blackie. She shook the shoulder of the Professor none too gently.

His only response was a kind of groan. In his sleep the Professor raised one arm instinctively as if to protect his face, as if all his life had been so difficult and defeating that he lived always thus with one arm raised. Again she shook him and again. Then the eyes opened and looked at her with a glassy, dazed expression and he mumbled something completely unintelligible and, knowing all the signs only too well, she understood. The Professor was dead drunk again. There would be no moving him anywhere for twenty-four hours at least.

It was always like this. Whenever things began going well or whenever they had set up an orderly plan for existence, he ruined everything and the world collapsed about them, back into the impoverished, fly-by-night existence which was all she had ever known. For a moment she considered walking off and leaving him. It was easy enough. She could go to Denver and find some kind of a job, if it was only that of a chambermaid in a hotel. If some of the anger and humiliation had not worn off she might have acted thus, but now, faced by this fresh crisis and suddenly a little ashamed of herself for her rudeness below-stairs, she became paralyzed by two things—one, the knowledge, born out of long experience that there was really only one kind of work that a girl so pretty and so young as herself could get. The other was the old knowledge that no matter what happened she could never desert the old man. Even as she stood there she knew that if she went to Denver, she would only return by the next train to look after him. She knew suddenly that it was the Professor who had become the child and it was herself who had all the responsibility.

So after a moment, she leaned down and loosened the high celluloid collar he was wearing and managed even to get him out of the long black, rumpled Prince Albert coat so that he would not suffer so much from the heat. Throughout the operation he remained limp and dazed, merely moaning a little now and then.

As she worked to make him comfortable she understood for the first time how old and how tired he really was. The grey old face was flabby and mottled. The neck thin and wattled like that of an ancient tom turkey. The fine, sensitive old hands, eloquent of so much ruined promise, hung limp.

When she had straightened the pillow beneath his head she picked up the bundle containing the drawers, the battered parasol and went to her own room. Here she took off layer after layer of clothing until at last, clad only in a chemise and drawers, she lay down on the bed in the dry heat of the mountain air.

For a time she considered the air and blamed it for her irritable behavior and for the fact that here in Silver City it required only half as much liquor to make the Professor drunk, and as her anger faded away, her reason returned. Out of a hard life she had developed a considerable amount of maternal common sense and even of calculation.

Lying on the bed, she indulged in a long dialogue with herself which ran something like this:

Mademoiselle 1—What would you do if you ran away to Denver?

Mademoiselle 2—God knows! You don't know anything about anything. You'd be on the streets!

Mademoiselle 1—What would happen if you waited and took the Professor with you?

Mademoiselle 2—You'd be no better off than you are here. You'd still have him on your hands and he's getting feebler all the time. Here at least you have a roof over your head and three meals a day and you'll get paid five hundred dollars for singing. That's the most money either of you have ever seen at one time or even in a whole year.

Mademoiselle 1—But you've got everyone against you. All these Dagoes and Polacks are doing their best to lick you.

Mademoiselle 2—(A very tough Mademoiselle, Irish in extraction) What if they are against you? You can beat them anyway. You certainly out-look that battered old hag, the "Eyetalian Nightingale" and probably you can out-sing her. Why don't you stay and show them?

Mademoiselle 1—All right, I will. But I've got to have a piano to practice with and I've got to have some help in the fight.

Mademoiselle 2—You've got P. J. Meaney on your side and he's the boss of the whole town and the state. Isn't that enough? And what's more, that boy, young Dick, wants to help you if you weren't so damned disagreeable.

Mademoiselle 1—I'm disagreeable because every man, young or old, I've ever met has only one thought in mind.

Mademoiselle 2—Well, maybe he's got it in his mind too, but he's different. You know that!

Mademoiselle 1—How do I know it?

Mademoiselle 2—Don't try to get out of it. He acts like a gentleman.

Mademoiselle 1—He acts like a yokel—blushing and stammering.

Mademoiselle 2—Well, maybe you'd rather have him act like his brother—like a dog chasing a bitch up the street.

Mademoiselle 1—That's not very nice language for a lady.

Mademoiselle 2—Well, who ever said you're a lady? You've lived all your life like a tramp. He's nice and kind and a gentleman.

Mademoiselle 1—He doesn't seem to know anything about anything, he and his friend—that Limey.

Mademoiselle 2—He probably hasn't had any experience as a lady killer. Once they've had experience it changes everything. They know what it is they want and go for it.

Mademoiselle 1—I don't like that kind of talk.

Mademoiselle 2—You're getting awfully hoity-toity for a lady of your background.

Mademoiselle 1—You said I wasn't a lady.

Mademoiselle 2—Well, you aren't and I'll stick to it. You've never even met a lady unless it was Mrs. Meaney. She looked like a lady and acted like one while everybody else was behaving at the reception as if they was in the back room of a saloon.

Mademoiselle 1—Watch yourself! You should have said, "as if they *were* in the back room of a saloon" not "as if they *was*."

Mademoiselle 2—Well, what do you expect? I never meet anyone who talks right except the Professor.

Mademoiselle 1—What about young Dick? He certainly talks like a gentleman and right too.

Mademoiselle 2—What makes you keep going back to him?

Mademoiselle 1—Because he's the only nice feller I've ever met.

Mademoiselle 2—What do you really want? Have you ever made up your mind?

Mademoiselle 1—Yes. I want to be a respectable married woman. I want to have a nice home of my own with golden oak furniture and some brats.

Mademoiselle 2—There you go! You were blowing me about my grammar and you use words like "brats"!

Mademoiselle 1—All right! All right! Children then. I wish I was a man. Then I could do things.

Mademoiselle 2—If you was a man, you'd probably be running up and down Eudora Street chasin' yourself just like young Dick's brother.

Mademoiselle 1—There you go again. It isn't "you was." It's "you were."

Mademoiselle 2—All right! All right! But let's get on with the business. If you want a home and quiet and security how are you going to get it?

Mademoiselle 1—I don't know. I never met anybody who could give it to me. I only meet tramps and cheap actors and chippy-chasers.

Mademoiselle 2—What about young Dick?

Mademoiselle 1—Oh, him! I never thought of him.

Mademoiselle 2—He's right here under your nose all the time. He'll have plenty of money too.

Mademoiselle 1—I never thought of that.

Mademoiselle 2—Well, you'd better begin thinking about it. Only you'd better change your manners and be a little nice to him. The way you behaved downstairs to him just now is enough to drive off anybody—humiliating him in front of all those people. He only wanted to help you.

Mademoiselle 1—Yes, I'm ashamed of myself. What should I do?

Mademoiselle 2—You ought to go downstairs and write him a note apologizing.

Mademoiselle 1—I just can't apologize.

Mademoiselle 2—That's rubbish, unless you want to stay a tramp all your life.

Mademoiselle 1—What should I say?

Mademoiselle 2—You should humble yourself and be kind of buttery.

Mademoiselle 1—All right. I'll think about it.

Mademoiselle 2—Only it won't do any good if you go on losing your temper. You've got a nasty temper.

Mademoiselle 1—I inherited it from my father.

Mademoiselle 2—That's no excuse if you want to get anywhere. And you've got to stop worrying about every man who looks at you as if

[111]

you were the only woman in the world and that they couldn't get it anywhere else.

Mademoiselle 1—I don't!

Mademoiselle 2—Oh, yes you do. You're getting so you think it's so precious that no man is good enough for it. You'll end up an old maid in the poorhouse.

Mademoiselle 1—Well, if they didn't always keep bringing it up! They're always after me.

Mademoiselle 2—Well, you're pretty! That's what does it. And out here women are scarce as hen's teeth, let alone good-looking women. There's ten men for every woman. You ought to feel sorry for them.

Mademoiselle 1—Well, what do you want me to do—set up business?

Mademoiselle 2—No, of course not! But instead of just locking everything you've got up in a strongbox and putting a chip on your shoulder, use it to get what you want. Women have to do that. Men can get out to be cowhands or prospectors or businessmen, but a woman's got to use what she's got. Get your lazy carcass up off that bed and go downstairs and write a nice note—a charming note.

Mademoiselle 1—I can't be charming. It isn't in me.

Mademoiselle 2—Well, you'd better begin and learn. Get up now and write that note.

Rising from the bed, Mademoiselle put on again all the upholstery and went down to the parlor where at one end there were three writing desks. Here she had to wait for a time in line for there were many more letter writers than there were desks, but at last there was a desk free and she seated herself and began to write.

It was not an easy task for Mademoiselle was unaccustomed to letter writing. This particular note was in fact the first real letter she had ever written and there was another difficulty, a very great one—that she was humbling her pride to write a letter of apology.

After several false starts which involved the destruction of a considerable amount of Grand Hotel and Boarding House stationery, she took an envelope and wrote on it—"Mr. Richard Meaney, The Castle, Silver City, Colorado." Then she began all over again, with a number of other false starts. Sweating and fuming and chewing the end of the worn and scratchy pen, she finally produced a letter.

It read thus—

Dear Mr. Meaney:
    I wish to apologize for my impolite behavior this afternoon. I was
under great stress and strain and not myself. I hope you will accept my
apology and forget and forgive. I am

> Yours cordially,
> La Belle da Ponte

In one draft she had written, "I was under great stress and strain having been pursued all afternoon up and down Eudora Street by your brother." But this she cut out of the final draft, believing that it unnecessarily raised an issue. She had also tried many ways of closing the letter and finally decided upon "yours cordially" as the best way to leave the door open.

When she had finished the letter and licked the envelope she went to the door and called one of the Indian boys squatting in the shade of the veranda. She gave him a silver dollar to deliver the note at the Castle. After that she felt better, believing that at last she had taken hold of life and embarked upon a plan, the plan advised by Mademoiselle No. 2.

On his way up the hill to the Castle after leaving the hotel, young Dick kept up cursing and swearing to himself, "To hell with that girl!" He kept saying, "To hell with her!" "Let her look after herself." The sooner she got out of town the better. She had the whole of the Opera Company in an uproar, and when you tried to help her all you got was rudeness.

When at last he reached the great pile of prison-grey Colorado granite which P.J. called "home," he went up the stairs to his room, threw down his hat and seated himself in one of the big rocking-chairs. The chair stood by chance opposite the tilted mirror of the huge walnut bureau so that it reflected the whole of his figure clad in cowhand's clothes, and suddenly, without desire or plan, he found himself looking straight into his own eyes. The sight fascinated him for a moment and he found himself saying, "So that's you—Dick Meaney! And what are you? You're no damned good. You don't belong anywhere."

And then began an interview dialogue very much like the one taking place at about the same time in the bedroom of Mrs. Sowers' Grand Hotel where Mademoiselle lay on her bed clad only in drawers and chemise. It was the kind of interior dialogue which takes place very frequently with young people of intelligence who are trying to find a place in the world into which they fit. It was the kind of dialogue which implies intelligence because people without intelligence know nothing of interior dialogues. They just live. They may be happier but they never get anywhere.

The dialogue ran something like this—

Dick 1—What am I doing around here anyway? Where am I going?

Dick 2—You certainly are a mess. Look at yourself. You've got an expensive education. You know French and Latin and Greek and you wrote a very erudite paper about the "Metaphysical Disputes of the Benedictines during the Thirteenth Century," but you don't know a damned thing really. You don't know anything about life and all that expensive education doesn't mean a thing out here in this frontier world. It may impress a few fellows who can barely read and write but what difference does that make?

Dick 1—Maybe I'd better clear out and go back to the East or to England.

Dick 2—Don't try to evade the issue. You know that wouldn't work. You were homesick for three years for this country and these people and you couldn't live anywhere else. If you went back there you'd only return here in a year or two. It's no good deceiving yourself or trying to run away.

Dick 1—It's not my fault, really. Look at the rest of the family—Pa and Blackie and Buck and Shorty and Eudora. They're not like brothers and sisters. They're like strangers.

Dick 2—That's not an excuse anyway. And maybe they aren't your full brothers and sisters. You can't tell about those things.

Dick 1—No, that's not possible. Ellie-May has never been anything but a good, honest and faithful wife—browbeaten all her life.

Dick 2—You know that isn't true. You know that Ellie-May has a mind of her own. If it's anybody who's browbeaten, it's P.J. She's a smart woman, Ellie-May. Remember how you've seen her put P.J. in his place right in the middle of one of his bellowing tantrums. And she's secretive too—like a squirrel. She knows a lot of things she never lets on knowing.

Dick 1—No, I can't believe anything like that.

Dick 2—Then how does it happen you're so different from the others? It isn't altogether environment. You don't even look like them. Or think or act like them.

Dick 1—Well, I've had a different education. Anyway, how would Ellie-May ever have a chance for such a thing?

Dick 2—She has the cottage up there in the high mountains where she never lets P.J. come. He's never even seen it.

Dick 1—She lived up there alone except for Esau and certainly I'm not Esau's son.

Dick 2—Don't try to be funny. This is serious. Did you ever think that about the time you were born Henry Caldwell was in charge of all the cattle on the Calamares Range. The cottage is right on the edge of it.

Dick 1—I can't imagine Ma doing such a thing.

Dick 2—Your Ma is a very sly woman. Don't forget that Mr. Huxley and Mr. Darwin both say that the brunettes are dominant. Mr. Huxley even says that it's impossible for a brunette married to a blond to produce a blond child. Look at all the other Meaneys. They're as swarthy as pirates, even Eudora.

Dick 1—Why didn't it ever occur to P.J.?

Dick 2—P.J. never heard of Mr. Huxley or Mr. Darwin. He just thinks you look like your Ma's folks. And P.J. is such an egotist that he can't imagine any woman preferring another man to him.

Dick 1—What are you trying to do with me?

Dick 2—I'm just trying to get things straightened out.

Dick 1—I must say it's funny the way Henry Caldwell has always been around. It was funny the way I found him in Ma's rooms the other day. And the whole atmosphere was funny. It wasn't as if they were just strangers or even friends. It was more as if they'd been happily married for a long time.

Dick 2—Which would you rather be—the son of P. J. Meaney or of Henry Caldwell?

Dick 1—Why, Henry Caldwell, of course.

[115]

Dick 2—Then what are you worrying about? It clears up a lot of things.

Dick 1—What if P.J. ever found out?

Dick 2 —He'll never find out. Even if he did he'd never believe it. An egotist like him wouldn't dare believe it and he'd never dare admit it because it would make him look foolish and that's one thing he can't stand.

Dick 1—Well, I must say, you've got me all mixed up. But it isn't only that. I'm such a damned fool. I'm as big a damned fool as Cecil with his dressing up in cowhand's clothes and having tea with Eudora and Rachel.

Dick 2—Don't be too sure that Cecil's a damned fool. He's just expanding, that's all. Maybe Cecil was a natural born cowhand and pioneer all the time and never had a chance, being cooped up at Oxford and the vicarage all his life.

Dick 1—But Cecil doesn't know anything about women or about anything.

Dick 2—Don't get superior. What do you know? You're as inexperienced as a babe. That's what made you mad the other day when P.J. began kidding you about being a virgin. Look at this Mademoiselle—you're interested in her and you don't know what the hell to do about it.

Dick 1—I don't know whether I'm interested or not.

Dick 2—You never felt like that about any other girl.

Dick 1—I've never known any girl like her. I never met any while I was away—only women like Cecil's old maid sister and the professors' and tutors' wives.

Dick 2—Well, there's all those women down at Madge's place—just for the taking. Look at Blackie—he lives down there.

Dick 1—I don't like that kind of women.

Dick 2—All right, Sir Galahad. You'd better find some other kind then. Remember St. Paul who said, "It is better to marry than to burn." You're a husky young man. You just admitted that you felt something for Mademoiselle. Better do something about it. It's different from anything you ever felt before, isn't it?

Dick 1—Well, yes, it is!

Dick 2—It gives you all kinds of new feelings, doesn't it?

Dick 1—Well, yes.

Dick 2—Makes you know what it's all about, doesn't it? You know what I mean?

Dick 1—Yes, I do. I've got all kinds of new ideas.

Dick 2—Well, why don't you do something about it? Maybe P.J. was right when he said he guessed being a traveling salesman gave him a better education than Oxford University.

Dick 1—Well, what do I do?

Dick 2—Try to make her get interested in you.

Dick 1—Well, how do I do that? Every time I try to talk to her, I don't know what to say. And when I do talk it seems to make her mad.

Dick 2—Well, she's probably had a lot of experience with men and what you do or say seems silly.

Dick 1—You mean I ought to go right after her?

Dick 2—What P.J. said was true. What you need is some experience. Act as if you couldn't wait. Seduce her. Carry her off her feet.

Dick 1—I'm afraid I don't know how.

Dick 2—Well, you'll never learn without trying. Act like Don Juan himself. You're not bad looking. You're big. What are you scared of?

Dick 1—It isn't as easy as that. Anyway down there in the hotel she just did everything but slap my face. She might just as well have slapped it—in front of all those people.

Dick 2—You've got to let her know you're interested. Press your suit. Be ardent!

Then for a moment, after Dick No. 2 had given so much bad advice, the dialogue broke off while Dick No. 1 regarded Dick No. 2 in the mirror. A kind of hypnosis fell over both of them, broken at last by the sound of a knock at the door. When Dick called out, "Come in," the ebony face and blue and gold clad figure of Esau appeared in the doorway. He carried a small silver salver on which lay a note. (The placing of the letter on a silver tray was a trick P.J. had picked up in Washington while engaged in paying off Senator Murgatroyd for services in keeping the government from laying hands on his cattle-grazing rights.)

The envelope carried the label of Mrs. Sowers' Grand Hotel and Dick opened it with misgivings, half-believing that it only contained more abuse and rudeness from Mademoiselle. When he read it a slow, broad grin came over his face. It was, he thought, like an act of God or the doings of Fate for it seemed to fit in exactly with all the advice that Dick No. 2 had just been giving him.

He put the note in his pocket, picked up his hat and set off again for the Grand Hotel.

Once inside the big parlor, he waited his turn to get at the writing desks and wrote a note which he sent upstairs by the colored porter. It read—

Dear Mademoiselle da Ponte:
Thank you for the note. Of course there is no question of apologizing. I understand the situation. I am downstairs waiting now if you could find the time to see me.

Yours cordially,
Richard Meaney

In five minutes the porter returned. He carried the same note. On the back of it was written—

Will be right down—La Belle da Ponte

He grinned again and thrust the note back into his pocket. Things were going well. Perhaps the advice of Dick No. 2 had been correct.

There wasn't much place or much privacy to undertake the campaign which young Dick had planned so vaguely in his room or on the way down to the Grand Hotel. Indeed there wasn't much place or much privacy anywhere in Silver City to undertake the slow, intense program of seduction and courtship as he had innocently conceived it. In the town there was no place to go except saloons, dance halls, gambling establishments and eating places, always packed day and night, or Moe Hirshbein's Emporium which was scarcely a place for a seduction or a courtship. And in all the town and on the small area in which it was located there was no park or grove or field or indeed even so much as a sheltering cluster of bushes or trees. Beyond this area the mountains began abruptly in sheer walls of rock, broken only by steep trails and roads. There wasn't even any place you could take a girl for a buggy ride since most of the roads and trails were too steep and rocky for vehicles and in any case there wasn't even a real buggy in the whole region but only open, flimsy and uncomfortable buckboards with no side curtains and no privacy whatever. You could not conduct a courtship, however ardent you might be, clinging to the sheer side of a mountain or on a barren pile of rocks. There was also that sense of immensity and grandeur and splendor in the whole of the landscape which seemed to reduce man himself to the insignificance of an ant and his amorous and mating activities to the level of breeding guinea pigs.

All of these things were physically and psychologically inhibiting and, together with the scarcity of women, may have served to reduce considerably the tendency toward old-fashioned, legitimate courtship and to augment the business of establishments like that of Madge Beakymer.

Rather gloomily young Dick, actually more in search of experience than of matrimony, considered all these facts as he waited in the crowded parlor with people going and coming amid the thin sprinkling of dusty, artificial potted palms growing from "dried earth" covered by a mulch of cigar butts, chewing gum, spit and ashes. After a survey he had staked out for himself a claim upon two chairs placed in a kind of nook beneath a turn of the staircase. He did not dare to leave the spot lest the claim be jumped by some passing cowhand, gambler or opera singer.

From this nook he saw Mademoiselle as she came down the stairs and stood for a second looking about the big, low-ceilinged room to find him. Unaware that she was being observed by anyone in particular, she looked innocent and pretty and at sight of her, young Dick's heart skipped a couple of beats and he felt those new and unaccustomed physical sensations which had marked each sight of Mademoiselle since the first day on the train.

He rose quickly and went a little way from the nook and the two chairs, keeping one eye upon them at the same time lest someone jump his claim while his back was turned. As quietly as possible, he called out, "Mademoiselle! Mademoiselle! Here I am!"

She looked at him and smiled. It was the first genuine smile uncorrupted by artificiality or boredom she had ever directed toward him and he found that it made her seem more desirable than ever.

As she moved toward him, he said, "I had to stay here to keep the place."

Then he bowed a little as she seated herself in a rocking-chair in the tiny alcove beneath the stairs. He was aware that his face was red and that he did not know what to do or say next. He found himself blurting out, "I wanted to thank you for the note."

Mademoiselle looked away from him and said, "I was ashamed of myself. I didn't mean to be nasty. I was upset."

"Is there anything I could do about it . . . to help?"

"No. It has nothing to do with you."

"I just came down to tell you that we'd be glad to have you and the Professor use the piano at the Castle."

"Thank you," said Mademoiselle, "I appreciate it."

"Anyway it will be better than trying to practice among all this bedlam here."

"Yes, that's true."

She was not altogether sure what the word "bedlam" meant but divined something of its meaning from the context. It seemed to her that he was always using words like that—big and elegant words which she couldn't understand. Because of the life which she had led, she had learned long ago to observe small things as well as large ones, to eavesdrop and almost without knowing what she was doing, to watch people. Thus she had watched young Dick and Mr. Chatsworthy and in their conversations together they had used very large and elegant words, the meanings of which were to her an utter mystery. Since she had had no education herself, save that imposed upon her casually by the Professor, she had an exaggerated respect for what was known as a "college education" and a corresponding sense of inferiority whenever she encountered evidence of such a thing. Big and elegant words made her tongue-tied and so after saying, "Yes, that's true," she fell silent, looking at her pretty hands, folded in a genteel way in her lap.

The same phrase, "Yes, that's true," seemed also to bring a dead stop to the flow of conversation from young Dick. Despite all his intentions, despite even the effect which she had upon him, he seemed to run out of words, thoughts, conversation and everything. Where did you go from here? What did you say now?

The silence became more awkward and oppressive until in desperation he asked, "I hope you are comfortable here in Mrs. Sowers' place?" He was aware that he had asked her this before on earlier visits and he was aware immediately that she had given him the same answer, "Yes, it's all right," before, not once but a couple of times.

Again there was a pause and he asked, "How is the Professor?" And she replied, "He's drunk again."

The forthrightness of the answer so startled him that once again he found himself blocked. He managed only to say, "That's too bad, but I expect he'll come out of it."

"He always does," Mademoiselle answered. "But the trouble is that he gets drunk all over again . . . more and more often lately."

She too felt ill at ease, not only because of her memories of the big words and the elegant way he talked but because she could feel that he was watching her, intently and warmly, while she sat there looking away from him, simulating the shyness which she did not really feel and behaving as she believed refined ladies behaved. She knew how he looked without seeing him.

While she regarded her folded hands in a refined manner, she was really seeing his good-looking young face, with the blue eyes and wavy blond hair. She even saw, without looking, the freckles sprinkled across the bridge of the straight nose. She thought suddenly, "I wish he was my brother. I'd like to have a brother like that." But there was a sense of malaise all the while in the background because the warmth which emanated from his whole presence was not essentially different from the warmth which emanated on occasion from men like his brother Blackie. It was simply less violent and more controlled. Why did men always have to be like that? And she was ashamed almost immediately at having referred to the Professor's condition in the realistic, forthright terms which were customary in the only world she knew. Almost immediately she felt that she could have bitten out her own tongue. She should have said, "The Professor is lying down. He's not feeling well," or something like that.

The pause in conversation was growing painful again, and she heard him saying, "Of course, you may use the piano any hour of the day or night. It won't disturb anyone."

"Thank you."

"In fact I've never heard you sing. It would be a great pleasure."

Primly she said, "I hope you'll like it." And then suddenly, the strain of behaving thus having become intolerable, she rose and giving him a single quick glance as if to refresh the memory of his pleasant young face, she said, "We'll be up tomorrow if the Professor is feeling well enough." She held out her hand with a sudden theatrical gesture as if she expected it to be kissed and said, "Thank you again, very much."

He took her hand and its vigor and strength and sudden warmth caused a surprising and unexpected reaction deep inside him.

He said, "We'll be waiting for you."

"Good afternoon."

"Good afternoon."

He walked with her to the bottom of the stairs and stood as she went up them, watching her until she was out of sight around the corner. Then he put on his hat with violence and said, "Damn!" and strode out of the parlor and up the hill to the Castle in the purple blue shadows which had already begun to fall on Silver City as the sun slipped down behind the great mountains.

The next day on the boards before the Opera House and in all the establishments in Silver City from the Emporium to the El Dorado appeared the announcement of the program for P.J.'s season of opera. At the top of the bill opening the season was *La Traviata* and in the role of Violetta was the name of Mademoiselle La Belle da Ponte. Within the ranks of the Opera Company the news spread like a prairie fire, roaring, crackling and hissing in a half dozen languages. Not only had the role of Violetta been taken definitely in the billing itself from Signorina Baldacie, they had even taken from her the right to open the season, an honor which had been hers since the Opera House was first established. Indeed the divine right of the "Eyetalian Nightingale" had been violated, in every possible way.

At first Signorina Baldacie raged and stormed publicly, on the wide front porch, in the big parlor, in the dining room. Within an hour or two the whole of Silver City was aware of the uproar and dissension. And then, suddenly exhausted, the diva took to her bed for a second period, during which she lay moaning while Signor Malatesta sat by her side, muttering Mafia threats and applying wash-rags dipped in cold water to her head.

After an hour or two the crisis passed into a third period in which the "Eyetalian Nightingale," loosening her corsets, sat up and went to work with Signor Malatesta. They began to plot and as their plotting flowered and bore fruit, all the experience of forty years of intrigue in provincial opera houses in Italy and second-rate music halls in America came into play. But there were other sources as well—Malatesta's experience and boyhood training with the Mafia and the profound genius for revenge, intrigue and murder which ran in their blood as it had run in the blood of the Borgias, the Medici, the Sforzas, the Colonnas. As the plotting progressed, the condition of Signorina Baldacie improved miraculously. Presently she rose, tightened her corsets again with the aid of a tug or two at the strings from Malatesta, and began walking up and down, talking and gesticulating wildly. But it was clear that her own ideas were too broad, too violent, too wild even to succeed in this new country, without sending them to jail or the quick vengeance of a posse of cowhands.

Malatesta, more cold-blooded, although scarcely less passionate than the Nightingale, kept throwing cold water on her plans. "*Non . . . non!*" he would say, "*Non troppo!*" He rejected poison or the dagger or vitriol throwing or even physical attack, all methods which in Padua or Verona or Messina or Naples might have been accomplished and passed over as the accompaniments of mere temperament. He had his own ideas of revenge, tempered by the knowledge that both of them were nearly sixty and had a few more years in which they had to earn their bread and butter. And presently as he began to talk, the violence of the "Eyetalian Nightingale" began to diminish slowly and translate itself into enthusiasm punctuated by rapid interjections of "*Si! Si!*" or "*Multe bueno!*"

By seven in the evening the Signorina had regained as nearly an attitude of calm as she had ever known since coming into this world more than half a century earlier in a pasta shop in Milan. By nine o'clock their plans were complete and they went down Eudora Street to the restaurant kept by a countryman called Lazzerno and there, surrounded by paintings on glass representing Lake Garda, Vesuvius, the Colosseum and other Italian scenes, they gorged themselves on antipasto, minestrone and spaghetti. Indeed so great was the enthusiasm of the plotters that when they left the restaurant, swollen with food and satisfaction, Signor Malatesta returned with the Nightingale to her room and for the first time in more than three years remained there throughout the night.

But the storm over the opening bill of the opera was not the only one brewing within the borders of Silver City and indeed of the whole State of Colorado. Like the distant rumble of an approaching thunder-storm or like yeast working in a brew, discontent was at work. For that movement, begun so moderately at the political meeting in the upstairs room on Eudora Street, was spreading. One heard of it in Leadville, in Meeker's Gulch, in Leaping Rock, even in Denver. Little groups of men came together in backrooms or upstairs rooms like the one on Eudora Street. Sometimes the men were miners, sometimes cowhands, sometimes sheepherders, sometimes prospectors. There were shopkeepers and politicians and plain good citizens and quite a sprinkling of vociferous madames and gambling-house proprietors and wherever there was a meeting Henry Caldwell was present or one of Henry Caldwell's admirers and lieutenants, for Henry, lean, grey-eyed, tough, was becoming rapidly the leader and spearhead of the revolt against the tyranny of P. J. Meaney. The truth was that, as Ellie-May had suggested, P.J. had pushed his game too far. If he had been content to stay within the borders of the kingdom he had set up in Silver City and the area around it, he might have been able to maintain his position without bringing about revolt, but P.J. in his hairy vigor was insatiable. He wanted not only to be King of Silver City. He wanted also to be King of Colorado and once he had achieved that power, what lay beyond? Who could say?

That he had begun as a big frog in a little puddle on a frontier where any shrewd, unscrupulous man could build the same or a similar sort of domain never occurred to him. He was convinced that he had succeeded only because he was P. J. Meaney and that there were no limits to what he might achieve.

[124]

In his "office" in the Castle, he received petitions, drew tributes from murderers and gambling-house proprietors and even from small shopkeepers.

He was never able to touch Moe Hirshbein because through the friendship of Moe's wife and Ellie-May, Moe was protected. Ellie-May would have no nonsense about Moe and his wife and daughter Rachel.

The truth was that, although P.J. never knew it, Ellie-May kept a little book in which she had jotted down a lot of memoranda about unsavory acts of which P.J. was guilty. She kept it hidden among the assortment of gadgets which filled one whole closet of her "apartment." Each time she got wind of something, she jotted it down with names, dates and details. It was indeed quite a book which involved P.J. in bribery paid to state representatives, connivance with crooks and gamblers and even with a couple of cases which came very close to collaboration in mayhem, manslaughter and murder. Ellie-May had no very clear idea what she meant to do with the book nor how she meant to use it, but her instinct, in reality far shrewder than that of P.J., told her that it was a good thing to have around.

Meanwhile she heard the distant but gathering rumble of the thunder. She knew about most of the meetings in Leadville, Meeker's Gulch, Silver City, Leaping Rock and elsewhere simply because Henry Caldwell told her about them whenever he turned up in Silver City. Each time she listened to him, each time she got out her little memorandum books, there flickered over her puckered face the shadow of a small and secret smile. Very slowly a plan was taking form, a plan in which retribution, satisfaction and power all played their parts. P.J. out of long experience, should have been suspicious of her save for the fact that he had long passed the point where he felt that he need worry about suspicions. He simply dismissed them with a twirl of his magnificent black mustaches. Colorado itself was very nearly under his complete and absolute control.

In Silver City and in the Castle itself there were small signs, small intimations of things progressing upon a considerable scale. Young Dick noticed some of these things and a few of them came through to Ellie-May and her friend Mrs. Hirshbein.

Not the least of these things was the change which Ellie-May noticed coming over her son Dick. Having no particular interest in Buck,

Shorty and Blackie, she concentrated upon Dick and among other things she observed that he grew nervous and irritable at times, that he spent a great deal of time hanging about the Castle while Mademoiselle did her practicing on the piano belowstairs. He would sit in the parlor across the hall filled with armor, palms and stuffed bears, listening to the accompaniment of the Professor while Mademoiselle went through the florid arias and lesser passages of *La Traviata*. On the days, about three times a week, when the Professor was "indisposed" and no rehearsal took place, Dick became a bull in a china shop, so far as the Castle was concerned, sulking, stalking about, visiting Eudora (which he never did under ordinary circumstances) or riding off wildly up one of the trails into the mountains.

On the whole, Ellie-May found the rehearsals of Mademoiselle and the Professor pleasant. The girl had a small but very true voice which she used very well under the guidance of the Professor and at first the sound of her singing, drifting through the huge hall and vast rooms of the Castle was pleasant enough. Even Eudora left the door of her room open to listen. It was only at the periods when Mademoiselle practiced scales or roulades or glissandos that the exercises became a little monotonous.

Ellie-May recognized the signs in Dick as a doctor might diagnose symptoms. He was, she knew, falling in love with Mademoiselle and he had not the faintest idea of what to do about it. Concerning the situation, Ellie-May was of two minds on the subject. One was that the experience would do him good. The other that Mademoiselle was a minx and was after him for his money. The latter doubt caused her considerable apprehension.

She did not care in the least whom Buck, Shorty or Blackie chose to live with either in lawful wedlock or in sin. As for Eudora, she would have liked to get Eudora off her hands for the simple reason that Eudora was becoming a bore. You had to give Eudora a certain amount of attention or she began hell-raising with Rachel, the servants and anyone who came within the zone of her existence. You had to keep remembering to pay Eudora a visit at least once a day or the cowbell by her bedside kept up a perpetual clamor demanding attention.

But young Dick was different. She had already made plans about him—how when he married she would visit him, how she would renew her own distant youth by taking care of his children and having them visit her. She wanted young Dick to get himself the right kind of wife.

Into this picture Mademoiselle did not fit. Certainly her background or as much of it as you could discover or divine, was not the ideal background for a wife for Dick. Ellie-May could not make the girl out. Her instinct told her that Mademoiselle was a virgin but her experience told her that this state of affairs was highly unlikely (what she did not understand was the fact that with Mademoiselle the protection of her own virtue had become the major and determining issue of her existence).

Mademoiselle seemed polite but cold, demure but resistant, innocent yet experienced; and indeed all of these things were partly true. But in a way Ellie-May misinterpreted them or at least mistook them for other things. When Ellie-May tried to become friendly and intimate, Mademoiselle seemed to withdraw and become suspicious.

Indeed, Dick himself made little more progress than his mother. He tried politeness without much response. When he displayed any degree of warmth, Mademoiselle turned upon him a fishy eye. If he lost his temper even to a small degree or uttered even a faintly sarcastic remark, she promptly outdid him, both in temper and sarcasm. So the courtship, if so tentative a set of maneuvers could be called that, resolved itself into a turmoil of attraction, resentment, sulks and sudden excitements.

The truth was that if at this time he had said bluntly to Mademoiselle, "Will you marry me?" she would have fallen into his arms with relief, abandoned her career and married him, if for no other reason than because, temporarily at least, it solved all her problems. But Dick did not know this and the girl in her stubborn pride would have been the last to enlighten him.

Slowly too, among the other small things, Ellie-May became aware of the change that was coming over Mr. Chatsworthy. The change had indeed been becoming clearer and clearer to all from the day he bought his first cowhand's outfit. The progress had been steadily forward, away from what might have been called the European manifestations of Mr. Chatsworthy's character toward what might have been called the New World manifestation. He was even beginning to lose his accent and to talk out of the side of his mouth like the cowhands he encountered along Eudora Street. He even took up riding and although he had believed that out of his occasional experiences with hunters on his cousin the Earl's estate, that he was a pretty good rider, he discovered that pounding along on a hard-gaited Pinto pony in a Western saddle was something fundamentally different from anything he had ever experienced before in the equine world. Stubbornly he mastered the new technique until he was able to swing himself on and off a hard-mouthed, disagreeable Pinto with little effort and even to remain in the saddle when the pony gave an exhibition of violent bucking. He received variously, a dislocated shoulder, a cracked collar-bone, a scraped face and a kick in the stomach, but returned each time to the struggle with all the dull and enduring stubbornness of the Anglo-Saxon.

Most of the lessons and practice took place in the corral on the edge of town about a quarter of a mile from the Castle itself. The corral lay in full sight of the Castle and all his exploits and injuries were watched by Eudora through her telescope. She even gave up her usual habit of spending all of the morning in bed cutting out texts in order to watch the performance. And as she watched, her admiration grew for the pallid little man who was clearly determined to become a tough cowhand even if it killed him. The invitations to her room to have tea with herself and Rachel grew more frequent and as Mr. Chatsworthy liked his tea and realized that this was probably the only way he would get it, he nearly always accepted.

It was about this time that the incident occurred that marked the beginning of his friendship with Madge Beakymer.

On one of those evenings when Dick sat mooning and listening to Mademoiselle's trills, Mr. Chatsworthy, feeling restless, wandered down into the town. A little earlier, such an adventure would have terrified him, but many changes, psychological, spiritual and glandular had been taking place inside the thin, somewhat puny body—changes which displayed themselves actually in his physique. The stringy muscles had hardened a good deal and the pallid face of the scholar had taken on the tan, if not the leathery wrinkles, of an authentic cowhand. Among the crowd which lined Eudora Street day and night he was no longer conspicuous. It was only when he opened his mouth to speak that his exotic origin betrayed him but even this defect he was struggling with considerable success to overcome. He was learning rapidly to speak through his nose with an authentic high-pitched twang and to use the local colorful flow of profanity and picturesque expressions.

On this particular night Cecil made his way directly to the El Dorado. The purpose in the back of his mind was to do some gambling.

During all the years since he had reached maturity, the maximum income he had ever achieved was the equivalent of sixty dollars a month with board and room as a tutor at Oxford plus three pounds or the equivalent of fifteen dollars received from a fund set up for him at birth by his great grandmother the Dowager Countess of Cantwell. Even though young Dick had paid all the expenses of the long voyage from Oxford to Silver City and Cecil had free room and board at the Castle, he still had only a reservoir of about forty-three dollars which was constantly being diminished by the spending of money for trinkets and souvenirs he sent home to various relations and for the cigars and chewing tobacco which gradually and determinedly, although somewhat painfully, he had learned to use. (Each morning after the going over he took from the Pinto pony, he practiced spitting for fifteen minutes in a corner of the corral.)

Like most gamblers he was bent, as he entered the El Dorado, upon making his fortune and, like all beginning and inexperienced gamblers, he was timid about the whole thing.

At that hour of the evening the place was crowded and noisy with the tables in full swing, the bars doing a capacity business, a vaudeville show in progress on the stage and a good deal of traffic by cowhands and sheepherders going up and down the stairs that led to the rooms overhead. For a long time he wandered inconspicuously from table to table watching the faro and roulette wheels and the red-dog and poker tables, trying to decide at which table he would risk half of his remaining forty-three dollars. In turn he rejected the tables of red-dog and poker because he did not see how, once he was in, he could withdraw after having lost only twenty-one dollars and fifty cents. Faro he rejected because he did not like the looks of the man running the game and in the end he settled for the roulette wheel which was being operated by a large and blowsy bleached blonde who was a cousin of Madge Beakymer's from back east in Jersey City.

Timorously he watched the turning of the wheel and the actions of the players and at last when he thought he had got the swing of the thing, he carefully brought one silver dollar from his pocket.

At the same moment a turn of fate, destined to shape his immediate career, occurred. As he pushed his way toward the table, Madge herself, moving majestically through the crowd with her eye on the proceedings, passed by and recognized him.

She slapped him on the back and said loudly, "Hello, Cecil! Glad to see you!"

He turned and shook hands politely.

"Trying your luck?" she asked.

"Why, yes," said Cecil, "I thought I'd give it a fling."

Then the expression on her face changed suddenly and she pulled him by the arm away from the table to a spot a little less crowded than the rest of the room. Here she said, "Haven't had much experience, have you?"

Cecil's face reddened. "Why, no," he said, "I just wanted to see what it was like."

"Well, take it easy," said Madge. And then she added cryptically, "and if you get a note from me, do what it says."

With that she slapped him again on the back and went on her way, returning the sallies that followed her progress through the room, greeting old customers in from the mines and the range, cracking lewd jokes and in general distributing vitality and good humor all the way to the stairs leading up to the balcony and her own "suite." Only once did she stop on her way and that was as she passed her cousin Lena who was operating the roulette wheel. For a moment she paused and said something and then went on her way up the stairs to P.J. who was drinking champagne and going over the account books.

Again Cecil pushed his way to a place at the table and timidly placed his silver dollar on the board. Lena yelled, "Here we go, boys," and spun the wheel. It went round and round and then slowly came to a stop—at the very number on which Cecil had placed his dollar. "Rake it away, boys!" called Lena and, prompted by a tough sourdough standing beside him, Cecil, bedazzled, took possession of a pile of silver dollars that Lena pushed toward him.

Upstairs Madge rejoined P.J. and poured herself a glass of champagne.

Without looking up from the account books, he said, "Business was sure good this month. How is it tonight?"

"Packed house. Everybody busy," said Madge.

P.J. ran his big fingers down another column of figures and Madge said, "Looks like we gotta expand."

"Expand?"

"Sure. We can't handle the crowds any more. Either we gotta expand or let in some competition."

"Always better to have a place crowded," said P.J.

"We ain't got rooms enough, even," said Madge.

He was still half-absorbed by the figures and did not answer her.

She took another sip of champagne and said, "You gotta understand this place is growin' up. The whole country out here is growin' up. You gotta keep up with the times. Every month there's more trade. Why, I hear all the tickets is gone for the whole Opry season."

P.J. grunted and Madge went on. "Anyway a little competition would help drain off some of the low-class trade. The place is gettin' spoilt and it's losin' its elegance and distinction. Too many tin horns. We could let in a cheap joint and keep it cheap. I ain't interested in volume. I like a classy joint and high rates. The place is gettin' lousy with tin horn sports that is always complainin' about being soaked. But that don't keep 'em away from what they want and gotta have. They come and get it and then give me a song and dance about how much it cost 'em."

P.J. closed the account book and said, "We let in competition and things'll get outta control."

Then Madge said, "And I wisht you'd get Blackie outta here. He stirs up a fight damned near every night. He's the kinda trade I'd like to get rid of. He'd like a cheap joint better. That's the way he is. He ain't got an ounce of refinement in his whole ornery body."

As she spoke, a change came over P.J. For the first time she seemed

[131]

really to get his attention. His face grew slowly darker and presently he interrupted her by saying, "I thought that so-and-so had gone back to the ranges a week ago!"

"Well, he ain't! He's still hanging around here. He don't go out except to follow that foreign opry singer up and down Eudora Street every time she leaves the hotel. It's like he was off his nut about her."

"Where is he?" asked P.J.

"I don't know, but I guess you might find him downstairs. He can't stay upstairs all the time. Nobody can! Not even a Meaney!"

P.J. grinned at the compliment and then frowned as he lifted his heavy body out of the chair. "He was supposed to be outta here last week. I'll throw him out!"

"Don't make no disturbance. It ain't good for the house."

As he started toward the door, there was a knock and the porter came in saying, "It's a note from Miss Lena. She wants an answer."

P.J. stood while Madge opened a bit of paper torn out of an exercise book. The note read, "How much longer am I to go on fixing it for him? He musta run his dollar up to about a thousand. Everybody's backin' the number he plays. It's costin' the house too much money. You can't get near the table."

P.J. looked at her and said, "Well?" as if they had no secrets from each other.

"It's about our friend, Cecil," said Madge. "He's playin' roulette and I told Lena to let him win." She crossed to the gilt *escritoire* bearing the scars of many "rampages" and took up a pencil and wrote on a piece of gilt-edged notepaper—"Dear Cecil. Better lay off now and come up here for a drink with P.J. and me." This she signed "Madge Beakymer" and gave it to the porter with instructions to deliver it to Lena to be passed on to Mr. Chatsworthy.

When the porter had gone P.J. asked, "How much did he win?"

"I dunno but everybody else is followin' him. Lena says to call him off."

"It ain't good for him," said P.J. "You oughtn't to have done it. He'll think it's always easy to win."

"Mebbe I'll tip him off."

P.J. pulled the Prince Albert coat down over his big stomach, opened the door and said, "Well, I'll go take care of Blackie."

At the table belowstairs it was as Lena had said. There was a big crowd around it watching the newcomer and his phenomenal luck. Whenever he put a pile of silver dolars on a number the space was quickly crowded by followers. Girls left neighboring tables to jostle their way to touch him just for luck.

Then the porter approached, passed the note to the busy, worried Lena which she read and passed on to Cecil. For a moment the play stopped while they read the message. Then Lena began yelling to the players to place their bets and spun the wheel.

But Cecil wasn't ready to quit. The pockets of his pants and shirt were filled to bursting with silver dollars and before him on the edge of the table lay four canvas bags provided free by the house that were filled with more dollars. His face was red with excitement and there was a glint in his eyes. If this went on he could become a millionaire. And then a wonderful thought came into his mind—he might never have to go back to England and Oxford. He could stay forever in this intoxicating country of mountains where silver dollars rained from the brilliant blue skies and anything could happen.

The real trouble was that Cecil had discovered that the more money he left on the table the more he won, so with each play he piled the silver dollars higher. As she watched, Lena grew more and more worried. The sweat came out on her big face and formed cakes of the rice powder she always applied too abundantly. She knew she shouldn't go on forever letting him win but she knew better than to disobey Madge's orders. Madge, she decided, had gone upstairs and forgot all about this excited little man. That was when, in desperation, she called the porter and sent up the note.

Cecil, shaking with excitement, ignored the message. He would, he decided, make just one or two more plays and double or triple the big pile of silver dollars lying on the table.

Lena gave him one more chance. He won and left his winnings on number eleven. The wheel spun slowly and then came to a stop on number 11. But the next time Lena decided it was time to act.

She called out, "Look out, boys! Here she goes!" and then with one high heel and shoe she tapped out the signal to the man in the cellar belowstairs to change numbers—to change to any number. The wheel spun again and this time, as a knowing groan rose from around the

[133]

table, it came to a halt on number 2 and Cecil saw his pile of silver dollars swept away by Lena's rake.

But at the same moment, something else happened. From the direction of the bar came the sound not of shouting but of bellowing, a sound recognized by the old patrons of the establishment. It was P.J. on a rampage bellowing like the Bull of Bashan. At almost the same moment a figure swept through the crowd around the table. The figure was half on the ground and half off it and the old-timers recognized it as that of Blackie, being propelled toward the door by his father. Nothing stopped the progress, neither cowhands nor miners nor gamblers nor girls nor tables nor chairs. All gave way to Blackie's paternally propelled progress—a progress accompanied by bull-voiced expletives, "Git out and stay out! And no arguin'! Git back to them sheep or I'll beat your brains out!"

Then at a distance of about ten feet from the entrance to the El Dorado, P.J. took a swing and let loose of Blackie. He shot through the swinging door and landed on the wooden sidewalk of Eudora Street.

Then, dusting his hands, P.J. made his way through the confusion until he came to Cecil who was busily engaged in thrusting all his winnings inside his flannel shirt. Here P.J. paused and said, "Better call it a night, son, and come and join Mrs. Beakymer and me in a glass of champagne."

"Thank you, sir," said Cecil.

Then P.J. turned to Lena who in the confusion was engaged in shielding with her body the winnings of the house. "Better come along too, Lena! You and Mr. Chatsworthy ought to get acquainted."

So Lena, pushing all the money off the table into a canvas bag and turning over the table to her assistant joined them and went upstairs to Madge's apartment.

It turned out to be a fine evening. The champagne, cold in the ice from the Grand Kalmath Glacier, flowed, as P.J. said, like water. Cecil, looking slightly pregnant with silver dollars, drank glass after glass and told Cockney stories and sang a couple of old English ballads in a quavering tenor. He was, Lena observed, a real live feller. Long after midnight, he departed, uncertainly, to make his way up the hill to the Castle, clanking as he walked. With each step he felt better and bigger, singing as he went. As he neared the Castle there came over him an irresistible impulse to serenade someone and, about two in the morning, he found himself in the brilliant moonlight beneath Eudora's window, singing lustily, "Drink to me only with thine eyes and I will pledge with mine."

The serenade did not go without response, for a moment or two after he had begun singing, Eudora's heavy figure appeared in the moonlight, leaning on a pillow she had placed on the window sill. Out of long experience, she knew that Cecil was drunk but this did not spoil her pleasure at receiving attention from a gentleman for the first time since her fiancé had failed to show up on her wedding day. When he had finished she called out, "That's wonderful, Cecil. Sing something else!" And he obliged with an old Morris Dance number he had learned during his anthropological studies at Oxford. The only thing which puzzled her was the clanking sound which arose faintly from the figure below the window every time he moved.

But other things were going on in Silver City that night. Not the least startling event happened to Mademoiselle just as she was preparing to go to bed. She had undressed and put on her long-sleeved nightgown and was putting up her hair in kid curlers when she heard strange sounds on the roof of the big veranda of the hotel just outside her window. The window gave out on the side next to the mountain and she had never troubled to pull down the cracked, green window blind. As the sounds—clearly those of feet advancing across the roof—reached her she turned just in time to discern beyond the grey, worn mosquito netting stretched across the window the all-too-familiar features of Blackie.

Strangely enough the sight did not terrify her. It merely infuriated her and, driven by the accumulated irritations of weeks of annoyance, she simply bent over and picked up the slop-jar.

"Get out!" she said. "Get out, before I holler!"

But Blackie didn't get out. He simply stood there looking at her with a tipsy, cowlike expression saying, "Don't get mad, Honey! I ain't gonna hurt a hair of your pretty head. I only aim to talk to you."

Mademoiselle felt the muscles of her arm contracting without any

[135]

effort or will on her part. She took a firmer hold on the slop-jar and repeated, "Get out! I give you one minute to get out!"

But Blackie's voice, with a little more edge on it now, came through tne netting, "Why do you have to be so mean to me? I ain't gonna give up. Nothing is gonna make me give up."

"One," said Mademoiselle, and then "two" and finally "three!" and then with all the strength of her vigorous young body she hurled the slop-jar, contents and all right through the mosquito netting. It caught Blackie somewhere about the center of his solar plexus. There was a grunt and an oath and then he seemed to vanish into moonlit space. The impact simply carried him, together with the slop-jar over the edge of the low roof into the street. Then Mademoiselle pulled down the cracked window shade, blew out the light and climbed into bed.

Down the street in Madge's apartment above the El Dorado the gilt chairs and tables were already scattered around the floor and the Turkish cosy corner had come apart again in a heap of shields, spears, canopies and pampas grass. That night Venus and Mars seemed to be in conjunction all over Silver City.

From the very first the rehearsals of the opening performance of the Silver City Opera season went well. Signor Malatesta had assembled a fair to middling orchestra mostly recruited from New Orleans, Cincinnati and San Francisco. P.J. paid good wages and he could get good musicians, because outside the beer gardens, there was never too much work in summer and in many a good musician there existed the almost universal urge to see the West. The few holes that remained in the ensemble, Signor Malatesta filled in with local musicians—a tuba player who, outside the opera season was a prospector, a cymbal and drum player who worked in Madge's place but whom, in her enthusiasm for opera, she let off for rehearsals and performances, and two fiddle players who played for square dances, one at Meeker's Gulch and the other at Leaping Rock. On the whole the ensemble was a fair one. The tuba player was only required to toot a couple of times during the performance of *La Traviata* and the two fiddlers, although flat in tone, exceeded the "foreign" players in actual agility. With a great deal of temperament and excitement Signor Malatesta whipped them into shape. The only real incident occurred when one of the fiddle players, by name Mike Hawk, got into an argument with an Italian fiddler called Vassari. It became an argument conducted almost entirely upon violins, each playing cadenzas at each other. Mike Hawk won on agility and Vassari upon tone.

The big curtain with the Lake Como landscape surrounded by advertisements was rolled up and the kerosene lights were filled and lighted and finally when the orchestra was considered in proper condition, the final three rehearsals began in earnest.

Of the singers, Mademoiselle as Violetta was the only one under fifty. Blavatsky, the Russian, played the father, which was suitable, but Alfredo, her lover, was a somewhat cracked tenor, Belgian in origin, who was, quite plainly, older than his father. The role of Violetta's girl friend fell to an ample mezzo with a voice of tremendous volume. The other characters and the "guests" and "country folk" were drawn from here and there, three of them girls whom Madge gave a holiday during the opera season. On the program, behind the designations of the principals appeared the names of the great opera houses of Europe and America—La Scala, the Paris Opera, La Monnaie, the Vienna Opera, the Berlin Staatsopera, the French Opera in New York and New Orleans, although there were no notations as to what roles they had sung or whether they had merely carried spears or sung in the chorus.

Surrounded by them, Mademoiselle was, for perhaps the first time in her life, genuinely terrified. All of them knew their roles. Some of them had sung again and again the parts they were singing and all of them had heard the opera countless times. She herself had heard it but once at the French Opera House in New York where she and the Professor had sat high in the gallery.

She had expected from the others in the cast some of the hostility she had encountered in the parlor and dining room of the Grand Hotel, but none of it appeared. On the contrary, they all seemed to be amiable and helpful even when she herself broke down or made some wrong move on the stage. Even Signor Malatesta who directed the stage production as well as the orchestra became almost fatherly. Only the Professor, seated far back in the darkness, watching, was suspicious— of what, he did not know, save that he had never seen in all his long experience any opera troupe behave so well and so amiably. There was something distinctly unnatural about it all.

He had trained Mademoiselle well and he knew that, although she

[137]

lacked experience and temperament, she was a better natural musician than many of the others in the cast. And, sitting there in the darkness, tired, alone and old, he suspected that but for him she would not be there at all on the stage among all those tired and sad performers, for in her soul there was none of that fire which he had himself known so long ago that he had almost forgotten what it was like save in those moments when, as on the afternoon of the reception, something had happened to him and he had played with all the fire and skill that were long since faded and dissipated.

Far back in the theatre he lost himself in the music. It did not matter that the shabby orchestra scarcely played together at all or that at times a violin or a clarinet or even a whole section of the orchestra lost its way and went on independently until the passage it was playing came to an end or the rest of the orchestra caught up with it. He did not hear the sounds being made by this fantastic orchestra in the Silver City Opera House. He was hearing with his memory the glorious sounds of the orchestra he had heard thirty years earlier in Europe when *La Traviata* was new. For him, even the wandering tactics of part of the band could not spoil the lovely sounds and tragic music, so much a part of his youth and of the middle of the century when there had still been in him faith and hope and the power to love passionately. All of these things were long since gone and they could never have meant much to the people of this wild, half-barbaric frontier town—a town which had no past and perhaps no future. And this opera, this music, for all its sentiment and romanticism was old music born of an old civilization which for him held a charm and a beauty and a continuity which no life in this new world possessed.

As the violins and clarinets struggled with the *tempi* of the first act, there came back to him all of his youth and for a little time he was happy again and almost young.

And as he watched and listened to the young girl who still had all her life before her, he became for a little time Mademoiselle herself, leaning forward, humming, articulating in his own withered, burned-out old throat the trills and roulades of the brilliant, flamboyant arias. And at the end, in the beautiful, half-spoken passages of the letter that arrives too late as Violetta lay dying, the tears came into his rheumy old eyes. He had trained her over and over again in that part of the

[138]

role which for him was the most beautiful and tragic music in all opera, and she had learned the part better than she knew for she seemed to become actually frail and dying and the very youngness of her voice produced an unbearable pathos. Listening to her just before the curtain fell on the last act, he knew that she could not fail to bring the whole house first to tears and then to applause and shouts of approval.

Who knew? It might be the beginning of a great career in which she would know some of the glory and triumph he had long ago thrown away so carelessly. If only she had the temperament and ambition there were no heights to which she might not go. And he knew too that in spite of their envy of her youth and her beauty the others in the cast must know how good she was and believe what he believed. Perhaps it was that the whole tired, raddled troupe were amiable and kind because they recognized what he himself saw. In his own pleasure and nostalgia and satisfaction he forgot all his long experience with musicians and with singers, most of all.

But at the death scene, he was not the only one who had tears in his eyes. In another corner of the big house, there sat a young man, big and blond, who felt his throat begin to throb and tears come into his eyes in spite of anything he could do. When the curtain came down to the last tragic chords young Dick blew his nose and dried his eyes and hid for a time in one of the boxes until he felt that all traces of his unmanly emotions had been eliminated. If he had had any doubts he knew now that he was in love and experienced for the first time those romantic yearnings and those sudden gusts of physical passion and desire of which he had read in the novels of the day.

On the day of the third rehearsal, the sufferings and death of Violetta became unbearably real. This time the old scenery, used so many times, dusted off and refurbished each year, was brought out—the party scene, the gambling hall, the garden of the country house, flat and faded, became as real to him as the granite of which the Opera House was built. They were a part of a world which he had never known, yet which was familiar. Even the fantastic figures of some of the singers and the familiar faces of Madge's girls among the guests at the party and in the gambling scene failed to shatter the sense of beauty and romance. Mademoiselle herself in the three costumes made by Mrs.

Hirshbein, looked more beautiful than he had ever seen her look. Rachel's mother had done well indeed.

When the curtain had come down and Dick had again eliminated the traces of his emotion, he went backstage through the little door beneath the box which by tradition belonged to the Meaney family and went straight to the dressing-room where the Professor sat with Mademoiselle while she removed the rouge and the make-up which the Professor had applied so skillfully. It was the first time Dick had ever seen the dressing-room of an "actress" but even its dusty shabbiness and the sight of Mademoiselle with a grey shawl wrapped round her shoulders, removing the illusion from her face, failed to dampen his enthusiasm. He saw her still as he had seen her on the sofa in the last act, dying in the presence of the lover who had tragically arrived too late.

As she saw his reflection in the spotty mirror, she turned and before she could speak, he said, "You were wonderful! Wonderful!" It wasn't the words he spoke which made the compliment impressive but the look in his eye and the eager sincerity of his voice.

The Professor got up and went out of the room so quietly that neither of them noticed when he had gone. Mademoiselle said, "Thank you" and the old familiar, awkward silence settled over the room and the two of them.

After a moment Mademoiselle said, "Sit down," and then after another moment in a sudden flare-up of vanity, she said, "Don't look at me now until I get the grease off my face." She went on removing the grease observing his reflection in the glass from time to time.

He sat down and said, "You'll be a great success, Mademoiselle." And then, almost passionately, she replied, "Don't call me 'Mademoiselle.' That isn't my name and my name isn't da Ponte either. My name really is Bridget—Bridget Moore. The Professor just made up the name."

Turning his ten-gallon hat awkwardly round and round, Dick asked, "What shall I call you then?"

"Bridget," she said. "That's my name."

"Then you'll have to call me Dick."

"That's all right—Dick."

The simple interchange of words broke down a barrier. Magically, it altered all the strained relationship between them. He leaned back in the chair and asked, "Where are you going when you leave Silver City?"

"I don't know. We never know. The Professor thinks I'm good enough to get a job singing in Denver. But I don't know. He always thinks I'm better than I am."

"Well, I do too."

In the back of his mind he was trying to find some reason to keep her in Silver City. He could, of course, follow her to Denver but things didn't seem far enough along for that.

"Do you like Silver City?" he asked.

"It's all right . . . like any place else if you always live in a hotel or a boarding house. But there isn't much to do for somebody like me. You can't even go out in the street alone."

He waited for a moment and then said, "I heard my brother Blackie has been making a nuisance of himself."

"Oh, I think I can manage him."

"I only heard about it after he'd gone back to the range. It isn't really his fault. He had a funny kind of bringing up. You see, he didn't have much education and since he was nineteen he's spent most of his time up on the range." She didn't answer him and he said, "I'm not making excuses for him. I'm just trying to explain. I want you to like Silver City."

"I like it all right."

She had finished taking off the make-up and wanted to get into her street clothes but he still stayed. It was a barren, dreary atmosphere—the dusty dressing room. She went on pretending to take off the make-up which was already gone, wanting him to go away and yet wanting him to stay and then idly, Mademoiselle No. 2 came to life again, causing her to wonder what it would be like to be married to him, to have a house she could call her own with something more than a couple of battered old trunks as the base of her existence. She still couldn't make him out—whether he was simply up to the old tricks, transposed into a new and perhaps European pattern, or whether he was just amusing himself or whether he was really interested in her at all. For a moment, out of the hard experience of the past, there came an impulse to turn suddenly and say abruptly, "Well, Mister, come

[141]

on! Out with it! Why are you sitting around here taking up my time? What do you want?"

But the impulse died as quickly as it was born. And suddenly for no reason she felt sorry for him and for herself because in this strange world of Silver City, there seemed to be no place for either of them and no place where they could go. In that whole world from the Castle to the Grand Hotel there was nothing stable or ordered or really decent, like the worlds which must exist somewhere but which she had never known, worlds in which families clung together and sat down at the table together for meals and shared affection and confidence. In Silver City everything was crude and exaggerated and disorderly, even more disorderly than her own life had always been.

And then, quite suddenly, she was very tired . . . and turned to say, "If you'll go now, I'll change my clothes. Thanks again for the compliment."

The color came into his face and he stood up, still turning his hat round and round in his hand.

"Well, good-by, ma'am. I'll be cheerin' for you tomorrow night." Then he bowed and went out, still troubled about what kind of girl she was or even whether she was a girl at all.

As he closed the door behind him, he encountered the Professor standing in the shadows. He seemed tired and shrunken and old in spite of the jaunty tilt of his hat and the bright red of the necktie with the false diamond in it, showing above the checked waistcoat.

The old man said, "Well, sir. Everything looks mighty fine—if she can just do it once again tomorrow night."

"She's wonderful," said Dick and then, suddenly, impulsively he asked, "What kind of girl is she, Professor? I can't make her out."

The Professor had never been asked the question before. Indeed he had never even speculated upon the subject of what Mademoiselle really was or what went on inside her pretty head. He coughed and then feeling an inspiration regarding the direction he should take, he said, "She's a remarkable girl, sir . . . being talented as you can see. She's got brains too and a lot of character. I've brought her up since she was a child and I'm mighty proud of her." Then, with his inspiration carrying him onward, he said, "And she's innocent too, sir. No man has ever laid hands on her."

[142]

He looked at Dick and saw that he was regarding his hat thoughtfully. Quickly the Professor added, "Of course, she's got a mighty quick temper but that's natural—her being Irish. But it goes away as quick as it comes and she's always sorry afterwards."

Then Dick looked up at him. "Thanks!" he said. "She seems a mighty fine girl to me."

He walked away and the Professor watched him until his figure was lost in the dusty shadows of the shabby scenery. His old mind had come alive again, that mind which for so long had worked overtime to devise ways and means merely of existing and finding lodgings, of escaping the poorhouse. It was trying now to decide quickly one of two courses of action—whether it would be better for him to have Mademoiselle marry such a rich young man and settle down or whether it would be better for her to go to Denver and begin that career which he knew lay before her if she would but choose to follow it. The old urge to see her in the realization of the things which had once been within his own reach and had evaded him forever, swept high. He knew that in a way, the decision lay with him and he knew too that he really didn't matter very much because he wasn't long for this world.

And then he acted. Briskly he walked to the dressing room door and knocked.

Mademoiselle's voice came back to him. "Just a minute more." He knew by the sound of the voice that she was not addressing him but the boy whom she thought was still waiting outside. He thought, "That young fellow doesn't know how to play his cards! He's pretty decent!"

Then the voice said, "Come in!" And he opened the door to find her standing up facing it with exactly the expression on her face that from the sound of her voice he knew he would find. It was an expression of surprise and then of disappointment and he thought, "So that's the way the wind blows?"

"Ready to go back to the hotel?" he asked casually.

"Yes."

She moved toward the door and he said, "He seems like a nice young feller—that young Meaney." And casually she said, "He's all right, only he doesn't know anything. He's just a yokel." Then she turned to him and asked, "Do you feel better?"

"Yes, I'm feelin' fine. All that dizziness is gone." The old man looked at her suddenly and then, very stiffly bowed and raised her hand to his lips.

For two days, patrons of the "Opry" had been coming in from the valleys and canyons, from the high ranges and from scattered settlers' cabins. The "Opry" marked the height of the season in Silver City. There were cowhands and miners and prospectors, sheepherders and even two Indians, chiefs of the Calamares and the Calgut tribes, by name One-Big-Foot and Eagle's-Pin-Feathers. To accommodate the crowd Mrs. Sowers put extra beds in all the rooms except those occupied by the opera troupe—a procedure which led to an unusual amount of brawling and quarrels and general disorder. Women in the town took in roomers and Madge allowed certain of her best clients to live in her establishment for the season. The two Indian chiefs had a simple solution for the housing problem. They brought tepees and set them up outside P.J.'s corral where the squaws, children, Pinto ponies and dogs created a lively village.

. In the Castle Mr. Jonathan Wright, the banker, and Mr. Cyrus Laidlaw, the lawyer, who had come out on the train with Dick and Cecil, put in an appearance occupying big high-ceilinged rooms on the second floor. For P.J. this was a signal honor and a symbol of triumph, for it meant that he and his kingdom were being recognized now in the distant East. They were coming to see *him* now instead of his going to see them. With most of Colorado under his thumb, they had to ask *him* when they wanted to put through a new railroad or buy in on a new mining concession. But they were a source of boredom and irritation to Ellie-May who was now forced to "dress up" twice a day for meals and assume her secondary personality as hostess and woman of the world.

Henry Caldwell appeared in town too, but he did not come for the "Opry." He came because the season brought in people from five hundred miles around whom he could see and talk to, thus saving himself hundreds of miles of slow travel, much of it by buckboard or on horseback. He appeared everywhere, in bars, at the El Dorado, in hotel and boarding house parlors, even at the sparsely attended evening

[144]

services of the Baptist and Methodist churches. He talked in corners, or leaning against the hitching-rail lined with buckboards and cow-ponies. He was well liked, Henry. The "peepul" liked his lean, straight toughness and the clear light in his grey eyes. He was one of them but he was smarter than most of them—a fact which they accepted. He was better educated, more aggressive, more courageous. He did not know what it was to be lazy or tired.

In the Castle or at Madge's place, P.J. received reports of what was going on. He knew that Henry was in town and that he was trying to stir up trouble and revolution inside the kingdom.

At noon-day dinner on the day of the opening of the Opera, Mr. Laidlaw, the New York banker, swooping back his sidewhiskers, asked, "Who is this man called Caldwell I hear about all over the state?"

P.J. laughed, "Oh, he ain't nobody. Just a crazy character. He used to be a partner of mine. He wasn't practical enough to fit in."

Mr. Wright, the lawyer, said, "Looks to me like he's kind of an anarchist."

Mr. Laidlaw added, "You see, Mr. Meaney, we have to keep ourselves informed about these things. *Sometimes* we have to keep up with politics."

P.J. gave a big belly-laugh. "Well, you don't need to worry about *him*. When folks get troublesome out here in *that* way we just remove 'em where they can't do no harm."

Then, for the first time, Ellie-May raised her eyes from the table and looked at her husband. She had been listening all the while with the demure air of a distinguished and worldly dove, and now she felt her temper rising. She did not like Mr. Wright or Mr. Laidlaw. She did not like any of the lawyers or bankers from the East who turned up at the Castle. She didn't like their smug air of condescension to P.J. and even herself. She did not like their slipperiness or the smooth insincerity of their manners. But most of all she hated their dullness. Whenever she had to talk to them, she found her mind wandering off to more interesting things. Even the dirty Indian boy who fed the ponies at the corral was more entertaining.

Now, as she listened, she felt her temper slipping as she heard P.J. and the two visitors ganging up on her Henry. She knew the insincerity that lay at the root of everything the two easterners were saying.

She knew that they hadn't even the vestige of real friendship for P.J. and that if Henry were, by any miracle, successful in taking over the state, they would desert P.J. and go over to his side, overnight. And as she felt her temper slipping, she said to herself, "Ellie-May, hold yourself in! This isn't the way to do anything! It won't do any good!"

So she bit her lips and turning to Mr. Laidlaw, who as the banker sat on her right, said, elegantly, "How is the season at the French Opera in New York?"

Her companion answered, "Well, ma'am, I couldn't tell you. When I'm in New York I'm so busy I don't have time for things like that."

Ellie-May thought, "Well, that doesn't get anywhere." So she tried again. "Tell me," she said, "how's the Erie Railroad doing?"

This opening was more successful, and presently she heard how the Erie Railroad was doing. She had no choice. Like the Ancient Mariner, Mr. Laidlaw fixed her with a glittering eye and told her how the Erie Railroad was doing. She didn't understand anything he was saying and she didn't care how the Erie Railroad was doing, but he told her, on and on for nearly twenty minutes. About halfway through she developed hysterical deafness, heard nothing but merely nodded her head from time to time and murmured, "Yes, how interesting!" All the time she was really thinking how she would set in the gores on Eudora's new dress, but Mr. Laidlaw was enchanted by her attention and her performance. It was the kind of thing that made bankers and lawyers say after meeting her, "What a charming, intelligent and clever woman. I wonder how that diamond in the rough ever found her?"

The problem of Eudora's dress had troubled her ever since early morning when a little after seven at the imperious sound of Eudora's cowbell, she had gone to Eudora's bedroom to find her on her feet rummaging through the drawers of her walnut bureau bringing out ribbons, gew-gaws, bits of jewelry and silk stockings that were old and had gone rotten during the long period of Eudora's retirement after her "disappointment."

At sight of Eudora, Ellie-May understood that the thing she had long dreaded was about to happen. Eudora turned toward her mother and spoke the fatal words, "I'm feeling so good, Ma, I think I'll go to

[146]

the Opry tonight." A coy smile suddenly illumined Eudora's big, dark face, "Cecil," she added, "is going to take me!"

Ellie-May's practical mind hit at once upon the difficulty. "What," she asked, "are you going to use for clothes? You can't get into your old ones and Millie Hirshbein hasn't got anything your size."

But Eudora had everything figured out. She was not for nothing P.J.'s daughter. She said, "We can run up something on your new sewing machine."

"What about stuff? Millie hasn't got silks and satins in stock for Silver City."

A sly look crossed Eudora's face. "I got that figured out too. You know them new red velvet curtains we got for the library? We can cut them up and I've got some old gold passementerie in the drawer here."

Ellie-May knew that she was defeated as she had been defeated many times by P.J. When you were licked, she believed, the best thing was to join in and make the best of it. It was clear that Eudora meant to quit her retirement; it was clear that her heart had been mended. Now there was no telling where it would end. The discovery that it was Cecil who had mended Eudora's heart both astonished and troubled Ellie-May. What chance would he have married to Eudora? Dimly, Ellie-May felt that there was something unfair about Cecil's position, as if, in his passion for this new country and this new life, he had somehow confused Eudora with the size and magnificence of the scenery, the storms and the general bawdiness of life in Silver City.

Weakly, Ellie-May said, "I don't know whether we've got enough time. I've got to go to every meal now with those New York fellers here."

But again she was checkmated by Eudora. Her daughter said, "I've got all that figgered out. Millie Hirshbein can help you. Rachel can take over the Emporium and Millie can keep the machine going while you're eatin' dinner."

Ellie-May bowed her head. She said, "All right, I'll go and get the curtains. Put on a shimmy and some pants and a corset and I'll send down for Millie. We'll have to make it up right on you. There ain't time to do it otherwise."

[147]

Within an hour, Millie Hirshbein, still excited by the news of Eudora's miraculous recovery, was on hand and together she and Ellie-May went to work.

The truth was that Ellie-May was at least a frustrated *grande couturière*. In another time and in another world she might have been a great designer and a great dressmaker and she found as she worked, cutting, fitting and basting, that her alarms and forebodings over Eudora's recovery largely faded away in the face of the immediate project confronting her. Even the problems of Eudora's overabundant figure, standing there in chemise, corset and pants, did not fill her with despair. As a potentially great dressmaker, the problems and difficulties of Eudora's heroic bust and jutting behind merely served as a challenge and a stimulus.

To begin with she draped the red velvet around Eudora and pinned it in place while she and Millie Hirshbein withdrew from time to time to a little distance to figure out the problem of cutting it. It was a long business and Eudora revealed the fact that she was strong as an ox by standing bolt upright without fainting throughout the whole of the performance. Just before they unpinned the stuff from Eudora's figure, inspiration came to Ellie-May.

"I know," she said. "We'll give it the Hussar effect. I've got some gold frogs and tassels laid away that'll do fine."

And a moment later, the red velvet curtains were on Ellie-May's big cutting-table and the scissors were snipping away at it. By lunch time it was cut and basted, with Eudora herself still serving as a dress form and, when at last Ellie-May had to change her dress and personality to go downstairs to lunch with Mr. Wright and Mr. Laidlaw, Millie took over the sewing of the seams.

When Ellie-May returned, the base of the gown was finished and it was again drawn over Eudora's head. Then Ellie-May fetched the passementerie and the gold frogs and tassels and pinned them on where they belonged. She used the passementerie as an insert to the *décolletage* which revealed a fine expanse of Eudora's magnificent bosom. The result was what great dressmakers are always seeking; it was both alluring and modest, both revealing and concealing.

Then with pins, Ellie-May arranged the frogs across Eudora's torso from the low-cut neck to the waist, shortening each successive frog with a snip of the scissors by an inch or two as they descended, thus creating the illusion of a wasp waist and a reduction of about fifteen inches in Eudora's waistline. The gold tassels she arranged in a cluster on the left shoulder and finally she draped the loose material at the back into a slight bustle and a short train. Then, standing at a distance, she and Millie Hirshbein reviewed the result.

It was magical. Eudora appeared no longer squat, wide and thick. She seemed taller and slimmer and the combination of red velvet and gold suited her swarthiness and whatever good looks she possessed. But perhaps most satisfactory of all, the dress, even with the frogs and passementerie pinned on did not look like a home-made affair. It was conceived and executed in the grand manner. It was suited to the opening of the opera and would have done credit to the upholstering talents of the Brothers Worth in Paris.

Before they set out upon the finishing tasks, Ellie-May said, "Wait a minute!" and went to the closet where she kept all her vast assortment of gadgets and the little book in which was written down the record of P.J.'s skulduggeries. After digging about for quite a while, she emerged with a box covered with purple velvet. Opening it she took out a parure of diamonds. It consisted of dangling earrings, a necklace, a bracelet and a low tiara. Without a word, she placed these on Eudora and then stood back again to survey the effect. It was truly magnificent. After a moment she turned to Millie and said, "I must say, you'd hardly know it was Eudora."

All through the afternoon the excitement kept mounting in the hotels, bars and other establishments of Silver City. It could hardly be said that there were in the prospective audience many real lovers of classical music. The more experienced ones familiar with the opera went to it each season because it was a "show" and because it offered romance in a life where that particular kind of romance was scarce. There were also many who had never seen before anything more elaborate in the way of a "show" than the performances put on by the men who sold "Swamp-root," "Peruna" and other cure-alls commonly used on the frontier as *apéritifs*, baby soothers, cures for female complaints and rheumatism.

Behind all the excitement there was an odd psychological feeling of an approaching crisis, even of doom which arose from nothing that anyone could define. It arose, perhaps, from the restlessness of the miners, the approaching political campaign and the fact that as the growing pains of the community augmented and Madge's El Dorado could no longer accommodate the sporting element, disorder became more frequent.

In all this sense of apprehension, the Professor participated, although for reasons of his own, little connected with the disorder and general strain which affected the community. His sense of suspicion regarding the quietness which attended the rehearsals of *La Traviata* had been growing steadily and was increased considerably by the sudden and complete retirement from the scene of the "Eyetalian Nightingale." On the day marking the beginning of the final rehearsals she had vanished from human sight. From the beginning she had been in the eyes of the Professor a bird of evil omen, and when she no longer appeared in the parlors and dining room of Mrs. Sowers' Hotel, he took the disappearance, out of his long experience, not with relief but with alarm. When he discovered that the Nightingale had not left the hotel but was simply keeping to her room, he knew that she was "brooding," a danger signal in any Italian opera singer, male or female. Of all this he made no mention to Mademoiselle for he did not wish to upset her. Privately, however, he was alarmed.

At least one other person suffered apprehension not connected with the economic and social problems of the community and that was young Dick. He had come to the conclusion that sooner or later he must speak up and put an end to the impasse which existed between himself and Mademoiselle and he had chosen the night of the opening as the occasion. It seemed a good time for he was certain that Mademoiselle would have a triumphant success. Afterward she would be at the party given at the Castle each year on the opening of the opera when all the company as well as the leading ranchers of the countryside and Silver City's most prominent citizens were invited to celebrate by the local Lorenzo de Medici, P. J. Meaney. Then would be the time to declare his suit, if not to propose—at least to make a flattering declaration of his admiration and intentions. As a prelude he had arranged to send her across the footlights the biggest, handsomest bouquet that Denver could provide.

All morning he rampaged impatiently about the corral, teaching Cecil who had now progressed to the stage of busting bronchos, new tricks in the handling of horses. At noon-day dinner he was fidgety and preoccupied and left immediately afterward to meet the Denver train bearing the bouquet kept carefully on cracked ice from the Grand Kalmath Glacier.

The train was, as usual, late, but when at last it puffed into the depot, the bouquet was aboard as fresh and crisp on its layer of cracked ice as if the flowers had just been cut. He fastened a card on it upon which was written "From your greatest admirer, Dick" and left it, still on ice, in the baggage-room to be fetched later by Esau and brought to the Opera House at the last minute.

When all this was accomplished, he went to the corral, picked out a pony, swung himself aboard and rode up the trail past the mines. He had gone off alone thus in order to prepare himself for the ordeal of the evening and as the pony picked its way up the mountain, the declaration took form in his head. It would, he decided, run something like this—"For a long time, Bridget, I've been thinking about you but I never knew how to say what was on my mind. But I've never seemed to get anywhere at all so now I'm saying it right out. I'm in love with you and I want to see more of you. It's pretty hard to court anybody here in Silver City but I guess we can do it. I hope you won't think I'm a fool. It is not a sudden thing. It has been coming over me ever since that day I first talked to you on the train."

He tried the speech around in many ways. It seemed foolish to him that such a declaration should be so difficult, but it seemed impossible to say simply, "Will you marry me?" There had to be some kind of preparations. Flushed with success, she would be in a mood for kindness. From there on, he hoped, things would be easy. The only element which troubled him was that in her triumph she might look upon him as a worm and cast from her all thought of anything so simple as matrimony.

When he had settled the speech he allowed his imagination to run into the future. Once they were married he would take her away, perhaps to San Francisco, and after that would stay away from Silver City, perhaps in Denver and he would find himself a job, for he knew by now that, although he could not bear to leave the West, he could not remain in the town where he was born. He had to get away and stand on his own, away from P.J. and Eudora and Shorty and Buck and Blackie and Madge and everything which crippled and stifled his existence. Maybe, he thought, he would take up with Henry Caldwell. Maybe he would go into politics. After all he was twenty-one and it was time he decided what he was to do.

All these things were going through his head as the pony jogged homeward down the trail with his back to the setting sun. He himself rode in the blue shadow while the mountains on the other side were illumined still by rosy light. Even the shacks and shanties of Silver City with the Opera House and the Castle rising high above them were softened and lovely in the fading light.

Then suddenly the Pinto reared and sprang forward so suddenly that Dick was almost thrown from the saddle. He was a good, steady pony, not given to shying but as Dick pulled him in, he reared again and then Dick saw what it was that had startled him A rock half as big as a man's head struck the pony on the forequarter. Then another glanced off Dick's shoulder and, looking up on the side of the mountain above him, he saw against the rosy sky the outline of three heads and a raised arm. The arm thrust forward and another rock whizzed passed narrowly missing the pony and himself. He gave the pony his head and a moment later they were both out of range.

On the edge of the town he pulled up the pony and leaned forward to examine the pony's shoulder. The rock had been sharp and cut through the pony's hide. If it had struck his master on the head it would have killed him. He knew suddenly that those three men had meant to kill or at least to injure him. Clearly they did not mind if, by accident, he were killed.

Over his shoulder Dick looked back again toward the mountain and the spot from which the rocks had come at him. They came from the ledge high above the road and just below the opening of the Ellie-May Mine. Now the ledge, lying in the shadow, appeared empty. Dick leaned down again and patted the pony's shoulder. "Someone," he said, "wanted to get us, Tex."

But who? Why should they want to kill him? So far as he knew, he hadn't any enemies in Silver City. He hadn't even lived in Silver City for nearly five years. Shorty had enemies and Buck and Blackie and certainly P.J. had them—enemies who would have drilled holes in each one of them if they had believed they could get away with it. Maybe they had mistaken him for his father or one of his brothers. "They"? Who were "they"? Perhaps men the Meaneys had swindled or cuckolded or beaten up or . . . Very slowly the possibility took form in his mind. Maybe it was a bunch of miners who wanted to kill or hurt any Meaney or anything or anybody connected with P.J. The rocks had come from a ledge just below the mine.

The thought depressed him. He hadn't believed that the trouble P.J. was having more and more often with the miners was as bad as that. They had been complaining of poor wages, of water in the mines, of quarters that were more like dog kennels than houses. Most of the miners were Irish but there were among them a few Polacks and a few Hunkies. They all spoke with one kind of an accent or another and they lived apart on the periphery of the life which centered about Eudora Street. When they came into town from the shacks on the hillside they were shoved about or told to shut up. He hadn't even thought of them since his return. Before he went away as a kid he had hardly been aware of their presence. They had always been there like the dogs and the ponies and the Indians.

He wakened out of his thinking as the pony stopped at the steps under the porte-cochere of the Castle. Bojo, the Indian boy, took the reins as he got down.

"Bathe Tex's forequarters with liniment," he said, and pointed out the cut to the boy. The Indian looked at the cut and then back again at Dick and said, "Fall?"

"No," said Dick. "Somebody threw rocks."

The Indian looked at him again and then made an incoherent sound, swung himself up on the pony and rode off. The expression on any Indian's face seldom betrayed what went on inside the head or heart.

In the Castle, everyone was making ready for the opera and Dick hurried to his room, forgetting for the moment the whole unpleasant incident and thinking only that in an hour or two he would be seeing Bridget again.

He took a bath in the big zinc tub with the swan-necked gold taps and when he crossed to his room and opened the door, he found Henry Caldwell, wiry and thin, standing with his back against the mirror.

He said, "Hello, Dick."

"Howdy. When did you come in?"

"This afternoon."

Dick threw off his bathrobe and opened the drawer of the bureau. "Going to the opera?" he asked.

"No."

Dick pulled out his underwear and Henry said, "You have grown into a husky feller." He grinned, "How'd you get that way on books?"

Dick began dressing. "It wasn't books. I played football and rowed."

"Yeah! I've heard about all that."

"Does Pa know you're here?"

Again Henry Caldwell grinned, "Not that I know of."

"How are things going? The campaign, I mean."

"All right! Pretty good!" Then he said, "What happened to your shoulder? The Pinto throw you?"

Then Dick looked at his reflection in the mirror and noticed that his shoulder was beginning to turn a fine shade of blue.

"Oh, that!" he said. For a moment he didn't speak, feeling an unaccountable unwillingness to tell Henry Caldwell the story. Then he found himself with an equally unaccountable impulse, telling it.

Henry listened, taking the pipe out of his mouth and leaning forward a little. Dick finished by saying, "I don't know who was trying to get me."

"I suspect I know," said Henry.

"Who?"

"Some of them Polacks."

"I thought that too . . . but I couldn't quite believe it."

Henry Caldwell knocked the ashes out of his pipe and then said with a curious twang of the voice which he used when serious, "Dick, there's goin' to be trouble around here one of these days. Some day them miners are going to cut loose and raise hell and it's the Old Man's fault. He ain't reasonable. He squeezes 'em too hard."

"I've been away so long I don't know anything about it. I guess I never did know anything about it even when I was home."

Henry was silent for a time while Dick got into his trousers. Then he said, "Funny! I came here to talk to you about that. Funny they pulled this afternoon to heave rocks at you! Funny they picked you of all the family that's had least to do with the mess."

"It wouldn't have been so funny if that rock had hit me on the head."

Henry went on. "I tried to talk to your Pa about it in the old days before we broke up altogether, but he wouldn't listen."

"Did Ma ever talk to him?" asked Dick.

"She tried, but he didn't pay any attention to her about things like that. He thinks wimmin ought to mind their own business."

"Yeah, I know!"

"Mebbe you could talk to him. It's for his own good."

Dick didn't answer for a moment and then he said, "I guess it wouldn't do any good. He thinks I'm a dude." The last sentence seemed suddenly to echo in his mind as if he had said it twice and aloud he said, "Maybe I am."

"Maybe you are," echoed Henry and when Dick looked at him, Henry was grinning.

"You mean it?" asked Dick.

Henry didn't answer him. He just grinned. The color came into Dick's face and Henry asked, "Got any plans since I last saw you?"

"Why, no . . . not exactly . . . nothing definite."

"When are you gonna start plannin'?"

"I don't know. I guess there's plenty of time."

"There ain't never plenty of time in this world. There ain't time enough, son, to get through half the stuff any he-man ought to get through before he kicks off. The sooner you begin plannin' the better."

Dick didn't answer him. He felt a sudden impulse to take off all his clothes and get back again into his shirt and chaps and forget all about the opera and go off with Henry up the mountains into the range country. The old doubt about his own relationship to P.J. returned. P.J. wasn't any father at all. He was a kind of noisy, animated, busy monument.

"What's all this about this here gal in the Opry?" Henry asked suddenly.

Again the color came into Dick's face. "Nothing, I guess. Who told *you* about it?"

"Your Ma," said Henry directly. "What kind of a girl is she? She ain't no trollop, I take it."

"No," said Dick. Out of the window he could see the carriages coming up to the porte-cochere, three of them—open Victorias with horses in gold harness and plumes, and he thought, "It looks like a goddam circus!"

"You ain't makin' much progress are you?"

Half sullenly, Dick answered, "I don't know."

"Had any experience with wimmin?"

Dick didn't answer him and after a pause, Henry said, "Most womanly wimmin like masterful men that knows where they're goin'." Again Dick didn't answer and then as he slipped on his coat, Henry put one hand on his shoulder and said, "Listen, son. If I can help you any way, call on me, see?"

"Yes," said Dick.

"The Old Man ain't much help. He never was any use to any of his children. He stopped abruptly as if to let his words hang in the air. Then he said, "I'm comin' back. Your Ma always knows where to find me if you want me for anything."

Then the door opened and Cecil stood there in his London "full-dress." Nervously, he said, "They're waiting for you downstairs. Your father wants us all to drive down together."

"I'm coming," said Dick. "Tell 'em I'll be right down," and he thought, "Always a goddam circus!" The thought of seeing Bridget again swept over him. He turned to Henry, "Good-by for now, sir. Are you going away?"

"No. I'll be hanging around for a time. I got political work to do." He grinned, "I gotta see that a lotta people don't get cheated out of voting." Again he slapped Dick on the shoulder, "Good luck, son." And Dick hurried off.

All Eudora Street was filled with the crowd moving toward the Opera House. Some had tickets for the opera and some were just going along to watch the show from the outside. Some were simply enjoying the occasion and some were roaring drunk. Every now and then a cowhand started a near-riot by throwing into the crowd strings of lighted firecrackers procured from Hu Chang, the laundryman.

Then as the crowd became packed near the steps of the Opera House three men on horseback broke a way through the crowd. They were Bill Jennings, the sheriff, and two deputies. Directly behind them came the three Victorias bearing P.J.'s party. The first barouche carried P.J. and Ellie-May, P.J. dazzling in tails and top hat with hair and mustache oiled and perfumed; Ellie-May dressed in purple taffeta, wearing diamonds, with an aigrette in her hair. On the seat opposite them rode precariously Buck and Shorty. In the second carriage rode Mr. Wright, the New York lawyer, and Mr. Laidlaw, the New York banker, and in the third, Dick, Cecil and Eudora, looking in her red velvet and diamonds rather like the Emperor Nero.

In a fourth carriage which had slipped in unobserved to take advantage of the wedge driven by the sheriff, rode Madge Beakymer and her cousin Lena like consorts or camp followers.

At sight of the procession, part of the crowd broke into cheers. More firecrackers were set off and the plumed horses reared and pranced. Ellie-May bowed to right and left as if she were royalty and P.J. with a cigar wedged beneath his teeth, raised his top hat in acknowledgment of the crowd's applause. In the second carriage the two visiting New Yorkers sat nervously on the edge of their seats watching the rearing horses and ready to climb out at the first sign of a runaway. Clearly, they found the spectacle both exciting and terrifying.

In the third carriage Eudora looked from side to side, her eyes bright with excitement over her first excursion into town in seven years. The look of animation, the red velvet gown with the gold frogs and braid and the diamonds, made her appear almost handsome in a monstrous sort of way. Young Dick felt merely uneasy and depressed and a little ashamed. The bruise on his shoulder had begun to hurt now. It was much worse than he had thought. He glanced at Cecil, as if to apologize, but Cecil was clearly enjoying the spectacle and the ovation. He turned suddenly to Dick and with a beaming face, said, "I say, isn't this jolly? Much better than Covent Garden."

In the fourth and final carriage Madge and her cousin Lena

accepted the ovation directed at them. Madge bowed slightly, smiling, in acknowledgment of the loud wolf howls and the cries of "Good old Madge!"

On the steps, other deputies of the sheriff cleared a path for the party and one by one the carriages unloaded their burdens and the rearing horses drove off. Then the crowd closed in again.

Inside the doors the Opera House was already packed and smelled of tobacco, horses, beer, cows, sheep, sweat, and cheap perfume. Down in the first row, three of Madge's girls who were not taking part in the performance as guests at Violetta's party, occupied a whole row of seats. The two Indian chiefs, accompanied by their Prime Ministers, had seats just behind, and near them Moses and Millie Hirshbein and their daughter Rachel occupied seats on the aisle. The remainder of the audience was made up of cowhands, gamblers, prospectors and mine foremen with a few women scattered here and there. In the front row just behind the conductor's podium sat the "Eyetalian Nightingale" in a very low-cut dress, aigrettes and a vast amount of false jewelry. On either side of her, in a kind of phalanx, sat the other members of the company who were not taking part in *La Traviata*.

The Opera House was constructed with only two boxes, highly gilded, one on the right, one on the left of the proscenium. Into one box piled P.J. and his party. Into the other came Madge and her cousin Lena, chastely and alone. At sight of the two parties the ovation broke out again, punctuated by cries of "Good old Madge!" and "Three cheers for P.J."

Then the curtain bearing the landscape of Lake Como and the garlanded advertisements of Eudora Street's activities rolled up, revealing an under curtain of faded, dusty crimson plush. One by one the kerosene lights were turned down by attendants and the hush which falls over the audience at that moment of expectancy swept over the house. Signor Malatesta appeared to the accompaniment of cheers, stompings and whistles. Twice he bowed and then turning, raised his baton. The first thrilling, expectant shimmering notes of the overture arose from the pit and the opera season in Silver City was open.

Backstage in the dusty dressing room, Mademoiselle and the Professor awaited her cue to go on. They were alone, with an aloneness which seemed to have increased during the last day or two before the performance. When they came into the theatre, the other singers had seemed to ignore them and now there was none of the going back and forth, none of the chatter and excitement which the old man knew always preceded an opening night performance.

La Belle da Ponte, her make-up finished, sat in the costume for the opening scene made by Mrs. Hirshbein, staring at her reflection in the fly-specked mirror. But she saw nothing of the reflection. She was waiting, thinking.

The old man watched her, wondering that she showed so little excitement or emotion of any kind, wondering indeed what went on in the mind which remained perpetually mysterious to him. This was the best chance they had had since Mademoiselle was old enough to perform, a chance which might bring them money and decent rooms and good meals and a chance to relax from the whole business of trickery, wits and humbuggery. The old man was very tired tonight and he was both hopeful and afraid. There were people in the audience who had come all the way from Denver who might carry the news of Mademoiselle's triumph out of Silver City into the world.

And presently he heard distantly, coming through the dusty crimson curtains and the door of the dressing room, the music of the overture and he leaned forward a little resting his elbows on his knees, his face buried in his hands, slipping back again into the past.

The pair sat thus for a long time and at last the Professor said, "The overture is finished. You'd better go into the wings and be ready."

That was the only word spoken between them. The old man opened the door and stood aside for the girl to go out and then silently they moved into the darkened wings of the stage.

It was an old-fashioned set where one could walk on the stage at any point from behind the high columns of painted marble. On the stage the party scene was in progress. The show was going well.

And then suddenly, the Professor said, "Now, honey. Now!"

Out of the darkness, quickly almost mysteriously, Alfredo appeared, fat, elderly and painted, at her side.

The Professor said, "Now, honey, now!" He kissed her hand

quickly and she walked onto the stage as the music rose for the entrance of Violetta.

In the gilded box on the right young Dick leaned forward between his mother and Eudora, watching the scene for the moment she appeared. Then suddenly she was there, young, radiant, beautiful— more beautiful now than she had seemed at rehearsal, and he experienced again the cold-hot shivering feeling. Tonight was the night he would speak to her. The echo of the speech he had prepared and memorized came into his head.

The crowd on the stage raised their glasses in a toast to Violetta and then she began the great aria, so filled with life and glitter, with youth and gaiety and zest in living. She seemed unafraid. She was singing it brilliantly and then suddenly when she was halfway through, a curious thing began to happen. The volume of the orchestra seemed to rise, at first imperceptibly and then noticeably. Slowly it grew louder and louder until it was quite impossible to hear the young, fresh voice of the singer. She seemed quite unaware of the rising volume and after a moment or two the effect became ludicrous for she appeared to be standing in the middle of the stage, grimacing, opening her mouth, and acting without making a sound audible to the audience. It was as if she were playing the role in silent pantomime. The audience leaned forward in its seats striving to hear the sound of Violetta's voice. Here and there people began to whisper or nudge each other. In some quarters resentment arose at having been swindled. What was this? A singer whose voice was so feeble it could not be heard?

In the box Dick felt that something had gone wrong but in his inexperience he did not know what it was. He only knew that it had not been like this at rehearsal. Even in the back of the theatre he had heard her voice quite well; now in the box immediately over the stage he could not hear her. The others in the box seemed at first to notice nothing. Ellie-May was the first to turn and look at Dick with an expression of questioning. He had told her that the girl was magnificent and now you couldn't even hear her voice.

Then suddenly the aria was finished and instead of the applause which always greeted any singer after an aria during the opera season in Silver City, even when he sang off key, there was only silence punctuated by a few handclaps. Dick's own vigorous applause rang out almost alone, so loudly that heads turned toward the royal box as if to inquire what all the clamor was about.

Backstage the Professor knew what was happening. He had heard the volume of the orchestra swell to proportions so tremendous that even the loudest-mouthed Wagnerian soprano could not have been heard above the noise. It was an old trick—when there was a feud between conductor and singer—to drown out the singer.

The old man knew that Mademoiselle, in her inexperience, could not know what was being done to her. Frantically he walked up and down trying to catch Mademoiselle's eye, to convey to her in pantomime what was happening. Even for a moment he considered rushing out to the front of the house to protest in person to Signor Malatesta, but he knew that such tactics would only ruin all hope of the great success he had counted upon. Helpless, he raged up and down. When the curtain came down he would go for Malatesta between the acts. With this in mind he returned to Mademoiselle's dressing room to take courage out of the bottle he had brought for just such an emergency.

But the worst was still to come. Near the end of the act as the guests at the party left and Violetta began her second aria, the volume of the orchestra again swelled to gargantuan proportions. Again not a note that Mademoiselle sang was audible; but toward the end of the aria, something even more fantastic and disastrous happened to the orchestra. Part of it—that part not recruited from local talent but which had played many times under Malatesta's direction—seemed to undertake a career of its own. While the tuba and the more agile, flat-toned violins (all recruited locally), continued on their own way, the rest of the orchestra changed key. At the same time, its volume diminished notably and suddenly the voice of Mademoiselle was heard singing freshly and clearly but disastrously off key.

Apparently the change of key had been a signal of some kind, for at the same moment there arose here and there in the audience loud boos, hisses and foot-stampings. Then a tomato was hurled and then another and then a few eggs.

The orchestra played on but in the midst of the stage Mademoiselle stopped singing. The elderly tenor, Alfredo, his arm raised above his head to protect himself from an ill-aimed egg or tomato, took to the wings leaving Violetta to face the sound of cat-calls and the barrage of vegetables alone.

For a moment she stood there as if frozen into stone while more and more vegetables, accompanied by the clinking sound of pennies striking the floor, came across the proscenium. Then a tomato struck Mademoiselle's bare shoulder and, as if it sparked her into action, she picked up first one tomato and then another and another and threw them straight back into the orchestra. One of them struck Signor Malatesta full in the forehead just below the line of his toupee.

In the audience fights broke out between those who were launching the attack upon the new singer and her partisans, who thought she was "mighty pretty" and did not care whether she sang on key or off or even whether her voice was audible. Then the curtain was lowered suddenly (by the Professor himself from behind stage) but the brawling out in front continued. A few peaceful music lovers like the Hirshbein family managed to escape from the auditorium, but the remainder of the audience, enjoying a good brawl, remained.

In the gilded box on the right, P.J. stood up and began to shout in the voice of Stentor, "Quiet! QUYUT! GODDAMMIT! QUYUT!" but no one paid any heed. At the back of the house the brawl had translated itself into a free-for-all between sheepherders and cattlemen. The "Eyetalian Nightingale," with a strange glitter in her eye, made her way out the side exit, along with other members of the company and their hired claque and retainers.

Then the sheriff and his deputies went to work clearing the house.

From the gilded box on the right of the proscenium the party of P. J. Meaney made its way down the stairway and out a side exit. Outside in Eudora Street the crowd still milled about and at news of the brawl inside the Opera House it made every effort to get inside and join the fray. Its entrance, however, was made difficult by the fact that at the same moment the sheriff and his deputies were engaged in driving the brawlers *out* of the Opera House into the street. The two crowds meeting in the foyer and the steps, the ranks of both were forced together and began a new fight.

Meanwhile P.J.'s party made its way into the alley. The carriages had gone back to the stables to await the normal time of closing and a boy sent to find the drivers reported that there was no trace of them, so there remained but one alternative—for P.J. and Ellie-May, Eudora, in her splendor, and Mr. Laidlaw and Mr. Wright to return to the Castle on foot and in ignominy.

P.J., fuming and speechless, save for a constant rumble of profanity, led the way through the back streets, past the Grand Hotel and Boarding House. All the way he kept interrupting the profanity by declarations of his contempt for opera singers and for opera in general as a form of art. He was through with opera. There would never be another performance. The ticket buyers could have their money back. He would turn the opera house into a warehouse. To hell with the whole program of culture for Silver City!

When at last the little procession reached the Castle, P.J. posted Esau at the door to announce that there would be no party and to turn away all the guests who appeared. No one had yet arrived, for most of the leading citizens were still trapped inside the Opera House, their way barred by brawling sheep- and cattlemen, augmented by outside elements of Silver City's population who simply enjoyed a good fight and had taken sides.

Inside the Castle P.J. retired to his own quarters followed presently by Ellie-May bearing a pot of mint tea and some dandelion wine to soothe his nerves. She found him pacing up and down his room, his collar torn off and his starched shirt front torn open, exposing his hairy, grizzly-bear chest. His face was beet-colored and his eyes bloodshot. If he had been in reality the despot he believed himself, the "Eyetalian Nightingale," Signor Malatesta and the other members of the opera troupe would have been hanged, drawn and quartered that very night.

Baffled and frustrated, he now stamped up and down the room, muttering, "Tomorrow they get out of town, that whole bunch of Dagoes and they go out of town on a rail."

When the barrage of vegetables began, he had understood the full extent of the plot.

In her heart Ellie-May did not really much care whether he had a stroke or not. His behavior and appearance betokened such a catastrophe but even while Ellie-May, rustling up and down the room in her purple opera dress, kept mollifying him and trying to persuade him to take a sip or two of the mint tea, another part of her mind was engaged in a lively speculation of how blissful the future would be if P.J. suddenly collapsed and died. She saw the Castle empty or turned into a hospital and herself dividing her time between the cottage in the mountains and a house in Denver where she could garden and cook and pedal the sewing machine to her heart's content, with no more dressing up to be bored by people like Mr. Laidlaw and Mr. Wright, no more necessity to assume the secondary personality as hostess which she found more and more tiresome.

"Come P.J.," she said aloud, "stop that ranting! It isn't gonna do you any good and it's likely to throw you into a fit (I hope). And it ain't gonna do you any good to persecute those poor ignorant Eyetalians. Just fire 'em and ship 'em!"

At last when P.J. had worn out something of his own prodigious, unquenchable vitality, he lay down, still sputtering, and drank his mint tea like a tired little boy.

Ellie-May kept saying, "You aren't as young as you once were, P.J. Your arteries are beginning to harden up." It was almost as if she were persuading him to have a stroke.

Downstairs, the others found it too early to go to bed. The anticlimax of the debacle which marked the opening of the opera season had left them with nerves unstrung, expectancy unsatisfied. Eudora in her red velvet and diamonds, felt especially frustrated. After sitting about for a time she ordered up champagne and led Mr. Wright and Mr. Laidlaw and Cecil into a game of whist. Buck and Shorty knew what to do. They got out of their fancy clothes as quick as possible and into store clothes. Then, happily, they both headed for the El Dorado which had been on their minds ever since they had arrived from the range late that afternoon.

It was only after the whist game was in progress that Eudora observed, "Dick ain't here. Where do you suppose he could be?"

"I think I know," said Cecil.

"Where?" asked Eudora.

"Backstage, talking to Mademoiselle."

But Cecil was only partly right. It was true that at the moment the curtain came down, Dick left the box and went backstage, but

[164]

by the time he reached there Mademoiselle was already locked into the dusty dressing room.

What he found backstage resembled, on a smaller scale, the brawl which was taking place in the foyer and on the steps of the Opera House. In one corner was the Professor held back by Alfredo and Alfredo's father from committing an assault with a fire ax upon the person of Signor Malatesta. Elsewhere, three of Madge's girls, having taken the side of the Professor and Mademoiselle, were calling other female members of the company a rich assortment of names, embroidered with the fruity language of the El Dorado. Through the midst of the fray, Dick made his way to the door of Mademoiselle's dressing room.

He knocked without receiving an answer, once and then again, and then gently he turned the knob and tried to enter, but the door was locked. It was then he heard the faint sound of sobbing, and for a second he stood uncertainly, listening to it.

Upon his already agitated nerves, the sound produced a prodigious effect. Love, frustration and the confusion of emotions arising from his half-adolescent passion turned him into a White Knight bent upon rescuing a damsel in distress. The proper course of action came quickly into his head. He would break down the door, rescue Mademoiselle and carry her off, out of Silver City, out into the world. With that idea in mind he thrust his big, muscular shoulders against the door to break the lock, but at the first shove the voice of Mademoiselle came to him through the closed door.

"Who is it?" asked Mademoiselle.

"It's me—Dick. Let me in!"

There was a little silence and then the voice, no longer softened by sobs, came to him again. This time it was colored by icy fury, a fury so concentrated in its contempt and scorn that it was like a jet of ice water full in the face. What the voice said was even worse.

It said, "Get the hell out of here! I don't want to see anything called Meaney again—ever! I don't want to hear the name Silver City! It's a hick town full of white trash and the Meaneys are the worst of all. If you try to get in here I'll kill you! Get the hell out and never try to speak to me again!"

The sense of the words was bad enough but what collapsed all his indignation, his admiration and for a moment even his passion was the discovery that the girl whom he loved, the girl who was so pretty, so soft, so desirable could use such language in a voice so terrible. He had meant to talk, to argue, or plead with her, even to carry her off, but the speech and the quality of the voice in which it was uttered both chilled and paralyzed him. He simply stood staring at the door.

But the voice had not finished. It said, "I hate the whole place and everything called Meaney from that gorilla brother of yours through your old man. They ain't even civilized and you ain't any better with your soft la-de-da manners. You don't even know how to treat a woman! You're nothing but a silly calf! Get out and leave me alone!"

Then the dazed paralysis in Dick turned into wild anger, akin to the apoplectic rage consuming P.J. at the same moment. He answered back, saying, "All right! Nobody gives a damn what you think! To hell with you!"

At the same moment there appeared out of the shadow what might have been mistaken for an animated funeral offering moving forward under its own power. It was the bouquet from Denver carried by a boy who was completely hidden behind it. Its arrival could scarcely have been subject to worse timing. The sight of it seemed only to augment Dick's rage. Turning, he seized it from the astonished messenger, tore off the card, so carefully worded as a tribute to Mademoiselle's expected triumph, crumpled it and flung it on the floor. Then he threw the bouquet violently against the door, crying out, "Take your goddam flowers!" and stalked blindly through the gloom and shadows toward the stage door.

On the way he noticed, without being aware of it until some minutes later, two things. Three or four stage hands were carrying out something feet first and at the same time out of the shadows there appeared the ample, bedizened figure of a large woman with bleached yellow hair. It was only after he reached the street that he understood the meaning of the two brief, incomplete pictures that had registered upon his consciousness. The something that was being carried out feet first was the Professor, and the bedizened figure with bleached hair was Madge Beakymer. Vaguely it occurred to him that she was moving in for the kill but in his rage at the insults projected through the dressing room door, he did not care what Madge was up to.

For a long time he walked the back streets fuming, oblivious to the interest he aroused among the miners and Indians at the sight of his black suit with long coat tails, a high starched collar and a white necktie. At last, when he had cooled off a little he found himself walking up the hill to the Castle. He entered it by a back door and cautiously made his way up the stairs to his own room, where, as rapidly as possible, he stripped off the tight uncomfortable black clothes.

Madge Beakymer could read signs and portents, especially when they concerned men and women who for twenty-five or thirty years had been her business, and so, as she came through the backstage shadows, moving indifferently through the arguing, brawling members of the opera company she observed three things which, for her, had great significance. She noticed first the broad retreating back of young Dick and then the crumpled bouquet flung against the door of Mademoiselle's dressing room and finally the crumpled card lying near by. Picking it up she held to her eyes the *lorgnon* which she carried only on such grand occasions as the opera opening, and by the dim light of the kerosene lamp nearby, read what was written upon it.

These three things pieced together told her the story. As she read, the big, hard, experienced face relaxed into an unconscious smile. It was the smile of a realist and a cynic who was eternally amused by the ructions and goings on which complicated the lives of other people. Not for at least a quarter of a century had love, passion or jealousy actually disrupted the even, straight, steely course of her ambition. She had known what she wanted and gone for it, using whatever weapons and advantages she could lay hands upon. From the moment of her "ruin" at the age of sixteen, which she never took too seriously but regarded as merely the first move in the natural course of biological events, she had wanted just such an establishment as she now possessed. She now regarded the retreating back, the crushed bouquet and the crumpled card as mere symbols of that biological pressure and confusion which along with tradition, habit, morality and convention, complicated the lives of so many people. She was neither troubled by nor concerned with any such thing as the romance or mysticism that complicated the lives of Tristan and Isolde or Abelard and Heloïse. In fact, she had never heard of them. All these signs and portents she had just uncovered meant only one thing to her—that young Dick and the singer wanted each other and why didn't they just get together and call it a day? All these attendant complications simply gave her an unexpected opportunity and she had never been one to overlook an opportunity.

The fact was that she had wanted Mademoiselle as an entertainer in her establishment since the first appearance of the girl in Silver City. Having observed the effect of the girl since the day of her arrival upon the overpopulation of males on this particular frontier, she divined that her presence would be like that of honey to flies. But more than that the girl would give "tone" to the establishment. Until now the ambition to engage Mademoiselle as an entertainer had appeared unattainable but now opportunity was showing an unexpectedly benign face.

Knowing women and being shrewd, she did not attempt to seek immediately a personal interview with Mademoiselle. She knew well enough that in the agitation of the moment she would get nowhere. So she did not knock on the door and attempt to speak to her. She simply bent over, with some difficulty, owing to the tightness of the steel casing of her corset, and thrust underneath the door a note she wrote quickly on the back of a program. Then quietly she vanished again and joined her cousin Lena who was waiting in the shadows and together the two women made their way, accompanied by occasional plaudits and tributes from male passers-by, back to the El Dorado.

Inside the dressing room, the rage and tears of Mademoiselle presently wore themselves out and she began to take off the gay first-act costume designed by Millie Hirshbein for Violetta's party. As she took it off she understood that she would never again wear it on the stage of the Silver City Opera House or perhaps on any other. Then as she began removing her make-up, it occurred to her that it was strange that the Professor had not put in his appearance. She considered opening the door and looking for him but she dared not do so for fear that she would find young Dick standing outside, moon-eyed and reproachful. And in her humiliation and hurt-pride she wanted to see no one, the Professor perhaps least of all, for he had counted on this performance tonight as a last gamble for success, security and rest. She could not bring herself to face him.

As she took off the make-up, shaking now and then with the hysterical echo of a sob, she regarded herself in the worn mirror, thinking, "There's a curse on you. The wicked fairies were present at your birth. Everything is against you!"

Then Mademoiselle No. 2 made her appearance again and said, "So you're going to pity yourself and lie down and quit! So you're going to let them lick you! A fine way to act!" And suddenly she was angry all over again.

As she threw the ball dress into the corner of the room, she noticed the bit of paper thrust under the door. Going over to the door she picked it up suspiciously, as if it had been not a simple piece of paper but a stick of dynamite. It was, she was certain, a note from Dick and suddenly she did not know whether she hated him or was in love with him, whether she believed him a damned fool or was sorry for him.

Then she discovered that the paper was a program with her name at the top as star of the opening performance of the Silver City Opera Company and that the back was covered with writing. It was not Dick's small, careful handwriting which she knew by now; but big, sprawling, careless script. The note read:

Dear Mademoiselle:

I am writing to congratulate you on your wonderful performance. The hub-bub was a plot. Anyone could see that. It's what comes of bringing Polacks and Dagoes into Silver City.

Will you accept an offer to sing at the El Dorado? I would pay well and you would have the special rights of a prima donna singer . . . no drinking at tables and such like. I would look after your protection personally.

Your admirer,
Madge Beakymer
Proprietor the El Dorado

Quickly she tore up the letter. No matter how much money she was offered she would never sing at the El Dorado. She would not even stay a day longer in Silver City. She could not make up her mind whether the letter was sincere praise, whether it was an insult or whether it was merely a trap. It did appear, however, to be a plot against that virginity which, all else having failed, suddenly became of even greater importance than it had been in the past.

Then she dismissed the whole business from her mind as already a part of the past. The future—the immediate future—offered troubles enough. There was the business of packing and of finding enough money to take them both as far as Denver. Out of long experience she was inclined to believe that the Professor had no cash in reserve. It might even be necessary to borrow it—but from where or from whom? P.J. had not yet paid her any salary but she would not ask him for it if she starved to death or had to walk to Denver, and she could think of nowhere else to turn.

Then the second Mademoiselle said to the first Mademoiselle, "You'd better stop mooning about and pitying yourself. You'd better get to work on escaping from town."

At last she put on a brown dress and tied a bonnet over her head and unlocked the door. She was a little afraid of opening it for fear of what or whom she might find outside. For a moment she stood quite still listening but she heard no sound save the mewing of the theatre cat. Opening the door carefully she discovered that the place backstage was empty and dark save for an oil light burning beside the door which led into the alley. As she crossed the stage, she heard the voice of the old man who tended the door during the opera season. He said, "Good night, Miss! And don't let it worry you. It was a stinking shame!"

"Good night!" she said. "Thank you."

That was the triumph the Professor had hoped for.

Then she opened the door on the side street. It was empty now and still. Between the shabby buildings there appeared overhead a deep, cobalt blue sky brilliant with stars that seemed to move and glitter in the dry, still clearness of the mountain air. For a moment she remained there, looking up at the sky. Then she took a deep breath and felt her courage return.

In his room Dick, dressed now in the old cowhand clothes, packed some odds and ends into a saddle bag and turned out the lights. As he passed Ellie-May's apartment he opened the door and by the dim light from the hall he left an envelope on the sewing machine where she would be certain to find it. Then he closed the door behind him and went quietly down the back stairs through the back hall and out into the brilliant starlit night.

Quickly he turned in the direction of the corral, outside which the two Indian chiefs were camped with their delegations. An Indian dog howled somewhere in the distance but otherwise the night was still.

At the same time an old man climbed the hill from the railroad station. He was carrying a telegram in his hand addressed to P. J. Meaney which had come over the railroad wires from Denver. The old man who had worked for P.J. in a small way for more than twenty years knew that it was important.

At the door of the Castle, the colored boy, Esau, admitted him and led him straight to P.J.'s room on the second floor. The old man had orders to bring every telegram to P.J. no mattter what hour of the night it arrived.

It was P.J. himself who opened the door, clad in a long nightshirt with red embroidery about the cuffs and neck which Ellie-May had run up for him. With his black hair tousled and the black hair on his chest pushing its way through the open neck, he looked a little like a gorilla female impersonator and his appearance clearly startled the little old man bearing the telegram who took off his cap, averted his eyes as from a mystery and went into a series of bobbing bows.

Then P.J. tore open the telegram and read the message, muttering aloud, "Well, I'll be goddamed!" When he recovered he took a five-dollar bill out of his bulging billfold and gave it to the old man, saying, "No answer, Marle. Go on home to bed."

When he was alone again, P.J. sat down on the edge of the big, double bed and read the telegram again. It read:

CAUCUS HELD TODAY MAKES CERTAIN DEMOCRATIC NOMINATION HENRY CALDWELL CLEAN UP CAMPAIGN PLANNED

VIC McGINTY

Then slowly P.J. tore the telegram into small pieces and threw them on the floor. For the fraction of a second he was afraid, perhaps

[171]

for the first time in all his life. But the fear passed quickly and turning out the gas light he lit a cigar and lay back on the bed.

He had already begun plotting.

At Mrs. Sowers' Grand Hotel, Mademoiselle came in by the back door that opened on the alley. She didn't want to see anyone, much less any of the opera troupe. She found them upstairs in the hall on the second floor. Even as she climbed the stairs she heard them, arguing and chattering angrily in two or three languages or in broken English, for the word from the Castle had already reached them by way of Mrs. Sowers who notified them that their contracts were ended and that their rooms would be needed the next day. The center of the disturbance seemed to be in a room where the voices of the "Eyetalian Nightingale" and Signor Malatesta were heard, engaged in violent recriminations, interrupted only by occasional sobs and screams from the Nightingale. From out the doors along the corridor there appeared singers of various nationalities carrying odd bits of clothing which they were in the process of packing, to throw into the general bedlam remarks and observations of their own.

Mademoiselle passed quickly along the corridor, ignoring them, aware now that the plot had misfired and that as a result all hell had broken loose. Out of long experience she was prepared for physical violence but she received nothing worse than black looks. The fury of the company seemed to be directed less against herself than toward Signor Malatesta and the hysterical Nightingale.

She was headed for the room of the Professor to talk over with him their plans for the future, whatever they might be. At the end of the long hall she discovered that the door of the Professor's room was open and that there was a light shining from it into the hallway. As she reached the doorway she discovered that he was not alone. He was lying on the bed with his coat off and his shirt open at the neck. His eyes were closed and beside the bed sat a man dressed in a black suit, with a bald head and long flowing side whiskers. He was holding the Professor's wrist with one hand and a gold watch attached to his vest by a heavy gold chain, in the other. At the foot of the bed stood

Mrs. Sowers herself with a forbidding yet triumphant expression on her battered face.

At sight of Mademoiselle standing in the doorway, Mrs. Sowers moved toward her. She held her finger to her lips and the drooping lines of her raddled face took on a new expression of condolence and bereavement which betokened only the satisfaction which she had always felt in disaster, even in her own disaster and disillusionment in having picked a drunkard and wastrel for a husband. With the mournful look of an injured bloodhound she led Mademoiselle to the head of the stairway and, despite the racket still continuing in the far end of the hall, said in a whisper, "He has had a stroke!"

Then quickly she poured out the story, "It seems," she said, "that the Professor tried to kill the Signor Malatesta with a fire ax and just as he was about to bash in his head the old gentleman fell down in a fit." Then she sighed quickly and added, "Lots of things happen in Silver City but there was never a night like this." And she made a clucking sound, which indicated satisfaction rather than alarm.

"How is he?" asked Mademoiselle.

"I guess he ain't gonna die," said Mrs. Sowers, "but he's pretty bad off."

When Mademoiselle re-entered the room, the doctor had finished taking the Professor's pulse and was standing by the bed. Mrs. Sowers introduced him and he said, "Your father has had a stroke. I think he'll get over it but he may not be much good afterward."

"When will you know, doctor?"

"Not for four or five days. In the meanwhile he'll have to have someone with him all the time, night and day."

"I'll stay with him," said Mademoiselle. Then she added, "He really isn't my father. He just brought me up."

"He's all right for now," said the doctor. "If he should start getting purple in the face, you can send for me. There isn't anything I can do and there are a lot of broken heads in town that need mending."

Mademoiselle thought desperately of the escape she had planned from Silver City and asked, "When will we be able to move him . . . I mean, out of town and back to Denver?"

"I don't know, but not for quite a while. You'd better not count on moving him that far for a long time."

She felt a sudden weakness in her stomach. The doctor picked up his hat and bowed, "Mrs. Sowers'll know where to find me," he added.

When he had gone, Mrs. Sowers closed the door behind her and her expression changed from that of a saddened bloodhound to that of a rather smug weasel.

"There's one thing," she said, in a refined voice, "it's about the bill. . . ."

Mademoiselle's temper flared suddenly, "This is a hell of a time to talk about bills. I'll take care of it in the morning."

The weasel expression of Mrs. Sowers softened a little. "You understand, Miss. I have to make ends meet here. P. J. Meaney is a hard man. I've got a contract with him and I have to pay up regular and in Silver City there's always three people for every bed."

"Sure, I understand. And now please go away."

Mrs. Sowers opened the door and then turning, stood there for a moment. "And there's another thing," she said. "It ain't good business to have people dyin' in the house."

Perhaps as a result of long experience, she quickly went out the door and closed it behind her.

When she had gone Mademoiselle took off her bonnet and sat down wearily on the chair. On the bed the Professor breathed heavily and noisily, a sound interrupted only by the shouts and accusations from the running quarrel which continued among the performers at the far end of the hall.

As she sat there, bolt upright and very tired, it seemed to Mademoiselle that she had come to the very end of the tether and that everything which had happened since the Professor chose the ill-fated train to Silver City had led steadily toward this end in the dreary bedroom with its hard bed and washstand and slop-jar and the dreary, grey, sagging mosquito netting on the window.

In a kind of weary bewilderment she watched the Professor, his breath coming noisily, his Adam's apple moving slowly up and down in the withered turkey throat. While she sat there she kept speculating upon what she should do and the more she tried to find a way out the more difficult everything became. There were complications of money, of pride, of virtue, of reputation, complications which involved Madge Beakymer, P. J. Meaney, Mrs. Sowers and many other

[174]

people. At last as the first rays of the sun turned the view of the great mountains outside the window to a pale, glowing pink, she reached a conclusion.

She would humble her pride once more and send a note up the hill to Dick. Now in her weariness, with all her bad temper washed away, he seemed more desirable than he had ever seemed before and she began to regret the harshness of her behavior. Maybe his softness and shyness weren't so bad after all. Maybe they really weren't just a means of getting round her. Maybe he acted that way only because he was decent and civilized; but she really didn't know what civilization was or whether she had ever known anyone civilized in all her existence. She saw him clearly now in her imagination—his blond curly hair and bright blue eyes, the big shoulders and the full lips. Maybe she had been a plain damned fool. In any case, he was her last hope.

By eight o'clock she had composed a careful note and sent it up hill to the Castle by one of the half-breed boys who hung about the hotel.

It read: "I'm sorry I lost my temper last night. The Professor is sick. He had a stroke. I don't know what to do. I need advice. Can you come to the Grand Hotel?"

Then she sat down to wait and in half an hour the half-breed boy returned. He gave her back the note she had written unopened.

In his pidgin English the boy said, "Mister Dick gone away. Nobody know where he gone."

She gave him the last silver dollar that remained in her purse and sent him away. Then she sat down again and remained thus for a long time staring in front of her, and at last about the time the opera troupe had begun to straggle out of the hotel toward the depot, she took up the scratchy pen again and wrote a note to Madge Beakymer.

Dear Mrs. Beakymer:
I am interested in your offer. My stepfather is sick. He had a stroke last night and I have to stay with him. Could you come to the Hotel?
                                        Yours sincerely,
                                        La Belle da Ponte

Finally she went downstairs and gave the second note to the half-breed boy to deliver at the El Dorado. When she returned she stood for a long time at the window watching the procession of artistes leaving the hotel. Most of them walked, carrying Gladstone bags and valises. A wagon drawn by two skinny cayuses carried the trunks and at the rear of the procession came Signor Malatesta and the "Eyetalian Nightingale" in the one open hack for hire in all Silver City. It was clear that they were still quarreling. The Nightingale in purple with plumes occupied the main seat with her luggage packed about her and on the folding seat opposite her sat Signor Malatesta. Mademoiselle suspected, rightly, that there had been a quarrel over which one should have the prestige of a carriage and that in the end a compromise had brought them together thus, sitting opposite each other without speaking.

As the procession vanished around a corner bound for the depot, she experienced a sudden feeling of relief which for the moment wiped out even her weariness. At least everything was cleared away. Whatever happened now she had all the reins in her own hands. She was through with operas and careers. In that moment she said farewell forever to whatever remained of childishness. She wasn't a girl any more but a woman.

PART IV

━━

IT WASN'T ALTOGETHER TRUE THAT NO ONE AT THE CASTLE KNEW WHERE
Dick had gone. One person knew and that was Ellie-May but she kept
the secret. And in the way in which chance determines all too often
what happens to us, Ellie-May never knew that the half-breed boy had
brought a note up the hill from the Grand Hotel and Boarding House.
The boy never got any farther than Esau at the door and Esau only
knew what he had been told by Ellie-May along with the rest of the
household—that Dick had run off to some unknown destination. If
Ellie-May had met the boy at the door and guessed the note was from
Mademoiselle, the whole of the story might have been different. But
she wasn't at the door and knew nothing about the note.

At the moment the boy arrived and was sent away Ellie-May was in
her own apartment, humming to herself and pedaling on the sewing
machine. She was happy because Dick had gone away out of Silver
City and she hoped that his departure meant that he would never return and settle down as a kind of deputy for P.J. as the other three
boys had done. It would mean that he had escaped and that he
had prepared a way for her own escape later on.

She scarcely thought of Mademoiselle at all save that she was sorry
for her humiliation on the night before and glad that it had brought
about P.J.'s headlong decision never again to bring an opera company
to Silver City. She had never enjoyed that kind of music much. It had
always seemed high-falutin' and false, and it meant that each year for
a couple of weeks she had to get all dressed up, ride through the
streets like a Ten-Thousand-Dollar beauty in the circus parade and sit,
covered with jewelry, in front of all Silver City like a monkey in a cage.

She knew well enough that Dick had been troubled by a lot of

[177]

things and that the longer he stayed in Silver City the worse his unhappiness and restlessness became. Vaguely she supposed the girl had something to do with it but how much she did not know and Dick never chose to tell her. Long ago she had suspected that his experience with women was what might have been called "perfunctory" rather than functional. So now she was not much troubled on that score. By the time Dick returned, if he did return, the girl, good or bad, would be gone for good and all out of his life.

So Ellie-May pedaled and sang, cheered by the brightness of the morning and the look of the river winding like a stream of liquid silver through the cottonwood trees of the distant valley.

She had too another cause of happiness and that was the telegram P.J. had received late the night before. He hadn't told her or anyone else about it but she had her ways of finding out things that happened in Silver City and this time the information came direct from the source—from Henry Caldwell himself. Early that morning before he left town he had sent word by way of Millie Hirshbein that he was to be the Democratic candidate for Governor. Indeed, she had known it in her bones for a long time past, and now the knowledge made her happy because she thought the time was just about ripe.

Although she seemed to know little about politics, she was in her bones a better politician than P.J. and she knew a great deal that he never suspected her of knowing. It came to her in a great many ways, from the pompous men and the characters who came to stay at the Castle, from Millie Hirshbein's varied sources of gossip centered about the Emporium and she learned a lot from the Irish and Chinese and Polacks who worked the mines. She and Millie were the only ones in the town who ever gave the foreigners a thought; and she had among them many friends. Some of them she had supplied with food and medicine when they were ill. For some she had paid doctors' bills. For the dozen or so who had wives and children she had helped out with winter underwear and bedclothes run up on her sewing machine. And Addie Hardenfelt, wife of the old man who had brought the telegram, kept her informed of every message of any interest that came in. She had paid for Addie's operation when Addie had "everything taken away."

She was glad because it seemed to her that Henry Caldwell was at last coming into his own and getting the recognition he deserved. It had always seemed to her that Henry held himself too cheaply, just because he began life as a cowhand and didn't speak elegant English. Lately he seemed to have gained stature and confidence and people all over the state seemed to be recognizing the change. She knew that he had behind him all the ranchers and cowhands, who had had a good deal of trouble with P.J. and she knew that Wentworth Talmadge (P.J.'s candidate for Governor) was a miserable specimen who cringed whenever P.J. bellowed. The contest would not be between Henry and Wentworth Talmadge but between Henry and P. J. Meaney. And here she was caught right in the middle.

Pumping her machine a little faster and chuckling to herself, she thought, "I kinda relish that!"

She had, she reflected, a good many cards up her sleeve. Chuckling she thought of those women in the East she had read about who were agitating to get the right to vote alongside the men. The poor fools! If they only knew how to operate they already had a lot more power than the vote would ever give them.

"Yes," she thought, "I think I'm going to enjoy this campaign."

And presently she fell to thinking of Eudora and in that direction too fortune had seemed to be smiling on her. Eudora had certainly enjoyed her excursion to the opera and a first-hand view without a telescope of the brawl that had taken place at the Opera House. And then she had organized the game of whist with Mr. Wright and Mr. Laidlaw and Mr. Chatsworthy and sat up playing long after Ellie-May had gone to bed. It was clear that Mr. Chatsworthy, resembling so closely the fiancé who had walked out on Eudora, had caught her fancy. The question was whether Mr. Chatsworthy had taken a fancy to Eudora. Only time would tell. Anyway, Mr. Chatsworthy seemed to like the western country and that was a help.

Indeed, thought Ellie-May, as she gayly pedaled, things were moving and beginning to open up. Tomorrow, she decided, she would go down and spend the afternoon with Millie and have Millie read her horoscope. She hadn't had a reading for nearly five years. Maybe at last Saturn was out of the way and things were looking up.

At noon she dressed up and went down in her role of "consort" to lunch with Mr. Wright and Mr. Laidlaw, but it was a gloomy lunch.

P.J. was in a black mood and Mr. Wright and Mr. Laidlaw didn't seem very sprightly. Eudora and Mr. Chatsworthy had gone off in a buckboard taking a picnic lunch with them. When she heard the news, she thought, "I hope Eudora isn't overdoing it."

In the middle of lunch an argument broke out between P.J. and Mr. Wright over the sudden departure of the lawyer and the banker. Mr. Wright said that he and Mr. Laidlaw would have to leave for Denver that afternoon. P.J. complained that they hadn't finished their business with him and that too many things had been left in the air. But Mr. Wright, who was smooth and cold and slippery, wasn't to be persuaded and although P.J. fumed and cursed, nothing changed the plans. Even to Ellie-May, the sudden decision to leave seemed mysterious and even suspicious. But Mr. Wright and Mr. Laidlaw bored her and she slipped away as soon as possible after bidding them a gracious and elegant good-by and urging them to return soon. She had an idea that they had been somewhat shaken by their experiences at the opera the night before, and that she might never see them again. The thought did not trouble her.

At about five o'clock Eudora burst into the room. And as Ellie-May turned from the machine she saw at a glance that the picnic had been a success. Eudora was flushed as a schoolgirl and looked almost pretty in a swarthy, elephantine fashion. She gave a brisk account of the drive to Meeker's Gulch and of Mr. Chatsworthy's fascinating, sophisticated conversation and then said suddenly, "Have you heard about that girl, Mademoiselle?"

"No," said Ellie-May.

"Well, she's gone to the El Dorado. Everybody in town knows it. She's gonna sing there beginning Monday night."

"Well!" was all Ellie-May could say, although she was thinking very rapidly.

"I wish I could go and hear her!" said Eudora.

"Now, Eudora, don't begin getting ideas. Remember you've been sick for seven years. You'd better take things easy at first. You know no respectable woman has ever been inside the El Dorado."

"Yes, damn it!" said Eudora. "Sometimes I think it's a pity to be so respectable."

"Eudora!" said Ellie-May as severely as possible.

"Well, I mean it. When I think of all the things a man like Cecil is able to do."

Then Eudora went away and Ellie-May settled back to her sewing. She wanted to finish the child's red flannel petticoat she was working on so that she could go down to Millie's for the astrological reading. Everything was turning out better and better. Now the whole matter of whether Mademoiselle was a virgin or a trollop was settled. If she had gone to the El Dorado she was a trollop. Probably that was what Dick had found out and probably that was the reason he had gone away. Anyway it cleared up the situation.

When the proprietress of the El Dorado awakened lazily after one of her more quiet nights (one in which the Turkish cosy corner remained intact) the old porter brought her Mademoiselle's note along with her coffee. She read it and lost no time to pluck this peach which was ready to fall into her lap. After dressing with care, she set out on foot for the Grand Hotel passing on her way the bedraggled members of the Opera troupe, already bound for the depot.

She found the girl in the Professor's room, still awake, still looking out of the window by the side of the stricken old man. The meeting was cordial enough and conducted entirely upon the most professional and ladylike plane. Madge had taken care to dress well and impressively in a stylish suit bought in Denver with a plumed hat, parasol, feather boa and gloves.

She took the girl's hand in hers and patted it, saying, "Now, you don't need worry about a thing. I'll take care of everything." She looked, admiringly, at the pale, pretty face with the dark circles of fatigue beneath the eyes and added, "What you need is some rest. I'll send over Mrs. Birdwell to set with your stepfather until we can get a regular nurse from Denver. Mrs. Birdwell is the housekeeper and very good and conscientious and you can really trust her. I've got quite a lot of property in this town and we'll find a small house where we can put the old gentleman. But you come home with me now and get some rest. I'll put you in the room I keep for Aunt Etta when she comes out from Cincinnati to visit me."

Mademoiselle looked away from her and was silent for a moment. Then she said, "But I can't pay for all this. I haven't any money."

"Don't you worry about that. I'll take care of everything. In a few days you'll be singing and earning money . . . lots of it." Then after a second she said, "Do you mean to say P.J. hasn't paid you anything?"

"No. He was supposed to be paying our expenses until last night. But I guess that's finished. Mrs. Sowers was asking for her money already last night."

"Why, the old skinflint!" said Madge and Mademoiselle didn't know whether she meant P.J. or Mrs. Sowers or both. "I'll see that he pays you all right. Just leave that to me!"

She looked out of the window and said, "Here comes Mrs. Birdwell now." She picked up the bonnet and placed it on Mademoiselle's head. "There now! Fix your hat. Mrs. Birdwell will take over here. She's had lots of experience. She often takes care of the lady artistes at the El Dorado when they're sick."

"But my clothes," said Mademoiselle.

"We'll send over for them. Mrs. Birdwell can pack them up."

The girl didn't protest. She felt herself sinking deeper and deeper into a morass of fatigue so profound that it seemed difficult even to move her arms or raise her hands to tie the bonnet strings beneath her chin. It was good—wonderfully good—to have someone taking charge of everything, taking care of her. But in the back of her mind a stubborn voice was saying, "But I won't give in! Nothing can make me give in!"

Then Mrs. Birdwell appeared in the doorway, a motherly little woman of about sixty-five. In an unexpectedly deep voice she said, "Well, Madge. Here I am!"

Madge took a nightshirt out of the cupboard and together she and Mrs. Birdwell raised the unconscious old man, undressed him in the most professional way and got him into the nightshirt. For neither of them was this an unusual or a recently acquired achievement.

"When is the doctor coming back?" asked Madge.

"He said he'd be in about ten o'clock."

"What's his name?"

"Carton, I think he said."

"That's good," said Madge. "He's the one who looks after my

girls." And turning to her companion she said, "You know how to handle him, Mrs. Birdwell? So that the old gentleman gets the best attention?"

"Sure, Madge!"

Then Madge turned and said briskly, "I guess that takes care of everything. We can go now." She patted Mademoiselle's shoulder, "You must be terribly tired, my dear."

Her manner was warm and pleasant. The odd thing was that the girl felt it was sincere. Then Madge said, "Come along. I've been in some tough spots myself till I got to be a business woman."

But the voice inside Mademoiselle kept saying, "But I won't give in! I won't give in!"

In the hall below they encountered Mrs. Sowers. This embittered woman, understanding what was happening beneath her eyes, tried to look scornful but scorn got her nowhere with Madge, for Madge knew that Mrs. Sowers knew that her own fate was inevitably in Madge's hands.

She said, briskly, "The Professor and Mademoiselle are leaving your hotel this morning for better quarters. Please get your bill together and send it over to my place."

Mrs. Sowers didn't answer nor did Madge wait for an answer or even act as if she expected one. But as Madge and Mademoiselle went out the door, Mrs. Sowers in frustration cleared her throat and spat into one of the dusty, potted palms.

Their progress along Eudora Street did not go unnoticed and although Mademoiselle was too tired to notice anything, Madge saw with satisfaction that not a man they passed failed to observe the pretty girl in her company. One man even quickened his pace and went ahead to the Gates Ajar Saloon and notified the customers who immediately leaned out of the open windows and over the swinging doors for a good view. All this meant business—so much business that Madge could afford to raise her prices all around and keep out the cheaper, more troublesome trade.

They did not go in by the main entrance of the El Dorado where the gambling had already begun but went up by the covered outside stairway used only by Madge and her close friends. Upstairs Madge led the way through the sitting room with the gilded "suite" and the Turkish cosy corner and down a short corridor. There she opened a door and said, "There we are. This is Aunt Etta's room. I keep it just for her."

It was, Mademoiselle noticed, a really gorgeous room. The furniture like that in the sitting room was gilded and the lights were all covered with soft, pink shades. On the far side of the room stood an enormous gilt bed covered by a spread made entirely of what appeared to be gigantic rose petals. There seemed to be mirrors everywhere.

"Isn't it pretty?" asked Madge. "Aunt Etta made a good marriage in Cincinnati—a brewer. She's used to luxury. She kind of raised me until I was sixteen so I've always been very good to her—nothing but the best."

For a moment, Mademoiselle just stood there, as if dazed. Then she said, "Yes, it's pretty . . . especially the bedspread."

"All rose petals," said Madge. "See!" She bent over and lifted the border. "See! All the leaves and thorns around the edge." She gave a deep-throated laugh. "Symbolic! Never a rose without its thorns." She began undoing the buttons of Mademoiselle's dress. "But you get to bed. That's what you need. And sleep as long as you like. Mrs. Birdwell and I will take care of the old gentleman. D'you want some breakfast?"

But all Mademoiselle could see or think of was the great gilded bed with its cover of silken rose petals. It hypnotized her. "All I want," she said, "is to sleep and sleep."

Madge went to the bed, removed the rose-petal cover and folding it carefully, placed it on a chair and turned back the bed.

"Well, honey, if you want anything just pull that gold rope beside the bed. You just sleep all you like and when you wake up we'll talk business even if it's day after tomorrow."

Then she went out and in a little while Mademoiselle, half buried in the great, gilded bed was fast asleep.

Thirty-six hours later, Mademoiselle awakened, slowly, so that as she opened her eyes the reality of dreams and the reality of the pink, silken room filled with mirrors were for a time blended together in a haze of consciousness. Then slowly, emerging from the haze, the room became the reality and she remembered bit by bit the whole sequence of events from the nightmare moment when the vegetables began flying in the Opera House, and presently she knew where she was and how she had come there and remembered Madge Beakymer's admonition to pull the gold rope beside the bed in case she wanted anything.

Sitting up in bed she saw by the light on the distant great mountains outside the windows that it was evening, and she thought, "What has happened to the Professor?"

So lazily she tugged on the bell pull and in a little while there was a knock on the door and Mrs. Birdwell entered. In her deep, masculine voice, she asked, "Well, how do you feel?"

"Fine," said Mademoiselle.

"I suppose you'd like some breakfast?"

"Yes, but I can come downstairs."

"No. Madge wants you to eat up here. She wants to talk to you. You leave it to me. I'll send you up a good, big meal. You'll be needing it."

Then Mademoiselle asked about the Professor.

"He's all right," said Mrs. Birdwell. "I've got him moved into a cottage Madge owns down by the river. She had to throw out the tenant. He was a bartender at the Gates Ajar—and I've got him a good woman to look after him."

"Has he come around yet?"

"No. He opens his eyes now and then but he just mumbles."

"What does the doctor say?"

"He says the old gentleman will be all right. He may never be able to walk but he'll get back his senses." Mrs. Birdwell's face puckered into a smile. "Doc says he's a tough old bird. A stroke like that would have killed most men his age." She crossed the room and opened a door. "The bathroom is in here," she said. "Hot and cold running water, marble tub, silver taps. San Francisco hasn't got anything better—mighty nice! Well, I'll send you up some breakfast. Madge is just getting dressed up for the evening. She'll be in to see you as soon as she's ready."

When Mrs. Birdwell had gone, Mademoiselle got up. She hadn't any nightgown and for a moment she stood regarding the strong, young body in the mirrors. They were arranged so that standing in one place she could see herself from every angle. It was a Narcissistic pleasure she had never experienced before and she was a little astonished at the beauty and perfection of her own figure. It was like a statue she had once seen called, "The Greek Slave."

Then suddenly she was ashamed of herself and crossed the room to the bath. It was, as Mrs. Birdwell said, mighty fine. The silver taps were all in the form of swan's necks. But still she did not escape from her own vanity and immodesty for the walls were made of mirrors set in gold frames and again she found her nakedness repeated over and over again into infinity.

When she had bathed she put on the clothes she had worn and while she was still putting on layer after layer of pants and petticoats and chemises there was a knock and Madge came in.

She was dressed magnificently in yellow satin with the handsome bosom well exposed. The blond hair rose from her brow in a complicated structure of puffs, curls and waterfalls and she wore a whole parure of diamonds very nearly as fine as that worn by Eudora at the opera.

"I'm all dressed up tonight," she said. "The Governor and P.J. are coming in for a little champagne supper." Then she seated herself and said, "Go on dressing, honey. Don't mind me. I suppose you want to go over to see the old gentleman?"

"Yes," said Mademoiselle.

"Well, while you finish dressing, I thought we might talk business." Mademoiselle didn't say anything and Madge continued, "I've got it all figured out. You'll supply the tone to the place. It'll be just like I said in the note. You don't have to do anything but sing. Of course, now and then, there'll be gentlemen here—important gentlemen like the Governor—and when they come I'd like you to help me entertain them—you know—kind of help me as hostess. It would help me out a lot. My Cousin Lena ain't much good. She's sort of common and what I like is tone. Nothing, you understand, but be pleasant and chatty and only with important guests. You understand what I mean?"

"Yes," said Mademoiselle dully.

"You'll be entirely on your own to do just as you feel best. If

[186]

anybody gets fresh with you just let me know and I'll take over. I've got it all figured out." She was silent for a moment and then said abruptly, "You are a virgin, aren't you?"

"Yes," said Mademoiselle.

"That's how I figured it. Well, we'll keep you that way. It's an asset if you're serious about settling down later on. It can be an asset to an entertainment establishment too, especially if it gets around. Now as to the act . . ." She looked in the mirror and began reassembling the assortment of puffs, curls and waterfalls. "I think you might sing opry now and then to give tone and then some good songs like 'The Baggage Coach Ahead' and 'She May Be Somebody's Mother.' You know the kind that makes 'em cry? They cry easy out here where women are so scarce. And we'll get you some fine clothes—lady's clothes—refined and everything to give tone. We don't need sequins and bugles and short skirts with fringe. They get plenty of butt-shaking out of the other girls. I want you to be a lady. I want you to remind 'em of their mothers and sisters."

As Mademoiselle finished dressing it was Mademoiselle No. 2 who was listening, curiously, with that instinct for self-protection which had grown so strong during a long, hard life. Mademoiselle No. 2 didn't see any objection to the terms thus far.

"Come here and let me button up your back," said Madge. Mademoiselle obeyed and while Madge went on with the buttoning she said, "Of course you may get a chance to marry some important bloke. It's a big opportunity. You'll meet a lot of them here . . . mine operators, ranch owners, politicians and all kinds of people. I'll make it clear to them that you're a good girl and brought up refined."

The last of the buttons was buttoned and Madge said, "How about fifty dollars a week to start with?"

For a moment Mademoiselle caught her breath. Fifty dollars a week coming in steady was more money than she and the Professor had ever known. Usually they got along on fifty dollars a month or less and even that had been dwindling steadily for the last two or three years. Fifty dollars a week!

"Paid in silver dollars of course," said Madge.

"Yes . . . yes," said Mademoiselle. "That would be fine."

"And now as to the billing," said Madge, "I've been giving it a good deal of thought but I haven't come to anything. Mrs. Birdwell says you're like a dove and you ought to be billed as the dove of something or other but I can't think of what. With your Eyetalian name I got out the geography and looked up some Eyetalian towns but it all sounded too much like the Eyetalian Nightingale and that old warhorse has worn out the Eyetalian shindig all through the West."

"But I'm not really Eyetalian," said Mademoiselle. "My real name is Bridget Moore. Mademoiselle La Belle da Ponte is just made up."

"Irish," said Madge. "Well, that's just wonderful. That gives me a whole lot of new ideas." She tilted her head to one side speculatively, "Let's see! . . . Blarney! . . . That's no good. The Dove of Cork . . . no, that's no good . . . sounds like a bottle stopper. The Dove of Dublin. . . . No." Then a look of inspiration came into her eyes. "I've got it! The Dove of Tralee! How's that? Mademoiselle Bridget Moore, The Dove of Tralee! How do you like that?"

"It sounds all right," said Bridget.

"That's it! The Dove of Tralee. It fits right in with bein' a virgin and refined. I can see it now, out in front—'The Dove of Tralee!'"

Then the door opened and the old porter came in bearing a tray weighted down with food—a bowl of fruit, creamed chicken, toast, waffles, potatoes, pie, a bottle of wine and coffee. It was, at that moment, the most wonderful of sights. As the fragrance of the food reached Bridget's nostrils she thought suddenly that she would faint before she could attack it.

"We'll go up to Denver tomorrow," said Madge, "and get some clothes for you. You can begin singing next Monday. That suit you?"

"Yes," said Bridget, between bites of creamed chicken.

"The Dove of Tralee!" said Madge, "The Dove of Tralee! That's it."

Mr. Wentworth Talmadge, the Governor, was as Ellie-May believed, a poor thing and no more than a tool of P.J. and one or two other less rich and powerful individuals of the state. He was a graduate of Harvard, tall and thin with drooping mustaches and sidewhiskers, which gave him a look of weak distinction among the rougher citizens of the frontier, and he made a point of developing the distinctive quality of his looks, since indeed he had little else to commend him. This made him pompous without the pouter-pigeon look which should go with pompousness. He wore high "gates ajar" collars which always stood reluctantly away from his long, thin neck and prominent Adam's apple. With the high collars went a long, full-skirted black Prince Albert coat. He had a gift of elegant speech and elaborate phrases which impressed the frontiersmen even more than his appearance. But with all these things he lacked both brains and character. He was but a hollow vessel periodically filled with the substance of P.J.'s plots and ambitions.

He had been summoned posthaste from Denver on the day after P.J. received the telegram. It was notable that P.J. did not go to the Governor; the Governor came to him.

The telegram had created, as if it were a focal point, a curious effect on P.J. It was as if it drew together and crystallized the doubts, rumors and suspicions which had been creeping over him, despite his boldness and conceit, for a long time. Largely speaking, they were the same rumors and intimations of which Ellie-May had been aware.

But the visit of the Governor only depressed him. The tall, thin Mr. Talmadge, who had always carried out orders without doubts or misgivings now seemed in the face of possible crisis a poor thing, empty as a hollow reed growing along Sauter's Creek. Not only did he fail to have any ideas about what to do; he didn't even seem to know what was going on. And worst of all he bored P.J. who in his great vitality was not easily bored. And P.J. found suddenly that he had nowhere to turn. He did not trust his fellow conspirators and Madge never had any ideas but those based upon direct action and violence. Blackie, Buck and Shorty were no good at all. Dick might have been some use but he seemed to be a nincompoop and didn't know anything about politics and anyway he had run away, at least for the time being. On the whole horizon, there remained, as far as he could see, only Ellie-May . . . good old Ellie-May. Sometimes she had more sense than you gave her credit for.

About four in the afternoon of the Governor's visit P.J. decided that he couldn't stand any more of Mr. Wentworth Talmadge's tired and empty conversation or even of his undiluted presence. There was no way of getting rid of him until the following day, so he sent down word to Madge to fix something up for supper about eight o'clock. Just one other girl for the Governor. All they wanted was a quiet evening—champagne, Puget Sound crab, some thick steaks and brandy.

So when Mademoiselle returned from visiting the Professor, whom she found in exactly the condition described by Madge and Mrs. Birdwell (unconscious but resting peacefully in the care of a gigantic Irish nurse), she found Madge already in the Rose Petal Room with one of the ball dresses made by Millie Hirshbein for the role of Violetta laid out on the bed.

"It's a little old-fashioned," she said, "but you look wonderful in it. It'll be a surprise in these times." Then in a bustling mood, she added, "Get out of your clothes and I'll fix up your hair. I took a course in hair-dressing once. Aunt Etta wanted it. She thought a girl ought to be able to earn her own living. I never finished the course but I've done all right supporting myself without it."

As she spoke Mademoiselle noticed that on a silver tray on the dressing table there was laid out a whole array of articles for "enhancing beauty"—a rouge pot, rice powder, Eau de Cologne and a bottle of perfume so voluptuous and heavy of scent that Mademoiselle could smell it halfway across the room before it was opened. As she smelled it, the voice inside said firmly, "But I won't give in! I won't give in!"

"We'll have to keep on the move," said Madge. "P.J. doesn't like to be kept waiting." And then as a kind of afterthought she added, "Not that it matters."

So to the distant accompaniment of the bawdy music which indicated that "butt-shaking" was in progress belowstairs, the two women went to work and a few minutes past eight Mademoiselle was ready. Before leaving the room she stood for a moment turning her head slowly to regard her reflection from all the angles revealed by the endless mirrors. And for a moment she was weakened by the sight of herself. Maybe after all, this virtue business wasn't all it was cracked up to be. . . .

But Madge interrupted her thoughts. "Come on, honey! We mustn't keep the gentlemen waiting!"

It wasn't a very merry evening. So far as the Governor was concerned any gal, as Madge remarked later, was safe as a church. He had never been the amorous type and whatever passion he may have known was long since withered at the source by thirty years of married life with a woman who considered that such things were beneath contempt.

In the Gold Room with the Turkish cosy corner, a table covered by a damask cloth had been set up with an immense and extravagant heap of fruit—melons, peaches and plums, piled in a huge silver epergne. Champagne stood in a silver bucket filled with ice from the great glacier. Then the food came on. It was a meal such as Mademoiselle had never seen before, beginning with turtle soup, followed by crab ravigote, followed by pineapple sherbert and then thick, juicy pink steaks, potato soufflé and new peas and a French salad, *bombe glacé,* coffee and brandy. It was nearly ten o'clock by the time the meal was finished. The Governor was not a heavy eater. As P.J., who had *two* thick steaks, observed scornfully, "He picks at his food like a puny quail."

The black mood of P.J. brightened gradually as one bottle after another of champagne disappeared. And as he brightened, Mademoiselle noticed that a certain light came into his eyes, a light with which she was familiar through long experience. It was the kind of light which flickered and glowed each time he looked in her direction. And about the middle of the meal Bridget noticed that she was not the only one aware of that light. Madge, a woman far more experienced than herself, was aware of it too and Bridget thought, "Here goes everything! Here's where I get thrown out!"

When dinner was finished they went out on the balcony overlooking the gambling floor and the stage and sat there watching the entertainment while P.J. and Madge drank more brandy. It was then that Mademoiselle became aware of a gentle, tentative touch of a foot upon her own silver slippers. Thinking it an accident, she withdrew her foot but after a little while, the pressure was renewed and she withdrew a little farther, suspicious now that the pressure was not an accident. She could not believe the Governor guilty of such tactics. In any case he was turned away from her and was watching the prancing chorus of girls. Then she observed P.J. slipping a little lower in his chair and even though her feet were withdrawn as far as possible, the pressure was renewed

It was Madge who put an end to the campaign of foot seduction. In a fierce whisper, she said, "Sit up, P.J.! I know what you're slumping down for."

The situation might have been disagreeable but for the fact that their attention was attracted by the sound of heavy breathing and as they turned toward the sound they discovered that the Governor had fallen sound asleep while watching the girls.

P.J. muttered, "He never could drink anything. Better send him home."

So he shook the Governor and said, "Better get up the hill, Governor, and get some sleep."

Then they went back to the gold sitting room and P.J. pressed the Governor's hat and stick into his hand and sent him, dazed but still capable of locomotion, down the covered outside stairway.

When he had gone Madge turned to Mademoiselle. "Better go to bed, honey. I'm going to stay up a little longer. P.J. and I have got some business to talk over."

When Bridget had gone a remarkable scene took place in the Gold Room.

First Madge said in a commanding voice, "Unbutton the back of my dress!"

While P.J.'s big, bear-like hands were engaged in this operation she said, "You leave that girl alone!"

"I didn't do nothin'," said P.J., sullenly.

"Now loosen them corset strings," commanded Madge.

As he obeyed, she said, "That girl is something special and I want you to get that into your head. She ain't no floozy! She's an artiste!"

P.J. grunted. The corset strings gave way, the figure expanded to its natural lavish proportions and the ample bosom fell about five inches. It was a little like the air going out of a balloon. But the spirit remained, and Madge said, "When men your age begin going for the young ones, it's the beginning of the end."

She retired to the adjoining bedroom and returned, minus ball-gown and corset, clad in a flowered kimono bordered with pink maribou which matched the maribou on the slippers.

"I got a special career planned out for that girl. She's got looks and talent and some day she's gonna make a rich marriage if I can steer things right." P.J. didn't answer; he was still brooding sullenly over her remark about "a man of your age." Age, hell! He'd never thought about age.

Madge poured herself a fresh glass of champagne. "I ain't jealous, you understand. I just can't see you makin' a fool of yourself." He still sulked and suddenly she made a strange remark. "I had a baby that died when she was about four years old. If she'd have lived she'd be the same age as Mademoiselle."

The thought seemed to soften her and she rose and crossed over to him. She touched him on the shoulder with a gesture of affection that was almost shy. "Neither of us is gettin' any younger. I got an idea you'd better attend to your knittin' until after election. If they took it into their heads to clean up the state neither of us would be in very good shape."

In the morning when Mademoiselle was dressed she went into the Gold Room to find Madge, but Madge wasn't up yet. In her place the old porter was at work painfully and carefully restoring the spears and shields and Cashmere shawls and the pampas grass to the original pattern of the collapsed cosy corner. Two gold chairs were overturned and the table pushed against the wall.

"What happened?" asked Bridget.

"It's P.J. and the Boss," the old man said. "They kind of have disagreements now and then. It used to take me a long time to get the cosy corner together again but I've kinda got the knack of it now."

But the next day there arrived two dozen roses by the train from Denver addressed to Mademoiselle da Ponte. Inside was a card on which was written "P. J. Meaney." When Mademoiselle showed them to Madge with the card, Madge said, "Why, the ornery old bastard!" And then on second thought she said, "Maybe he meant to apologize." Only she knew that he never apologized for anything and that it would never occur to him to do so.

When Dick left the corral, he turned the Pinto up the narrow road that led past the mine where the day before he had had the narrow

[193]

escape from the rocks. But it was dark now and there wasn't much danger even by the light of the moon that was coming up slowly behind the mountains on the opposite valley. As a boy in the saddle he had known every inch of the road and of the rough trail into which it turned as it petered out high above Silver City. From then on the trail led down again into the canyon and then alongside a rushing stream for a distance of twenty miles, climbing slowly all the time until with a sharp ascent it followed a crevasse in the canyon walls to come out finally upon a high grazing plateau where one of P.J.'s great herds pastured all during the summer months. Here the trail followed a small, clear stream that ran from pond to pond carved out among the rocks and the rich, red volcanic soil.

The horse knew his way even when the road turned from a road into a narrow trail. Dick gave him his head and sat back in the saddle as the moon rose and turned the rocks and running water and the pine trees to silver with deep black shadows. High up the air was cool and brilliantly clear and as he slipped down the steep side of the mountain on the other side of the high saddle, it seemed to flow, cool and refreshing, like the water itself down the deep valley.

The shoulder where the rock had struck really pained him now. Each time the Pinto slipped on the rocky path, a paroxysm of pain shot down one side of his body. Between the painful jolts he fell to thinking again about the miners and why they had tried to kill him. It was a good trick. If one of the rocks had cracked open his skull, he might have died there on the road and no one would have known what happened. They would simply say that he had been killed by a rock fall. It happened often enough.

The idea of killing shocked him. He thought suddenly that things must have gotten much worse since he left Silver City as a boy of sixteen. He knew that the town was worse, that it had grown bigger and dirtier, bawdier and noisier—a Babylon in the wilderness, and a wilderness of almost incredible beauty and grandeur. It was as if man himself were a corruption, and he remembered Ellie-May's observation —"Where every prospect pleases and only man is vile."

He was certain that he had done the right thing by running away. For a long time he had been restless and at times he had come close to a willingness to compromise, join P.J. in his corruption and become a part of Silver City and of that kingdom over which P.J. ruled as a despot. Once or twice he had been almost willing to sink to the brutish level of Buck, Shorty and Blackie.

Maybe, he thought, it was a good thing that Bridget had called him names and made him lose his temper. He tried to speculate what would have happened if it had gone the other way; if her performance had been a great success; if he had proposed and she had accepted him and he'd married and settled down in Silver City. It might have been awful. Now by running away he was going to have time to think and get things straight. And as he rode, the old doubts kept returning— why he seemed so different from Buck and Shorty and Blackie and even Eudora.

Then he was aware, as he followed the trail along the winding water, that overhead the moon was slipping down the other side of the sky and was turning pale and that high above him the top walls of the canyon were taking on a faint glow of pink. It was an unreal beauty like the description of Heaven in the Book of Revelations and he thought, "This is where I belong—high up here in the mountains." He didn't want a life like that of London or New York or Denver and certainly he did not want the life of Silver City.

Then as the light increased and the surface of the rushing stream turned pink and silver, he pulled up the pony, got down and led him to an open, shallow break between the boulders where the pony could drink. Upstream he knelt and put his lips to the clear, cold water and when he had drunk his fill, the impulse came suddenly to him to bathe in the crystal water. It might help the feverish pain in his shoulder.

So there in the deep canyon he turned the Pinto loose and stripped off his clothes and plunged into the deep pool. The water was icy but after the first shock it seemed pleasant enough. When he came out he dried himself with his shirt and slowly a glow seemed to steal over him and with it a reluctance to dress again and go on his way. He was proud of his body. It was straight, muscular and in the rising morning light, very white, almost like marble. As he lay there on the sand with his head thrown back he saw something moving high up in the pink light that bathed the wall of the canyon on the opposite side of the stream. Lying very still he saw that it was a flock of mountain goats, a big buck, three does and three half-grown kids. Slowly they picked their way from ledge to ledge, dropping downward across the face of the brilliantly colored precipice. The big buck went first, picking the way and after him followed the three ewes, each with her kid just behind her.

The chill of the morning air began to steal over him but he remained quiet until the little herd of goats had turned past a shoulder of the rock into a crevasse which opened to the peaks beyond. Then slowly he rose and put on his clothes, caught the Pinto and climbed aboard. The animal, by instinct, turned into the trail which led toward the upward end of the canyon and into the high Savannahs where the cattle ranged.

He was aware that he had experienced a moment of almost pure happiness in which, somehow, he had lost himself and all that troubled him in the vast beauty of the mountains. Then, he knew a sudden loneliness and understood that if there had been someone with him to share his satisfaction, the moment would have been one of complete fulfillment, and he found himself thinking of the girl who had locked the door in his face. It was not, he saw clearly now, that the trouble, the quick anger, the regrets had anything whatever to do either with her or himself; it was all the complications of life itself that lay between them, complications with roots which ran deep into the pasts of both of them, complications which had to do with P.J. and the Professor and his own brothers and the "Eyetalian Nightingale" and Signor Malatesta. If all these things could be uprooted, if both of them could tear themselves free, everything would have been easy and different.

But how to do it? How to be sure that he was not deluding himself? How to escape from all the complications and the weight of all the other circumstances and people? He was running away but he would have to come back one day. Up here in the mountains it might be that he could find that freedom. At least he could think clearly, without all the other things crowding in upon him. And presently, as the Pinto climbed out of the canyon on to the great plateau, he began to understand a little why his own nature was so complicated and why in time of action he became paralyzed. He should, perhaps, never have gone away from Silver City to the East and to England where he had learned so much that his father and brothers did not know or understand and never could know. If he had not gone away he would perhaps be happy and at peace with his surroundings, content as the others were with a simple existence, concerned only with the physical facts of living—with eating, carousing, whoring around, so profoundly unconcerned with the things which troubled him that they were completely unaware of their existence. In the case of the girl, they would have made a direct and brutal attack to get what they wanted and if they failed would simply have found quick physical compromise and consolation elsewhere. They wouldn't feel any pity or try to understand her. In reality love would have nothing to do with the whole affair. And perhaps they were right. Perhaps there was a greater physical and even a greater spritual happiness to be found in the direction of their physical approach. Perhaps that was exactly what a girl like that desired. Perhaps he himself was just a plain damned fool!

The sun had risen higher by now and the mountain chill had gone out of the air. On the great plain that spread out all about, the level pasture lay a foot or two high. As the warmth increased the scent of the mountain plants came to him in waves—the smell of the grasses, the lupines, the small creeping plants. Once he passed a low pool bordered by bullrushes and wild flag and a great blue heron flew up matching the grey-blue of the sky itself so that as it flew off it merged into the color and became invisible save for the blurred movement of the great grey-blue wings. And once again his spirits rose, buoyed by the physical animal pleasure of the warmth, the perfume, the color of the vast plain.

Half-heartedly he had wished that he would encounter one of the great herds but now the desire was gone in this new sense of belonging here on the high plateau, of being actually a *part* of the whole thing, of the grasses and mountain wild flowers, the sudden glimpse of the agile goats, the splendor of the canyon under the rising sun. Once or twice he had wished that he had brought Cecil with him, but that desire vanished too in the knowledge that Cecil would only have admired all of these things extravagantly in an objective, bookish way without ever really understanding them or being a part of them. He knew well enough by now that all Cecil's extravagant admiration for this new country and his valiant efforts to become a part of it were both superficial and a little ridiculous. He might be happy here, happier

[197]

than he had ever been in grey, compact, crowded, history-burdened England but he would never really belong as somehow the simplest, drawling, ignorant cowhand belonged.

It was nearly evening when he came in sight of his destination. He turned off the main trail near a small lake reflecting the brilliant blue of the sky. The side trail leading toward the big grove of trees was nearly grown over and as the pony's feet trod the grasses and wild flowers, their fragrance rose rich and heavy in the heat of the late afternoon.

And presently on the edge of the woods the outline of the cabin itself became visible, small, low, grey like the trunks of the trees all about it.

The cabin was what Ellie-May called the cottage, where in the past she had taken refuge again and again, where she had never permitted P.J. or any of the others to come, and as he rode toward it, he suddenly understood what he had never understood, that the place had been necessary to her if she were to go on being P.J.'s wife and live the life of the Castle and go on being the mother of Blackie, Shorty, Buck and Eudora. And he understood that he had fled to it for the same reasons which had driven his mother there when life became intolerable. She was, he knew, a simple woman who did not talk of such things nor even perhaps consider them very clearly. At least she never gave any sign. He had come to understand her lately as he had never understood her before—that by clinging with desperation to the small things like the sewing machine and the window boxes and her friendship for Millie Hirshbein, by fleeing to the cottage, she had managed to preserve herself and the good values of her own life and to escape the blindness, the ambition, the greed and the grossness of all the others. It was thus she had managed to save her soul. She knew, as none of the others ever knew or ever would know, the sterile emptiness of P.J. and his glittering life, the small things like the fragile and touching loneliness of the bonds that held together people like the Professor and Bridget, the pathetic refuge of Eudora in imaginary invalidism when her pride had been hurt. She understood perhaps even the animalism of poor, stupid Blackie and the odd long-standing relationship between P.J. and Madge which would have humiliated most women but oddly enough did not appear to touch her. Again it occurred to

[198]

him that perhaps the small, withered woman, whom he had taken for granted for so long, really possessed greatness.

The doors and windows of the cabin were boarded up, just as Ellie-May and Esau had left them a year earlier. Grass and weeds, spindly in the thick shade of the dark pines, had grown up around the steps and brilliant green moss grew thick upon the roof.

He lifted off the saddlebag, unsaddled the pony, hobbled it and turned it loose by the spring, and then spent the rest of the afternoon taking the planks from the doors and the windows and chopping wood for the kitchen fire. As he worked, the squirrels watched him, flirting in and out of the speckled sunlight on the dark branches of the pines. And as he worked it struck him as odd that nobody had molested the cabin, pried loose the planks and rifled it of the pans and dishes that were so often precious to cowhands and prospectors and to solitary wanderers who drifted across the high plateau in their escape from civilization and the law. Perhaps, he thought, it was because they knew it was Ellie-May's cabin. They knew her—all of them—in Silver City and throughout all the mountain country.

Tomorrow, he reflected, he would have to ride down the steep mountain on the far side of the plateau to buy supplies at the trading-post in Meeker's Gulch. In his quick escape he had brought only enough for a day or two. He did not know how long he would stay up here alone in the wilderness, but he knew that unless something violent happened which would change everything, he would stay until he found himself.

Down in Silver City the campaign was getting under way and as it developed old P.J. became slowly aware of more and more small signs and omens he had never noticed before. Henry Caldwell was nominated as Democratic candidate but this, in itself, did not alarm him, since it was a foregone conclusion. It wasn't even that he was afraid of Henry. It was the little things.

They began with the abrupt departure of Mr. Wright and Mr. Laidlaw and their haste to get back to Denver leaving their work and negotiations only half-finished. They departed almost without excuse or at least an excuse that was so flimsy as to be insulting. What had they discovered? What did they know? Had it been that they believed that they were backing the wrong horse and that P.J.'s day was finished? They wanted loans and concessions, ranch land and mines and rights of way to railroads. For nearly twenty years P.J. had been pretty well able to deliver these things. They wanted to control and exploit the riches of the incredibly rich new country. And now suddenly they seemed to have lost interest.

But the real trouble was that as the days and weeks passed it became clear that they were not losing interest; they were merely transferring it. They didn't go back to the East but remained in Denver; they had been seeing Henry Caldwell and the men on the other side.

Like a great black spider, P.J. sulked, plotting, in his office in the Castle. He considered abandoning that sickly fool governor and joining forces with Henry, but two elements made that impossible. One was the fact that he would have to abandon the whole machinery of his organization; the other, far more important, was that he knew there was no chance whatever of trying to strike a bargain with Henry. Henry was a damned incorruptible. He himself knew, better than anyone, what high-falutin' ideas Henry had about honesty and about something he called "the people's rights."

Down in the town there were other signs and omens. He had news of meetings and lately there had appeared placards in the town, here and there on walls and telegraph poles and buildings which read, "Give Colorado back to the people!" When he heard this P.J. spat into his big silver-plated spittoon and said, "The people! Hell! The people haven't got enough sense to run anything."

He received constant reports from henchmen who came from all parts of the state, from ranches, from mining towns, from Denver, but what they told him, however cheering, did not cheer him. His outfit was too old, and like all political organizations it had grown smug and lazy. His henchmen only told him what he wanted to hear. In his shrewdness he knew that they were afraid to tell him any bad news, even if they believed it.

Worst of all he couldn't get directly into the fight himself. If he himself had been the candidate instead of that milk toast Wentworth Talmadge, he could have gone out over the state and made speeches and bellowed and raised hell, but he couldn't. He had to sit back and let Talmadge, with his high-falutin' phrases and pompous manners carry the campaign. If P.J. so much as opened his mouth, the first cry of the opposition would be, "Who's running for governor, Wentworth Talmadge or P. J. Meaney?" He couldn't do anything but sit back and worry and as a last resort—lay plans to steal the election.

But worst of all there came into his mind for the first time, doubts which had never troubled him in all the days of his power. They were doubts about things he had done in the past and things which he was doing at the moment. If he lost power, the others might jump on him. It was just possible that he might end up in jail.

In the midst of these doubts there came an afternoon when he thought again, "Maybe I'd better have a talk with Ellie-May."

In the beginning when they were living from hand to mouth with the family growing all the time, it was Ellie-May who had urged him to give up the fly-by-night existence of a drummer and go out to the new country where there were big opportunities for any man willing to work. Grudgingly, he admitted to himself that but for Ellie-May he wouldn't be a millionaire or sitting in this Castle. But of course, it wasn't just Ellie-May who had made him rich and powerful. It was his own energy and smartness. Nevertheless. . . .

And so one afternoon he went along the hall and opened the door to Ellie-May's suite.

He found her watering the window boxes, a little sadly, because the early mountain frosts would finish off her blooms before many days more.

He said, "Busy, Ellie-May?"

"Not especially," she answered, continuing her task.

"Well, set down for a minute. I want to talk about something."

"Very well." She put the watering can on the sewing machine and stood there looking at him.

"Set down," he repeated. "I've got a lot to say."

She sat down, a small, thin figure with a face like one of her own flowers which had passed its prime.

"It's about this here election."

"Yes," said Ellie-May.

"It ain't goin' right."

"Yes," said Ellie-May, "I'd kinda noticed that."

"I thought maybe you'd have some ideas."

"Could be," said Ellie-May. "Tell me about it."

Ponderously and with great difficulty, P.J. related to her all the long record of his doubts and misgivings. While she listened she rocked gently in the patent rocker covered with red plush, interrupting only to say "yes" now and then. When he had slowed down a little, she asked, "Is that all?"

"Yes . . . I guess so."

She looked out of the window for a moment and then turning back to him she said, "You know, P.J., long ago in McGuffey's Reader I read a story called 'The Frog Who Would Be An Ox.' It was about a bullfrog in a pasture beside a little pond. He was a great big bull-frog in a little pond but he got envious of the ox that came down every day to drink. He was a big ox and in spite of being a big bull-frog, the frog had to get out of the ox's way so he wouldn't get squashed. So the bullfrog decided he'd blow himself up till he was as big as the ox and he blew and blew and blew and suddenly he busted right open and when it was all over there was nothin' but a frog skin hanging off the lower branches of the willow tree beside the pond."

As she finished speaking, P.J. who was not one to understand parables or fables, sat for a moment looking at her in bewilderment. She did not help him and presently he said, "You mean Henry Caldwell is the bullfrog?"

"No," said Ellie-May, "I mean *you* are."

"Me! Why I'm the ox. Henry's nothing but a squirt!"

"Then what are you worryin' about?"

"It's ain't that I'm afraid of Henry Caldwell."

"No! But you're kinda skeered about all your skulduggery catchin' up with you. And you're just gettin' too big for your skin."

P.J. considered this ponderously for a moment and she added, "You're already too big for your skin, P.J. You ain't a big enough man to stand in the shoes you're a-wearin'."

"I'll be goddamned if I know what you're talkin' about, Ellie-May. I didn't come in here to get no Bible lesson."

"Well, if you're so dumb you can't see, I'll tell you right out. You're a smart man—shrewd-like, but you haven't got any real brains and you're unprincipled. If you was really smart you could have been a

[202]

great man but all you are really is a combination of that bullfrog and a skunk."

P.J.'s face grew purple and he began to sputter but Ellie-May said, "Now you shut up and let me talk. That's what you came in here for and you're a-goin' to listen. I never talked to you hard-like but once or twice in my life and this here is goin' to be the third time." She paused for breath and then continued. "If you were a really big man you could have done a lotta things for this state and the people in it."

Then he burst out, "Who's developed this state more than I have, I'd like to know?"

"You haven't developed anything. All you did was exploit." He looked puzzled and she said, "Exploit means when somebody takes everything and gives nothin' back. That's what you been doin' all your life and the people are gettin' kinda sick of it."

The speech seemed to make a faint impression on him and seeing her advantage, Ellie-May pressed forward. "Excuse the language, but what the hell do you want more than you got? You've got millions. You've got power. It's about time you relaxed. What do you care if Henry Caldwell is elected and you don't run things any more?"

P.J. looked puzzled and said in a feeble voice, "What would I do?"

"You've got enough to do just managin' what you've got already. You're gettin' old, P.J., and don't try to palaver me about feelin' just as young as you felt when you was eighteen. The night the Opry blew up you came awful near to havin' a stroke. And now you're runnin' after that girl down at Madge's. If that ain't a sign of gettin' old, I don't know what is . . . you telegraphin' over the railroad wire to Denver for flowers—as if you thought Madge and I wouldn't find out. I suppose you call it romance." She clucked her tongue. "The Dove of Tralee! A fine dove with an old vulture like you a-swoopin' down on her—competin' with his own sons. Oh, I heard about Buck hangin' around and that Blackie a-chargin' down from the sheep range every two or three weeks like a ruttin' goat. Some night they'll be carryin' you up hill on a stretcher. Why don't you stick to Madge? I've never mentioned her name all these years. She's a smart woman. She can take care of you. I haven't got anything special against Madge. She minds her own business and I know a man like you has got to run around. I always knew it. Just stick to Madge!"

Now that she was under way, things began to pour out of her. "There's some things I kinda admire about you, P.J., or I wouldn't still be here livin' in this monument. It ain't a home. It's a mausoleum. Some day somebody is goin' to have to look after you. Mebbe you'll be lyin' flat on your back, helpless. I wouldn't be stickin' around here if there wasn't some things I like and some things I remember about you from long ago. I've done my duty and kept things goin' when sometimes they would have blown up but it's comin' to the time when I need a rest and when you do too, and if you haven't got enough sense to see what's ahead, I have. I was always for you up to the time you split up with Henry and from then on I've just kinda let you go your own bull-headed way, but it looks to me as if mebbe I'd have to take over again now that you're gettin' old and childish."

"Old and childish," repeated P.J. in indignation. "Why, I never. . . ."

"I know," said Ellie-May. "You keep trying to kid yourself."

"Is that all you've got to say? If it hadn't been for me you might still be livin' in a boarding house."

"And maybe a good thing too. You and your Castle! Why, I'd like to see the whole damned thing burn up. And that ain't all I got to say. There's something else. It's that I'm against you in this here election and I hope you get licked for your own good before you get shot or end up in jail. And go ahead and order me out of your fancy Castle. I'd get out like a shot. Why, you couldn't see me for dust!"

The purple had gone out of P.J.'s face by now. When she had finished he sat there for a moment. Then he said, "Is that all you got to say?"

"No, but it'll do for the present."

"Well, it ain't much help."

"No, but it's for your own good. Are you still gonna worry about this here election?"

"What do you want I should do? Lie down and quit?"

"No, I didn't expect anything like that, but when you get beat, don't come and cry to me. The people of Colorado want their state back."

P.J. perked up at this and asked, "Where did you hear that?"

"Why, it's wrote all over town. It's wrote all over the State of Colorado and Henry is gonna give it back to them."

"The goddam squirt!" said P.J.

Quietly, Ellie-May said, "I just wanted you to know I was against you."

"Well, you can't do nothin'."

Ellie-May *might* have answered that one but she chose not to. She merely thought about the little black book with the record of his skulduggeries over a period of ten years carefully set down with dates, names and details.

Ellie-May rose and picked up the watering can. "That's all, P.J., I just wanted you to know."

"A fine thing when a man can't count on his wife."

"A fine thing when a wife can't count on her husband. You've taken hold of the wrong end of the stick, P.J."

Then he went out slamming the door and Ellie-May returned to watering her flowers.

When she had finished she sat down at the desk and got out a piece of paper and pen and started writing a letter to Dick. She had been writing him regularly but she had found that there wasn't much to say beyond the gossip and that Eudora had forgot all about being an invalid and put away her telescope and had given up sending texts to the prisoners altogether and that she and Cecil seemed to be getting on all right. She had avoided writing anything about Mademoiselle on the principle that it was better to let sleeping dogs lie.

While it was fresh in her mind, she wrote him all about the scene with P.J., saying, "If it can be done, I'm going to see that he's licked. The whole thing has gone far enough. It don't make sense any more."

Near the end of the letter she weakened and wrote, "As to that girl, Mademoiselle, she's reigning like a Queen at the El Dorado. Buck is after her now and even your Pa is off the rails like a Longhorn bull. It looks like she's found the place where she belongs."

At the end of the letter she wrote, "If Henry Caldwell turns up tell him to get in touch with me."

Then she sealed the letter, put on a hat and went down to the corral where she gave it to one of the Indian boys (one she suspected was a by-blow of Buck's) and told him to deliver it to the cottage.

On the high plateau the first signs of distant winter had begun to appear. In the morning there was a fresh white rim of frost over the meadows and along the edge of the woods which sheltered the cottage. The herds had begun to move in slowly toward the trails that led downward to the lower meadows, away from the danger of the sudden blizzards which sometimes swept down overnight covering the rich grasses and half-burying the cattle. Like all else in that great western country, the weather, on a vast scale, was spectacular, violent and unpredictable.

Young Dick took part in the vast round-up, moving with the cowhands a little lower down with each day's grazing, sometimes driving the bellowing herd even after darkness had fallen. He was happy again, riding the quick, good-tempered little Pinto across the great meadows under the brilliant autumn sun. It was as if he had gone back again to his boyhood where there were no complications regarding the future, no devouring restlessness, no uncertainty but only the bright, clear days filled with the satisfaction of hard physical work in the saddle followed by the brilliant night when, rolled up in a blanket, he slept on a bed of fragrant grass and lupines beneath the stars.

He knew most of the cowhands from his boyhood and liked them because they led hard simple lives high up on the range varied only by the wild and violent bouts of dissipation on those occasions when they went into Silver City. At first he seemed a little strange to them with his different way of speaking but presently they forgave him his correct grammar and the fact that when he spoke he did not drawl and whine as they did.

But even after they had gotten used to each other again, a remote indefinable strangeness remained which he did not come to understand until nearly three weeks had passed. He noticed it most of all in the evenings when they set up camp. Again and again it happened that when he approached a group of cowhands talking together, they would suddenly fall silent or, quite obviously, change from what they had been talking about to wander awkwardly and haltingly into new fields of conversation. And then one night he discovered the reason for their behavior and for that strangeness which marred somehow the full realization of comradeship.

He had been sitting alone behind the cook wagon, leaning against a flour barrel where he was hidden from view, smoking and thinking again about what he was to do with his life. Beyond the wagon five cowhands were seated about the fire talking. At first he had not been aware of their conversation and then slowly it began to filter through to his consciousness.

They were talking about P.J.

One of them said, "The kid is all right. It isn't his fault that he has a sonofabitch for a father."

Then another said, "The kid sure is different from the rest of the family. I wouldn't give a plugged nickel for the lot of 'em . . . except maybe for the old woman."

"The kid's like her."

There was a silence and then a new voice entered the talk. "If you ask me, I'd say the kid ain't any relation to old P.J. I've heard once or twice that he's really Henry Caldwell's kid."

"Could be," said a deep voice. "It's funny the way P.J. and Henry broke up all of a sudden."

"It didn't need nothin' like that to break 'em up. Henry Caldwell just couldn't stomach the old bastard any longer."

Then a silence and a voice said, "Someday, somebody is going to plug the old man. When I went down to get fresh grub, I heered that he was chasin' the new singer they got at Madge's place."

"I heered she is mighty pretty and that the old man ain't gonna get anywhere with her."

"Not unless he buys his way."

Then the voice of the man who had gone down for grub said, "That sonofabitch Buck is after her too."

There was a coarse laugh and a voice said, "I'd hate to be in her situation with them two after me."

"I heered that when she was living at the Grand Hotel, she emptied a bucket of slop over Blackie when he was tryin' to peek in her winder."

This raised another coarse laugh followed by a deep voice saying, "Well, she can put her shoes under my bed anytime only I reckon I ain't got the mazoola to pay for it."

The laugh subsided and a voice said, "Well, I heered that the one she really liked was the kid only he didn't show no interest and ran away up here to get away from her. Can you figure that? Runnin' away from a lollypaloozer like her. I hear Madge says that's how come she went to singin' at the El Dorado. She was broke and that old man she was travelin' with had a stroke and the kid wouldn't give her a play and she said, 'To hell with it.' "

In the darkness behind the barrel Dick rose very quietly and walked across the vast meadow. He had heard enough. He knew now what the strangeness was and why it existed. Why, the bastards! They were like a lot of old women gossiping at a sewing circle. He felt hot from head to foot with an impulse to go back and punch a couple of the gossipers, but he knew that by doing so he would only make himself ridiculous. But worst of all he knew that he was on the outside again, hopelessly on the outside, first because he was P.J.'s son and second because he didn't have the same coarse, direct approach to life of the cowhands seated around the fire. In their hearts they thought he was a damned fool. And this stuff about Henry Caldwell!

He walked for a long time, in a circle and presently out of the darkness, he came suddenly upon his own pony, hobbled and grazing. The pony wickered at sight of him, and then the impulse came to him. He unhobbled the pony and led him back toward the faint glow of the dying campfire. The place was silent now, the cowhands rolled in blankets, soundly asleep in the thick grass. He found his saddle and blanket, saddled the pony and fastened the bags behind the saddle, then climbed aboard and, looking at the starlit sky and the great snow-capped peaks lying to the south, found his bearings and turned the pony's head toward the distant cottage.

For three hours, he traced over and over in his mind all the things he had heard and out of them all the thing that troubled him most was what he had heard them saying about the girl. Worst of all he found that he hadn't escaped her at all. She was still there in his heart. He knew suddenly that the cowhands were right. He was a coward and a damned fool. He had run away from her and from everything. He hadn't solved anything at all; he couldn't go on forever living alone in that cottage like a hermit. As he rode, certain things became clear to him—that he could never go back to Silver City to live the rest of his life and that he had to do something about the girl before it was too late.

And presently the dark low mass of the woods which sheltered the cottage came into sight in the starlight exactly as he had calculated.

Then as he drew nearer he saw a light twinkling from among the trees. It came from a window of the cottage. At the edge of the trees he got down from the pony and threw the bridle rein over its neck. Then on foot he made his way through the trees until he reached the cottage itself. Cautiously he approached and looked in the window.

There seated in front of the fire smoking a pipe, sat Henry Caldwell. At sight of him Dick experienced a sudden feeling of having come home, of finding what he sought and needed most of all, and at the same time he *knew* deep inside and for the first time that what the voice had said in the darkness by the campfire was true. He had been a fool not to have seen it all along. And suddenly he was grateful to his mother and loved her more than he had ever loved her before.

PART V

MADGE'S PLAN FOR THE DOVE OF TRALEE HAD WORKED EXACTLY AS SHE HAD expected it to work. She raised the price of drinks, the take at the tables and all the other fees concerned with an establishment like the El Dorado and still the place was packed all night and most of the day. For a salary of fifty dollars paid to The Dove she was making two thousand dollars more a week.

It began with the cloud of rumors which had reached even the high range. The enthusiasm mounted on the famous Monday night when The Dove was unveiled to a house that packed the El Dorado to bursting. It was a tough audience filled with curiosity, for in that frontier world women, any kind of women, were objects of interest, and a new beauty in any community was likely to create mayhem, assault, shooting frays and every kind of disorder. And The Dove, tricked out shrewdly by Madge in demure clothes, was undeniably and by popular acclaim, a beauty. If she had been pretty enough to create excitement as she passed along Eudora Street in ordinary dun-colored clothes, she became dazzling on the stage of the El Dorado. Madge understood the game. The Dove was the demure type, however false the demureness may have been, and Madge played up the demureness.

On the opening night, after the chorus of "butt-swinging" girls and the middle-aged soubrette had finished their act (with little or no attention from the drunks and gamblers) Madge herself stepped onto the stage to a loud and fancy fanfare from the cornet player. With a showmanship which had made her the most successful "business woman" in the West, she had dressed herself in a plain black gown with a white fichu gathered modestly over the famous bosom. But for the brilliant gold hair and the somewhat battered face, she might have been mistaken for a distinguished governess or somebody's mother.

By the time the fanfare was finished, the attention of the drinkers and gamblers was directed full upon the soberly clad maternal figure in the spotlight. A hush, broken only by the mutterings of two or three drunks and the occasional tinkle of glasses at the bar, fell over the big room. Only one false note occurred when a drunk leaning on the bar called out, "Has somebody died, Madge?"

Madge waited until they threw him into the street and then in her deep, whisky voice she said, "Gentlemen!" There were a few self-conscious glances about the room and the audience gave its full attention.

"Gentlemen!" repeated Madge. "I have for you tonight a great surprise. As an added attraction to the entertainment provided by this establishment, I have engaged a new singer. She is Irish and known professionally as The Dove of Tralee. I have brought her here at great expense after a series of sensational engagements in New York, Boston, Baltimore, Philadelphia and Washington, *Dee Cee!*" Here Madge glanced down at the paper she held in her hand—a paper prepared earlier in the day by Cecil Chatsworthy in a union of his and Madge's best styles. "This is a new kind of entertainment for the El Dorado but one I am sure you will appreciate."

At this moment, Madge's eye caught sight of something in the audience which temporarily distracted her attention so violently that she was forced to glance at the paper and repeat herself. . . . "But one I am sure you gentlemen will appreciate. Considering the distinction of the singer and the great expense involved in bringing her here for your entertainment, I am sure that you will be willing for a moment to transfer your attention from the bar and the gaming tables to the stage." She paused and then said, "One more word. The Dove of Tralee is an artiste and will play no other part in the entertainment of this establishment!"

Once more she paused, "Gentlemen! I have the great honor to introduce The Dove of Tralee!"

With a final glance toward the audience and the sight which had startled her, she stepped into the wings and the orchestra struck up "Kathleen Mavourneen." After about ten bars, the curtains at the back of the stage parted and The Dove of Tralee, dressed in pale pink with a wreath of forget-me-nots in her hair, appeared.

For a moment there was a complete silence and when Mademoiselle moved down stage, there arose a tremendous sound of stamping, clapping, whistling and cheers. The Dove bowed again and again and then as the ovation died away, punctuated by an occasional shrill whistle or a rebel yell, she began to sing.

She sang well and prettily and she looked like a child, the very apotheosis of innocence and purity. The effect was, as Madge had calculated, sensational. Tears filled the eyes of the gamblers and cowhands and prospectors. Near the end of the song one Irishman, overcome, fell forward on the bar, upsetting his beer and buried his head in his arms, sobbing.

She then sang the "Sempre Libera" aria from *La Traviata* (just to show them after the fiasco at the Opera House) and followed this by "My Old Kentucky Home" which wrought havoc among the Kentuckians and finished with "The Harp That Once Through Tara's Halls."

The triumph was as great as the fiasco at the Opera House had been. She returned eight times to bow in response to the deafening ovation and after the eighth time Madge, standing in the wings, bustled her away upstairs to the Gold Room. She said, shrewdly, "I always say. Never satisfy 'em! Always make 'em come back for more."

Upstairs in the Gold Room, P.J. was waiting with champagne already opened to celebrate. They raised their glasses and drank to The Dove of Tralee! Then Madge turned to Mademoiselle and said, "Well, I guess you fixed that old hag of an Eyetalian Nightingale. Nobody with any sense'll ever dare put her on a stage again." She kissed the girl and said, "What did I tell you, honey? The opry ain't your forty. Let the fat old women sing them oprys."

And quickly she turned to P.J. and asked, "Did you see what I seen out there?"

"No, what?" asked P.J.

"I seen it plain as life. Eudora settin' at a table on the balcony along with Cecil."

P.J. put down his glass with such violence that it shattered against the surface of the table. "Eudora!" he bellowed, "in a place like this! My little daughter Eudora . . . I'll . . . I'll . . ."

He started toward the door, sputtering, but Madge stopped him at the door. "Wait a minute, P.J. . . . wait a minute! What are you goin' to do?"

"I'm gonna throw her right through the swingin' doors!"

"Now, listen," said Madge. "Calm down! You can beat up Blackie and throw him out but you can't do that to Eudora. Eudora's a lady. And anyway she'd be kind of hard to throw out. She's kind of hefty!"

He looked at her, the agitation subsiding a little. Madge continued, "You'd better have it out with her when you get home."

"I'll whale the daylights out of her!"

"Anything you want but not here, P.J. Eudora's a strong-minded woman. She ain't no delicate flower."

Again P.J. began sputtering, "I'll . . . Why, I'll . . ."

"Sit down and take another glass of champagne or you'll bust a blood vessel."

He followed her advice and she said, "Things are changin', P.J. Women is gettin' more independent." As she poured out the champagne, she added, "Why, in the East I hear women are even agitatin' to get the vote."

She was interrupted by a knock at the door and the old porter came in. "Sorry," he said, "but there's a lot of men wantin' to pay their respects to Mademoiselle."

"How many?" asked Madge.

"About fifteen or twenty."

"Just tell 'em Mademoiselle ain't here. Tell 'em she was overcome by the excitement and went home to rest." When he had gone out she turned and said in a voice acid with scorn, "Men! Men! They ain't got no artistic appreciation." Turning to Mademoiselle she said, "Now you go to bed and get some rest, honey."

As Mademoiselle went out of the room, Madge's eyes were on P.J. As she heard the door close, she said, "As for you, you get your mind back on the champagne. I ain't gonna have a property like that spoiled by no dirty gossip!"

In the Gold Room that night no amount of champagne had served to raise P.J.'s spirits. It seemed to him that Madge herself was slipping

[214]

away from him. She behaved as if she didn't need his protection or cooperation. Perhaps, he brooded, she was already feeling her way toward an alliance with the other side. It became suddenly clear to him how precious was his power. If it was lost he would have money but little else. And money in comparison with power didn't matter.

All this really lay behind the sudden explosion and the violence of his behavior over the discovery that his own daughter was sitting at a table in the El Dorado. Her behavior became simply one more betrayal of his authority. Tomorrow, he knew, all Silver City as well as the up-country would know that P.J.'s daughter Eudora was sitting in the El Dorado like a common trollop . . . his Eudora for whom he had named Eudora Street.

The sense of humiliation kept growing the longer he sat drinking with Madge and presently he put his glass down violently and said, "I'm going back to the Castle. If I can't whale her in public the way I whale the others, I'll whale her at home."

Madge only shrugged her shoulders. "Eudora," she said, "ain't no child. She's thirty-one years old."

"It's that damned Englishman with his fancy ways," he said, rising and picking up his hat. "I'll whale him too!"

"You got a better chance with him than with Eudora," said Madge. "She might whale you back!"

It was after one o'clock when Eudora and Cecil climbed the steps of the porte-cochere into the hall filled with armor, stuffed bears and potted palms. They let themselves in and were crossing the hall when P.J.'s stentorian call of "Eudora!" startled them. As they turned they saw him among the palms and bears at the doorway leading into the sitting room. His face was purple and his eyes bloodshot.

Eudora turned and said, "Yes, Pa?"

"I want to speak to both of you. Step into the sitting room."

They followed him and he said, "Sit down!"

They sat but P.J. remained standing. With his hands behind his back, he began pacing up and down. After a time he managed to say, "What were you doing at the El Dorado tonight?"

[215]

Eudora was expecting exactly what was coming and had prepared herself for it.

She said calmly, "I wanted to hear the new singer."

"Don't you know a lady doesn't go to such places?"

But Eudora had an answer for that one, "Whoever said I was a lady?"

"You're the daughter of P. J. Meaney!"

"That ain't no help," said Eudora, with a marked defiance in her voice.

"And I don't want any lip!"

"I'm not givin' you no lip, Pa. I'm talkin' facts. I'm old enough to take care of myself. I know what I want to do and I'm goin' to do it!"

"You're my daughter and you're still dependent on me."

Bluntly, Eudora said, "To hell with that stuff! Women ain't what they used to be. Why in the East they're wearin' pants and talkin' about votin'."

"That sort of woman ought to be horsewhipped. I've a mind to give you a horsewhipping myself."

Eudora looked at him with a queer glint in her eye, "You lay a hand on me and I'll bash you!"

The statement stopped him in his tracks. "Why . . . why . . . I'll" . . . But before he could find words, Eudora followed up her advantage, "You're gettin' to be an old man, Pa. Ef'n you get so mad, you're like to fall down in a fit."

Then he found words. They came tumbling out in a torrent. "I ain't as old as that and don't think I am. By Gawd, I'm still ruling this roost!"

Then Cecil who had watched until now with a kind of shaking awe tried to speak. His words came out high-pitched and shaken like that of a choir boy whose voice has begun to change. "But Mr. Meaney," he began.

With that P.J. plunged toward him like a bull aware that here was no challenge, here was something he could bowl over and trample. But Eudora was too quick for him. She took up a position between P.J. and Cecil.

"Ef'n you lay hand on him, I'll bash you . . . you big brute!"

Behind her, Cecil got out of his chair, as if uncertain whether to take flight or to get to his feet so that he might use Eudora as a shield. Being on his feet gave him the advantage of mobility. The sight of little Cecil avoiding him seemed to increase P.J.'s rage.

"Takin' my daughter to a place like the El Dorado! Why, you little piss-ant!"

"But Mr. Meaney . . ." began Cecil again.

"Shut up!" bellowed P.J.

"Let him speak, Pa," said Eudora.

"But Mr. Meaney, I didn't take Eudora there. She took me. She said she wanted to see what it was like and she said if you could go there she could too."

"Ef'n you'd been a man you'd have protected her innocence."

"Innocence, hell!" said Eudora. "Where do you think I've been for thirty-one years?"

Cecil was still peering from behind Eudora. "But Mr. Meaney," he began again.

"Let him speak, Pa," said Eudora. "He's got something to say."

"Well, say it!" bellowed P.J.

It came out of Cecil with a rush, almost before he himself was aware of it. "Eudora and I want to get married!"

"Married!" said P.J.

"Yes," said Eudora, "married! Is there anything funny about that?"

Then P.J. began to laugh and Cecil came out from behind Eudora. P.J. laughed and laughed.

"Married!" he kept saying, "Married!"

"I wish to ask your consent," said Cecil.

"Consent? You have my consent." In a rush the awareness that this was a marriage made in heaven came over him. It took care of Eudora for good. "Are you going to take her back to the Old Country?"

"No," said Cecil. "I'm going to stay here. I thought I might become a rancher."

"A rancher? Sure, I'll give you a ranch if that's what you want . . . for a wedding present."

"Thanks, Pa," said Eudora.

"Here," said P.J. "Let's shake on it!" He took Cecil's small hand in his own big paw and shook it violently. "Well! Well!" he said, "I'd never calculated on havin' a Limey for a son-in-law!" He stood back

[217]

and regarded Cecil critically. "Well!" he said, "Ef'n you're going to marry Eudora I guess it's up to you to keep her out of the El Dorado. And I wish you luck. Sometimes she can be as ornery as her brothers." He lighted a cigar and said, "I guess we'd better wake up your Ma and tell her."

"There ain't no need," said Eudora. "She knows it already. She knowed it was coming, all along!"

At the same moment Madge, in the Gold Room, had a visitor who was helping her drink up the champagne that P.J. hadn't finished. He had appeared a few minutes after P.J. had left, as if he had waited for the old tyrant to leave.

Buck was the best-looking of the Black Meaneys and probably the least ornery just as Blackie was the ugliest and the most ornery of the three brothers. He had the same darkness and hairiness that character-ized old P.J. and the two brothers but in him these characteristics were somehow refined and whittled down. His features were not quite as over-sized nor his hands quite so like the paws of a gorilla. Now and then his dark face was illumined by a grin in which there was a trace of charm. He was dressed now in the store clothes which he wore when he came into Silver City off the range—a black suit, a black ten-gallon hat, boots and a flowing black tie set against a liver-colored shirt.

It was the first time he had ever been permitted the intimacy of Madge's salon and he sat forward on the edge of a gilt chair, his feet raised on the toes to balance himself while he drank the champagne.

"I've come a-courtin'," he was saying, "in the proper sense. You understand, I want to marry that gal."

"She came in here a virgin and she's goin' out a virgin," said Madge, firmly.

"I ain't proposin' nothin' else," said Buck. "There's a lot I could offer her and when the old man kicks off there'll be a lot more."

"She's refined," said Madge, "and used to a luxurious life. She ain't no Indian squaw."

Buck smacked his lips and held out his glass to be refilled. "Ef'n it's that squaw you're a-worryin' about, I sent her back to the tribe. She was gettin' more and more bossy and I ain't the type of man to tolerate bossiness." He leaned forward confidentially, "You see, Madge, I'm thirty-five years old and it's gettin' time I settled down. Wimmin is scarce around here. I can't go up to Denver and pick one out. I ain't refined enough. And I ain't gonna marry just the first woman that comes along."

Madge didn't say anything. She was thinking. By now she suspected that the girl could take care of herself and handle someone like Buck. By the time he'd done his courtin' and won her, if he ever did, she herself would have got all the value there was out of The-Dove-of-Tralee angle. And after all Buck had a lot of money and there were worse men around lookin' for wives in a country where women were scarce. Anyway, the girl couldn't be so choosey and with the old Professor dying she couldn't run around alone and unprotected in this frontier country. Some ape, like Buck's brother, Blackie, might kidnap her. With P.J. gettin' along in years and liable to pop off at any time in one of his rages, it might be a good thing for herself to be in on the ground floor with his successor Buck.

All these things were going through her head before she said, "You understand, Buck, it's got to be a proper courtship—no pantin' or pawin'."

"Sure," said Buck, "I can be genteel when I have to be. What about bringin' her in and introducin' her?"

"No," said Madge, "not tonight. She's tired. Mebbe tomorrer night." He looked at Madge sharply. "What about the old man?" he asked.

"I can manage him," said Madge. "Only I'd keep out of his way if I was you."

"Some day the old man and me is gonna have a set-to." He ran his big hands through his long black hair. "And what about that elegant brother of mine?"

"Blackie?"

"No. Dick!"

"You don't need to worry about him."

"I ain't a-worryin' about him. I was just worryin' about gossip I heered."

"He's gone away . . . for good. It looks like."

"That ain't what I asked you. What I was askin' was what she felt about him."

Madge sighed. She was at heart a match-maker and she had been thinking that Dick would have been the perfect match. "I dunno," she said. "But it looks like he'd run out on her."

"We understand each other," said Buck, standing up.

"Yes," said Madge. "But no monkey-business, remember that."

"Sure!" said Buck. "No monkey-business!"

"In a lotta ways, you ain't exactly what a woman would call a catch."

"You don't know nothin' about that," said Buck.

"No," said Madge. "But I can guess!"

In the days that followed, the success of The Dove of Tralee continued unabated. The news of her presence at the El Dorado traveled rapidly and far into mining towns and sheep and cattle ranches. After the third night Madge no longer appeared, dressed discreetly as the headmistress of a lady's boarding academy, to introduce her latest attraction. It was no longer necesssary. Twice an evening, once at seven and once again at ten, The Dove of Tralee made her appearance, the gambling and drinking stopped, the few noisy drunks were ejected by popular action, and the audience wept into its beer over the sad songs and cheered over the trills and roulades of the fancier arias.

There was one element in the success which was missing from that of all other performers in the West. This was the element of curiosity based upon the legend of embattled virtue and virginity. A good many miners, prospectors, sheepherders and cowhands came for the first time to witness the spectacle of virtue existing undefiled in the midst of vice. In their world the only virtuous women were those who were plain or were married before the age of fifteen. The Dove of Tralee became in reality a sociological and psychological phenomenon. Each evening, after she had performed, she vanished abovestairs leaving behind her varying degrees of desire, frustration, sentimentality and downright loneliness, all of which contributed to the growing success and revenues of Madge's establishment.

There were, of course, those evenings abovestairs which Madge referred to as "inteem" when favored old friends of Madge's were invited to the Gold Room for champagne and buffet supper with Madge and Bridget acting as hostesses. The guests were a hand-picked lot of which Madge made the scrupulous choice, and the evenings were conducted upon a high and refined level, with conversation, euchre or pinochle (none of the gambling games played belowstairs were allowed) and occasionally music furnished by The Dove of Tralee herself. There were mine and ranch owners, businessmen and bankers from Denver. Sometimes P.J. himself was present.

During the first three weeks the parties in the Gold Room netted for the Dove of Tralee seven legitimate proposals of marriage and nineteen more or less veiled propositions.

But among all the suitors, Buck was the most ardent and persistent. He neglected his duties at a time of the year when his thousands of cattle were being moved down from the range. He wore his best clothes and even shaved and took a bath every day. During all the courtship he kept out of P.J.'s way so thoroughly that the old man never knew he was in town instead of where he belonged, on the range. Twice at the sound of P.J.'s heavy footsteps on the stairs, Madge spirited him out to the balcony and downstairs.

During all of this something was happening to Bridget. She had no longer even the faintest illusions concerning her whereabouts and circumstances, nor the reasons why now and then she was asked for the loan of the Rose Petal bedroom for a night for an important guest who was certainly not Madge's Aunt Etta from Cincinnati. She learned plenty but what she learned came gradually not to concern her. In the immediate circumstances of her existence, she had no complaint and long ago, out of her own hard life, she had learned not only to mind her own business but to be tolerant or at least indifferent in the broadest sense. And after a hard life in the cold rooms of cheap and disreputable boarding houses and hotels with no companionship but the Professor, with her embattled virtue constantly under assault, she knew for the first time in her life security and comfort and even luxury. But more precious than all she had made the discovery of female companionship and the luxury of female protection, and possibly no female in the world was more qualified to protect her than

Madge Beakymer. It was possible now to go to bed quietly in a vast, warm bed, to rise in the morning and have a bath in a marble tub with swan-neck taps. There were clothes in abundance and not just two worn dresses, and suddenly she realized for the first time the pleasures of clothes and mirrors, of scents and powder and silk. And in the process of this realization the rather pure, almost hard beauty of the girl softened and grew more luxuriant.

And always in the background was the knowledge that the old man in the cottage down by the river was as comfortable and as well off as it was possible for him to be. Each afternoon she went to see him, sometimes on foot and sometimes with Madge in her carriage. That she drove through Eudora Street side by side with the proprietress of the most notorious gambling house in the West, that some of the more grim-faced women of Silver City averted their faces, did not disturb her, for she had never known convention or respectability or an ordered society and so could not be an outcast from it. Nevertheless when she encountered Mrs. Hirshbein or Rachel or Eudora and they smiled or waved a hand to her, a warmth crept through her whole body. Once while walking she encountered Ellie-May and oddly enough, Ellie-May did not turn aside. She stopped and said, "Good afternoon, Mademoiselle. It's been a long time since we met."

The encounter and Ellie-May's behavior so startled the girl that for a moment she could think of nothing to say but Ellie-May carried on. She said, "It's nice to hear you're having such a success after that bad business at the Opry House. I'd come and hear you if I could."

"Thank you," said Bridget. The girl knew, as Ellie-May knew, all that went unspoken behind that remark. It wasn't as if Ellie-May could come with dignity into Madge's establishment. With Eudora, it was different.

Then Ellie-May said, "Maybe sometime you'd come up to the Castle and sing for me."

"Yes, ma'am, I'd be glad to," said Bridget.

Then they said good-by and went their ways and until Ellie-May was out of sight, Bridget struggled with the temptation to run after her and ask her if she had any news of Dick.

Sometimes the old Professor knew her and sometimes he didn't and she was not certain which was the worse experience. He was only able to mumble a few words but she managed with difficulty to converse with him, enough to tell him about her success and to know that he was pleased with it. But he was tired and sick and very gentle with a gentleness she had never seen in him before. All the old humbug and cockiness and defiance of life was gone for good. It was as if he were resting for the first time in all his vagabond existence, as if he were waiting for the time when he would go to sleep without ever waking again.

Each day when she had finished her visit, she went back to Madge and dressed and went out on the stage to fresh triumphs, fresh proposals and fresh propositions.

The suitors were of all kinds. Some were old men, some middle-aged, some young, and if she had been free she might have chosen one of them, not out of love or even perhaps out of affection, but because some of them at least represented security and stability. There were three she like—a middle-aged banking widower from Denver, a youngish cattleman who came four or five times all the way from Cheyenne and, oddly enough, she liked Buck.

He had, even Madge admitted, a kind of animal charm and vitality, as P.J. himself had had long ago in the days when Ellie-May had been in love with him. And in all his courtship there was a kind of humility and awkwardness which reminded Bridget of young Dick despite the fact that they were so different in appearance. Buck brought her flowers and gave her presents and tried to talk in a refined way and he held out vigorously against getting drunk.

The only trouble was that with Buck, as with the other two suitors she might have married, there always came a moment even while she was talking to them or playing cards with them, when the image of young Dick intervened. It was as if she saw through and past them, as if they dissolved before the image of young Dick's blue eyes and blond, curly hair. He was different from the others and when she attempted to discover what the difference was, it resolved itself inevitably into the same thing—that he was fresh and young and unsoiled. Once, lying awake in the Rose Petal bed half the night trying to make up her mind what she should do and to discover a little what lay ahead of her, she came very close to understanding him, for it seemed to her suddenly, that despite all the money and the flamboyant background of the Castle, he knew much the same complications and difficulties that she herself knew. And always there was in her mind the picture of the two of them escaping; of leaving behind them Silver City and the lives they had both known to go off together.

And then one Sunday night when there was no party and no visitors and she and Madge were left alone, Madge brought up the subject of marriage.

"Of course," she said, "you're young yet, honey, and you've got plenty of time, but you're passing up opportunities that don't come to most girls. I'm just wondering whether you're doing the right thing."

Bridget didn't answer her and Madge said, "I've been around women long enough to know that you like the banker from Denver and the cattleman from Cheyenne and you like Buck. Most girls out in this country would give their right arms for such chances." She was silent for a time and then said, "Maybe you want to go on with your career."

"No," said Bridget. "That's not what I want."

"I can tell you," said Madge, "that Prince Charmings are all right only they don't come along every day and they don't always turn out to be Prince Charmings. For my own money, I'd take a good sport before I'd take a Prince Charming. They wear better in the long run."

Again the girl was silent and Madge said, "It ain't young Dick, is it?" When Bridget didn't answer, she continued, "I wouldn't count on him. He's kind of flighty."

Bridget was thoughtful for a moment and then said, "I don't want any career. I want to get married and have a home . . . more than anything in the world." She looked away from Madge and put down the embroidery she had been doing. "If he don't show up soon, maybe I'll marry one of them . . . maybe Buck."

"It don't look as if he was goin' to show up," said Madge, "and you can't go on forever monkeying around with Buck. He's likely to turn nasty."

That was all that was ever said about it, but when Henry Caldwell showed up in town about a week later, Madge sent word to him to pay her a visit to discuss something important. She told him to come after dark and use the outside covered stairway and not to come up unless the shade of the middle window was halfway up. She was never a woman of unmixed motives and she knew a great deal more about the lives of people in Silver City than most people credited her with knowing. Friendship or at least good relations with Henry Caldwell might be valuable in the future but P.J., for the moment, mustn't know anything about the visit.

On the night specified, the shade on the middle window was half-drawn as Henry passed along the wooden sidewalk on the opposite side of the street. With his ten-gallon hat drawn well over his face, Henry walked to the end of the block, crossed over and followed the sidewalk until he came to the mouth of the long tunnel leading upward to Madge's apartment. Then he vanished from circulation.

After young Dick recognized the figure of Henry Caldwell sitting by the fire in the cottage, he went back, unsaddled his pony, hobbled him and turned him loose. Then he returned to the cottage, climbed the steps and opened the door. As the door swung clear he saw Henry Caldwell standing, gun drawn, covering the door, with his back to the fire. At sight of Dick, Henry laughed.

"Oh, it's you, son!" he said and put the gun back into the holster. "I wasn't going to shoot. I'm just a little nervous. I've been havin' pot shots taken at me lately."

Dick flung the saddlebag on the table and shook hands.

"How you been?" asked Dick.

"All right! All right!" said Henry. "If I can hold out without gettin' shot for a couple more days, it looks like I'll be governor."

"Who's been shootin' at you?" asked Dick.

Henry started to speak and then quite apparently changed what he had meant to say. Grinning, he said, "Don't know. Can't imagine who'd want me out of the way." Then he walked over to the stove. "How about a cup of coffee? Just made some fresh."

"Sure," said Dick.

Henry poured the coffee and they both sat down. For a moment they drank in silence, both of them aware of a certain awkwardness and restraint.

Presently Henry said, "I was afraid I was goin' to miss you."

"Lucky I came back," said Dick. "I didn't leave camp until after dark. I didn't make up my mind till the last minute. I was going to follow the cattle."

There was a long silence and then Henry said, "Been enjoyin' yourself?"

"Yes."

"Got things sort of thought out?"

"Better than they were," said Dick.

"That's the reason I dropped in," said Henry. "I had some things to talk over."

"Yes?"

"Dick, how'd you like to work with me when I'm governor. You know, as a kind of secketary?"

Dick thought for a moment and then said, "I might not be much good."

"Mebbe it sounds like countin' our chickens before they're hatched but it looks kind of good. Seems like P.J. himself is worried for the first time in his life."

They were both silent for a time, drinking their coffee and smoking. Outside in the woods an owl hooted gloomily and from further out on the range the faint wail of a coyote arose in the frosty moonlight. Inside the boy, the sight of Henry Caldwell so soon after what he had heard by the campfire had started the turmoil all over again. He kept wondering whether he should come straight out and tell Henry what he had heard. He kept thinking, "It must have happened right here in this cabin—the whole thing." And, despite himself, his imagination kept trying to reconstruct what had happened, so long ago. Once or twice, furtively, he glanced at Henry who sat comfortably facing the fire, his long, lean figure slumped in a chair, trying to find the answer and the truth in the leathery, lined face.

"Maybe," thought Dick, "that's why he's offering me that job. Maybe that's as near as he can come to telling me."

"When are you going back down?" asked Henry suddenly.

"I don't know!"

"It doesn't do any good to run away, son."

A silence filled with night sounds fell between them again, and then Henry struck out on a new course. Very casually, he said, "That

girl . . . you know the one . . . that Mademoiselle what's-her-name . . .
is sure packin' 'em in at the El Dorado."

"I heard that," said Dick.

"I kinda feel sorry for her."

Dick didn't say anything and slowly Henry drawled on.

"Madge was tellin' me about her the other day . . . says she's a
mighty fine girl who's never had any luck . . . a straight girl too . . .
straight as a die."

"Then what's she doin' at Madge's place," asked Dick.

Henry went on without looking at him. "I guess she had to take
what she could get what with the old man a-dyin' and everything."
His eyes crinkled up at the corners. "Madge has made a kind of campaign out of the girl's virtue. She's tryin' to get her married off. Seems
like there are a lot of good candidates. The leader seems to be your
brother Buck."

"Buck?" said Dick.

"Yeah. You'd hardly know Buck. He shaves and takes a bath every
day now. Wears his store clothes and even sports a kind of perfume
called cologny water. Maybe she'd straighten Buck out. . . . Seems
like the girl has a lotta character. I guess she must have to go right
back to singin' after all that business about the opry . . . and making
'em all eat out of her hand too." Then he looked directly at Dick and
said, "I heered you was kind of sweet on her yourself when she first
came to town."

Dick didn't answer and Henry pressed his point. "Was there anything in it?"

"Yes."

Henry sighed and relighted his pipe. "Ridin' around between places
I get a chance to do a lot of philosophizing. And I've been doin' a
lotta thinking about you. Sometimes it's kind of like you was my own
son. You see you growed up while I was still in business with P.J. . . .
and it always looked to me like you didn't get much chance. P.J.'s
never got time for his family. The other boys was the same way only
they ain't no good to begin with. You can't make a silk purse out of
a sow's ear. It was kinda like you was brought up a half orphan.
That's why I came all the way up here from Meeker's Gulch for the

[227]

night . . . coz I was interested in how you was gettin' on with your problems."

He poked the fire and threw another balsam log on it. "You're the kind ought to get married, Dick. You ain't the sort that likes whorin' around. And I asked myself . . . who's he gonna marry? It ain't easy findin' a girl out here and for somebody like you with all that special education it's twice as hard." He shifted his chair and went on. "Oh, I ain't against all that education. I pushed your Ma into bullyin' P.J. into it. But it makes it kinda hard for you."

Then he broke off again. "D'you hear the latest? Eudora's gettin' herself married to your friend Cecil. I suppose your Ma sent you word."

The news startled Dick out of his depressed mood. "No," he said, "I hadn't heard it."

"Sounds to me all right. A girl like Eudora could never marry a big, strong-minded guy. She had to have somebody who'd be more a wife than a husband. I guess it's a load off your Ma's mind. Eudora was always troublesome." Henry went right on. Dick had never heard him talk so much in one stretch in all his life. "Sometimes," he went on, "I regret not havin' got married, but I never met but one woman I ever wanted to marry and she was already hitched."

He didn't look at Dick and Dick suddenly was sure that he knew the reason. Bit by bit, in a back-handed way he was trying to tell Dick everything without ever admitting anything. With a kind of frontier sense of honor he was protecting Ellie-May. Dick tried to remember what Henry and Ellie-May were like nearly a generation earlier just before he was born, what the meetings must have been like here in this cottage, then newly built. No one could have known anything about it but the colored boy Esau and Esau had never told. Maybe Ellie-May had bribed him, but almost at once he knew that this was unlikely. Ellie-May never needed to bribe people. Somehow, always, they were loyal to her and kept her secrets without being bribed. Funny that Esau should be the only one to know anything about what had happened so long ago.

Henry was talking again. "I guess Madge and me must seem a funny pair of cupids, but we've got the same idea in mind. We think it'd be a good idea if you tried to marry that girl. I ain't a man to mince matters and certainly Madge ain't. I don't know how you feel about the girl. She's strong-minded. Even Madge says so, but a woman without a strong mind ain't worth much. That's always what I liked about your Ma. She looks kinda small and puny but she's got a mind of her own." He turned toward Dick. "Well, son! What do you think?"

"I don't know!"

"D'you think about her much? I mean at night when you're alone?"

"Yes."

"D'you want to help her out but your pride won't let you?"

"I guess that's it."

"D'you worry about people sayin' later on 'He married her right out of the El Dorado'?"

Dick's face turned a dull red. He hesitated and then said, "Yes."

"Well, don't let that worry you. This is a new country, son. A man's gotta take a woman where he finds her. In a few years it ain't gonna matter where you found her and I can testify that Madge is right when she says the girl is pure as a lily. Madge wouldn't lie to me. We've known each other too long. Why, *I* introduced her to P.J."

"What d'you think?"

Dick was silent for a time. Then he said, "I think yes."

"Then, Prince Charming, you'd better go to the rescue before it's too late. A girl in her position ain't gonna wait around forever in a den of wolves. It ain't natural." After a moment Henry stood up. "Guess we'd better get some sleep. We can get an early start tomorrow. We can go down by Meeker's Gulch and Binghamtown. That'll take a day or two longer but you can kind of get acquainted with politics and the people over there and get in line for that secketary job. I never had much education and I'm gonna need an educated fellow around me to write letters and look after them slickers from the East that comes out here to sell us gold bricks."

In the bedroom Henry Caldwell fell asleep almost at once and snored loudly, but Dick couldn't sleep. He had the sense of a decision made, as if somehow all the circumstances had come together to make a decision for him. He was going to belong to this wild beautiful country for the rest of his life and it wasn't any good taking a soft woman to go through that life with him. And now he knew that inside him it was Bridget he wanted. It was Bridget he wanted with his body, tormented and frustrated. He had known that for a long time. But Henry had somehow made it all clear now. Now he wanted her with his mind and his reason as well. The idea of Buck, black, stupid, greedy, even thinking of her, filled his mind with suppressed fury.

And he knew another thing, something he had always wanted to know for sure—that he was no relation to P. J. Meaney. Since the moment the sun had gone down far out on the range, it had been a big night.

Nobody ever quite understood what it was that set off the chain of events which led to what became known in the history of Silver City and Colorado as the Battle of the Ballots, an event remembered to this day by the old-timers, an event which has become a legend for citizens who were not even alive at the time it happened. Mrs. Hirshbein, poring over her astrological charts afterward in her bedroom, above the fire-singed Emporium could find nothing to explain the explosion. She finally gave out the opinion that the whole thing was caused by spots on the sun.

The Professor died quietly in bed one late afternoon with Bridget sitting in a chair by the side of his bed while Madge waited below-stairs with the doctor and the nurses. Dying, the old man clung to her hand. It was as if in all his wandering, unstable, fruitless life she were the only thing in which he had ever found any satisfaction. A little before he died he regained enough clarity of mind to recognize her but he never regained the power of speech.

He died very quietly. He simply closed his eyes and stopped breathing and the grasp of the hand relaxed suddenly. Gently she laid his hands across his chest and went down the stairs. To the doctor and nurse she said, "I think you'd better go up." And then in Madge's arms she began to cry.

They buried him two days later in the little graveyard bordered by cottonwood trees along the rushing little river.

The only mourners were Bridget and Madge following the hearse in Madge's Victoria, both dressed in black, Madge wearing more crepe than they had ever seen before in Silver City. The service was read by Father O'Malley, a little, old Irishman who was Priest of the tin-roofed adobe church where the Irish railroad workers went to Mass and made their sulphurous confessions. It was an unorthodox proceeding on the part of the old Priest but it was not the first unorthodox action of a Roman Catholic Priest in that frontier country. Although Bridget never really knew, she guessed that the Professor must have been a Roman Catholic because in the past whenever their luck had seemed at the end of things, the Professor would go to Confession and Mass.

Madge paid for a Mass and insisted upon paying half the price of the tombstone. They ordered one of white marble, inscribed simply "Alonzo da Ponte, born January 23, 1823 at Trieste, Austria. Died November 3, 1888, Silver City, Colorado. Home at last after the long journey." It had been a long, disreputable voyage from Trieste to Silver City. Bridget wasn't even certain that Alonzo da Ponte was his real name but she thought that probably God would know who the tired old man was, when he arrived at the Gates of Heaven.

For two nights she did not sing on the stage of the gambling room and on the third night when she returned from the stage she found Buck waiting for her in Madge's Gold Room. He stood, sullen and awkward, leaning against the upright gilt piano. He was, as usual, dressed up in the ill-fitting store clothes and at first sight she was glad to see him.

He said, "I was right sorry to hear about the old man a-dyin'," and moved across the room toward her. It was then that she noticed something peculiar about him, that he walked unsteadily and that his eyes were bloodshot. His jaw thrust forward in an ugly way. She thought, "Madge doesn't know he's up here. He must have come up the outside stairway."

"Thank you," she said.

Then she noticed that craftily he had maneuvered his big body between her and the door.

"But that ain't all, Miss Nicety-Nice."

She didn't answer him and suddenly she was afraid, for she knew that he had at last turned nasty as Madge had predicted.

"Now the old man is dead I guess you can marry me right off."

She managed to put the gilt table between herself and him. "I'm not marrying anybody!"

"It ain't gonna do you any good to get behind that there table and it ain't any good tryin' to yell because Madge can't hear you. That there door behind you is locked and I'm gonna lock this one."

He turned quickly, locked the door by which she had come in and put the key in his pocket.

"Now, Miss Nicety-Nice, we're gonna settle this. You've been teasin' me long enough. Buck Meaney ain't used to bein' teased by wimmin. Wimmin don't fool around Buck Meaney."

She saw now that he wasn't only drunk; he was a little crazy. He wasn't any longer the big, awkward brute who had won a kind of pitying affection that she might have had for a bad boy. This was the real Buck Meaney and he didn't make a pretty specimen. She was frightened but she wasn't as frightened as she was angry. After all the long fight she had had to keep her virtue she wasn't going to have it taken away from her now by force. She picked up a vase off the table and said, "You keep away from me, you dirty ape!"

"Dirty ape, am I? I wasn't no dirty ape when I was givin' you presents and flowers and cologny water. What do you think you are— posing like you was a Saint in a place like this?"

He started toward her and she slipped to the other side of the table and then the idea came to her. In his drunkenness he had forgotten the bell rope. The only chance was to get to the rope, pull it and then get back behind the table again. She moved a little in the opposite direction, hoping to lure him far enough away so that she could reach the bell. The feint worked for a moment but as she moved quickly in the direction of the bell rope he saw what she was up to and acted quickly with all the craft of a half-mad drunk. He got to the bellrope first and jerked it off the wall.

"And you ain't gonna use that either." Then he took off his coat and threw it on the floor. "Now Miss Dove of Tralee, we're gonna see who's boss around here."

This time as he came toward her, he simply picked up the big table and threw it in the corner. At the same moment she let fly with the vase. It struck him on the head and broke. The blow stunned him for a moment. He put his hand to his head and it came away covered with blood. Then slowly a maniacal look came into his eyes and he started toward her.

"You think you can knock out Buck that way? That's the kind of thing Buck likes. If that's what you want you're gonna get it."

As he came toward her she dodged aside and like a cornered mouse, started running along the wall of the room. She knew now that it wasn't as if she were dealing with lust alone. She was dealing with a drunken maniac. Twice she managed to escape him and then he forced her nearer and nearer to the cosy corner and at that moment the inspiration came to her. As he started toward her for the last time she turned quickly and dived headlong into the Turkish cosy corner itself. Mercifully and ironically this altar to lust behaved as she hoped it would behave. As she landed, the whole thing came down on top of her in a mass of draperies, spears, shields, tassels and pampas grass. A moment later she felt Buck's drunken body on top of hers. She felt his big, hairy hands groping for her among the Cashmere shawls and shields and pampas grass, and she managed to roll out of his way, wrapping herself more and more tightly in draperies. She could hear his drunken cursing and once she felt his hot breath on her face, but the more they struggled in the complicated wreckage the safer and more inviolable she became. In a minute or two she was swathed like a mummy from head to foot.

Then just as she became so entangled that she could no longer move, she became aware that he wasn't there any longer. Faintly she could hear sounds of violence and crashing but they were no longer near her but somewhere else in the room, a little way off. As she managed to disentangle herself sufficiently to achieve vision with one eye, she witnessed an awesome spectacle.

Opposite her the door leading to the balcony was standing open and shattered, its paneling splintered from top to bottom and in the middle of the room two big, black, hairy men were fighting. It was a terrible fight in which slugging, scratching, biting and eye-gouging were all playing a part. One was Buck, his face covered with blood, the other was old P.J., panting and puffing, his coat torn half off his back. For a moment or two she watched, fascinated, before disengaging her other eye. And as she watched she saw Buck take a gigantic swing which landed on the corner of P.J.'s heavy jaw. The old man's

[233]

head swung back and he fell on the floor and lay still. Then Buck landed a half-hearted drunken kick at the prostrate body, pushed the long black hair out of his eyes and began to swear. At the same moment Madge appeared in the shattered doorway. She was in full eyening dress, very décolleté with the diamond butterfly in her hair and carrying a shotgun.

She raised the shotgun and pointed it right at the middle of Buck's abdomen. The sight of the gun and the pressure of the muzzle against his middle seemed to sober him up. Out of long habit, he raised the hands covered with blood over his head.

"Now!" said Madge. "You black-livered son-of-a-bitch! Get out of here! Keep them hands up and back out that door!"

Slowly Buck obeyed her. He backed through the shattered door along the balcony and slowly down the stairs, Madge following with the muzzle of the gun still pressed against his belly. By the time the pair had reached the bottom of the stairs, their advance had been noted by a half-dozen gamblers and three or four drunks at the bar. Slowly the progress backward continued across the big room between the tables as bit by bit all play stopped so that the customers might watch the fun. Hoots and jeers arose and at length when the pair reached the swinging door Madge gave an extra hearty poke with the gun barrel and sent Buck backward into the street.

Then, turning, she swung the shotgun under her arm as if she were returning from a quail hunt and made her way back through the cheering drunks and gamblers, up the stairway and back into the Gold Room.

Bridget, having meanwhile disentangled herself from the cosy corner, was bending over P.J. She had loosened his collar and was bathing his face with cold water. Madge laid down the shotgun on a chair and knelt beside P.J., slapping his face violently. In a moment he opened his eyes and sat up looking about him. Then he said, "Where is he?" Groggily he got to his feet and said, "I'll beat the bejeezus out of him. Where is he?"

But Madge took his arm and led him over to a chair. "There now," she said, "sit there and I'll get you some brandy."

She took a bottle from the cupboard and poured him a glass filled to the brim. "It's all right," she said. "I threw him out. He ain't likely to come back here again. If he does he'll get a belly-full of buckshot."

P.J. drank and she said, "It took a shotgun to fix him. He was so crazy a revolver wouldn't have done no good, but a shotgun blows a hole as big as a stovepipe right through a man. It affects the imagination." Then she turned to Bridget who was sitting on a chair now, white and shaking. "You were smart, honey, to go for the cosy corner. God knows what would have happened to you if you hadn't wrapped yourself up in them draperies.

Then she noticed the crowd standing in the doorway and said, "Get the hell out of here, all of you!" She picked up the shotgun again and the crowd of mocking, leering faces moved away while she shut what remained of the shattered door. She didn't want them to see the shame of old P.J. whose own son had beat him up.

He sat there drinking the brandy and shaking his head in a dazed way like an old bull who has been driven out of the herd. After chastizing his sons for years, it had happened at last and now everybody in Silver City would know it—that the rule of the titanic old man was over.

"That's right, buckeroo!" said Madge, like a mother addressing a naughty child who had hurt himself. "Drink it right down!"

Then she turned to Bridget. "A little of this wouldn't hurt you, honey," she said and poured out a glass. "I guess you haven't lost anything but it was lucky we came along when we did. When I found the door locked, I knew something was wrong. So P.J. just smashed it open."

Then she noticed Buck's coat and ten-gallon hat and crossing the room she picked them up and walked to the window. With one hand she opened it and with the other she threw the coat and hat into the street.

When she came back to P.J. he was moaning and groaning faintly. She knew it wasn't the physical pain that hurt him. It was the humiliation.

"Better come on into my room and lay down," she said.

At seven the next morning P.J. made his way back up the hill to the Castle. Ellie-May, always an early riser, encountered him in the upper hallway. He would have preferred not seeing her but there was no escape and there was no concealing the fact that he had been through some kind of brawl. One eye was blacked and there were long scratches down one side of his face where the drunken Buck's fingers, attempting the eye-gouging technique, had slipped.

Ellie-May on encountering him said, "Good morning, P.J.," casually, as she had done every day for years and then a second look led her to follow him into his room. There he sat down heavily on the bed as she closed the door behind her. He sat there silently, glowering at the floor.

For a moment Ellie-May looked at him, presently aware that something serious had happened, something serious enough to have deflated him badly. He sat there like a discouraged, broken man, and she said, "Well, what have you been into now?"

He raised his head and looked at her out of his one good eye. "It was your son who done this, Ellie-May."

"Which one?" she asked.

"Buck."

"Well, he's the strongest. He's the most like you. I felt this was comin' on for a long time. You can't go on treatin' big grown men like they were still in diapers. Where did it happen?"

"At the El Dorado," said P.J. "He was tryin' to violate that little girl singer. Had her locked in a room. I had to break down the door and when I saved the girl and tried to throw him out, he hit me."

It struck her that there was almost a whimper in the voice. Considering the story for a moment, she began to fill in the gaps and, out of long experience, she came very close to the truth. She couldn't see P.J. in the role of the White Knight saving the lady no matter how hard she tried. She knew, instinctively, and out of experience, that this was a fight over a woman and the old bull had been licked.

"Everybody in Silver City knows about it," said P.J. "There was a lot of 'em lookin' in. They're all goin' around this morning saying 'D'ja hear—Buck Meaney beat hell out of his old man last night.' "

"Who got rid of him?" asked Ellie-May, following out the line of the story like a prosecuting attorney.

"Madge," he said, "with a shotgun."

"She didn't shoot him, did she?"

"No. Just paraded him out the door with the muzzle stuck in his belly."

Ellie-May considered this for a moment and then said, "Well, Buck must have looked awful foolish. It looks to me like you came off about even." Then, as usual, she embraced action rather than talk. She said, "Get off your clothes and go to bed and I'll get some beefsteak for your eye."

"A fine thing to happen!" he was mumbling, "and Election Day only day after tomorrow."

"Well, I guess you won't want to be seen around between now and then. The less you're seen the less talk there'll be. Now you get off your clothes and get into bed."

She left him then and went downstairs to the kitchen. She wasn't upset by the shame of the scandal as gossip and scandal were unimportant save that they might at the last minute diminish P.J.'s prestige and contribute to the defeat of his candidate and the wrecking of his power. But after all that was exactly what she was hoping for. For weeks now she had even been working for it, out of the little black book. She wouldn't need to tell any of Henry's men about the brawl. Already, it would be spreading all over the state. What mattered to her was a very simple thing. It was this—that in the old man sitting on the edge of the big walnut bed, she had seen for a moment something of the young man she had married, the man who came to her with all his discouragements and troubles, the man who was a little like a child, the man whom she had fallen in love with and married, the man who was a little like a boisterous small boy. That was the P.J. she had loved before the intoxication of success and power had turned him into a crook and a bully. For the first time in years she saw a chance of getting him back, of escaping from the Castle and all that life which had steadily grown emptier and drearier with the passing of each year.

There was always beefsteak in the big hanging-room, iced with ice from the glacier. Briskly she borrowed a knife from her friend, the chef, and cut off a large, flat hunk. Nobody in the kitchen paid much attention for she had a way of coming in and taking out of all the abundance good beef and fresh trout to feed the stray dogs and cats that hung around the stables and lived off her bounty. Then she climbed the stairs and stopped by her own apartment to tear a bandage off a worn, clean sheet and progressed along the hall toward P.J.'s room. And all the time she was thinking, "If things just go bad enough, everything'll turn out all right. P.J. isn't so old that he hasn't got a lot of good years left if he don't have a stroke. We can leave things to Eudora and Cecil and the boys and go off travelin' to Europe and down East. We can patch things up all over again."

In her heart she was almost gay.

When she returned, he was in bed, the great body spread like a mountain range beneath the sheets. He was smoking a cigar. At sight of him she repeated what she had said a thousand times in the last few years, "You're gonna fall asleep and set fire to yourself one of these times. Now set up and hold still while I fix this steak."

She was leaning over him tying a knot in the bandage when the explosion occurred. It came first as a distant rumble and then mounted quickly into a violence which rattled the windows and shook the pictures on the wall. The bandage and the beefsteak fell out of her hands and P.J.'s head struck the solid walnut head of the bed. For a second they were silent and then looking through the window, Ellie-May saw where the explosion had come from. At a spot about halfway up the mountains there rose a great, billowing cloud of white and grey smoke and Ellie-May said, "It's at the mine."

P.J. sat up quickly, "The mine!" Then he put one leg out of bed and stood up in his nightshirt. "I gotta get up there," he said.

She moved toward the door and stood with her back to it. He was already pulling on his trousers.

"You ain't goin' up there," she said quietly.

He paused with one leg thrust into the trousers, and she continued, "If that's what I think it is you ain't goin' near the mine. They'd jump on you and kill you on sight."

"Kill me?"

"They've been gettin' madder and madder because you wouldn't spend the money to put the mine in shape. I knew it was goin' to happen and now it's happened! Unless you want to get killed you stay right in this room."

"I ain't afraid!" said P.J.

"It ain't a question of your bein' afraid," said Ellie-May. "It's just

[238]

a question of you gettin' the daylights beat out of you. D'you want that to happen right on top of this other thing? Are you crazy?"

Slowly he removed his leg from the trousers and let them fall on the floor. Then he moved slowly to the window and looked out. Fire had quickly followed the explosion and at the mine the flames were leaping higher and higher. And there was a new sound now. It was a confused, distant sound of uproar and shouting that came from the town itself. Ellie-May at the other window, saw people running out of houses and bars and lunchrooms. They were jumping on ponies or driving off in buckboards, all headed one way toward the road leading to the mines.

Presently she turned away from the window. "Now get back to bed, P.J., and stay there or get the hell beat out of you. Let me get that beefsteak back on. I've got to get out of here. I've got to get down to the Emporium. Millie and I have got a job to do."

Like a little boy he got back into bed. She fastened the piece of steak firmly over the damaged eye and hurried out to get the horses and every available vehicle ready to transport the injured and the dead.

It wasn't only that Ellie-May was at heart a good politician; she also had great talents as an executive and organizer and she and Millie Hirshbein represented all there was as an organization to cope with a disaster such as that which fell upon Silver City that bright November morning.

The explosion had come at the worst time, when the morning shift of Poles, Chinese, Irish and Italians were going to work. Somehow, something had set off the explosions in the main building where the dynamite should not have been stored. Its violence in turn set off a kind of chain reaction in the dynamite wherever it was stored in the area and even in the mine itself. Then fire followed the explosion. And Ellie-May and Millie Hirshbein found use for all the old sheets and shirts they had been hoarding away for just such an occasion.

Women are indispensable in times of disaster, and women like Ellie-May and Millie are less likely to lose their heads than men. Somehow the non-essentials seem to drop away, leaving the essentials clear and uncomplicated. In Ellie-May's mind, once she had reached Eudora Street and discovered the magnitude of the disaster from the stream of wounded and dying already being brought down the mountain, one thing became clear—that she and Millie could not manage things alone. In the past she had speculated sometimes upon just whom she would call upon for help if a disaster occurred and always she had arrived, reluctantly, at the same conclusion—Madge! Madge would be better than any man. She could handle men better than any man or woman in the town and she had had long and thorough practice in handling hysterical women. Now, Ellie-May saw, was the time to call on Madge.

Without hesitation, once she had sent Millie armed with bandages and salves up to the mines, she went up the covered stairway.

She found Madge in the process of changing out of a dressing-gown trimmed in maribou into a suit of durable heavy brown cloth. The two women did not mince matters, although actually they had never even met each other before. They did not even trouble to exchange "Good mornings."

"You'd better go right up to the mine and help out Millie," said Ellie-May. "That's where the confusion is. It'll need some bossin' around up there and Millie is goin' to have her hands full just bandagin.'"

"Sure," said Madge. "That's what I had in mind."

She put a snood over her brassy yellow hair so that it wouldn't get in her way, fastened a holster and revolver around her waist and she was ready.

"I can use the downstairs here," said Ellie-May, "and the upstairs too."

"Sure," said Madge. "Use it any way you want." She started out the door and then turned.

"The old man had better keep out of sight," she said.

"Yes, I've taken care of that," said Ellie-May. "It's up to you to see they do what Millie wants. I'll take care of things down here."

"You can count on me," said Madge, and went down the stairs.

At the hitching rail, two or three ponies still stood, unclaimed. Selecting the sturdiest of them, Madge swung herself aboard with some difficulty and set off at a gallop along Eudora Street and up the road toward the mine.

Ellie-May found Mrs. Birdwell and the old porter and a couple of hysterical girls and a bartender and set them to work turning the El Dorado into an emergency station. The whole thing she put in charge of Mrs. Birdwell. Then she thought of the Opera House. There was a lot of room there and for once that big warehouse could be of some real use.

Until well into the afternoon they were busy laying out the dead and carrying down the wounded, and after the first emergency was met, new tasks arose. There was a train coming from Denver with doctors and nurses and supplies. There was the question of food. When the worst was over, Ellie-May set up an office at one of the counters near the door of the Emporium. Madge took over the duties of sheriff and Bridget became a kind of messenger. Millie was everywhere with water and drugs and bandages.

It was only then, after the first of the confusion was reduced to a semblance of order, that it occurred simultaneously to Ellie-May and Madge that the whole thing was complicated by the fact that the next day was Election Day and that plenty of trouble could be expected, disaster or no disaster. And so, late that night after the Denver doctors had begun to take over, they organized a kind of Vigilante Committee. It wasn't any good looking for the sheriff. He was P.J.'s man and like P.J. he was hiding out for fear of being mobbed.

It was Madge with her intimate knowledge of nearly every man in Silver City save the Priest and the United Brethren Preacher, who selected the committee. She chose the tough ones she could count on, a score of them—bartenders, cowhands, and prospectors—and set them to work. When she gathered them together she delivered a kind of address.

She said, "Now, men! You know there's gonna be plenty of brawlin' and fightin' round here. Things has got to be kept in order and it's up to you. There's a lot of hurt and dyin' people around here and we can't have any more trouble. And the elections has got to be held because they're sacred. If you want any instructions you'll find me at the old stompin' ground. Now go out and do your duty and if anybody gets too ornery, just shoot. Don't try to kill 'em! Just pink 'em and put 'em out of action. There's a lot of good men who get ornery as hell on Election Day."

The sun had fallen behind the great mountains and the whole valley was already slipping into the shadow of night on the evening of Election Day when Dick's pony turned down from the high ranges. He had been riding all day in the hope of getting from Meeker's Gulch to Silver City before nightfall but the pony had gone lame late in the afternoon and all hope of hurrying him had to be abandoned.

The boy had made up his mind now and was impatient to carry through his decision. He was headed straight for the El Dorado. He meant to find Bridget and ask her at once to marry him. The imagination which set him apart from all the others in the family but Ellie-May had been working overtime. He would propose that they get married at once and go away and when he came back he would take the job as "secketary" to Henry Caldwell and go to live in Denver. And, all day, as he rode he kept building up step by step their life together. In his imagination he saw the kind of home they would have. He pictured what love, of which he knew very little in practice, would be like. He even imagined what the children would be like. And all the time, with each mile he gained, this girl whose image had tormented him night after night as he lay rolled in a blanket in the high grass of the range country, became more desirable.

From the beginning he had planned not to get to Silver City until sundown. That had been Henry Caldwell's idea and advice. Henry said there would be trouble between his supporters and the cohorts of P.J., how bad he did not know, but under the circumstances, if P.J.'s outfit felt the election was going against them, they would, said Henry, resort to every kind of measure even to stealing the ballot boxes. Under the circumstances, young Dick had better keep out of the way during the daytime while the balloting was in progress.

Despite the advice of Henry Caldwell, love and the hot young blood of youth kept driving him on, until the pony went lame and by now as he rode slowly along the edge of the rushing river in the darkness, he knew that he would not arrive until well after dark.

As he reached the lower end of the canyon where the trail led downward past the mine into Silver City, he became aware slowly of a strange, rose-colored glow in the distant sky. It resembled the last rosiness of one of the famous Colorado sunsets at that point before the color changes imperceptibly into a pale green and then to the deep transparent blue of night in the high mountains. But the rosiness was not so beautiful as it was terrifying for the "sunset" was not in the west but in the east and presently Dick thought, "There is a great fire somewhere in the valley. It must be in Silver City."

The discovery only heightened his impatience but he knew that at-tempting to hurry the pony would only make him break down al-together. In his frustration his imagination began to work again. He saw the whole town in flames, the El Dorado, its flimsy wooden structure reduced to ashes, and Bridget perhaps injured or dead. He began to believe that he had the worst of luck, that he was a fool and that all the world was against him.

In this desperate mood he made as good time as he was able until he reached the point where the trail rounded a shoulder of the mountain and the valley with Silver City came into view. Then he saw that the whole town was not in flames. Here and there a building was burn-ing but the great fire which illumined all the sky came from one place halfway up the slope above the town. He knew at once what it was. There could be no mistake for the fire was so far advanced that the flames leaping from the windows, illumined and silhouetted the whole crumbling structure of the Castle.

Quickly he got down from the pony, tossed the reins over his head and started running the two miles or more that separated him from the stricken town.

The fights began almost at once after the polls had opened. In the beginning they were mostly small disorders which involved fists and eye-gouging but no shooting. The opponents knew each other on sight and the followers of Henry Caldwell kept a close watch on P.J.'s faction for any kind of shenanigans. Both factions had head-quarters operating in the town, Henry Caldwell's faction basing on the second story of the building across the street from Mrs. Sowers' Boarding House and Grand Hotel, P.J.'s from the long established headquarters near the depot. From the very first it was clear that P.J.'s faction was going to be out-voted in the balloting, a fact which only made them uglier. Throughout the morning and until well into the afternoon things were kept under control, largely by the constant patroling of Madge and her Vigilante Committee.

But there was one element on which none of them had counted and this was an element which had no votes at all and was not even permitted to vote. It was the miners. Out of the disaster about two hundred of them still existed unhurt but in a desperate mood.

For hours after the disaster, they had remained scattered and half-dazed, some of them looking for best friends and comrades, some of them drinking in the cheap saloons. There were Poles, Italians, Irish, Chinese and as they found friends or comrades, burned, disfigured and injured and drank more and more, they gathered into little groups and began talking violence. They had been until now a downtrodden, outcast group of foreigners who, in this new world, had been forced to accept whatever treatment was given them. But rebellion had been smouldering for a long time and now the disaster seemed to bring everything to a head. The growing fury began to reach a climax about the middle of the afternoon of Election Day when one little knot of miners joined another group and then that group joined still another and presently grew into a mob.

The first clash came in front of the headquarters of P.J.'s faction near the depot when a gang of miners broke all the windows and smashed in the door. By the time they got in, the place was empty for the cohorts of P.J. knew real trouble when they saw it and already had made their way to safety out of the back door. Down by the river they held a conference and decided that instead of taking to the mountains they would go back and fight. By the time they returned to the headquarters, all the furniture including the big enlarged, framed photographs of P. J. Meaney and Wentworth Talmadge had been dumped into the street and the wooden building was going up in flames.

In front of the building where Eudora Street turned off from Depot Square, a mob was gathered about a bonfire above which swung from a telegraph pole a dummy figure made of a suit of store clothes stuffed with straw wearing a placard bearing the legend, "P. J. Meaney."

At sight of this, P.J.'s little army retreated and set out upon a new course, to steal the ballot boxes and burn them. At the first polling place they ran into opposition from Henry Caldwell's supporters and gun-fighting broke out.

It was about this time that Madge appeared at Ellie-May's headquarters in the Emporium. She swung down off her horse and ran up the steps.

She found Ellie-May in the little room where Cecil had once tried on the cowhand's clothes that changed his whole life. Inside the room she closed the door behind her and asked, "Where's P.J.?"

"Up to the Castle!" said Ellie-May.

"Well, you'd better get the old buzzard out of there and quick! They'll be goin' up there next and if they catch him they're likely to hang him to the nearest lamppost. Them miners is on the loose proper and they're drunk as goats. Get him into one of the barouches and drive him out of town. It ain't any good his tryin' to hide any place. They're likely to burn the whole town down."

"Anybody'd recognize him. You can't hide him."

"Well, get him out, Ellie-May. In another hour there won't be any holdin' 'em. Get goin'! I've got things to do! By Gawd, they're not goin' to burn down the El Dorado if I have to shoot all of 'em!"

Then she left the room and hurried out to her pony.

For a moment Ellie-May stood there, trembling a little from excitement. Then she tied her bonnet under her chin and set out on foot as fast as she could go to the Castle. Getting P.J. out of town wasn't going to be easy. Because the mountains rose almost straight up behind the Castle he couldn't take to the woods in that direction. If he escaped she'd have to get him some way through the town itself and the town by now was in the hands of the half-crazed miners or Henry Caldwell's cohorts.

Then just as she reached the porte-cochere, panting with fatigue the idea came to her and instead of going into the Castle she went around it to the stables to tell one of the men to hitch a horse to a phaeton.

But she found the stables deserted. Not to be defeated she harnessed a horse called "Old Doc," who was a pensioner, to the phaeton, put up the top and drove him up to the hitching rail by the back door of the Castle. There she tied him and ran into the Castle. It too seemed to be empty as she climbed the stairs and felt her way in the darkness along the big hallway. When she got to Eudora's room she turned in and struck a match from the box she had picked up in the kitchen on the way upstairs. She didn't want to light one of the lamps for fear of attracting attention to the darkened Castle so, holding the match with one hand, she opened the door of Eudora's closet and selected an old velvet dressing gown and a shawl.

Then as the match burned itself out she made her way along the dark hallway to P.J.'s room at the end. The room was in darkness but the sound of P.J.'s gruff voice came to her from the bed, "Who's there?"

"It's me—Ellie-May. Get out of that bed quick and put on these things."

"What's the matter? What are you talkin' about?" said the voice.

"Don't argue with me. All hell's breakin' loose in town. They're burnin' you in effigy down there and when they get the idea they'll come up here and get the real thing. I ain't foolin', P.J. There ain't nothin' can stop 'em!"

"I ain't gonna run away!"

"Get up off that bed and stop arguin' with me!"

She took the big, hairy hand and tried to pull him up, "If you don't wanta get killed, get out of here!"

P.J. sat up. "I ain't gonna go!"

She knew he was still sulking over the humiliation of Buck, over the humiliation of not being able to stride up and down the streets of Silver City the way he had used to do on Election Day.

"Listen!" she said. "You hear that?" In the silence the sound of yelling voices, smashing windows and an occasional gunshot arose from the town. She heard the bedsprings creak as P.J. lifted his great weight from the bed. Then by the faint glow from the window, she saw him standing beside her.

"Look outta that window!"

He moved toward the window and what he saw was worse than anything she had anticipated. Up the road leading from the town a mob was moving toward the Castle. It was carrying election parade torches and bits of flaming wood and by the light of the torches they saw that the big ringleader was carrying about forty feet of rope.

"Come on, you damned fool and get out of here!"

The sight had put the fear of God into him and he said, "All right. Let's git!" and followed her quietly through the hall, down the back stairs and out the back door to where Old Doc stood patiently hitched to the rail.

Outside the rosy glow from the fires illumined the figure of the old horse and the phaeton. "Here!" she said. "While I unhitch the horse, put this on and put the shawl over your head. We gotta drive through the town and anybody'd recognize you."

"I ain't gonna dress up in no woman's clothes," he said, stubbornly. She knew that for him this was the ultimate and final humiliation and she used strong language. She said, "Mebbe you'd rather be hangin' by a rope, a-chokin' and bein' riddled like a sieve."

The wild sound of the mob advancing on the other side of the Castle added weight to her words and P.J. acted. While she untied Old Doc, he accepted the final indignity. He slipped his arms awkwardly into the velvet dressing gown. "Now put that shawl over your head," said Ellie-May. Thus attired he climbed into the phaeton. Ellie-May took up the whip from the socket and brought it down over the rump of Old Doc so fiercely that the old horse sprang forward into a slow gallop. Ellie-May steered him behind the stables and out along the back side of the corral where, even in the light from the fires, they would be invisible to the approaching mob. She headed by a back lane for the river and as they cleared the fence of the corral, the first and most perilous stage of the journey was over. At least they had escaped the direct action of the mob whose purpose was unmistakable.

Then as she let Old Doc slow down out of a broken-down gallop, she said, "If we meet anybody, you're gonna be Eudora. If they stop us just pull the shawl over your face, put your hands up and be cryin'."

In order to get out of the town Ellie-May had to take a course through the back street past the kitchen end of the Grand Hotel and Boarding House down the alley by the Opera House. It seemed safe enough since most of the rioting appeared to be taking place along Eudora Street. They had already turned the corner by the Opera House and were emerging from the alley into the outskirts of the town when they came suddenly upon a dozen rioters.

[247]

At sight of the carriage one of them grabbed Old Doc by the bridle and two others came up to the side of the phaeton and peered in.

"Where are you goin'?" asked one of them in a drunken voice.

"We're just a couple of women tryin' to get out of town," said Ellie-May.

"Whose wimmin?" asked the drunken voice.

"I'm Mrs. Meaney and this here is my daughter, Eudora. She's poorly and I'm tryin' to get her out of here on account of her nerves." Then she turned to the figure by her side with its face buried in the shawl, sobbing. "There now, Eudora," she said, "don't take on so. These gentlemen ain't gonna harm a lady."

"Naw!" said a voice. "We ain't gonna hurt no ladies."

Then another voice said, "No son-of-a-bitch around here is gonna lay hands on Ellie-May so long as I'm around . . . not after what she done for us yesterday."

He was a big Irishman and he was very drunk but he was in a chivalrous, protective mood and belligerent about it. He pushed aside the two men who had been peering into the phaeton. He took one careful look at Ellie-May and said, "Yeah, that's her all right! Nobody's gonna touch a hair of her head while I'm around." Then he patted the sobbing, shawl-enveloped figure gently on the velvet-covered knee. "There now, little girl," he said, "there ain't nothin' for you to be skeered of. You and your Maw just drive right along." Then in a stentorian voice, he bellowed, "Leave go of that bridle, you son-of-a-bitch" and removing his hat, and making a low bow, he said, "Drive on, Florence Nightingale!"

They were out of the town among the cottonwood trees when at last Ellie-May spoke. She said, "It was mighty lucky Eudora grew up to be such a big girl!" But P.J. didn't say anything.

A hundred yards further down the road, Ellie-May pulled in the old horse and said, "I'm goin' back to the Emporium. You get goin' and don't stop goin' till you get to Denver."

She left him there and set out for the Emporium on foot and as she reached the first turn she saw that they had escaped not a second too soon. The Castle was afire and the flames were coming out of the windows as high as the third floor in the battlemented west turret. At the sight, Ellie-May began to chuckle. Everything was going all right. Nothing could save the place even if anybody wanted to save it.

A little later she reached the Emporium and was at work again helping Millie with the wounded victims of the Battle of the Ballot Boxes. Most of them were drunk and the victims of what was merely a wild celebration of Henry Caldwell's great victory—news of which was already beginning to come in over the railroad telegraph.

Meanwhile the drunken band that had held up the phaeton, having made their way up to Eudora Street, was considerably puzzled when they broke into the Grand Hotel to find Eudora herself seated in a room on the second floor, watching the burning Castle through a telescope, apparently with enjoyment and even gusto. They were too drunk to suspect what had happened. They were either scared or attributed the apparition to their condition. In an awed silence they went away leaving her to the enjoyment of the grandiose spectacle of destruction.

It was very likely that the presence of the injured miners at the El Dorado preserved the establishment eventually from looting and possible destruction. They lay in rows on the floor of the gambling room and in some of the rooms upstairs and all through the day and the night the "butt-shaking" girls spent their time giving them water and whisky and tending their needs. Millie Hirshbein divided her presence between the El Dorado and the Opera House and when she was absent at the Opera House she left Bridget in charge at the El Dorado. Before long Millie discovered that the girl had a great many of the good qualities of Ellie-May with some of the good ones of Madge thrown in. She was calm and efficient and never lost her head and managed to keep the "butt-shaking" girls of the chorus in order through the worst of the disaster, even slapping one of them, who became hysterical, back into sanity.

During the two days and one night of the rioting and disaster Madge dropped in now and then to see how things were getting on and her robust and bawdy presence served to calm and reassure even the suffering men lying on the floor. The fact was that Madge should probably have been a general or a revolutionist for it was in this atmosphere of disaster and rioting that her best qualities came out. The more the excitement, the rioting, the disorder, the more calm and more capable she became.

Late in the afternoon of the rioting, she dropped in for a special reason which concerned Bridget. She found the girl lying on her own bed, sleeping for the first time in thirty-six hours. For a moment she stood looking down at her, hesitating as to whether to wake her or not even for the most important of news, but at last she reached down and began stroking gently the girl's forehead so as to wake her slowly.

But the girl wakened quickly, sat up and asked, "What is it? What's the matter?"

"It's nothing serious. It's good news! I just seen a man that came over the mountains from Henry Caldwell. Henry sent a message by him."

The girl, still half lost in slumber, looked up at her with a puzzled expression.

"Henry Caldwell?" she asked.

"Yes. Henry Caldwell. Young Dick's father!"

The remark only appeared to increase the girl's bewilderment, until Madge explained. "Sure, he's young Dick's father. Any lunkhead would know that. I thought you'd like to know that Dick wasn't no relation of the Old Buzzard. That's private, of course, between you and me!"

"You mean . . . ?"

"That's what I mean. Ellie-May ain't as big a fool or as meek as some people think. But what I wanted to tell you was that young Dick is on his way here and he's gonna ask you to marry him."

It was then from the look on the girl's face, which nothing could have suppressed, that Madge really discovered what she wanted to discover. You couldn't have that look without being in love.

"How does Henry Caldwell know?" Bridget asked.

"Because he talked it all out with Dick. He just wanted you to know so you'd be ready for it when it came and not make any mistakes. If you ask me, sister, you're doin' all right when you get that boy. What d'you think?"

"I think yes."

And then out of the weariness both of immediate experiences and out of the long and lonely past, she began to cry. It was a pathetic kind of weeping, wholly uncontrollable and filled with happiness. And after a moment Madge began to cry too, and in a strange way it was the same kind of weeping, almost voluptuous in quality, for her own past and for the years ahead and for the disaster and the men belowstairs. It was the kind of weeping in which women indulge together upon cosmic occasions like weddings and births and funerals. Clinging to each other they wept for many minutes and presently Madge asked, "D'you feel better now, honey?"

"Yes," said Bridget, sniffling.

"I always say there's nothin' like a good cry. I feel a lot more calm myself." She stood up. "But there's one thing you've got to watch— that's that bad temper of yours." Then as a kind of afterthought, she added, "Of course, now you won't have to be so professional about bein' a virgin."

Then she straightened the belt of her holster and yanked down the short skirt she was wearing. "Now you go back to sleep so you'll look nice and pretty. He's ridin' over from Meeker's Gulch and ought to get here some time tonight."

Bridget took her hand and said, "Thanks Madge!" That was all she was able to say.

"It wasn't nothin'," said Madge. "Now get back to sleep."

Then she left and for a long time Bridget lay awake simply because happiness would not permit her to sleep, but in the end the sheer weight of physical weariness won out and once more she fell into a doze.

How long she slept she did not know but gradually the sound of the rioting and yelling and shooting in the street died away in a fog and then after a long time she was awakened by what at first seemed to be a nightmare.

Standing above her were two figures. They both wore black ten-gallon hats and their faces were covered by bandanna handkerchiefs. One of them held a gun and the other had a flowing red beard that projected far below the handkerchief. The bearded one carried a length of rope. For a second she did not know whether she was awake or asleep and dreaming and then one of the men—the one without the beard said, "Now, don't make any trouble, lady. We're going to take you away." She started to open her mouth to scream but no sound came out. It was exactly like a nightmare.

The man with the black eyes said, "We ain't gonna hurt you." Then he turned to his companion, "Grab her hands, Jake." And quickly before she could even struggle, they had tied her wrists and ankles tightly with bandannas. Another bandanna covered her mouth.

"There," said the dark man. "Truss her up a bit, gentle-like. She's too pretty to hurt."

They had just trussed her up loosely with a length of clothes rope when in the doorway appeared Minnie, one of the girls from the chorus. The room was dark save for the glow of the fires outside and Minnie couldn't see very clearly what was going on.

She called out, "Mademoiselle!" and then the man with the red beard grabbed her and put his hand over her mouth. She fought like a wildcat but it wasn't any good. In less than a minute they had trussed and gagged her and laid her on the floor.

Then the dark man said, "Come on, let's get the hell out of here! Take her feet! I'll take her head!"

As the man with the red beard bent over, he said, "What about the other one? We gonna take her too?"

The dark man said, "Forget her! We got enough trouble with this one." And in a hurt voice, the bearded one said, "I was only thinking about the rest of the boys!"

"Come on! Out we go!"

Then feet first they carried her down the outside stairway and quickly across the three feet of sidewalk which separated the bottom of the stairway from a waiting buckboard attached to a pair of ponies. They laid her gently in the bottom of the buckboard and pulled over her a tarpaulin, smelling strongly of sheep, climbed up and drove off at top speed down Eudora Street.

As he neared the town young Dick stopped running and advanced with caution. After the experience with the rock on the same road, he had no intention of exposing himself again to attack. The cowhand's clothes were a partial disguise, especially in the darkness, but to protect himself further he pulled the brim of the worn ten-gallon hat lower over his eyes.

The outskirts of the town seemed empty but as he neared the Depot Square he saw crowds about the embers that were all that was left of P.J.'s political headquarters. Near the Square the light from the isolated fires, but most of all the great sheet of flames from the burning Castle, added their light to that of a great full moon that was rising above the cottonwoods.

From there on he made his way cautiously as far as the El Dorado and there he disappeared up the private stairway to Madge's apartment. In the Gold Room, one oil lamp was lighted and the room was empty. For a moment he stood looking about him and then in the doorway of Madge's bedroom, he noticed something wriggling on the floor. Moving toward it, he discovered that it was a woman trussed and gagged.

Quickly he bent down and freed her. She was hysterical and for several minutes he could get from her nothing that made sense. Then suddenly she said, "They've kidnapped Mademoiselle! Go after 'em quick!"

His heart missed a beat and then he shook her and asked, "Who kidnapped her? What are you talking about?"

"Blackie did! The handkerchief fell off his face when I was fightin' with him. It was Blackie and a fella with a red beard!"

"How long ago?"

"It must have been about an hour."

"Where'd they go?" But all the answer he got was, "How do I know? I was tied up here on the floor."

A whole stampede of thoughts went through his brain. If his pony hadn't gone lame he'd have been here in time. And Blackie had the kind of dull mind that would make him think he could get away with this kind of thing. That was what made Blackie dangerous—he wasn't quite bright. Then, sobering a little, he tried to think where Blackie would go, and he understood there was only one place. He wasn't a town dweller; he was afraid of towns, even of Silver City. He was certain to head straight for the sheep range.

He found that he had been holding the hysterical girl by both arms. Suddenly he freed her and said, "Tell Madge what's happened! Tell Madge I'm heading out the river road for the sheep trail."

Then he left her and dashed down the stairs three steps at a time. He had planned to grab the nearest horse, but there weren't any horses in sight save two ponies, galloping wildly down Eudora Street, panicked by the fire and shooting. The saddle of the horse hung under his belly.

All fear of being recognized or shot at had gone out of him now and he started toward the Grand Hotel. There in an alley-way in the back stood an old cow pony, tied to a cottonwood tree, his head lowered, asleep. It didn't look like much of a pony but it would have to do. Untying it quickly he swung himself aboard and lashed the old pony into a gallop. In a little while he passed the last house on the river road and was in the valley that led up to the sheep range. They had a start of an hour and a half and very likely were driving a buckboard hard until they had put Silver City well behind them.

In the beginning the idea had come to Blackie by accident, born perhaps of the long and lonely brooding aggravated by the "French" pictures which had marked the whole of the long summer among the sheep high on the range. When he came down to vote, Jake, the man with the red beard, had come with him. They had voted early and had a good deal to drink and during the afternoon they had enjoyed themselves for a time, smashing windows and even helping to burn the effigy of P.J. in the Square in front of the depot. Then they had some more to drink and Jake's imagination, a sluggish affair which only began to operate under the stimulus of a quart or two of rot-gut whisky, began, ponderously, to operate. As for Blackie it wasn't only that he was stupid, he was drunk as well. If he had merely been stupid he would never have attempted the project.

Jake said, "What about going around to the El Dorado?" But Blackie countered with, "Madge would throw me out! She ain't havin' me there any more."

"Madge hain't there!" said Jake. "She's sorta ridin' round the town."

Then they drank some more and Jake said, "Looks to me like a good opportunity to lay hands on that there girl."

"What girl?" asked Blackie vaguely.

"That girl that nobody hain't allowed to tech . . . that girl you been talkin' about in your sleep all summer." Blackie didn't answer him and

Jake's stimulated imagination brought forth another pearl, "Eff'n you'd get her alone and let her get acquainted with you you might get somewhere with your courtin'."

Again Blackie didn't answer him. He was brooding now.

"Some wimmin," said Jake, "like bein' carried off. It kinda stirs 'em up!"

Then for the first time, Blackie spoke. In his dull brain it seemed to him for a moment that Jake's idea was a good one. Mebbe he hadn't made the right approach to a girl like that. . . .

"How would you do it?"

"One more drink!" said Jake to the bartender of the Gates Ajar saloon.

"No more drinks," said the bartender, "I'm closin' down and boltin' the door!"

"One more drink," said Jake sullenly, "or d'you want trouble?"

"I don't want no trouble," said the bartender. "But this here one is sure the last."

"Sure," said Jake, and then resuming his conversation with Blackie, he said, "I'd get a length of rope and truss her up and carry her off!"

"Here's your drink," said the bartender. "Put it down, I want to close up."

"Sure," said Blackie.

And immediately Jake said to the bartender, "Another quick one." The man said, "I told you I was gonna close up."

Jake placed his gun on the bar in front of him. "One more," he said, "and quick!"

The bartender didn't say anything this time but simply removed the empty glasses. Jake returned eagerly to his plotting and so did not notice that the man was slower than usual in preparing the drinks, nor did either of them observe any of the preparations.

When at length the drinks were placed before the pair, both raised their glasses and again downed the drinks at a gulp. Almost immediately an expression of doubt came over the weatherbeaten face of the red-bearded Jake. It hung there for an instant while he stared into space, lost in reflection.

Then he looked at Blackie. "That taste funny to you?"

"No," said Blackie, "I didn't taste nothin'." He was planning now about the buckboard and the rope . . . Jake stood up. "Come on," he said. "Let's go ahead and do it." Then as they went out the door Jake shook his head like an old ram and said, "That there last drink tasted to me like sheep-dip smells."

Now, three hours later, they were driving along the road in the moonlight, not feeling too well. Bridget freed from under the tarpaulin was sitting up between them. She still had her ankles and wrists bound and the handkerchief tied over her mouth. A little earlier they had stopped and taken off the gag but the flow of language and abuse that came out immediately startled and sobered them.

Jake said, "That ain't no way for a lady to talk and I ain't a-goin' to listen to it" and they gagged her again, not tightly but enough so that Jake couldn't hear what she was saying. Now all that came from under the handkerchief was an indistinct and angry mumble.

Meanwhile Blackie kept up his courting. He kept saying, "I don't aim to do you no outright harm, lady. I just want to get acquainted better and Jake here and me couldn't figger out no better way." Then with a kind of bearlike tenderness, he said, "You're gonna have a nice house up here, right in a field full of pretty daisies and then we'll get acquainted. I kinda think you'll like it. And then after you get used to me we kin get married."

They had gone this way for about fifteen or twenty miles, lashing the ponies to a smart trot until they were well away from the town, when Jake began to gulp and hiccough.

"What's the matter?" asked Blackie. "You ain't sick, are you?"

"No, I ain't real sick but I don't feel so good."

And then a little further on after they had passed Bullwinkle Trading Post in the moonlight, Blackie began to gulp and hiccough too and all conversation came to an end. For a long time they rode in silence save for the clop of the ponies' hooves and the occasional angry mumbling from under the handkerchief that covered Mademoiselle's mouth.

Blackie began to shiver and pulled the worn buffalo robe higher over the knees of the three of them. Jake leaned over the side and heaved and after a little while Blackie said, "You take the lines and drive a spell, Jake," and he, in turn, was sick.

After a long time Jake said, "I ain't been so sick since I had cholera morbus when I was a kid. It musta been somethin' that sonofabitch put in the drink. I knowed it didn't taste right."

Then both of them were silent, wilted and miserable. The reins hung on the dashboard and the ponies slowed down to a walk, their backs steaming in the frosty moonlight.

Beneath the old buffalo robe, Bridget's hands were working swiftly and deftly. At first she could only loosen the handkerchief that tied her wrists by spreading and twisting them. And then slowly she worked one hand free and then the other. After a glance at the huddled, miserable figures on both sides she cautiously drew up her legs and began working on the knot that bound her ankles. Once or twice Jake or Blackie stirred and she quickly abandoned her efforts, but each time they stirred only to lean over the side of the buckboard and be sick. Jake kept groaning and muttering about having been given a horse pill or a dose of sheep dip.

It was Bridget who heard the sound of the hooves first. They came faintly but distinctly in the still, clear air of the moonlit mountain night. For a moment she stopped working on the knot about her ankles, uncertain whether the sound was born of her imagination and her hopes or whether it came in reality out of the night. Then suddenly there was no longer any doubt. The sound was the sound of hoofbeats coming nearer and nearer. She went to work again on the knot and Jake said, "Hark, Blackie! There's someone a-comin' on a horse."

With a great effort Blackie raised himself and listened. Then he brought the heavy whip down over the rumps of the steaming ponies and whipped them into a gallop.

The race through the moonlight began with Blackie's urging the horses on along the river and finally up the long rise that marked the beginning of the trail that led to the high range. And Bridget straining every nerve, listening and tugging at the knot, heard the sound of the hoofbeats gaining on them. As they reached the rise, she looked

[257]

behind and far down below in the moonlight discerned the black figure of a horse and man.

She thought, "It's Dick! Who else would be trying to catch us?" And her fingers tugged harder at the knot.

Then one of the tired ponies stumbled and the three of them were pitched forward in their seats against the dashboard. The tired animal regained its feet and went on and Jake, his beard whipping in the wind, called out, "He's a-gainin', Blackie!" And at the same time beneath the buffalo robe the knot gave way and Bridget's feet were freed.

The horse and rider were close behind them now and Jake had taken out his revolver and, aiming drunkenly, he fired three times.

It was then Bridget acted. Leaning over, she snatched the buggy whip from Blackie's hand and brought it quickly and firmly down on Jake's head. The revolver dropped from his hand and he pitched forward out of the buckboard to the side of the road. Blackie seemed scarcely to notice what had happened and with a fresh blow she felled him too. As he pitched forward against the dashboard she seized the reins and drew in the ponies.

The rider, hatless in the moonlight, was suddenly at her side and swinging out of the saddle into the buckboard. He cried out, "Bridget! Bridget! It's me!" At the same time she pulled the gag out of her mouth and suddenly, without knowing how, she was in his arms and he was crushing her against him.

The ponies stopped, heaving and panting, and Dick said, "Are you all right?"

She began suddenly to cry, uncontrollably. "I'm all right!" she managed to say. "Oh, Dick! I thought you weren't coming!"

He kissed her silently and then holding her head close against his, he said, "I'm here, honey! I'm never going to leave you again!"

There was nothing difficult about it all. It happened simply and easily as if it had always been meant to be that way.

When she had stopped crying, she began to talk, pouring out the whole story.

"It doesn't matter now," he said. "We're going back now! I'm going to look after you always and forever!"

Then they remembered Blackie still huddled forward against the dashboard. Young Dick shook him violently but got no response. It was difficult to tell whether Blackie was unconscious or merely drunk.

Dick said, "Wait till I get the pony I stole and hitch him to the back."

The tired pony was easy enough to catch. Dick knotted his bridle to the back of the buckboard, climbed in and, taking up the reins, turned the buckboard around and drove back to where Jake lay beside the road. He had come to and was sitting up, still moaning and groaning and heaving. Then Dick pulled up the ponies, got out and laid the unconscious Blackie beside him on the grass.

He poked Jake with his foot and said, "If you want the buckboard, you'll find it tied in front of the Emporium in Silver City. It's a nice, moonlight night. I hope you two bastards enjoy the hike back. If you weren't so drunk I'd beat the hell out of both of you."

Then he climbed into the buckboard and settling Bridget close beside him with her head on his shoulder, he leaned down, pulled up the buffalo robe and tucked it about her. Picking up the reins, he clucked to the ponies and they moved off at a slow walk.

There wasn't any hurry now for Dick had found what he wanted and Bridget was safe where she had always wanted to be. Now and then he leaned toward her and kissed her, thinking it improbable that any such happiness could ever have been known to any other man since the beginning of time.

And after a long time in which neither of them cared whether the morning ever came, there appeared far down the valley in the direction of Silver City a deep, rosy glow which painted the tops of the mountains all about them a faint pink. This time it wasn't the glow of the burning Castle. The fires in Silver City had burned themselves out. It was the glow of sunrise, of a new day being born.

WELL, MY FRIENDS, THAT IS THE STORY OF SILVER CITY AND THE Meaneys. Henry Caldwell got elected all right and young Dick became his "secketary" and together they did a lot to clean up the corruption that old P.J. represented and for which he was responsible. And young Dick made his own career in politics and got to be Senator for a time in Washington. After he retired from politics he continued to live there as principal defender of the "Silver Bloc" and became a director of several large corporations. No longer did men like Mr. Laidlaw and Mr. Wright dictate to or swindle the West, for the shoe now is on the other foot. Mademoiselle became a famous hostess, entertaining Ambassadors and Presidents and Senators and Congressmen. She was and is quite a character and, in this changing world, the legend that grew up about her as the gambling house singer whom Dick Meaney married out of the El Dorado, became an asset rather than a liability. If you were "anybody" in Washington, you were invited sooner or later to the Meaneys' big house on Connecticut Avenue. A large part of every summer old Dick Meaney and his wife spent in Colorado at the big house which they built on the site of the cottage, high up on the edge of the cattle-range country.

The Senator Meaneys had four sons and three daughters for it seems that Mademoiselle got what she wanted when she married young Dick—which was a home, a fireside, domesticity and a lot of children. So far as anyone knows Dick never looked at another woman. And they had fourteen grandchildren and eleven great-grandchildren with the books not yet closed. One grandson was killed as a Navy flier during the war.

P.J. after a quiet old age, largely spent in traveling under the domination of Ellie-May, died in 1920. Ellie-May continued for a long time to enjoy the success both of young Dick and of Henry Caldwell. She remained bright and birdlike and filled with common sense and was the friend of Ambassadors and Senators until the end, which came when she died quietly in her sleep at ninety-eight in the big house on Connecticut Avenue.

Out in Colorado the Meaneys became known and identified as the Black Meaneys and the Blond Meaneys. The Black Meaneys, everyone said, were always ornery and no good. Blackie went on herding sheep and never married. Toward the end of his life he grew queerer and queerer and died at last alone in a cabin with only a tame coyote as a companion. His intimate friend Jake preceded him in death by fifteen years.

Buck finally settled down and married a big, raw-boned Mormon girl. Their offspring are scattered over the ranching country and they have been virtually lost and forgotten.

Shorty took heavily to drink and died of cirrhosis of the liver at the age of forty-five.

Eudora and Cecil were known as the "in-between" Meaneys. The marriage was a success and Eudora had six children including two sets of twins. On the birth of the second set, Ellie-May observed, "It's always the little men who produce litters, I've noticed."

Cecil turned out to have a first-rate head for business and Eudora became more and more political minded as time went on, with plenty of money to back up her ambitions. After the women got the vote she became chairman of the State Republican Commitee for two years but lost the job eventually out of unpopularity because of her "bossiness." She displayed a great interest all her life in prison reforms and spent much time in visiting penitentiaries, reform schools and jails, possibly a hangover from her early interest in convicts during the period of her invalidism when she sent them mottoes and biblical texts embellished with garlands of forget-me-nots and roses.

Perhaps strangest of all was the fact that Eudora ended her life as a countess. Through a series of family deaths Cecil succeeded late in life to his cousin's title and became the Earl of Cantwell. He refused, however, despite Eudora's protests, ever to return to England or to use the title. The West had claimed him for good and he was buried at

[262]

last, on the ranch high in the mountains he had loved, as simple Mr. Cecil Chatsworthy. Throughout his life he managed somehow to dominate Eudora and even to survive her, perhaps because in their relationship he was like the male of that strange Brazilian species of spider—noted long ago by Darwin—whose small size permitted it to spend a life running over the body of the female and thus to escape the usual postnuptial death and immolation to which most male spiders are subjected.

As for Silver City, the Battle of the Ballots marks probably the high point of its growth and glory. From then on it went downhill more and more rapidly as the mines were worked out and the main lines of the railroads passed it by. Today it is a dead city inhabited by a handful of old-timers and eccentrics who find in its decaying bars and ruined boarding houses a suitable and sympathetic background. But once a year it comes back to life when an army of highbrows descend upon it from all parts of the nation. Then the dusty gilded Opera House is opened again for performances of operas and plays and the old lamps of the El Dorado are relighted and whisky and beer flow like water across the long-deserted bar. The Gold Room with the Turkish cosy corner which saved the virtue of Mademoiselle and the room with the rose-petal bed have long since fallen into decay.

The ruins of the Castle have taken on the look of an authentic European ruin of the Middle Ages. By day the coyotes hide among the great tumbled blocks of granite and at night they come out to raise their voices toward the brilliant unchanged skies and howl, perhaps over the desolation which is all that is left of the vanished orneriness, the vice, the color, the vitality and the tawdry splendor that was once a part of Silver City and an authentic part of the frontier history of a great nation.

Oh, yes, as for Madge, she retired with a large fortune a few years after the Battle of the Ballots, and, with her cousin Lena, went to live in Paris where presently they became members of the Ladies Altar Guild of the American Church. I used to see them sometimes at Rumpelmeyer's, where each afternoon they stuffed themselves with hot chocolate and rich pastries. As very fat and very respectable and respected old ladies they died within a year of each other shortly after the First World War.